Contents

Prologue

· ·

Toxicity
(Rated Mature)

Jeremy and Samantha have already been through so much in their relationship. Even with every hardship and struggle they have faced, they always have a way of finding each other again. However, they may have come across their most difficult hardship. Join the couple as they see if fate will win once again when they find each other back in the same space.

*

"Take off your clothes."

"W-what?" I pry my eyes away from his lips to meet his bright blue ones.

"I am going to strip down to my boxers. By the time that happens if you are still wearing any clothes I will rip them to shreds, do you understand?"

**

*Disclaimer***

This book contains harsh language, themes of rape, physical and mental abuse.

***

<u>Samantha Geraldine Kage.</u>

1

22 years old

5'10

Black

Born and raised in Harlem

Aspiring Wedding planner.

Dark skin, Dark hair, 4c coils, dark brown eyes.

Slim thick.

****

Jeremy Bresset

24 years old

6'4

Italian American

New York city

Corporate office

Bright blue eyes, Dark hair, chin stubble, tattoos

*****

Started July 2021

Finished September 2021

******

All Rights Reserved

Chapter 1

Samantha Kage

. . . .

"And I know we weren't perfect, but I never felt this way for no one!" We yell out as the music roars and the sound of cheap wine and alcohol flow into glasses.

It's girl's night, a much-needed girl's night at that. After all the shit men have put us through this year especially Jeremy Fucking Bresset, we deserve a fun night. Jeremy Bresset, the same man that ripped out my heart almost two weeks ago.

Everyone in this room has their own man problems but mine was the freshest in my opinion. I don't even want to be here, I have a flight in the morning but I needed my girls to distract me from the pain I'm feeling and help me to remind myself that I am a bad bitch and no man should be making me feel the way I currently am.

I feel like shit.

You miss the way his dick makes you feel though.

Here goes my inner goddess.

Maybe I should put down these drinks.

My best friend Annabelle comes to plop down next to me just

as Pussy fairy by Jhene starts to play in the background and Harper grabs the bottle of barefoot and starts to sing into it. We both look at each other and then look at her like she's crazy.

We are both trying to figure out what good pussy she is singing about when her man cheats on her at least once a week and she goes back to him like a dumb ass.

Who am I to judge when I keep tapping my phone screen to see if Jeremy texted me after two weeks of silence?

An idiot that's who.

"UGH! Men are so dumb!" I exclaim to Anna. "I mean he literally accused me of cheating on him with my brother like a fucking dumb ass. My fucking brother! If he had only listened to me when I tried to tell him that the person in the photo he saw was my brother and not some random man!" I stop myself as I feel my eyes get heavy and the tears start to form. Anna rests her head on my shoulder as a way to comfort me but it just makes me mad. I want to storm over to his house and kick him in his limp dick.

Girl, you know his dick ain't limp.

"After finally getting out of an abusive relationship, I thought I found the one and now he's gone because he likes to act like a little bitch," I say with my voice cracking a little.

"He doesn't deserve you bitch!" She yells drunkenly while pointing two fingers in my face.

I stare at her like she's out of her mind for a few seconds.

"There is better dick, better connection, and better-looking men out there for you. You're a beautiful dark skin queen!" She yells with her eyes squinted. I'm not even entirely sure she is looking at me.

Dam she's drunk as fuck.

"Okay, I think you've had enough," I giggle as I get up and grab both of her arms to pull her off the couch. "I'm going to put you into bed so you can sleep this off."

"No, I want to call Angel, I miss him," she slurs as we walk to the guest bedroom in Harper's house. I quickly call my uber so it will be here by the time I put her into bed. "I want my phone now!" She yells as I place the covers on her.

"Fuck that dusty Spanish nigga," I mumble under my breath. I hate Angel and he hates me and that's perfectly fine.

"What?" She says as she weakly holds her head up.

"I said your phone is locked in the drunk drawer where it will stay until you wake up sober. Love you," I say quickly as I kiss her forehead and close the door behind me.

The drunk drawer was the best invention we could have ever come up with. The drawer is locked with a combination lock that non sober people should not be able to open. Plus, after the drunk dialing fiasco of last year where someone's boyfriend showed up thinking they were cheating, the drunk drawer became a necessity.

I check my phone to see that my Uber is 2 minutes away. I grab my bag and jacket off the counter and say my goodbyes as I head out the door into the cold winter air.

I hate New York City winters, I can't wait to go to Florida tomorrow. I am going to go meet my brother and his new girlfriend. The further away from Jeremy and New York I am, the better.

I get home and walk straight into my room. I strip naked and throw on Jeremy's t-shirt like the weakling I am. I lay in bed and I couldn't help but think about the last time he fucked me before our untimely breakup.

Are you really this dickmatized? At your big age?

I ignore my inner monologue and decide to focus on myself instead.

I slowly move my hands down from my neck to the lower part of my body, caressing my breasts and thighs pretending they were his hands before I close my eyes to give myself a better picture of the toxic man doing things to me that make me wet just thinking about them. I reach down between my legs, sliding in between my folds that are already soaked just from the thought of the way he fucks me.

This is going to be fun.

Chapter 2

Samantha Kage

. . . .

I am laying on my stomach on his king-size bed naked, as he massages my butt with coconut oil. "Tell me what you want me to do to you Samantha," he whispers in my ear as he smacks my ass sending a chill from my spine to my already sensitive clit. All he has to do is touch me and my body will respond accordingly.

A man should not have that much power over me.

"Anything you want baby," I whisper seductively. He lets out a low groan as he smacks my ass hard with both hands and grabs them to spread them. I feel the spit land on my asshole as he uses his tongue to spread it out. My eyes immediately roll into the back of my head as a moan escapes my lips. He continues to massage my ass as he uses his tongue to devour me. I moan even louder when I feel his spit dripping all the way down to my pussy.

He stops, sits up, and flips me over in one swift movement.

He examines my body taking in the sight before him while stroking his long dick as he settles himself in between my legs. He licks his lips as he pushes my legs back and slides down to lick my throbbing clit one time before positioning his tip at my entrance. He bites his bottom lip right before he positions his hard dick to slide into my-

The sound of a car alarm makes my eyes fly open and I almost cry as I look at my phone and half debate destroying the thing that just woke me up from that dream. I look at the time.

6:59 am

My flight is in exactly 2 hours so I haul ass. It's a good thing I live close to the airport.

As I get up from the bed, I feel an overwhelming sensation of wetness.

Did I wet the bed? What the fuck?

I turn around and look at the bed only to realize that all the moisture I am feeling in between my legs is a result of dreaming about Jeremy all night.

How ghetto.

I hop in the shower and almost like I have PTSD, the thoughts of our break come flash in my mind. It's almost like it was yesterday.

"You're a whore! A lying cheating whore!" Jeremy yelled as he got close to my face. I stood there staring at this white man turning pink with the most confused look on my face. What the fuck is he talking about? I just walked into the fucking house.

Is this the white man rage that people warned me about?

"What are you talking about," I whispered confused as tears started to fill my eyes. My voice stays soft because I'm too scared to speak up.

Past abusive relationships have traumatized me and his yelling triggered a memory I didn't need. Nor did I know how to properly handle it.

"You've been dating another man and you two looked fairly

fucking close! Someone sent me a picture Samantha, so don't even try to deny it." He shows me his phone and I see a picture of me sitting at a table with a black man and I'm hugging him.

Immediately I recognize the figure. It's my brother. It was the day we met for the first time after he tracked me down. I didn't tell anyone about me and him because I wanted to keep something like that private. Before I can correct him, hand him his ass on a silver platter, and prove him wrong, he says something that breaks me.

"I always knew you were a slimy person just after my money. You're a gold-digging whore, look at you. You recognize him don't you, you can't even think of an excuse."

"Jeremy y-."

Before I can finish my sentence, he grabs my arm the way he who shall not be named used to and shoved me in the direction of the door. "I want you out. Out of my house out of my life out of my fucking face, I should have never given a gold-digging whore a chance! Oh and I fucked Tiffany while we were together."

His ex that I hated

I looked up at him in disbelief and I couldn't believe he had just said that to me. My sadness turned cold fairly quickly. The tears stopped and I looked at him nodded my head, grabbed my stuff, and walked right out the door without saying a word. At that moment my pride was more important than fighting for my relationship and I was over it. I knew he was lying. I knew he wouldn't cheat on me.

Right?

I shake off the thought. But I get how badly he wanted to hurt me. Instead of fighting for someone that had already made up their mind about me, I chose to leave and not look back. If it was so easy for him to treat me like that, then maybe I was wrong about the way I thought he felt about me. Fuck him. I made the right decision.

Right?

I land in Miami around 11 am and I texted my brother letting him know I arrived safely. He let me know to take an uber since he couldn't pick me up. He paid for my hotel so the price of an uber to South Beach really didn't bother me.

As I'm waiting for my Uber, I take in the Florida sun that I've missed so much. I came to Florida twice with Jeremy, it feels weird to be here without him. I must stop thinking about this big dick toxic man.

It's becoming bad for my health. I need to remember I am here to enjoy myself.

I make it to the hotel and Steven is waiting for me in the lobby. I've been to this exact same hotel before with Jeremy. He said he liked it because he liked the way the rooms and hallways smelled.

Weirdo.

I greet my twin brother with a big hug. When we met about a month ago we were all we had. Both of us were adopted but we were both left with trust funds the size of Mt Everest. I think back to Jeremy scolding me about wanting his money but he doesn't know I'm rich. He doesn't need to know, his money seems to make him feel like a man so I'll let him have that.

Plus, I am assuming the women in his past only valued him for his money so that seems like a problem he needs to work out with a therapist and not take out on me.

"You ready to go meet my girlfriend? She's at the beach with a bunch of friends," Steven says excitingly.

I forgot about that part. Steven just told me he needed to tell me something important. I wonder what it was.

"Yea I just need to put down my bags first."

"Yes, yes of course. Andrea's waiting for us though so don't take too long."

I look at him skeptically for a second. What kind of leash does she have him on that he rushing me? I think my protective sister instincts are just kicking in randomly.

I head up to my room and throw my stuff on the floor. I quickly shuffle through my bag to find my neon pink bikini. I throw it on along with some jean shorts and slides. I stop and examine myself in the mirror and admire how neon pink looks against my dark skin.

Who says dark skin girls can't wear bright colors?

I throw up my knotless braids in a bun then spray my skin with sunscreen because protection bitches, and I grab my phone, room key, wallet, and my towel. I throw them in my beach bag and head out of the room to the elevators.

"You ready to go?" I ask as I walk out the elevator doors into the lobby

"Of course," he says excitingly. I can tell he's just eager to go see Andrea.

We walk out of the hotel and I see something familiar. It's a car, it's the 2020 white Lamborghini Huracan Evo to be exact. The same car that Jeremy rented last time we were here. We fucked all over that car. Was this here when I walked in? Oh well.

Chapter 3

Samantha Kage

. . . .

We walk over to the beach lost in conversation. The closer we got to the water, the more voices I heard calling out stevens name. We head over to a group of guys who are apparently my brother's friends.

We make our introductions as the long-lost siblings and make small chit-chat with a couple of the guys. I do my best to ignore any attempts of any of these men trying to flirt with me in front of my brother.

He doesn't seem too pleased with it though. I simply brush it off.

Me and Steven decide to go for a walk to find Andrea since she met up with some other friends. We have his friends watch our stuff but I keep my phone and wrist wallet on me. We are currently at 12th street beach and decide to head south along the water until we find her.

We get lost in a conversation talking about how we both grew up in New York City and we never met. I grew up in Harlem with a foster mom that passed when I was 16. I loved that woman. In a life of bouncing around foster homes, she was the most consistent and caring one. I was with her for 5 years.

I applied for early emancipation after she died and I have

been on my own ever since. Steven grew up in queens with his adoptive family who he is fairly close with. Apparently, the family didn't want a daughter just a son, so they only adopted steven when we were babies.

I can't be mad at random people I don't know. At least he had a better life than I did. I can be happy for him. I am working on letting go of the past and being happy now.

In the midst of our conversation, I see a girl running towards us from a group of people, she has the most perfect body I've ever seen. She's about 5'4, has a fat ass and big boobs, and at least a double D. She's also a Latina. She's wearing a bright red halter bikini and her blonde hair flows perfectly. She sprints towards me and I make a face until she jumps into my brother's arms.

"Baby!" She squeals as she covers him in kisses. He immediately giggles as he wraps his arms around her. It's almost a little sickening.

Sigh, I am so single.

 She finally turns her attention to me and just stares at me eyeing me up and down and I respond with the same face.

Girl if you don't...

Steven notices the awkward encounter and quickly steps in. "Andrea baby this is my sister that I told you about," he says nervously. Her face softens and she looks a little relieved.

"Oh my god, it's so lovely to meet you!" She yells as she quickly pulls me into an uncomfortably tight hug wrapping her arms around me. She is so little yet strong. I'm often not comfortable with certain people I don't know touching me so I kind of just stands there awkwardly.

"Come over here I have some friends I want you guys to meet!" She screams as she runs in the direction of a small group of people while pulling Steven's arms. I look at him confused and he shrugs and smiles before he grabs my hand pulling me along with them. I follow behind while keeping an eye on her because why is she yelling? She talks like El from Legally blonde. The first part of the movie.

We walk over to her group of friends by the water while my brother has his hand wrapped around her waist. As we walk over to the crowd I notice a familiar face and my feet pause for a second. It's Jesy, Jeremy's sister.

God? I don't ask for much. But please let a wave wash me away at this moment. I beg of you.

I had only met her one time when me and Jeremy had taken a weekend trip down here. She doesn't live down here but she just happens to love taking trips. She goes to Florida and Cali all the time. "This is my best friend," Andrea yells as she ushers to Jesy, we make eye contact and offer each other a casual smile.

I know you remember me bitch and I bet your brother told you all lies about me.

The introductions go on but I need to get out of here. I start to look around looking for some way to escape where I am standing. Being close to Jesy feels too close to Jeremy.

My anxiety starts to rise with the most outrageous scenarios. I'm scared I might see him. I'm scared I might not see him. I'm feeling way too many emotions at the moment.

I don't even know why I am panicking. There is no way Jeremy would pop up in Florida on this random ass February day while I am in Florida.

Right?

Yea, there's no way. I'm overreacting. I still don't want to be standing here though.

 I would much rather be creepily flirted with by my brother's friends than stand here for one more second with Jesy and all her friends. God knows what's going on in her mind right now. She too probably thinks I cheated on her brother.

Enough times passed and my anxiety has finally decreased, and I visibly relax.

I am finally calm. And then I hear it. I hear the words I have been dreading. "Oh! And this walking towards us is Jesy's brother Jeremy," Andrea said in a high-pitched squeaky voice. Why is she so fucking excited?

Maybe if I run now he won't see me, he will only see a sand-shaped cloud where my body used to be. Do I say hi? Do I turn around? Do I run? What is he doing here? When did he get here? I want to see his face. No! Fuck! I hate him, Oh my god. Keep your head down. Don't look at him Samantha. Be a bad bitch, not a sad bitch.

I look up for a second and our eyes lock.

Fuck.

He walks straight toward me and I can't help my wondering eyes as they hungrily drink his body in. I can't help but let my eyes wander down to his perfectly chiseled abs that lead down to that teasing V line that holds my favorite 11 inches.

No! Focus! We hate this man! We are mad at this man.

I'm trying to control my thoughts but the sight of him and his blue eyes distract me and the heartbeats growing between my legs are not helping the thoughts in my head.

"Can we talk?" He asks in a low voice as he walks up to me. I look at him shocked and I couldn't even form the words to respond. I started to open my mouth but he cut me off.

"Tonight? Over dinner?" He urges while he grabs my hand sweetly. I stare at him in disbelief after I glance at my hand.

Finally, my mouth finds a way to form some words and what comes out shocks even me.

"No," I say quickly as I pull my hand away from his.

His eyes widen and he starts to look confused. At this point, I have completely forgotten everyone else that is on the beach and it's just me and him. "I have dinner with my brother and Andrea tonight," I say quickly.

There, he can't question me.

"We will talk after then," he says coldly as he walks away.

Bitch I didn't say yes.

What in the entire fuck could he want to talk to me about? I'm sure he realized now that the person in the pictures I was hugging is simply my brother, but I can't forgive him for the things he said to me that day. The way he grabbed me most of all.

My anxiety's coming back. I can't do this right now. I grab my brother off to the side.

"I have to go back to the room in a little tired, early flight and all. I'll meet you guys for dinner later though, where is it?"

"You sure you don't wanna stay here for a little longer and chill?" He looks a little disappointed. At this point I know I won't be any fun.

"No, my eyes are closing, long night, just text me the address and time." Before he can object I quickly turn my back and walk away and throw a "later," over my shoulder.

I need to get off this dam beach.

I start to head back over to my brother's friends to grab my bag to head back to my room. I can't be here right now. I wanna slap him and cry in his arms at the same time. I miss him but the things he said to me that day were so hurtful.

"Leaving so soon?" One of my brother's friends says in a cool low tone. He flashes me his pearly whites and runs closer to me dripping wet as he's coming out of the ocean. The body of this man is truly a masterpiece by god but I'm trying and failing not to stare at it. I nod my head as I start to walk away but he runs in front of me blocking my path.

I'm looking down because the sun is in my eyes. As a result my eyes immediately meet the bulge in his royal blue swim trunks. I try to look away but it's basically challenging me to a staring contest.

"You want to go grab lunch? I'm kind of over the beach too." I try to focus on his words and not his glistening wet body and big bright blue bulge.

"No, I'm good. I just need to get out of here," I said annoyed. I'm your friend's sister how much more of a dick can you be.

"You know I can just make you come with me right," he says with a flirty smile.

I stop walking. "What did you say your name was again?" I said turning to face him with a smile.

"Isaiah, and your name is Samira, right? Your brother mentioned it earlier," he says looking me up and down taking in the sight of my body. I don't miss how he bites his lip.

I give him a soft smile and look him up and down so he can see that I'm taking in the sight of his body. I walk around him taking in his 6'3 dark skin perfectly chiseled body by looking him up and down and letting him see that I am examining him.

I make it back to his face and I give him one more look up and down while licking my lips as I take him in from bottom to top stopping to stare at his dick a little longer than the rest of his body. He notices and smiles. "You like what you see?" He asks cockily.

I stop to meet his eyes, he is clearly looking very pleased with himself. I take a step closer to him and I lean in and whisper in his ear, "not at all. I'm good."

"Aw, come on," he laughs.

"Also my name is Samantha," I say with an attitude while rolling my eyes and stepping back.

His jaw drops as I walk away. I sway my hips so he can get a great view as he watches me walk away.

As I start to walk off the beach towards my hotel I hear him call out, "I'll see you soon Samantha!"

"Don't count on it love!" I yell back as I exit the beach.

Chapter 4

Samantha Kage

. . . .

I enter the hotel and get in the elevator as quickly as possible. I check my room key and hit the button for the 4th floor. The quicker I get to my room and relax in the AC, the better . Just as the doors start to close a hand pushes itself in between, stopping the doors from closing. I look up startled as I see Jeremy enter the elevators. He pauses after entering the Elevator and sees me standing there.

We lock eyes with surprised expressions without moving for so long that the elevator lets out a loud beeping noise that indicates it wants to close its doors. It snaps us out of our trance. He steps in and pushes the 4th floor button without saying a word. I stare into the corner avoiding looking at him.

Great. We are on the same floor. Please don't be on the same side of the hall.

The elevator stops and opens as he lets me walk out first. We both start to walk in the same direction and we both stop moving when we realize the maids are cleaning the rooms. He looks over my shoulder realizing that his room is clean and continues to walk towards his room.

I realize the maid is cleaning my room so I lean on the wall and watch Jeremy walk past the maid to a door that's already been cleaned. He looks back at me and looks disappointed. He stops opening the door and walks back to me leaning on the wall in front of me.

"You want to come and sit in my room until they are done?"

Bitch don't go.

I look at him in disbelief. "No, I'm okay I need to take a shower before I sit down anywhere, I feel sticky," I said looking away.

Bitch you are doing a good job. Proud of you.

"Come shower in my room you can borrow my clothes, that way we can talk now and you can be comfortable and not sticky," he says towering over me.

My inner thoughts start to throw hands with me.

"Jeremy I-" I start to protest before he steps closer to me and glares at me a little letting me know that any argument I try to put up will not work out in my favor. I lick my lips, look around, and let out an annoyed sigh as I walk past him and stop at the door he was standing at earlier. He follows behind me, opening the door for me while looking pleased with himself.

I hate his ass.

I walk in to see a perfectly clean room. I stop in front of the bed in the middle of the room with my arms crossed. He walks to his bag and grabs a T-shirt and boxers. He hands me a towel and sits down on the bed. "Take your time," he says looking up at me. I sigh and walk away.

I walk into the huge bathroom that has a see-through shower door and I turn on the shower. I put my stuff down on the sink and strip down naked to step into the shower. Before I step in the shower I throw my braids up in a bun so my hair won't get wet, and I grab one of the wash cloths in the bathroom.

I take time showering, trying my hardest not to think about what's waiting for me on the other side of the wall.

I begin to get lost in my thoughts humming to myself when I feel fingers on my waist. My eyes immediately snap open as I turn around alarmed. I turn around only to see Jeremy's naked body. We stare at each other for a moment before he steps closer.

"Jeremy," I begin to say in protest but he pulls me closer to him in response.

Our naked bodies are just barely brushing each other under the steaming shower water.

My breathing unintentionally picks up a little. Why does he make me so nervous? Why does he still have any effect on me?

Before I could even open my mouth to say anything else, "I'm sorry," is all I heard him say under his breath before crushing his lips to mine. I don't kiss him back immediately, solely because I am in shock but soon after my mouth opens to invite his tongue in as my hands reach up to his face and the back of his neck pulling him closer.

He deepens the kiss and I immediately tangle my fingers in his hair.

The kiss becomes greedy as our tongues start to fight for dominance with his winning. He is in control right now, and my weak ass is letting him.

I get lost in the kiss and his hands start to explore my dripping wet body. His hands greedily explore my back and move down to my ass all without breaking the heated kiss once. He caresses my nipple piercing with one hand while the other hand slides down to my sweet spot where I miss his touch so much.

A moan escapes my lips once his fingers find my clit and his other hand starts to pinch my nipple.

"Fuck," I whisper against his lips. He knows what he is doing to me. So fucking evil.

He finally breaks the kiss looking down at me greedily.

"I missed you," he whispered as he started to roughly suck on my neck the way he knew I loved.

He trailed the kisses down my body making sure to take both his hands and grab my dripping-wet breasts. He made sure to stop at each nipple, sucking and savoring each one roughly causing me to cry out.

I automatically threw my head back once he started to suck on my nipples harder going back and forth to each one, biting, sucking, and nibbling. The pleasure was turning me on so much that my legs were getting weak. I had to grab onto his shoulders for balance.

He moves down on one knee placing kisses on my stomach. "Hold on to that," he says sternly while pointing to the rod holding the shower curtain. I grab it and at the very same time he throws one leg over his shoulder, grabs my hips, and presses his tongue on my throbbing clit.

If Jeremy couldn't do anything, he could eat pussy. He started to hit me with the suck-and-lick combo and my grip on the shower rod tightened.

"Jeremy just like that baby, oh my god!" I scream as I reach my peak. To make things worst, he stops sucking and spits on my clit. He takes a finger and slides into me before leaning back in to devour me. It's been so long since I have been touched that the second finger sliding in made me cum immediately. My god, this feels so fucking good. I start to buck my hips and grab onto the bar tighter for support as I ride out my orgasm.

"That's right baby girl, cum on my tongue, I fucking miss the way this pussy tastes." That's all it took, hearing him call me baby girl, that's all it took for me to throw my head back and find my second release in a row. "Oh my god," is all I can form as he continued to devour me and refused to let me come down from my high.

He finally let go and my body relaxed a little. He stands up to turn off the shower and crushes his lips to mine again leading me out of the shower. I love the way I taste on his lips.

Our naked bodies are dripping wet as we walk back to the bed with neither one of us breaking the intoxicating kiss. We continuously bumped into things on our way there. I must have been moving too slow for him because he reached down and put both hands under my legs picking me up and wrapping my legs around his waist.

He quickly made his way to the bed and we both collapsed with him on top of me while resting between my legs. I can already feel his length resting on my thigh. He finally broke the kiss and stood up looking down at me with hungry eyes and biting his lips as he started stroking my favorite 11-inch dick. "God I missed you," he says as he licks his lips before he leans back down and settles himself in between my legs. Sometimes he could be rough, sometimes he could be gentle. This was clearly not going to be one of those times.

He places his tip at my dripping-wet entrance. No one can make me wet the way he does. I can't believe I am this soaked.

"I want to hear you," he says while looking me in the eyes and slamming into me hard. I had no time to adjust to his length after so long. "Tight ass wet ass fucking pussy," he grunted as he pushed himself inside me. I screamed at the amount of pleasure and pain that gave me sending my nails straight into his back. "You're screaming already and I'm not even all the way inside yet baby." My eyes widened as I felt him push the rest of himself inside of me.

My moans came out in curses and shaky breaths before he smiled to himself. He started going so fast and hard that I could barely think straight.

"You feel so good baby," he whispered as I wrapped my legs around his back, my arms around his neck, and screamed his name constantly never breaking eye contact with him. My god, this was intense. I let out a moan with every deep hard thrust.

He chuckled to himself for a second. "I need you louder," he said in a demanding tone before stopping. He pulled out of me and moved my body further up onto the bed. I could see his long dick covered in my juices. He took both of my knees and pushed them back into the mattress next to my shoulders, he had me listening to my own feet. I couldn't move, as he positioned himself at my entrance, this time he entered me dangerously slowly.

"Look at it," he said and I quickly obeyed. I looked down watching his dick covered with my juices slide back into me slowly disappearing one inch at a time.

I look away for a second and he slammed into me. "Bad girl," he said with a smile.

"You know I missed you so much baby," he whispered in the sexiest way possible. Right before he put his weight on my body and nuzzled his face in my neck biting it as he slammed into me over and over at a pace that my body couldn't handle as I let out ungodly screams.

"You like that don't you baby?" He whispered in my ear not breaking his pace.

"Jeremy please," my voice cracked, "it's too much, I can't take it." I start to scratch at his back because it's the only thing my hands can actually reach.

"Be a good girl and take it for daddy," he grunts in my ear and I whimper a little.

Why does it hurt but feel so fucking good?

He quickened his pace and I felt a pressure building in me that needed to be released. "I'm going to come baby," I said weakly. He started fucking me harder and deeper all while at the same time placing slopping kisses on my neck. I let out an earth-shattering scream of pleasure as I came around him with my walls clenching and I could feel my wetness dripping down to my ass. Literal tears were coming out of my eyes.

He thrust into me 4 more times harder than ever before he threw his head back and stilled releasing himself inside me. My name fell off his lips as I felt all his heat and moisture enter me and the feeling almost made me cum again. He collapsed onto me and we both lay there out of breath.

Did that really just happen?

Chapter 5

Samantha Kage

. . . .

"Ready to talk?" He asks sweetly.

"While you're still inside me?" I said turning my head to him slightly while raising an eyebrow.

"I'm comfortable here, what about you?" He said in a joking tone.

I simply glared at him until he got the point. How he can act like this is normal behavior is beyond me. He rolls his eyes and slowly slides out of me letting my legs slowly fall so I can relax a little.

I can't believe my dumb ass folded that quickly.

I can't believe your dumb ass folded that quickly either.

As I get up to walk to the bathroom I almost collapse as my adrenaline fades and my body becomes sore from the position he had me in not even two minutes ago. My legs shake but I slowly get up to walk to the bathroom so I can grab his shirt off the counter. He doesn't need any distractions for this conversation. I hear him snicker behind me after noticing the pain I'm in.

I look at my naked body in the mirror. I notice the dark purple marks near my nipples and on the lower part of my chest.

He's such a dick! He knows I have to wear many bathing suits.

I stand still as I feel his fluids from earlier running down my leg. I smile to myself as I use a napkin to wipe them away. The feeling of the warm liquid sliding down my thigh turned me on a little. I love it when he cums inside me. Reminds me of the time he did it 8 times in one night.

Focus girl.

I throw on the shirt with nothing underneath and stomp back into the room. "You wanted to talk, so talk," I spat.

He sits up looks at me and sighs sheepishly. "Are you just going to stand there or are you going to sit down?"

This nigg-

I walk over to the counter that's in front of the bed and sit on that instead. A small attempt to keep some sort of distance between us. I don't miss how he glances in between my legs and licks his lips a little. I pull his shirt down and pull my legs together feeling a little exposed in front of him.

He was literally just inside you and now you're worried about distance and him not seeing the goods?

Bitch please.

"I want to apologize, I was misinformed about the situation. I said some things that were out of pocket and you didn't deserve that. When I found out the truth I regretted it and I thought about calling you but I didn't know how to approach the situation. I didn't even know if I should have approached you considering how harsh I was. I decided to let you go, I figured you were better off without me. I knew you would never forgive me for saying the things I said. Also considering I told you I fucked Tiffany while we were together was a low blow. I know you knew I would never do that, I just wanted the words to hurt. I wasn't even going to try to enter your life again, but then I saw you on the beach today and I thought maybe it was fate. Then you were staying in the same hotel and I took it as a sign that I had to do whatever I had to do to make this right." He stops speaking and starts to search my face for a reaction with his sad eyes.

However, I was fuming.

"16 months.." I trailed off holding back the tears. I took a second and looked away because he was not about to see me cry. He was not allowed to. I had to gather myself to get ready. I took 3 deep breaths and was ready to go.

"16 fucking months Jeremy!" I yelled with my voice cracking. "You think I would cheat on you, and you didn't even give me chance to explain myself! Then you have the nerve to call me a gold-digging whore? Was there no trust at all in that entire time? Why was it so easy for you to believe someone texting you a random picture, over your girlfriend who you supposedly lov-" I stop yelling and look around for a second lost in thought. My eyes snap back to his. "Who sent you the picture?"

"It doesn't matter now."

"Who sent the fucking picture Jeremy." He could tell I was serious.

"Tiffany," he said as he put his head down and rubbed the back of his neck.

The tears actually just went back into my skull.

I saw red.

"Her again," I said nodding my head while chuckling. "Well, I guess she won this time because she got exactly what she wanted. I'm done with you," my voice cracked a little but I wanted him to know exactly how hurt I was. I quickly head for the door wanting to put as much distance between us as possible.

He flew up off the bed and grabbed my shoulders a little to harder than he meant to. I flinched at the all-too-familiar feeling from someone else. He quickly let go. "Baby please, I'm sorry, tell me what I have to do to make this right. I need you I can't lose you again. It felt like my life fell apart these past two weeks without you."

I stared at him feeling the tears in my eyes saying nothing

"Baby yell at me, kick me, punch me, do something please you are too quiet."

"You don't even deserve it. You two deserve each other," I say with disgust.

"Please I love you, you're my world. What can I do?" He said pleading.

"Do you realize almost every fight we have ever had is because of her?"

I stared at him coldly. My face only softened a little when I saw him tearing up a little.

Don't fall for it queen! My inner goddess yells at me.

"Baby girl tell me what I can do to make this right. I'll do anything you ask, literally anything," he pleads while standing in front of me.

"It's crazy how you think doing one thing can fix this shit you caused," I said coldly

"Baby girl-"

"I need time. Preferably time away from you." I said cutting him off.

He nods his head in understanding before we start to stare at each other in silence. I start to walk past him to the door hoping the maids are done with my room. I need a nap.

Then again I felt like being a petty bitch today. I stop at the door and I look back at him watching me.

"You'll do anything?"

"Yes, anything baby."

"Fine," I said walking back towards him.

I approach him slowly until I stand before him and I look up into his bright blue eyes. "You're going eat my ass right now."

"That's it?" He asked while looking at me confused. "Not a problem."

"No, I expect groveling, a whole fucking lot of it. But this is a start in the direction you want to go in." A wide smile spreads across my face.

He licks his lips while looking down at me. He begins to wrap his arms around me while biting his lips.

"Wait," I said stopping him in his tracks.

He stares at me searching my face for clues about what I'm going to say next.

"FaceTime her while you do it. And if she doesn't answer then I won't let you taste it."

I brace myself for an argument or for him to protest so I can walk out and erase him from my life. I was looking for any excuse if I am being honest. However, what he does next shocks even me.

He throws me on the bed face down. Walks over to grab his phone, throws it on the bed then proceeds to snatch me up to yank the shirt off over my head before throwing me back on the bed on my stomach. I hear the phone ringing as he places kisses on my ass cheek. I'm surprised but at the same time turned on by his actions.

As soon as I heard the bitch says hello, I feel him use one hand to move my ass cheek out of the way, giving himself more room to use his entire tongue to lick my hole. I let out a loud moan and I know she heard me. I know she knows it was me.

I heard the phone hang up but I didn't care if she did it or he did. His tongue felt so good on me that I couldn't focus.

"Oh fuck baby," I cried out.

He dropped the phone using his now free hand to spread the other cheek so he had better access to my hole. My moans didn't stop, they grew louder as his kisses got wetter. He pushes me up on my knees opening my legs and pushing down on my back into an arch. I feel so exposed in this position.

He licked my hole one more time before moving his lips down to my dripping pussy. He started to use his tongue to devour me from behind. As he was licking my clit he started rubbing my thighs sending shivers up and down my spine. I was still mad at him but boy did his touch do something to my body. He stopped licking my clit to stand up. I look over my shoulder to see him staring at me and biting his lips.

"What are you doing?" I ask between muffled breaths.

"Enjoying the view," he says before smacking my ass hard. So hard that I felt a heartbeat build inside me

He leaned back over using his hands to spread my ass cheeks and shoved his tongue inside my dripping hole once more. Using his tongue to fuck me, he started rubbing my clit in circular motions at the same time. I started to scream and shake feeling the pressure build inside me. He sped up his rhythm of double pleasure as my body began to shake. "Jeremy baby oh my god!"

Feeling his hot wet thick tongue enter me over and over made my eyes roll back into my head and my legs started to shake uncontrollably. I could feel the powerful orgasm building inside me as he took over my body.

I screamed as I came all over his tongue. I could feel the juices running down my thigh as he continued to make slurping sounds.

Was all that coming out of me?

He stood up and pushed himself inside of me. He took a hand full of braids and started to fuck me hard. He would stop ever so often to place a hard smack on my ass. I think he just liked the way it sounded.

He pushed my face into the bed causing my back to arch more and fucked me deeper than before. He pulled himself out of me before I felt his hot cum landing on my back and my ass.

I collapsed into the bed defeated with aftershocks hitting me constantly.

He climbed into bed with me wrapping me in his arms. "Relax," he said kissing my forehead. I accepted defeat and was asleep in no time.

Chapter 6

Samantha Kage

· ·

I wake up in a dark room being crushed by a set of arms. I didn't even realize we had fallen asleep. I didn't even know when I did.

Maybe after he fucked you into submission.

I slowly slide out from his bear hug carefully trying not to wake him up. I see him stir a little in his sleep which causes me to slow my movements. I grab all my stuff as I stand by the door to check my phone. I see a message appear from Steven.

Steven: I made reservations for Dinner at 7:30.

He sent me the address of the restaurant and upon clicking the link, I saw it was black-owned. A small smile ran across my face, anyone who knows me knows I'm all for black businesses. I look at the time seeing it was 6:23 and quickly hurried out the door not wanting to be late.

I sneak out and close the door slowly careful not to make any noise. I didn't bother putting on anything besides his t-shirt with nothing under it because I was only going a few doors down.

I enter my room, throw everything on the counter, and run into the shower for what feels like the 3rd time today. If I don't lotion properly I'm going to be ashy as fuck.

I hop out of the shower and quickly dry myself while I dig through my bag for a dress. The restaurant looks not too fancy, so I decided to go with a short flowy light blue wrap summer dress. It had a lot of cleavage but I didn't care, I loved my breast, I loved my thicker curvy body. I get dressed, lotion, and put on deodorant as quickly as possible. I start to brush my teeth while I draw on my eyebrows. I knew how to make them look as natural as possible, it was all the makeup I needed anyways. I didn't feel like putting on much if I'm being honest with myself. I take a little powder foundation and cover up the marks Jeremy had left on my skin from earlier. An unintentional smile plays across my face when I think about the day we had.

I was basically ready as I looked in the mirror, I noticed my hair. I quickly let my braids down out of the hot mess of a bun it was in. I looked at my baby hair and started to curse myself.

"Be natural they said. It would be fun they said," I said to myself as I attempted to make myself look like someone's child with these baby hairs. 4c baby hairs were a full-time job. I was getting frustrated. I checked the time to see it was 7:17. I rolled my eyes and attempted to swoop these hairs one last time. After 5 minutes I finally managed to do a little something and I grabbed my wallet, threw on my wedges, and called my uber. The restaurant was about 6 minutes away by car but I was late.

Your Uber is 3 minutes away my phone screen flashed.

I quickly dig in my back for my body spray. I sprayed myself about 20 times as I do, and darted out the door.

I finally arrive at the restaurant and walk inside. The

restaurant has a purple ambiance and flowers everywhere. I get greeted by the stewardess but I see Steven raising his hand at me. I walk over to see him sitting alone. He's wearing a black V-neck shirt and wine-colored slacks, classy and relaxed.

"Is it just us? I thought Andrea was coming," I ask as I take my seat.

"She is, they are meeting us here in a few. I wanted a chance to talk to you," he said with a straight face.

I furrow my brow immediately.

The waitress comes over and gives us two glasses of water, and two menus and tells us she will be over shortly to take our drink orders. We nod at her politely.

"About what," I asked confused taking a sip of my water. I mean yea we had a lot to talk about, but I don't think any of it was as serious as he was making it seem in this particular moment.

"When we first met I wasn't honest with you," he said and my body froze. "I told you I didn't know anything about our birth mother. I was lying. I wasn't sure if you were ready for the truth since when we met you openly expressed how you wouldn't care for someone who would give up her kids, twins nonetheless," he said sadly.

I sat uncomfortably in my seat. I didn't know if I was ready for this conversation.

"Okay, so what do you know about the woman who abandoned us," I said with a slight attitude.

He looked at me sadly and let out a deep sigh before he began. "Have you never wondered where the money came from? From our trust funds."

"I haven't given it much thought really. I just thought she wanted us to be set just in case we needed to emancipate ourselves or something," I said shrugging my shoulders.

It's not a subject I liked talking about. Nor was my wealth something I shared with people.

To be honest I never wanted to think about it. I didn't understand growing up how a couple who had so much wealth didn't want to take care of their children. I often suppressed the thoughts instead of dealing with them.

"Well, I might as well tell you. When I got curious and started digging into where I came from, I found out more than I bargained for. I hired a private investigator, and he helped me find everything I needed to know, including the fact that I had a fraternal twin sister which led me to find you," he said with a small smile.

"Apparently our birth mother, Serenity was her name, loved us very much. She was very excited to be a mother. Our father had died as soon as she became pregnant so she couldn't wait to welcome us into the world. I don't know much about him. She didn't have a big family and she wasn't wealthy but she had enough money to keep herself and us happy. During her pregnancy she befriended a man named Gerald Hoge, he was in the same grief group as her after his wife died, he was a very wealthy lawyer. They would meet up outside of the group and hang out fairly often. He was with her through most of her pregnancy, he was even there the day she gave birth."

"I'm so confused. What does this have to do with anything? She still gave us up," I said urging him on.

Just then the waitress comes over asking us for our drink orders. He orders a jack and coke & I teasingly call him an old man. I order a strawberry martini as she ushers away to grab our drinks.

"Please let me finish, it will all make sense in a few," he said as he started again. "Apparently the day she gave birth, had a C-section actually, she held both of us, fed both of us, and sang to us. See she never gave us up. She loved us. She was ready to take us home. Later on in the day, the same day we were born, she continuously told the doctors something wasn't right, she kept telling them she was in pain for hours. The doctors shrugged her off and told her it was probably just the stitches and her body adjusting to the procedure she went through. In the middle of the night while we were all sleeping, she had a pulmonary embolism and died from a blood clot that could have been treated had the doctors listened to her-" he stopped talking as he saw the tears coming out of my eyes. "She suffered before died, she was in pain for hours," he said sadly.

"She wanted us?" I said with a shaky breath looking at him. I start to think to myself about all the nights I stayed up hating her. Not understanding how someone can give up their child. Now I know that she didn't throw me away, but that she was brutally taken from me.

"Gerald was there with her that whole day, also hence why your middle name is Geraldine. He had become her best friend. After she died Gerald sued the hospital for racial discrimination and negligence. The hospital tried to settle but Gerald wasn't having it. He got a big payout and split it between us not keeping a penny to himself. The trust funds as you know were to go into effect on our 19th birthdays so that if we had greedy foster parents they wouldn't be allowed to touch the money and we could use it if we needed to start our lives over at that age."

The waitress brought over our drinks and looked at us confused and asked if we were ready to order shyly. At that point, I don't think either of us had even looked at the menu. I turn my head away to hide the tears and I hear Steven tell her to give us a minute.

This was a lot of information to take in. I didn't know how to feel about the fact that my mother didn't give me up but rather she was taken away from me.

"I know this is a lot to take in but there's more," he said slowly.

"What is it," I said while wiping away my continuous tears.

"Gerald wants to meet you."

"You met him?" I said shockingly

"Yes, most of the information the private investigator got was from him. He lives not too far in Rye, New York. When we go back try to visit him. He wants to meet you."

I nod my head in agreement. I didn't realize I was crying again but I couldn't stop. It was a lot of information to take in at once. I wasn't sure how to properly process it much less how to feel. He moved over to my side of the table and put his arm around me attempting to comfort me.

"If she could only see her babies now, at the age of 22 finally together as she wanted in the first place," he said kissing me on the forehead through my sniffles.

"Me being the older more handsome brother by 1 minute," he said jokingly. I laugh rolling my eyes at him. For the first time in what seemed like an hour, I actually let out a giggle.

"Excuse me." I hear a voice say. It was the waitress again. Our heads snap up to look at her interrupting the moment. "Uhm sorry, but the rest of your party is here so you guys can move to the larger table now sir."

"Thank you," he said moving to take my hand and walk me to the other table.

"Besides Andrea, who else is here?" I asked in a low tone trying not to cry again but I couldn't help it.

"I have no idea, that woman made the reservation," he said shrugging his shoulders.

The waitress leads us to the back of the restaurant that is outside but still inside, I look around and take in the room that is surrounded by pink and white flowers everywhere. We walk around the corner both shocked to see almost everyone from the beach there. I quickly turn around and try to wipe away any evidence of tears.

Everyone is mostly talking amongst themselves. I scan the faces to lock eyes with the man who make me cum about 4 times today. He's wearing a white button-down dress shirt that has the first 3 buttons open, some dark blue slacks, and his dark hair is slicked back perfectly. I take in the sight of this gorgeous man staring right into my soul.

He immediately stands when he sees my face, I must still look sad after all the information I just processed. He walks over to me taking my face in his hands as my brother lets me go to go greet Andrea.

"Baby girl, are you okay?"

I offer him a small smile and nod my head as he places a kiss on my forehead, wrapping me in his arms. I was still mad at him but his touch and embrace were all I wanted at the moment.

I take my seat next to him and acted like nothing was wrong as we continued on with dinner.

We finally made our way out of the restaurant. It was a nice night so we decided to walk back to our hotels. I was a little annoyed since I was wearing wedges but none of the other girls in six-inch pumps seemed to complain. Jeremy never left my side. He continuously held my hand and toyed with the small of my back. He even kept intertwining his fingers with mine, not saying a word. His touch was reassuring to me and it was what I needed.

20 minutes later we finally make it back to our hotels.

Andrea, Jeremy, my brother, Jesy, and her girlfriend are all staying at our hotel. We make our way into the elevators and floor by floor the goodbyes, goodnights, and see you tomorrows were thrown in the air until it was just me and him.

We step out of the elevator walking together and that's when my tears start to fall again. I start to sob when Jeremy steps closer to me and wraps his arms around me leaning down to place kisses on my forehead.

"Tell me what's wrong baby girl, please. You haven't been yourself tonight."

I look up at his concerned blue eyes, "Can I sleep with you tonight?" I ask through my sobs.

He doesn't say a word as he takes me to his room, which is probably cleaner considering the mess I made while getting ready. He sits me on the bed and takes off my shoes. I lay down as he sits on the edge and begins to rub my aching feet. He knows me so well.

"I know you will tell me when your ready baby girl," he says continuing to rub my aching feet. As I lay there I feel myself getting deeper into my thoughts and I decide I need a distraction. I get up, straddle him, and place a kiss on his lips.

He stares at me as I pull away.

I go in for another kiss this time biting his bottom lip so I can hear him moan. Just as he moans I take advantage and stick my tongue in his mouth at the same time. I go as far as grinding my hips on his lap.

The kiss becomes greedy as his fingers dig into my waist. I feel his dick harden in between my legs as I continue the motion of my hips. I'm letting out moans against his lips and suddenly he stops me, pulling his face back and looking at me with both of us out of breath.

"Baby girl not while you're like this," he says looking me in the eyes.

I look down at first, but then I start to get into my thoughts again. "Please," I said quietly with my voice cracking.

He placed a soft kiss on my lips and slowly turned me over and climbs on top of me in the bed.

Chapter 7

Samantha Kage

• •

I can't help feeling like I forgot to bring something on this trip.

Your dignity?

Self respect?

Common sense?

Was it my glasses? A certain outfit? Oh well. I am sure I will figure it out.

The sunlight peaked through the curtains of the room. I woke up feeling robbed. Robbed of a mother and robbed of an orgasm, considering Jeremy refused to fuck me last night.

Bitch ass nigga.

I have to admit though, it was nice to talk to him about everything. I move to get out of bed, when strong arms pull me back down, nuzzling his face in my neck. I shouldn't find this much comfort in being in one person's arms.

"Good morning beautiful," he said while trailing kisses on my neck down to my chest. "I want to take you on a date tonight, actually I wanna spend the whole day with you starting with breakfast. I wanna spoil you before you go back to New York tomorrow."

"When are you going back to New York?"

"The day after."

"Oh, where are we going?" I asked with a bright smile. I stare into his dark blue eyes waiting for him to say something but he just puts on a mischievous grin instead.

"It's a surprise baby." My face moved from a smile into a frown. Everyone on gods green earth knows I hate surprises. Something about them just doesn't sit right with me.

"Jeremy," I warn but it does nothing to phase him. He gets up and stretches, giving me a great view of his body. Every time I lay eyes on the body of this man I get so turned on. I feel myself getting wet just watching him move around the room.

"Stop looking at me like that," he warned. I hadn't even noticed I was biting my lip.

"I don't know what you're talking about," I said eyeing him while crawling closer to the edge of the bed where he was standing. I make sure he doesn't miss me licking my lips at the same time.

He leans over me to meet my eyes. He looks at me licking his soft pink lips. I could feel the heat building inside me the closer he moved to me. The heat of his body being so close to mine sent chills down my spine. His scent is enough to make me wet.

Please touch me.

He bites his lips taking in the sight of me, only inches from my face, he reaches up to touch my face using his thumb to softly stroke my cheek. I could feel the trail of goosebumps it left behind. I close my eyes, getting ready for his tender lips to touch mine. Instead, he leans over to my ear, and the feeling of him breathing on my neck makes the heat inside me grow even more.

"I'm not putting out until after tonight," he whispers in my ear before backing away and heading into the shower closing the door with the lock.

The shower had a lock?

I fall back into bed before rolling my eyes. Fine, he wants to play that game I can play too. I will make him touch me.

I quickly pull his shirt off over my head. Good thing it was the only thing I was wearing.

I lay back on the bed. I wait to hear the shower turn off before I start my devious plan. I open my legs, licking my hand, and I slowly start to slip my fingers into my soft hot wet folds. I place slow circles around my clit applying a small amount of pressure at the same time, not wanting to lose control too quickly before he could see me.

I use my other hand to start tugging on my nipple ring before I start to slowly caress my breast. A slight moan escapes my lips as my clit slowly grows more sensitive under my fingertips. My hips start to move along with the rhythm of my fingers. I hear his footsteps, and immediately I look over at his dripping-wet body walking over to the bed with nothing but a towel over his waist. He stops moving completely when he notices me, he cocks his head to the side to take in the sight of me.

He looks me up and down, but the sight of him makes the pressure inside me build even more making me let out another moan, arching my back off the bed. He knows what's about to happen. He drops his towels and quickly makes his way over to me to grab my ankle, his touch feels so good against my skin.

He clenches his jaw out of anger. Little does he know looking at me like that only fuels me more. He knows what I am about to do. He moves to grab my hand but it's too late. I let out one more loud moan riding out my orgasm on my fingers.

I relax back into the bed biting my lip and letting out a deep sigh. I slide my fingers out of my folds, slipping them up to my lips as I lick off my juices. His eyes never leave me as they grow darker.

"You're going to regret that," he says staring into my soul. I slide off the bed stretching. I watch his eyes trail down to my naked body, while he raises an eyebrow.

"I don't know what you're talking about," I said innocently before turning away from him and sashaying into the shower. I could feel his eyes on me.

I locked the shower door and an exciting smile appears on my lips. He hates when I have an orgasm that doesn't come from him.

Girl, he gon fuck that pussy up later.

I almost did a happy dance.

I stand in the shower thinking about the beautiful day I just had. He went out of his way to make me feel special today. Jeremy started off the day by taking me to breakfast at a little cafe that had some of the best cheese Danishes I ever had. After breakfast he booked me a massage at the Fountain Bleu spa, leaving me to relax for a couple of hours. He said I needed time to myself after the night I had. I think I moaned out loud when the masseuse touched me, I wasn't even embarrassed, she knew what she was doing, those fingers were magic. He picked me up from the spa to take me shopping. Part of me thinks he's only doing this so he can be in a relationship with me again, but he's still on punishment. Not pussy punishment but some sort of punishment for sure. He doesn't get to call me his girlfriend again, not yet anyway.

I really wasn't an in-store shopper but I knew I had to pick something up in at least one store or Jeremy would pick it up for me. Jeremy worked for his father's company that did some sort of buying and selling companies, he had told me about it multiple times but I could never understand it. I just knew he had a fuck ton of money, but then again, so did I. I ended the afternoon with a Louis Vuitton Wallet, three new Brandon Blackwood bags, *you know we love black businesses out here,* and a pair of white Christian Louboutin wedges that Jeremy picked out. He knew I wanted them but I would never buy them for myself.

I was enjoying myself too much down here. I wasn't ready to go back to New York or go back to work. I was an event planner for birthdays, lunches, and weddings, I loved doing weddings the most even though they took up most of my time. Don't get me wrong, I'm a city girl through and through, but something about the hot weather just makes me happier.

Make his pockets hurt!

He didn't let me get ready in his room, apparently, there were more surprises in there. What more could this man possibly have in store?

I look at myself in the mirror at the white long Beach dress I was wearing. The dress had a very deep cut in the front. It sat perfectly on my chest as the slit on the side of the sundress went all the way up to my waist. I pray the wind doesn't blow too hard tonight because ya girl surely isn't wearing underwear tonight. My knotless braids are in a half up half-down hairstyle. I take a second to look in the mirror admiring myself. I am not perfect, I have love handles, a little bit of a stomach, and my thighs could be shapelier. I could sit here all night and focus on the negative, parts of my body, or all the positive ones.

Bitch you look good!

A knock on the door shakes me out of my thoughts. I open it to reveal the man of my dreams standing there holding a single blue rose in his hand. He has a button-down white long-sleeve t-shirt that hugs his muscles so perfectly, with the top few buttons exposing his bare chest. It's tucked into some dark blue slacks that hug his lower half so perfectly. Taking in the sight of him I don't even notice I start to bite my lip. His chin stubble makes him look adorable and his perfect smile just warms my heart.

"Stop looking at me like that baby girl, or we will miss the evening I have planned," he warned.

"I can't help it baby," I said in a low whisper.

He hands me the rose, before taking a step back so I can come outside. I grab my dark blue Telfar off the counter and proceed out the door.

Our hotel was on the strip across the street from the beach. As we exit the hotel he takes my hand, pulling me in the direction of the beach.

"We are going to the beach?" I ask confused.

"Something like that," he said quietly. Boy do I hate surprises. He leads me across the way and moves me in front of him to cover my eyes from behind.

"You know Jeremy If you wanted to kill me, you could have just said so," I joked.

"Oh shut up," he said letting out a chuckle. I feel us walking for what could be 5 minutes. I can hear the waves crashing but I know we are not on the beach because it almost feels like a boardwalk under my feet. As soon as my clumsy ass tripped over something I was over it.

"Jeremy," I warned. He let out a laugh as he steadied me before I fell. We finally stopped walking but he didn't take his hands off my eyes. I guess he was building anticipation, but I was still mad that he made me trip.

"Are you ready?" He whispered into my ear.

I nodded my head. As I opened my eyes, I saw a beautiful table at the end of the wooden walkway leading to the beach. The table was under a wooden canopy that had twinkle lights and flowers hung all around it as the different color lights danced around on the flower petals. The soft sounds of R&B played in the background as he took my hand and led me to the table slowly.

"Jeremy this is-" my voice started to crack as I took in the sight in front of me. "Nobody has ever done anything-," I take a deep breath trying to hold my tears. I look up at him meeting his dark blue eyes. "I love it, thank you baby."

He leans down placing a small kiss on my lips with a satisfying smile on his face. He pulls out my chair for me to sit as waiters come out of nowhere to place wine glasses and water down on the table. No, seriously they came out of nowhere, I literally noticed not one other person on this beach before we sat down.

We got lost in conversations about work as we ate, drank, and laughed. I was in love with the man sitting in front of me, and he was in love with me. This is the man I asked god for, I manifested him. There was no doubt he was the one for me.

Sure lets pretend you didn't hate him two days ago.

"You ready for dessert?" He asked while taking my hand in his. I was kind of full from the appetizer and entree but I wasn't about to say no to him.

As I open my mouth to give him an answer, the waiter came and placed a plate in front of me with a small navy blue velvet box and a white ribbon on it.

"What is this," I asked nervously eyeing Jeremy across from me.in front

"Open it." He commanded never breaking his gaze on me. I release my hand from his and slowly take the box in my hand.

I open it to reveal a diamond band with white Opals in between each diamond. I hold up the ring and turn it around in my fingers and trace the lines of the diamonds and my birthstone.

I feel the tears start to fill my eyes as I look up at the man in front of me. "What is this?" I ask between shaky breaths trying not to cry

"It's a promise ring baby girl. It's my promise to you that I will love you and work to be the man you want me to be. I know things between us aren't exactly perfect right now, but this is my promise that I will work hard to get us back to where we were. I love you Samantha, I am in love with you Samantha, and god dammit woman, I want to marry you once we have fixed everything between us. I am promising you right here and now, that I will never hurt you again. My heart wouldn't allow it, I love you way too much."

I stare at his glossy eyes, tears running down my face. I cannot possibly look attractive right now with the way I'm crying.

"You are the woman of my dreams and you deserve the world. And I promise you that I will be the one to give it to you my love. You are the moon and the stars and I feel like god made you for me and I for you. There's no one I want to share these moments with other than you. I love you. Now I know it's too soon but will you please do me the honor of being my girlfriend again."

"Yes," I said quietly through my tears. If he asks me to be his girlfriend like this, I can only imagine how he will propose.

"Yes," he asked surprised raising an eyebrow. "Yes!" He yelled into the air before picking me up and spinning me into his arms before placing me down and taking my face in his hands placing a small kiss on my lips.

"I love you so much Jeremy."

"I love you too baby girl." Using his thumb he wipes away the tears on my face. I could stay in this moment with him forever. We stand there for a minute, in each other's arms, slowly taking in each other's features. I really do love this man.

Girl you need to suck the nut out of this man's ball

"Can we go now I said moving closer to him?"

"You don't want dessert?" He asked quietly.

"I surely have something I wanna swallow, but I can't do that here," I said sweetly.

His Jaw clenched, letting out a sexy low groan before looking over to signal the waiter to wrap everything up. He paid, grabbed the bags, and grabbed my hand to lead me off the beach as quickly as possible.

We are back in his room in no time, kissing and wrapping our arms around each other greedily. He reaches his hand up the slit in my dress to be greeted with the wetness that has been waiting for him. He breaks the kiss looking down at me. "Baby girl, don't tell me you went outside with no panties," He asked while placing a hard smack on my ass. I let out a moan while biting my lip and laughing.

"Looks like I'm going to have to add to your punishment."

"What? I'm still getting punished?" I pout as I reach my hand to stroke the length inside his pants.

"Yes."

He turns me to face the bed as I see another box.

"Open your punishment," he whispers in my ear.

I grab the box ripping it open like a kid on Christmas. The box revealed a small red silicone rose inside with silk ribbons. I hold it up in my hands examining it confused. "How exactly will this punish me," I ask raising an eyebrow.

"You'll see," he said a little scarily. "Undress Samantha. Now."

I don't hesitate, I stare into his eyes biting my lips as I slowly slip the straps off my shoulders, letting the dress fall into a pool at my feet.

He eyes me up and down licking his lips and rubbing his chin taking in the view. I twiddle nervously at the ring on my left hand which seems to put a smile on his face as he notices. He slowly strides towards me and slowly pushes me to lie on the bed before taking the silk ribbon and tying my hands together. He places a kiss on my now snug wrists before placing them above my head and standing up.

"What am I going to do with your baby girl?" He asks with a

mischievous smile.

He slowly takes off his shirt button by button. I lay on the bed restricted from moving just watching the beautiful sight unfold in front of me.

He leans over me, spreading my legs, and placing a hard slap on my pussy causing me to moan loudly. "What did I tell you baby girl?"

"I don't know," I smile playing dumb.

He lifts one of my legs placing another slap on my pussy from under causing me to scream out again. I quiver at his soft touch on my ankle. "Didn't I tell you that every time you cum, I should be the one to do it?" He asked while grabbing my ankles and spreading them far apart. I wouldn't dare move my hands. The look in his eyes showed me he wasn't about to show me any mercy if I did anything wrong.

He leaned his head between my open legs spreading my folds to place a soft kiss on my clit before spitting on it. He used his tongue to slowly spread his wetness around the area, careful not to let his tongue touch my actual clit. I wanted to buck my hips up to him so badly but I didn't want to add to my already pending punishment.

I was afraid to respond to him I had no idea what this man was up to. He lifted me to stand up so I was facing him. He dropped his pants and boxers, kicking them away from his feet. "Get on your knees," he said sternly.

Anything for you daddy.

I quickly oblige getting my knees in front of him. "Suck," he commanded. I don't hesitate before I open my mouth and take half his length inside my mouth as quickly as possible. He let out a sharp breath. "Fuck," he moaned as I started moving my head back and forth swirling my tongue around half his length. I let go of his dick and licked his shaft from the tip of his balls to the tip of his head before taking his back into my mouth again even deeper this time. I continued to use my throat to pleasure his long dick taking him deeper and deeper in my mouth as his dick became more lubricated from my juices. I could cum right now from the moans that were escaping his mouth. I reached down to try to touch myself but he quickly stopped me. He grabbed my hair pulling my mouth off his dripping wet dick. He pulled my head back so my eyes met with his while he was inches away from my face.

"Did I say you could do that?" He asked seriously while staring into my eyes.

Fuck

"No daddy," I responded before he quickly pulled me back up to stand and pushed me back onto the bed roughly.

"This is going to be fun," he said under his breath ."Open your legs for me baby girl."

I wanted him to touch me so badly but I knew he wouldn't. The lack of his touch was part of my punishment.

He walked over to grab the rose I had in my hand earlier. Climbing back over me, he lifted my thighs to place them to rest on his thighs.

We had used vibrators before so I wasn't too worried. The vibrator looked small, how much damage could a little rose do?

He placed the little hole on the rose over my clit after spitting on my clit again. He looked at me in my eyes. His eyes suddenly became dark as a crazed smile came over his face. "Just know I still love you after this is over."

The fuck?

Okay, now I was scared. He slowly places the tip of his dripping-wet dick at my entrance, and at the same time, I heard him press the button. I felt the pleasure of his throbbing cock slowly slip inside me as I let out a small moan but just then the rose sprung to life as he quickened his pace.

The rose latched onto my clit in a sucking motion as it began to suck my clit and vibrate at the same time while he started to slam into me. I didn't even realize I was screaming until he put his hand over my mouth.

"That's right baby," he said fucking me even harder. "You better relax or you're going to make daddy cum quickly if you keep moaning like that," he says through his grunts.

I continue to writhe around and scream under him. I felt the heat building inside me as my legs started to shake uncontrollably. "Jeremy oh my God!" I cried out as my walls clenched around his girth, the eruption inside me that was building was so intense that I started to shake and my eyes rolled to the back of my head. I threw my head back and arched my back off the bed unable to handle the pleasure that was pulsating through my body, I came so hard around him but he wouldn't stop.

I was running and crying while the rose was going and he was still fucking me as I was still cumming. A few hard thrusts later and he pushed himself inside me cumming so hard that I could feel the hot fluid filling me. He turned off the rose and dropped it on the bed before collapsing on top of me with both of us out of breath. Tears streamed down my face.

Did I just die? I think I'm dead.

Chapter 8

Samantha Kage

· ·

I finally touch down back in New York around 5 pm. I almost missed my flight being wrapped in the bliss of my baby. I couldn't have asked for a better way to spend my morning. Getting sucked, fucked, and licked into oblivion. I even stole that rose toy from him. I wonder if he knows.

I send a quick text to Jeremy letting him know I landed but he didn't respond.

Me: I just landed baby. I love you. Call me after your dinner meeting.

Jer Bear: Okay baby girl. Love you too.

Me: Promise?

Jer Bear: Promise my love.

I call my Uber from the airport to my apartment in Harlem. I honestly think I'm ready to move. I'm a little tired of it here in the city. I want to be in more of an open area. More of a bigger house.

I throw my bag down, get undressed and hop in the shower washing the airport off my body. I throw on some shorts and a sports bra before texting my brother that I'm home.

I decide to call Annabelle to let her know what she has been missing.

The FaceTime call rings, and she doesn't answer.

What is this bitch doing that's more important than answering my phone calls? How rude.

I roll over groaning. I want to tell my best friend about the wonderful weekend I had in Miami getting back with my boyfriend. Where is she? Where is everyone? Is my phone even working?

I feel my phone vibrate, I expect it to be a phone call from Jeremy or Annabelle, but instead, it's an unknown number.

"Hello."

"Hello?" I said confusingly as the man on the phone has a very deep voice that I didn't recognize.

"Hello is this ah....uhm Samantha."

"This is she...." I trailed off waiting for someone to say something else.

"Hi umm this is weird, but your brother gave me your number, I don't know if he told you who I am. Uhm my name is Gerald. God, I don't know why I'm so nervous."

"Yes! Oh my god. I'm so sorry. Umm hi, how are you doing."

"Oh, I'm fine, I'm fine, I was actually calling to ask you something, more of a favor really."

"Uhm sure anything what do you need?"

"I was wondering if you would want to come to lunch at my house tomorrow around 3 pm. Steven's coming as well."

"Oh, sure just send me the address, do you need me to bring anything?"

"No, and don't worry about driving I'll be sending a car for you by 2 o'clock.

"Oh okay, see you tomorrow sir."

Sir? What the fuck is wrong with you? Was that weird to call him that?

"Oh, and Samantha," he trailed off... "It's my honor to meet you."

"As is mine," I said smiling before he ended the call.

I send him a quick text with my address in it.

I roll over to sigh and stare at my ceiling. I decide to rewatch season one of Demon slayer and relax my mind for a while. I didn't know how to feel about all of these life changes occurring in one weekend.

But I need to put my big girl pants on. This man made sure I was set for life the least I can do is meet him for lunch. I check my schedule to see if I don't work until the day after tomorrow and I only have a couple of appointments. Nothing serious enough that I can't make time to see Jeremy after lunch.

Jeremy.

I don't know why he just randomly crossed my mind.Where is he? I check the time I texted him seeing it was 5:24 PM. The time now was 10:24 pm. I really do lose the concept of time while I'm watching anime. I wonder if he's still at his business dinner. I mean I guess men can get carried away, but I suppose he will call me later.

My phone vibrates again, and I pick it up excitingly to see if it's Jeremy, A small frown plays across my face to see Annabelle's face flashing across the screen. Oh well, I had to talk to her anyway. I answer and tell her everything that happened over the weekend. Everything with my mom, Jeremy, and the promise ring I keep twisting around on my left hand.

"Bitch!" She yelled. "That was a lot of shit to happen in 3 days."

"Bitch I know! I don't know how I survived it but, umm why didn't you answer me the first time I called you, hoe?"

"Oh, lol. Hmm. I was getting strokes sis."

"Strokes?" I exclaimed, "from Angel?" I ask in disbelief.

"Yes bitch. From whom else?"

"I was hoping it was someone new." I shrug. "But do whatever makes you happy I support you. No matter what," I said with a sarcastic smile.

She knew I didn't like him. He never appreciated her, and he never will. He hasn't even told his family he's dating a black woman. Then again neither has Jeremy in a way. I've met his mom a couple of times, his sister obviously, and his favorite cousin but never his dad. His mother and his father had a nasty divorce which led to Jeremy wanting to keep me away from his father at all costs.

"Don't come for me, cause I ain't send for you. Okay bitch?" We both started laughing and continued with our conversation talking about fuckery until we fell asleep around 2 am.

The next morning, I woke up around 10 am. I roll over to check my phone, and I see a couple of notifications from Instagram and a couple of random text messages. But nothing from Jeremy. Now I'm worried, I quickly call him but there was no answer it just kept ringing.

I got up and started pacing my room before I swallowed my pride and called him again. This time the phone went straight to voicemail. I began to worry and when I worry, my inner goddess starts to talk to herself and answer her own questions

Could his phone be dead? No, it couldn't have considering it rang the first time, but this time it didn't ring, it went straight to voicemail. He's probably with another bitch. Girl you know he's not with another bitch. Is he okay? Is he hurt? Did something happen last night in Miami?

My eyes widen at my last thought.

I quickly send his sister a text. By now I'm sure she knows the whole situation and doesn't care to hate me anymore. I hope.

Me: Hey Jesy, have you heard from Jeremy, he's not answering my calls, I'm beginning to get worried.

I start to get nervous waiting for her reply. Not even 30 seconds later my phone buzzed.

Jesy: Yea he called me this morning before his flight. I'm sure he's just on the plane right now.

I relaxed a little. I was panicking for no reason. What's wrong with me? I need to do better. I love this man, I trust this man. I still don't see why he couldn't text me back though. Maybe he thought I was asleep.

Whatever. I'll deal with that later.

I quickly grab my laptop and check my work emails that I have been ignoring all weekend. The only email that stood out to me was one from my boss asking if I wanted to take on planning a destination wedding. I happily obliged. I will be meeting with the clients when I get back to work.

I finally climb out of bed and turn on some music. I start to clean my apartment. It was a little messy but nothing that me and the vocals of Beyoncé couldn't fix.

I started to sing out loud and every time Beyonce got the words wrong I would get mad as if I wasn't the one actually getting the words wrong.

By the time I finished cleaning my apartment and wrapping up the third encore of my live concert. I checked the time to see it was 12:51 pm. "Shit!" I exclaimed out loud realizing I needed to start getting ready.

Why am I like this? The car will be here to pick me up in an hour.

I quickly run into the shower, and while in there, I try to decide what to wear. What do you wear to meet the man who was the best friend of your late mother?

I decide to go with a loose beige off-the-shoulder dress with lace ties in the front and some white sandals. I'm dark skin but the Miami sun made me even darker, and I loved it. People always ask me why I tan if I'm already so dark, I simply respond that the darker I am the prettier I feel.

I felt beautiful at this moment. As I looked at my glowing skin and my evened-out hyperpigmentation. I glance myself up and down in the mirror after getting dressed and putting on lotion. I still can't help but feel like I'm forgetting something. "Shit," I said out loud as I looked up and realized my baby hairs were just not it.

As I start to work on them, I look at the time seeing that it's 1:38 pm. Do I move in slow motion when I'm rushing to get ready? I don't understand how time flies by like this. My baby hairs are finally set, and it only took 10 minutes of my life. I sighed. I miss my wigs, but when I have my wigs, I miss my braids. I just can't win.

Black girl problems.

It's 1:51 and a text flash across my screen.

Gerald: Hey the cars downstairs waiting for you whenever you're ready.

I quickly grab my purse, wallet, and phone making sure I have everything I may want or need. I start looking for my keys only to find them next to a round pill case.

My birth control.

Fuck me. That's what you forgot bitch.

I lock my door and run downstairs. Not having time to worry about that other thing. I was greeted by a man in a white dress shirt, slacks, and sunglasses leaning on a black car.

"Samantha?" He questioned. I nodded my head, to which he responded by opening the door for me to climb in. The drive was quiet about 40 minutes out to Rye New York. We arrived at a giant red-bricked Victorian house with a lake in the background. I couldn't stop staring at the huge house in front of me. It was beautiful. I know Jeremy's mother had a house somewhere near here but I couldn't remember where. We had used it to get away for a weekend once while she was on vacation.

The driver opens the door for me and I step out slowly. He walks me inside and uses his key to open the door. I just realized I had no idea what Gerald looked like. As the door opened my mouth dropped so hard that my jaw hit the floor. I was in awe taking in the sight of the beautiful house. The inside of the house was so modern with glass and mirrors everywhere. The driver led me to the back yard where there was a table set on the grass. I looked around to see a couple of bodies walking over to me from the waterfront. I thanked the driver as he turned to head back inside the door. Walking towards me was Steven, two other men and a woman who to say was beautiful was an understatement. I don't know why but I instantly became nervous.

Steven started running towards me to pull me into a bone-crushing hug.

"You made it!" He exclaimed

I smiled as softly as I looked at the other three figures walking towards me. The two men obviously looked alike, the older one who I assumed was Gerald and the younger one just had to be his son. The woman seemed older than the younger man but not older than the other. Could be Gerald's wife I presume.

I lock eyes with the younger dark man. I know him. Where do I know him from?

"Isaiah!" I gasp remembering the boy toy from the beach that day. He looks like a younger version of Gerald; it has got to be his son.

"I told you I would see you soon, didn't I love?" He said grinning before reaching out to take my hand to shake it.

"Yea..." I said laughing awkwardly. I look around and see the older man walking up to me with what seems to be tears in his eyes. He has salt and pepper short hair and a cleanly shaven face. He Is shaped very well for his age. He has to be at least 6'2.

He was giving Handsome black sugar daddy. "Are you okay?" I ask.

"Ugh yes," he lets out a deep sigh. "You... you just look exactly like her." I could see the tears forming in his eyes. Before I could do anything else I walk up to him, pulling him into a warm embrace and hugging him tightly. He hugs me back before pulling away and wiping away his tears. "You are the spitting image of one of the most beautiful women I have ever seen in my life."

I feel the tears in my eyes as I take in those words.

I look like her. I didn't know.

The woman walks up to us, placing a hand on Gerald's shoulder. "I'm Genesis, Gerald's older sister," she said softly before shaking my hand. "We are so happy to have you here. You don't even know."

I smile softly looking around at the faces looking at me. Is this what it's like to have a family? I thought to myself again about what I was robbed of. I needed to get this negativity out of my head. I could tell I was surrounded by love.

After the introductions, we move to sit down at the table in the grass where there is an array of food. There are collard greens, baked mac, fried chicken, Jerk chicken, fried shrimp, rice and peas, fried whiting, potato salad, and a lot more. I double-count the five chairs trying to figure out who finna eat all this food.

"I hope you like the food," Genesis said from across the table. "I have been cooking all morning with little to no help from these two," she said eyeing Gerald and Isaiah.

"Aunty if we helped you cook, we would eat as we go and there wouldn't be any food left for lunch. We did you a favor," he said jokingly

"Shut up before you get no desert," she warned

"What did you make?"

"My carrot cake with the frosting from scratch."

"I'm sorry aunty," he said quickly bringing everyone to a laugh.

The afternoon was filled with laughter, jokes, and love as we carried on. I learned that Gerald had to raise Isaiah after his wife died and Genesis helped in the process seeing as she was the older sister and didn't have any kids of her own. I learned that Isaiah and Steven became very close after meeting each other about a month ago, close enough that he invited him to Miami.

"So, he runs out of the room with the diaper in his hands, throws it on the floor, and yells, NO! let me be free!" We all erupt in laughter as they explained that at 3 years old Isaiah decided he wanted to be a nudist and not wear any clothing.

"Aunty, please, you're embarrassing me in front of the beautiful lady."

I tried to hold back my smile while rolling my eyes at him.

We had moved into the dining room in the house for wine and conversation, but I had barely touched my wine. I wasn't sure if I should. We had moved way past lunch to the point where the sun was even setting

"So, where's this carrot cake I heard so much about earlier," I said looking around. I was stuffed but I needed to try it.

"Oh my god, I almost forgot," Gen said as she got up and ran into the kitchen. About two minutes later she came back carrying a tall 7-inch cake decorated on the side with nuts and orange flowers.

"Wow, you decorated that yourself?" I asked eyeing the beautiful cake in front of me.

"Yes, I did!" she exclaimed seeming very pleased with herself. "First piece goes to Samantha since she has never had my famous carrot cake." All the men at the table let out groans, but they are quickly silenced when Genesis shoots them a glare.

She places a slice of cake in front of me, as she and the other men watch me waiting for me to take a bite. I have no doubt that this cake will be amazing considering everything else she cooked today was beyond delicious. I place a piece of the cake in my mouth, and I make the most satisfying face letting my eyes roll back in my head.

"She loves it!" They all exclaim. No really, I loved it. I wanted to lick the plate; I would have had no shame in it either.

As the night came to an end, Genesis and Gerald walked me to the car that was waiting for me while I was carrying about 10 plates of leftovers. "Please come back soon, we try to do these lunches at least once a month. We know life can be hectic and sometimes we need to take some time and relax with family, and make no mistake Samantha you are definitely family."

I pull them into a big hug before letting out a thank you.

"What no love for us?" My brother yells while standing with Isaiah.

I walk over to them placing them in a big group hug. "I'll see you soon love," Isaiah whispers in my ear before I roll my eyes and make my way back to the car. Goodnight I yell back as I climb into the car to make my way back to the city.

This day was perfect. The only thing that would make it more perfect would be to hear the voice that I have been craving all day. I quickly set the food aside and grab my phone. I have been ignoring it all day.

I call Jeremy again, but straight to voicemail again. I furrowed my brow becoming increasingly annoyed.

Me: Hey are you okay? Please call me I'm worried.

I lock my phone before putting my head back in a deep sigh. My phone vibrates and I pick it up quickly to see that he texted me back. As I unlock the phone my eyes widen at the shocking message displayed on my phone screen.

Jer Bear: I'm fine. I can't do this. I'm sorry. It's over.

I'm flushed with a wave of hurt and confusion. I tried calling again but straight to voicemail. And again. 5 times in a row. I give up and text back.

Me: If this is some sort of joke it isn't funny Jeremy.

Jer Bear: It's not a joke. I don't want to be with you.

Me: So, what was this weekend? Talk to me Jeremy, please. I love you.

Me: You promised you would never hurt me. Are you serious right now? So, this ring means nothing?

Maybe: Jer Bear: Keep the ring. bye.

I cursed apple for that update. I tried to text again, but the bubbles just turned green. He blocked my number. I half debate throwing the ring out the window.

The tears began to fall from my eyes as I took the screenshot and sent it to Annabelle. she called me immediately and I couldn't contain my sobs while on the phone. I wanted to be home. I wanted to curl up into a ball. but I was alone in a car with a driver I didn't know and no Jeremy. I had never felt so alone before.

By the time we arrived at my house, Annabelle was already outside waiting for me. I spent the long night crying in her arms. I couldn't even sleep that night. My heart was broken, I was broken. I didn't know if I would survive this one. I couldn't understand why he would do this.

Chapter 9

Samantha Kage

. . . .

1 Year later

It was visit day. I wake up stretching sore from going to the gym the night before. I really need to stop hitting it so hard. Everyone said I didn't need it as much as I thought I did but I didn't care. It started off as a distraction suggested by my therapist, however, I was forced to stop. In the time I stopped I had come to miss the gym so much. It was a way to let out my frustrations.

God knows I have had a lot within the last few years.

I brush my teeth before leaving the room. The smell of pancakes hugs my nose as I make my way down the stairs of my new house. I had only been living here about 4 months but it was time to leave the city. I wanted to be closer to Gerald anyway.

For the past year, I had not missed a single lunch, dinner, or gathering at Gerald's house. He had become the family I never knew I needed. Ms.Genesis had also become a mother figure to me in a way and me and Steven were closer than ever.

"Good morning baby," I said as I watched the male figure walk over to me with a sleeping 3-month-old baby girl in his arms. He placed a kiss on my lips before handing Anya off to me.

"Hmm good morning beautiful," he said lovingly. I walk over to put the sleeping baby with the pacifier in her mouth in her downstairs sleeping room, turning on the baby monitor.

I make my way back into the kitchen taking a seat around the island next to him as he laid out the breakfast in front of us. "You were cooking breakfast with a baby in your arms? How the hell did you manage that?"

He took my hand in his and kissed it, "I'm not just good in bed yah know, I have many talents you wouldn't even begin to know about," he said smiling at me leaning over placing another kiss on my lips. I don't know when he became so lovey and touchy but I wasn't complaining.

I take a second to admire everything I have. A man who ate my pussy until I screamed last night, a beautiful baby girl, a new house, and a new car. Then I remember that I can't stay home and do nothing today.

"Ugh can't I just stay home today? I don't wanna go." I said pulling away from him and pouting

"The woman was by your side when no one else was. The least you can do is let her see her granddaughter once a week," he said shrugging. "You want me to come with you?"

"You know you shouldn't," I said smiling.

"I can still offer," he said as he snatched a piece of bacon off my plate.

"You eat my bacon I will beat your ass in this kitchen," I said eyeing him.

"I'd like to see you try love," he said sparking a grin to form on his lips revealing his pearly whites.

"Isaiah," I warned. He knew how much I liked to play fight, he would just find a way to bring out my inner child-like happiness.

"Fine," he said rolling his eyes to place the bacon back on my plate. He leaned up to kiss my forehead before he continued with his breakfast.

"Actually, you know what. You can drive me today. And you can pick me up. If you're not too busy that is."

"Perfect. I finally get to see where you disappear to once a week."

I roll my eyes. As much as I wanted to leave the thought of Jeremy behind. His presence would find its way into my life. His mother for example convinced me to let her see Anya once a week, even though her son knew nothing of her. It didn't take much convincing, the woman was there for me the day I gave birth. She was the only one there for me if I am being honest. However, I did want Anya to know as much about her family as possible.

I grew up without a family and I didn't want that for Anya. I grew up never feeling wanted and I would be dammed if I ever allow my daughter to ever feel that way.

Doing my best to break generational curses.

It's been a year. I haven't spoken to Jeremy since that day. I had tried calling, visiting his apartment, his job everything until I just gave up and accepted defeat. I started to feel desperate and I didn't like that for myself.

I had hit low points during those first few weeks after the breakup. Actually, it wasn't a breakup, after the ghosting, I should say.

But after finding out I was pregnant, things needed to change. I started going to therapy to fix myself. As a black woman I couldn't expect to raise a child without fixing myself first, especially a daughter. But now I was happy, I had things that when I was a child, I never thought were possible.

For starters, I have a family.

Sometimes I reminisce about the day I gave birth. A traumatic story that thankfully had a wonderful ending. And I owe it all to bubble tea. Taro bubble tea to be specific.

3.5 months ago

I walk out of the car after pulling up to the Asian market near my new house. It was like 1 pm and I wanted bubble tea and spicy noodles. I had no idea why, but the last time I ignored a craving, I was up being kicked all night because of the bundle of joy in my belly. She wasn't even born yet and she already had a bad attitude. And she was spoiled!

I wonder where she gets it from. I couldn't tell you, maybe she get her attitude from her sperm donor because I surely don't have one.

I was wearing grey sweatpants and a white cotton t-shirt, I was so over being pregnant and I was a week past my due date. The doctors said to take it easy, but my mind was set on this food. I was supposed to be on bed rest, but of course, my stubborn ass didn't listen.

I walk down the aisle looking for anything else I might need, I start to turn the corner when I spot a figure I hadn't seen in over a year. It was Mariella, Jeremy's mother. She hadn't noticed me yet, so I tried to slowly back up.

I knew she lived around here somewhere. I knew I wasn't crazy.

As I was backing up another lady wasn't paying attention and rammed her cart into my back, I immediately lost my balance and fell right on my butt. It sent a sharp pain through me that led me to cry out. The woman noticed what she did and immediately started to panic.

She needs to calm down, she is drawing too much attention to me.

"Oh my god, miss are you okay, I'm so sorry! Please try not to move," she said frantically.

Girl relax.

"No, no, I'm fine just help me up please," I answer annoyed.

Like, how did she not see me?

She moves to slowly help me up, but as I begin to rise I feel a small pain in my side causing me to cry out again. The worker runs over, telling me to sit back down which I happily oblige to after the pain I just felt. He lets me know he is going to call the ambulance, and at this point, I have no choice but to agree. I hope my baby is okay.

A small crowd around the store starts to gather but I just keep my head down while rubbing the side of my stomach. If I keep my head down maybe she won't notice me as I wait for the ambulance. As much as I didn't actually want to go in an ambulance, I wasn't about to risk my life driving myself to the hospital right now, anything could happen.

"Samantha?" Mariella stoops down looking at me questionably.

"Hey Mariella," I said awkwardly acting like there was nothing wrong.

"Are you okay, are you hurt, tell me what you're feeling Bambi?" I winced at the nickname she gave me. I wanted the earth to swallow me whole. She kept rubbing my back and telling me I was going to be okay, not once leaving my side.

This ambulance couldn't come quickly enough.

The ambulance finally came and neither the woman who hit me with her cart nor the Unbeknownst grandmother of my child left my side. Mariella of course refused to not be allowed to come into the ambulance with me, and the woman who accidentally hit me refused to not follow behind the ambulance to make sure me and the baby were okay.

Doesn't the pregnant woman get a say in this?

The ambulance was quiet until she finally spoke.

"Why wouldn't Jeremy tell me you were pregnant? I must call that boy, he barely talks to me."

"Yea well, he barely talks to me either," I said in a low harsh tone rolling my eyes.

Her eyes snapped up to meet mine. "What?"

I sighed rolling my eyes. "Ms.Mariella, I would really appreciate it if you didn't tell Jeremy you saw me, He doesn't know that I'm pregnant. He broke up with me and disappeared before he even knew I was pregnant, and I honestly have finally moved on and I want him out of my life if you don't mind. And I don't mean to be rude but if you're just going to tell him you saw me anyway, I won't hesitate to not allow any of you to see Anya."

It was harsh but I wanted nothing to do with Jeremy I couldn't even track him down to tell him I was pregnant in the first place so why should he deserve to know now. I didn't want a baby to be the reason he stayed with me anyway.

Her mouth moved to say something but instead, she looked at the floor. Her glassy eyes look back up at me. "Anya? It's a girl ?" Her face moved into a smile before I saw tears coming out of her eyes.

Before I could respond, a small monitor started beeping off on the side. "What's happening?" I quickly asked looking up at the EMT worker.

"The babies in distress, Eta two minutes to the hospital." I laid still and I started to panic, trying to control my breathing. The pain in my side and back hit again causing me to take in a sharp breath and rub the side of my stomach, they have been happening for the past 5 minutes. "Contractions seem to be about 4 minutes apart" the man yelled again.

We arrived at the hospital, not my hospital, not my doctors, and they immediately decided I should do a C-section.

The one thing I did not want. "No, I want to push," I said as I start to cry. I was genuinely afraid of a C-section after what happened to my mother.

The doctors told me I didn't have a choice because the baby and I were at risk. I couldn't stop crying as they tried to reel me away, I grabbed Mariella's hand as she was my only saving grace at the moment. "Please don't leave me," I say looking at her with tears in my eyes. I hadn't been able to call Gerald, Annabelle, Steven, or Isaiah.

In my scariest moment, she was all I had.

"I won't leave you Bambi." She started arguing with the doctors. They still separated us but as I got wheeled away I could hear her yelling at everyone. I got hooked up to machines on the table and I never felt more alone. I was cold, crying and I couldn't control my breathing. I didn't know if my baby girl was going to be okay or not. I didn't know if I was going to be okay or not.

Before I could get wrapped up in my thoughts, Mariella walked inside the room in white scrubs taking a seat by my head. "I'm hear Bambi," she said before kissing my forehead. For the first time since I fell, I had relaxed a Little. She didn't let go of my hand once and every time I would start to panic or cry she would be there to comfort me and sing to me. The procedure felt like it was going on for hours. My stress didn't waiver fully until I heard the sweetest sound in the world. I heard her cry. I heard my baby girl cry.

Mariella perked up at the sight of the baby. "She has his eyes," was all she said before breaking out into an uncontrollable sob. "I'm so proud of your Bambi," she said placing a kiss on my forehead.

But I didn't respond. I could see them working on the most beautiful dark-skinned baby I ever laid my eyes on. But my vision began to blur. I kept coming to and going out. I could see Mariella yelling, I could hear monitors beeping, and I was still unable to move. I was alone again as they ushered Mariella out of the room and took my baby girl away. The blurry vision took over and I was out.

It was hours before I finally woke up.

I woke up in a dark room, one of the hospital suites. My throat was dry. I blink to open my eyes to see Mariella sleeping on the chair in the corner, with Gerald in another one. I winced at the pain in my lower stomach and side. I look around unable to sit up and I don't see her. I don't see my baby girl. Where is she? I began to cry uncontrollably which led the monitors to start going off again. I couldn't control my breathing or my anxiety I just wanted to see her. Where was she?

Gerald and Marcella woke up at the same time alarmed, hearing the monitors. Both rushing over to me. Mariella ran out to call the nurse, and Gerald tried to calm me down.

"Where is she," I asked quietly through my tears, my voice hoarse. I couldn't focus on anything else. I just had to know she was okay.

"She's right here, calm down sweetheart, she's right here," he said

sweetly. I turn my head to the other side of the bed where I saw a baby fast asleep in a little tiny bed. I reach for her, causing the monitors to stop and my breathing to slow. I visibly relaxed, but all I wanted to do was touch her. The nurse comes into the room to check my vitals, monitors, and the bandages around my waist."

"What happened," I asked looking around at the people looking at me.

"You developed a blood clot during surgery, but we were able to remove it before It caused any serious damage. We worked very hard to save you, and not just because this woman over here threatened to burn down the whole hospital if anything happened to her daughter or granddaughter," she said giving Mariella smile.

"Is everything okay with the baby?"

"Yes, you have a perfectly healthy, 7-pound 3 ounce baby girl."

For the first time in hours. I finally feel like I am able to breathe.

"Wait. Gerald how did you get here, how did you know where I was?"

"I called your phone and Ms.Mariella here answered and told me what was going on. I dropped everything to drive down here. Your brother and Isaiah will be here in the morning. Try to get some rest," he said kissing my forehead." Oh, and Samantha, don't ever scare me like that again. I was petrified driving down here," he said with glossy eyes.

Once I knew Anya was okay and my mind was finally starting to relax, I realized just how exhausted I was. I was out like a light.

The next day I was showered with balloons, flowers, gifts, and love. Harper, Annabelle, Steven, Gerald, Mariella, Isaiah, Ms.Genesis, and the lady from the supermarket, Iris I think her name was, were in and out of my room all day. When I was finally able to hold my *baby I could finally take in her features, she was dark-skinned but not as dark as me, her eyelashes curled beautifully, and her eyes were dark blue, darker than Jeremys. With the exception of her eyes, she was my entire twin.*

The day before I was able to leave the hospital, Mariella had come to visit me, she was there every day so I wasn't shocked.

"I want to ask you something," she said standing nervously in the corner.

"Anything." I say smiling at her while breastfeeding Anya." I never knew how strong that connection could feel. Knowing I am the one that is nourishing her honestly made me happy.

"I want to be in Anya's life." she trailed off. "I don't know what happened between you and my son, and I don't care, if he wants to act like his father then so be it, But I will not let this little girl grow up not knowing she has me as a grandmother," she said nervously but sternly.

"Mariella," I smiled before continuing, "Her name is Anya Mariella Serena Bresset." Immediately tears sprung from her eyes.

"Are you serious?" She choked out between her tears.

"Yes, I wouldn't dream of her not knowing you," I said smiling at her.

Chapter 10

Samantha Kage

· ·

I get Anya dressed in a white onesie dress with sunflowers all over it with a matching headband. I throw on a yellow dress myself and start making my way out of the house down to the car.

"Diaper bag, extra breastmilk, change of clothes," I said to myself making sure I have everything. Not that I needed anything. Mariella had an entire room dedicated to gifts, essentials, and clothes for Anya.

I strap Anya in her car seat before making my way to the passenger side. Isaiah was already waiting for me in the car.

"You take forever to get ready woman."

"It takes time to look this good," I reply back with a smile and a quick kiss on the cheek. I am immediately greeted with a bright smile. I love his dimples.

"Who you looking so good for?"

"Me myself and I," I said while rolling my eyes on cue.

"Keep playing with me," he says before laughing.

I text Mariella to let her know I was on my way before we drove off.

In 15 minutes, we arrive at her house. Her house is twice the size of mine. I guess she must have won it in the divorce. It's a huge modern white house with windows everywhere and a pool in the back. It has to have at least 4 bedrooms inside. Isaiah steps out to grab the bags while I carry Anya up the stairs in front of the house.

Such a gentleman.

I use my free hand to grab the keys and open the door. I kiss Isaiah goodbye after he drops the bags at the doors and turns back out. I move to walk to the back of the house when I don't see her in the living room.

"Hey Angela," I greet her maid. "Is Mariella in her room or her study?"

"Good morning Bambi," she said sweetly. "And good morning mini Bambi," she says wiggling her finger at Anya. "Yes, Ms. Mariella is in her study. But I think there are some new clothes for Anya in the room. You should go look at them before you go to her study," she says with a little bit of urgency in her tone.

I look at her confused. "Nah, I'll just head up to the study. Mariella is very eager to see the baby today."

"You sure? They are really nice, I will even go look at the clothes with you."

"No, I'm good, thank you though."

She sighs and I make another confused face as I walk away from her to the stairs.

That little encounter was weird right?

I make my way up the stairs with a cooing baby in my arms. "Are you ready to see glamma?" I start to repeat over and over in my baby voice before entering the room.

We call Mariella glamma instead of grandma because she is glamourous.

I poke my head into the study without knocking to see two figures standing in the room and Mariella sitting in her chair looking concerned. When I enter the room her eyes dart to me widening in alarm. One of the figures turn around to see what Mariella was looking at. He immediately does a double-take before locking his dark blue eyes on mine. I look down at his arms to see that they are interlocked with a blonde bimbo on his side. The blue-eyed monster looks as though he wants to speak but decides against it. I decide to break the quiet to snap us out of whatever confusing trance we were in.

"Oh, I'm sorry Mariella, I didn't know you had company," I say as nonchalantly as possible.

"What is she doing here?" Tiffany has the nerve to part her lips. I feel nothing but fire, but I won't give him or her the satisfaction. I divert my attention back to Mariella instead.

"Mariella I'll be down the hall when you're ready for me," I said ignoring them and closing the door behind me. I make my way down to the double bedroom quickly. The bedroom is connected to a small opening connecting it to another room. Mariella had set it up for me just in case I ever decided to sleep over with Anya so we would have our own connecting rooms. Which I never actually did. I didn't feel right sleeping here, as badly as I know she wanted me to.

I close the door behind me and I really hope they leave soon. I want nothing to do with either of them. I don't need this negativity around my girl right now. As soon as I close the door to the room Anya starts to cry.

Great.

Shit her bottle is downstairs. She doesn't like drinking straight from the nipple because she thinks I'm trying to put her to sleep. But I'm going to try her with it anyway. "Please be nice," I whisper to her.

 I place a nipple in her mouth, she sucks about 3 times before letting go and starting to cry again.

She really only likes the nipple during bedtime.

Fuck it. I quickly go downstairs from the other staircase and I don't see anyone. I walk over to the bags on the floor grabbing a bottle to put into the bottle warmer. As the bottle is warming Anya is still fussy in my arms. I hear muffled arguments but I try to ignore them and focus on my girl. I don't care what they are talking about. That's their business.

I grab the bottle as soon as the timer goes off. As I start feeding Anya, I hear footsteps and see the big blonde bimbo herself stomp down the stairs. She stops walking and shoots me a glare while I'm standing in the kitchen. She looks like she wants to say something and I really hope she does. I hope she gives me a reason.

She goes to part her lips but stops once her eyes move to the baby in my arms and she softens her glare. A red face Jeremy comes down behind her and stops when he sees me. His eyes dart to the feeding baby in my arms, then back to me, then to the baby. His jaw tightens as he begins to look confused.

Did they not notice her before?

I try to pay them no mind as I lock eyes with the beautiful baby staring up at me. They are just standing there staring at me like a couple of weirdos.

Can they like...move?

"Her eyes," I heard tiffany say in a low whisper. I quickly turn around giving my back to them. I don't want that whore looking at my baby. I hear the footsteps trail off and the door slam behind me.

Bitch ass people made my baby flinch from the loud noise. I immediately roll my eyes.

They are not your problem girl. Fuck them. I hope they are happy together.

I hear footsteps and I turn around to see Mariella running down the stairs. "I'm so sorry Bambi, I didn't know they would be here," she says apologetically

"It's fine, he was bound to find out sometime," I shrug. "Not like he acknowledged her anyway."

"Did he say anything to you?"

"Of course not, why would he?" I said harshly.

I know it probably wasn't her fault but what if she set this up, would she really do that to me? Does she want him to know so he can take away my baby?

I quickly shake off the thought.

Just then the door flies open with an angry Italian man stomping through the door.

"How could you not tell me about this?" He asked as he stomped over to me while looking at his mother.

Okay, but if he talking to her, why is he standing so close to me?

"You don't even answer my calls, much less call me back, you want me to hunt you down and kiss your ass to tell you things? This could never be the child I raised dear lord," she said throwing her hands up in the air.

I am still looking down at my baby trying not to look directly at him.

"And you. Is this another play for my money?"

He not talking to me.

Woosah Samantha, Woosah. Maybe his money is the only thing that makes him feel like a man.

"Mariella. I will see you soon. Preferably at my house, if you don't mind," I say ignoring him. I move away to grab my phone to call Isaiah. Boy did I wish I drove myself today.

"Now hold on," she says before I grab my phone. "You will not talk to the mother of my granddaughter like that. This is my house"

"Are you sure the baby is mine?" He asks darting his eyes back to me.

I chuckle for a second. "I really fucking hate you, do you know that?" I said feeling the tears weld in my eyes. That was the first time spoke to him in over a year. Those were the first words I said to him and it felt so fucking good.

He had the nerve to look hurt that I said that. Is this man on crack? I quickly grab my phone to dial Isaiah's number. I pause before hitting the call button. I forgot I'm petty, I never worked on that in therapy.

"Let's get something straight, I am not here for you. I am here for my child to spend time with her grandmother, not only because she is her grandmother but when I almost died giving birth, she was the only one there for me not the sperm donor of my child. So yes, I visit this wonderful woman from time to time so she can see her granddaughter because all she has is a mother, a grandmother, and no father. And let's get something else clear, I haven't thought of you in god knows how long, and as far as I'm concerned, I didn't see you today, and I haven't seen you since Miami. You don't know I have a baby. You don't need to concern yourself with the fact that I have a baby because she or I am not your concern. And I am done speaking to you, you can like evaporate or something I don't know, but just don't do it around me or my daughter."

Harsh sis harsh.

"Mariella, I'll be in my room. I think I'm going to spend the night tonight". I said smiling before walking away and heading up the stairs.

Petty see petty do. Period.

I could feel his eyes on me. But I didn't care he deserved that. He put me through hell.

Jeremy Pov

Today is the day. Today is the day that I tell my mom that me and Tiffany have decided to get married. Per my father's request anyway. I would rather tell my mom myself than have her hear it through the grapevine as much as I wanted to try to keep it a secret. I lay in my bed in my room alone in my thoughts. Tiffany is down the hall in her room. I try to keep as much distance between us, she can be a bit much sometimes. All she really does is spend money and complain. But this woman was about to become my wife. I wonder if I made the right choices that lead me to be in the position I am in today.

I roll over and open Instagram switching over to my company's account. I type in her Instagram name to check how she's doing. I couldn't use my own Instagram because she blocked me. Thank god her Instagram was public. I do this at least once a week. Her most recent picture was a couple of weeks ago. A silly selfie with her and Annabelle. It was captioned, "Soon."

The fuck did that mean? Was she going on vacation or something? Why wasn't I told about this?

She looks happy, and she's glowing. I feel a smile come across my lips as I continue to stare at her face on my phone.

After god knows how long, I sigh putting the phone down. I hop in the shower, get dressed, and make my way downstairs to see Tiffany sitting in the kitchen. She ordered breakfast for herself.

Typical

"Good morning," she says with her eyes lighting up.

"Morning," I throw over my shoulder without looking back. "You almost ready? We should start heading to my mom's to tell her the news."

"Yes can't you see I'm dressed." I look over my shoulder to see she was wearing a skin-tight short Lacey pink dress looking like she took it out of a lingerie catalog.

"Change."

"Why," she pouts

"Whatever game you're playing won't work, I am not going to fuck you before we go to my mom's house. It will make us late. Go change now." I said rolling my eyes at her. She wanted me to fuck her every day, like some sort of animal. I could only get my dick hard for her once in a while.

"Ugh fine," she said hopping out of the chair and rolling her eyes.

I wait by the door and she comes downstairs wearing a pink spaghetti-strap crop top and some low-rise jeans and sandals.

Lord.

I don't even argue. I make my way out the door and start to walk toward my car. I decide to go with the BMW. She hops in before I start the 50-minute drive to my mother's house.

The ride is quiet as I turn a 50-minute drive into a 30-minute one. I park around the side of the house so no one will see my car. I wanted to surprise my mother. I feel like I hadn't seen her in forever.

I knock on the door of my mother's huge house. She lives here all alone, I start to feel a little bad that I don't visit her as much as I should. As I'm waiting for someone to answer the door, I look over to see Tiffany snapping pictures of herself with her ring.

Of course.

Angela finally answers the door. "Mr. Jeremy?" She asked confused.

"Hey Ang," I said smiling. "Is mom around?"

"Yes, she is in her study," she says looking at me cocking her head to the side. "Uhm Mr.Jeremy does your mother know you are here?"

"No. I was coming to surprise her. Can't a man visit his own mother?" I said confusingly.

"Erm yes, yes come in please," she says opening the door for us to walk in.

I look at her confused before I walk away. She has this look on her face that I can't pinpoint. Nervousness maybe?

I make my way up the stairs with Tiffany following behind me. I reach the doors of her study before knocking twice. I hear her feet scurry to the door and she opens the door with a big smile on her face. Her excited face turns to shock when she opens the door and sees it's me on the other side of the door. It turns into a frown when she looks over my shoulder to see Tiffany.

"Jeremy?" She exclaims diverting her gaze back to me. I've known the woman for 25 years and I have never once seen her look this confused before. "C-come in," she says stuttering while closing the door quickly behind us.

"Were you expecting someone else to be on the other side of the door?"

"What? no, no," she says laughing nervously. "I just didn't expect you to be here. You know since you don't love your mother and you never talk to me and all," she said stuttering through her words and laughing nervously.

What is going on with everyone today?

"Mom." I start to say in protest before she cuts me off.

"It's fine," she said holding up her hand. If she only knew why I did the things I did. "So to what do I owe this random visit," she asked while sitting down at her desk chair.

"Well mom, I-" I trailed off. "We have something to tell you," I said grabbing Tiffany's wrist.

She raises an eyebrow looking at the both of us waiting for her to continue.

"Well, we have decided to get married," I said clearing my throat right after.

She raises an eyebrow making a face of deep concern and shock, but before she could say anything, I hear the door open behind me. The voice sounds so familiar. It almost rolls off my ears like a soft wind on a summer day. "Are you ready to see glamma," the voice says.

The fuck?

I dart my eyes around to see the head of the most beautiful woman I have ever laid my eyes on. My eyes lock onto her beautiful silky bright brown eyes. Her hair is slicked back in a low bun. Her real hair. I've missed those coils. It's been so long since I have seen this beauty that my knees grow a little weak just at the sight of her. I watch as her eyes trail from me to me and Tiffany's arms locked in each other. Her once soft beautiful brown eyes turn cold.

She stops looking at me and diverts her attention back to my mother. Her eyes leaving me makes my chest tighten a little bit. I didn't realize just how much I longed for her presence until now.

"Oh I'm sorry Mariella, I didn't know you had company," she said diverting her gaze and completely acting like she doesn't know who I am.

"What is she doing here?" Tiffany says to me. But I'm still focused on the girl that just pushed her head through the door.

"Mariella I'll be down the hall when you ready for me," she said before ducking back out the door closing it behind her. I half want to run after her. Wrap her in my arms. But I don't deserve to even touch her.

I turn around to my mother giving her a questionable look. She just shrugs her shoulders.

"So you have your whore hiding at your mother's house," Tiffany said yelling in my face.

My hand twitched at her calling Sam out of her name. I don't hit women but I would surely slam the shit out of Tiffany with no second thoughts.

"Use common sense. I'm never up here. How would I have known that she was here?" I said shooting her a glare.

The stupid pointless argument goes on with my mother just staring at us from her desk chair.

"These two getting married," my mother said under her breath thinking no one could hear her.

I want nothing more than to leave this room and go see her again. But instead, I'm arguing with someone who doesn't know how to take her own head out of her ass.

"Fuck this, let's go," Tiffany says as she darts out of the room heading down the stairs. I have no choice but to follow behind her in hopes I get to see the beautiful goddess again.

I catch up to Tiffany seeing that she has come to a complete stop to stare at something. I walk over to look and to my surprise, my baby girl is standing in the kitchen feeding a young baby in her arms. By the looks of the sunflowers, it has to be a girl.

She had a baby?

"Her eyes," Tiffany said in a whisper.

I look closer to see the baby had dark blue eyes, Scarily similar to mine and my father's.

She had my baby?

I grab Tiffany's arm and drag her out the door. If she disrespects Samantha one more time, I would have to drop her and I don't want to do that in front of Sam. I don't need her seeing my violence anywhere other than the bedroom.

"Take the keys. Go shopping come back in an hour." I said to the blonde girl in front of me looking stressed.

"So you can have time alone with your whore? I think the fuck not."

"See this is what I'm talking about. You are in my mother's house. You're overheated and you are going to say something stupid. Go! Now!" I yell in her face.

Truthfully I just wanted her gone so I could spend some time with Samantha.

I think she missed me. Actually, I know she did.

"Fine," she says quietly as she grabs the keys from me. I wait until she drives off before heading back inside.

I'm mad. I have already missed out on god knows how long of my child's life. This is unfair to me. But I have no one to blame but myself. I burst back in the doors stomping over to Samantha, I needed to be as close to her as would be allowed without alarming her.

"How could you not tell me about this?" I said glaring at my mother. God knows how long she knew.

How long has she known? Why did no one tell me?

"You don't even answer my calls, much less call me back, you want me to hunt you down and kiss your ass to tell you things? This could never be the child I raised dear lord!" Mom said throwing her hands up in the air.

I look over at the beautiful sight in front of me. There is no way this little girl isn't mine. But she keeps her eyes on the baby. I want her to look at me. I want to feel her gaze. I need to make her look at me.

"And you." I said taking the opportunity to speak to her, "is this another play for my money?" I asked more harshly than I intended while watching her make the cutest faces at the baby. I would do or say anything to get her to look at me right now.

"Mariella. I will see you soon. Preferably at my house." she says ignoring me, moving away from me to grab her phone to call someone.

Who the fuck is she calling?

Now hold on," my mother says quickly "You will not talk to the mother of my granddaughter like that. This is my house!"

"Are you sure the baby is mine?" I said trying at one desperate attempt to make her at least acknowledge me.

"I really fucking hate you! Do you know that? "She threw at me through glossy eyes. Those words crushed my soul as they fell from her lips. At least I got her to look at me. I hope she didn't mean that. I couldn't help but be surprised that she felt that way. I don't think I made her hate me. Did I? I just wanted to wrap my baby girls in my arms, but I couldn't. Not yet. I watch as she grabs her phone again. I wish I could tell her everything but I can't.

If she is calling her man then he would die today. That's the only sane option.

"Let's get something straight, I am not here for you. I am here for my child to spend time with her grandmother, not only because she is her grandmother but when I almost died giving birth, she was the only one there for me not the sperm donor of my child. So Yes, I visit this wonderful woman from time to time so she can see her granddaughter because all she has is a mother, a grandmother, and no father. And let's get something else clear, I haven't thought of you in god knows how long, and as far as I'm concerned, I didn't see you today, and I haven't seen you since Miami. You don't know I have a baby. You don't need to concern yourself with the fact that I have a baby because she or I am not your concern. And I am done speaking to you, you can like evaporate or something I don't know, but just don't do it around me or my daughter." She said harshly putting extra emphasis on the, I's, and Me's.

Deadbeat? Died? What the fuck! Someone's going to get an earful later.

Her words cut through me like a knife but I know I deserved every word. Before I could even speak she diverted her attention back to my mother.

"Mariella, I'll be in my room. I think I'm going to spend the night tonight". She slowly walked away up the stairs with the feeding baby. Before I even realized it, I was running up the stairs right behind her.

Chapter 11

Samantha Kage

· ·

I quickly make my way back into the bedroom closing the door behind me. I place Anya down in her bassinet making sure any toy she grabs will be within reach so she doesn't start crying. I need to put her down and cool off.

I can't believe I just said that to him.

Why? He deserved it.

As she is safe in her playpen cooing away with her little toys, I start to pace the room nervously. Shaking my hands and try to calm myself as best as I can so I don't cry. Frustrated tears are more annoying than sad tears. Those don't fucking turn off.

I take a deep breath before sitting on the bed, I'm startled and confused when I hear a soft knock on the door.

I walk over to the door, expecting to see Mariella, but instead, I see a distressed man standing on the other side of the door. I finally take him in. His hair is slicked back perfectly, his face is cleanly shaven, I prefer him to look scruffy personally.

His hands are in the pockets of his black dress pants and he is wearing a black long sleeve button-down dress shirt to match. The shirt hugs his arm muscles so perfectly. I didn't realize how long I was staring at him until I looked into his eyes realizing he was doing the same.

"What?" I finally said making him take his eyes off my body and meet my eyes.

"I," was all he could choke out before I closed the door in his face.

He knocked again and I opened it.

"How can I help you?" I opened the door again.

"I don't know what to say Samantha."

He stays quiet for a few seconds before I shrug and close the door again.

Fuck he came up here bothering me for?

He knocks again and I roll my eyes before I open it.

"Can you stop?"

No.

I say nothing, I just stare at him. Did he come up here to just stare at me or what. I look dramatically around waiting for him to say something.

"I mean, are you okay?" He asked raising his shoulders.

"Am I okay!" I started to yell but I quickly stopped when I realized the loud noise made Anya starts to fuss. I dart my eyes back to Jeremy before rolling them. Letting go of the door I walk over to the bassinet picking her up and placing her on the bed. I sit next to her making sure she doesn't suddenly develop the ability to roll over. I try not to make her so used to being in my arms but Isaiah spoils her.

Like, let her have her dam tummy time.

"What's her name," he says quietly not moving from the door.

"Anya," I sigh "Anya Mariella Serena Bresset," I said looking away from him and mumbling the last name.

"You gave her my last name?" He says softly darting his eyes at me. I half expected him to yell at me for it but instead, he looked happy. In awe almost.

Shocked the fuck out of me.

"I did it because of your mother not because of you. Don't flatter yourself."

"Can I," he says clearing his throat. "Can I see her?"

"Uhm sure I guess. I didn't think you would want to."

"I'm sorry," he said.

Sorry for what exactly because you keep saying sorry and not saying what you're sorry for.

Ignoring him I reach over to cradle her in my arms as he walks over to us. She immediately looks up at him getting lost in his blue eyes. He reaches down and touches the side of her arm causing a half smile to form on the corner of her mouth.

"She's beautiful," he said slowly not breaking his gaze on her. He reached down and softly brushed her cheek and in response, she moved to attack his finger.

"She looks just like you," he finally said meeting my gaze with a smile on his face. He almost looked as if he was going to cry. I just look at him while nodding my head slowly.

I start to get an overwhelming rush of emotion watching him with her. She is finally meeting her father. I feel the tears filling my eyes. I can't be here. I can't be around him. I can't pretend everything is okay, not again. He hurt me. I won't let him hurt her.

I quickly grab my phone out of my dress pocket and dial Isaiah's number. I need to get out of here as soon as possible. Jeremy looks at me confused as he watched my actions.

"Hello," he says sleepily.

"Babe, can you come to get me? Now please." I said staring at Jeremy while my voice was a little shaky. He looked shocked at the word babe causing his jaw to tighten while he let out a huff of displeasure. Why is he mad right now? Isn't he in a relationship?

"Yea, I'll be there in 10 minutes. Are you okay?"

"Yea I just. I need to leave now. I'll come back tomorrow when there's not so much going on here." Our eyes are locked on each other as I'm speaking on the phone.

"Okay baby," he said before hanging up.

I move to stand even though Jeremy refuses to move from in front of me.

Does he think he is transparent? Can he move?

I move walking past Jeremy the best I can with him still in my way, and make my way downstairs.

"Samantha," he says quietly as I reach the doorway but I keep moving. I can tell he wants to stop me from leaving but there's something holding him back. Of course, he doesn't fight for me. Why would he? He never did before.

I make my way downstairs seeing Mariella in the kitchen talking to Angela. They both stop to look at me.

"I'm sorry Mariella I have to go, I can't be here," I said with my voice cracking. Just then the blue-eyed devil walked down the stairs making his appearance.

"What did you do," Mariella said her eyes darting back to him.

"I didn't do anything," he said staring at me and not meeting his mother's gaze. I look away and down at the floor. Why are his eyes on me so intense?

I could feel my eyes growing heavy with liquid again. At this point, these tears are getting really ghetto.

"Jeremy, you will not be the reason I don't get to see that baby, do you hear me? I'll be dammed if I let you treat Samantha the way your father treated me. I don't know why you idolize the man so much," she said angrily.

"Mariella it's okay, I'll just come back tomorrow. I'm free." I said quietly not wanting to cause any rift between them.

"I am nothing like father," he said quietly but coldly still not taking his eyes off me.

"Oh? And don't you think how you treated Samantha was very Justin-like of you?" She said looking at him and crossing her arms.

"You don't even know what I'm trying to do," he trailed off stopping himself.

"I do know. I know everything that happened between you two. And for you to walk in here after god knows how long just to tell me you're marrying a girl I cannot stand is very father like son if you ask me."

Marrying?

My eyes snap up at him in disbelief. He was marrying her. I could feel my face move from sad to cold in a matter of seconds. If I didn't hate him before, I know I did now. I can't even look at him.

It's like he goes out of his way to hurt me without even trying. I refuse to look at him. Instead, I look down at Anya who seems so innocent. She doesn't even know what's going on. The world hasn't had a chance to be cruel to her yet.

"Samantha," he trails off taking a step forward, causing me to flinch and take a step back. I couldn't look at him. I couldn't touch him. I didn't want to. I wanted to be as far away from him as possible.

Why today lord? I was having a good day.

He opened his mouth to speak again, but then there is a knock at the door. I move quickly to open it but not before wiping my eyes. I open it seeing my saving grace. Isaiah with some grey sweatpants on and a black V-neck t-shirt. He locks eyes with me and quickly strides into the house to take my face in his hands.

"Are you okay baby," he says looking deep into my eyes searching for what's wrong.

"Yes, can we just go please?" I said quietly.

He looks around and takes in the scene in front of him. Angela standing in the kitchen, Mariella looking upset with her arms folded glaring at something in the corner. His eyes trail over to see Jeremy standing in the corner leaning on the wall. If looks could kill, both of these men would combust into flames. I notice Isaiah's arm muscles tighten under his shirt.

I place my arm on Isaiah's chest causing him to snap out of the staring contest he was in. He looks at me before he softens his look. He lets out a sigh, grabs the bags on the floor, and takes them to the car. I follow out the doors behind him quickly trying to escape the weirdness of this day.

I make my way down the steps to turn around and notice Mariella running behind me. "I promise he won't be here tomorrow Bambi," she says whispering to me, pulling me into a tight hug before stepping back.

"Okay," I nod my head. I look up at the house to see he has made his way outside to watch me. Isaiah comes over to take Anya out of my arms to walk around and put her in the car seat. Jeremy's face immediately turns red. I could see his chest rising at the sight of Isaiah carrying Anya. I still don't see how he can be upset about this. No one caused this but him.

Isaiah comes back around to open my door for me but not before pulling me into a soft hug and placing a small kiss on my lips before stroking my cheek lovingly. He darts his eyes back at Jeremy who I didn't even notice had moved closer to us, way too close. I smile softly at Mariella before sliding into the car with Isaiah closing the door behind me. He throws one last look at Jeremy before he made his way around the car. He climbs in and hums the car to life driving off slowly. I lived less than 15 minutes away. The car was so silent even Anya had gone back to sleep.

When we arrive back at the house, we quickly make our way inside. He carried Anya to her play area placing her down.

"Do you wanna talk about it," he says walking over to me and placing his hand on my shoulder. I couldn't form words. I only shook my head and offered him a small smile.

"Can you watch her while I get some work done?" I ask softly.

He nods his head before diverting his attention back to the baby. I walk upstairs, close the door behind me, and grab my laptop. I sit on the bed and decide to throw myself into emails. The destination wedding was a few months away. I had a couple of emails with questions from the guests but that was it. I never really was a procrastinator, I did most of my work yesterday so I could have today free to spend with Mariella.

Look how well that turned out.

I decide to change out of my clothes and turn on old episodes of one piece. I just wanna spend the rest of the day wrapped up in the arms of Isaiah and Anya with Anime, it had become my happy place. Before I could get up to go get Isaiah and Anya, a message popped up on my computer.

Maybe Jeremy: Hey it's Jeremy. I need to see her again. I hope in time you will understand why I did what I did. I'm sorry. I hope you kept the ring. I love you.

Nah this nigga got me fucked up. The fuck does that mean. Someone needs to talk to apple about this maybe nonsense.

He loves who?

I actually did keep the ring of empty promises. I gave it to Anya. I keep it in a box on her dresser, wanting it far away from me. I ignore the message and close my laptop. I make my way downstairs to see the sight of a big man laying on the couch with a bubbly baby on his chest. It warms my heart to know she has someone for her who makes her laugh.

Wanna watch anime, stay in bed, have sex, and eat food? " I ask staring at him from the bottom of the stairs.

His head snaps up in excitement. "Umm is water wet?" He yelled back smiling.

We make our way back upstairs. As soon as we sit on the king-size bed and turn on one piece, Anya immediately falls asleep. She knows when mommy trying to get some. I place her in the crib in the next room grabbing the baby monitor. I make my way back into my bedroom seeing that Isaiah is already stripped down to his boxers.

"We have a good 15 minutes," I whisper looking at Isaiah ready to devour him.

"I only need 8," he said walking over to me before picking me up and throwing me on the bed. I pull my shirt off over my head and he climbs over my body quickly finding my lips. The kiss is so soft and sensual yet so greedy. He rests himself comfortably in between my legs letting me feel his length pressed against my inner thigh. We roll over with me on top of him straddling his waist without breaking our kiss. He traces my back with his fingers slowly moving his hands down to grab both of my ass cheeks, placing a hard smack on one of them. I grind my throbbing pussy against his rock-hard length.

He flips us back over breaking our kiss. He leans up to pull my shorts off slowly. I wasn't wearing any underwear, I think I genuinely don't like wearing panties anymore. He stands taking my thighs and yanking me to the edge of the bed. I let out a sharp breath as I move closer to him. He leans over placing a kiss on my lips, slowly trailing kisses down my neck, kissing my nipples softly, nibbling at my belly button, and then placing slow kisses tender kisses across my C-section scar that I was so insecure about. "Beautiful," I hear him whisper. It almost makes me cry.

He is so gentle with me.

He grabs my hips keeping them in place as he moves down to lick my soft wet folds. He sticks his tongue inside slowly licking and circling his tongue around my clit. "You like that baby," he says as he continues to take his time with my body. I start to arch my back off the bed as I put my hand over my mouth, careful not to wake the baby with the devilish sounds that have begun to escape my throat. He stands up and leans over to grab a condom off the nightstand. He slowly slides it on before leaning over to kiss me again. He seems to have a way of making me feel loved during sex.

He places his hard tip at my entrance and slides into me at a dangerously slow pace allowing me to get used to his size. We had only had sex once before this but it almost felt as if he was making love to me for the first time.

I still wasn't used to his size, especially after not having sex with anyone for over a year. He was so sweet, so sensual, so gentle with me, and so loving. He starts his strokes off slowly going deeper with every thrust, allowing me to feel every inch filling me up. Immediately I dig my nails into his back in response.

He takes one of my legs and places it on his shoulder leaning into me, I let out a too-loud moan which he quickly uses his hand to cover up. I push him off and quickly get up to push him down on the bed, I climb on top of him straddling him with his tip at my entrance before I slide down slowly on his length. "Fuck! I'm about to cum!" he moans out too loudly. He throws his head back in pleasure letting out a moan. I quickly kiss him to stifle his moans.

I start to buck my hips fast and faster looking him in his eyes as we bring each other closer to the edge. He looks at me as if I'm the only person in the room, the only person in his life, the only person in the world. It drives me to move even faster. I lean over to nibble at his ear which causes him to let out a sexy moan.

Our pace quickens as I feel the heat growing inside me. He

places his hands on my hips to match my rhythm from below thrusting into me harder than before. I throw my head back as I feel my orgasm start to build. A few more strokes and I come undone with my walls clenching around him as he thrusts inside me one more time stilling. I collapse on his chest out of breath smiling. He leans down to kiss my forehead still tracing patterns on my back with his fingers with him still inside me. I could sleep just like this.

And right on cue, the baby monitor goes off letting us know that Anya's awake.

"I'll get her, he said slowly sliding out of me and putting on his boxers and his shorts. He slaps my ass causing me to giggle before he goes into the bathroom to wash his hands and I watch him walk out of the room. I sigh deeply relaxing into the bed.

I need to change this blanket.

The three of us spend the day in bed, watching Anime, eating food, and enjoying each others company. It almost felt like we were a family.

Later in the night, I'm laying in bed tracing the face of a sleeping Anya. I like to stare at her sometimes and admire her beauty.

I did that.

"I want to take you out tomorrow."

"What?" I say causing my head to snap up.

"Yea, dinner specifically. I want to talk to you about something important." He stands up starting to get dressed.

"why can't you just tell me now?"

"Where's the fun in that? It will ruin the surprise."

Surprise? Y'all know I hate surprises.

I furrow my brow giving him a stank ass face.

"I guess I can leave Anya with Mariella, let me check if she's free?"

Me and Isaiah have never actually been on an actual date. With me preparing for the wedding and him working for his contracting company, we really spent most of our time together in the house with the baby.

"I don't see why she wouldn't be," he shrugs

Me: Can you watch Anya tomorrow night?

Glamma: Yes of course! Are you still coming over in the morning?

Me: Yes, we never talked about that thing you said you had to talk to me about.

Glam Ma: Oh just come over to relax. It can wait until mothers day in a few days. It's a surprise.

Me: Okay

I frown. I hate surprises.

"She said she can watch her." I smile looking up at him as he gets ready to go home.

"Good," I'll see you tomorrow at 6 love," he said placing a kiss on my lips and Anya's forehead before heading out the door.

Chapter 12

Samantha Kage

I arrive at Mariella's house the next morning a little later than I usually do, I ended up taking an Uber not wanting to drive. To be honest I was hesitant about coming back here after yesterday in fear that Jeremy would be here. I took my sweet time getting ready hoping that she would call and tell me he came back so I didn't have to come.

 If he was here again I would just simply leave and not come back. Mariella would just have to visit Anya at my house from now on. I am focused on protecting my own peace.

I use my key to open the giant white doors, and immediately my jaw drops as I take in the sight in front of me.

In the middle of the living room is a giant teddy bear with half a dozen giant pink balloons containing different size pink gift boxes surrounding it. In the mix of gift boxes are a bouquet of white roses. I know Mariella likes to shop for Anya but she could go a little easier.

Anya isn't even 6 months yet and she has more clothes than I do. And that's saying something.

Anya wouldn't fit half this stuff in a week or even a month. I would have to change her outfit four times a day just to guarantee that Anya will get a chance to wear the stuff Mariella had upstairs alone.

I hear footsteps, I look over to see Mariella hopping down the stairs toward me.

"Mariella, umm this is a bit much. I mean I'm grateful but Anya doesn't need this much stuff. We haven't even gone through half of the clothes upstairs. Also, what's the occasion?" I ask looking around.

"Oh no Bambi," she says pursing her lips, "this is not from me."

"Then who is it from?" I trail off turning my head back to the scenery of pink in front of me once the realization hits me.

I hand Anya to Angela before walking to the bouquet of roses taking up the note in the middle.

The note was handwritten, I would know that handwriting anywhere. I half expect this to be a letter of disappointment. It's probably going to tell me that he's disappearing again. For good this time.

Dear Samantha,

I'm sorry. Believe me when I say that this is not how I wanted things to be. Anya changes everything. Everything I did and why will come to light soon enough. Please try to understand when everything unfolds. When this is over, I will never stop apologizing to you.

I love you

What's with this I love you business?

This is the most confusing man I ever met. I feel like this is another attempt to play with my feelings and I won't give him the satisfaction. I shake my head while handing Mariella the note.

"What the hell does that mean," she asked confused.

"Beats the hell out of me. I wonder what could be so important that he would abandon me the way he did. It's inexcusable in my opinion. You can keep all of the stuff upstairs, I don't want any of it in my house.

"Bambi," she begins to say in protest but she stops talking to glance at the enormous amount of stuff and just nods her head in agreement. "So brunch at my house on mothers day?" She asks trying to change the subject.

"Umm sure that should be fine." Even if I could find an excuse to give this woman as to why I couldn't come to brunch she wouldn't take no for an answer. I understood where her son got it from.

"Jeremy is coming though, but I don't want that to change your mind, I want my children here and I want my grandbaby here. God knows I won't be getting one from Jesy anytime soon, she keeps switching from girls to guys, I can't keep up with her," she says smiling at me. "Oh, and the little blonde one isn't invited," she says shrugging her shoulders.

"Mariella I don't think-"

"Great! I'll see you here Sunday with my grandbaby," she says quickly cutting me off to take Anya from Angela and dart up the stairs.

I shake my head letting out a deeply annoyed sigh. I turn to eye the layout of pink gift boxes until my eyes stop at a small blue one with a white ribbon. I frown at the box considering the last thing that was in a box like this caused me to get pregnant.

I pull the ribbon opening the box to reveal a tiny bracelet with an engraving on a gold plate. Anya. I trace my finger over the words. Maybe this one gift isn't so bad. I'll keep this one. I look around at the giant teddy bear surrounded by gifts then it occurs to me. How the fuck did he do all of this in less than 24 hours? Is there a company that delivers baby gifts that I don't know about?

I know it's a bad idea but I decided to text him.

Me: Thanks for the stuff for my child.

Maybe Jeremy: Your welcome beautiful. Can we talk?

Why is he always trying to talk to me about something? He had all this time to talk to me but instead ignored me for a year.

Me: You had a year to talk to me.

Maybe Jeremy: And I will spend a lifetime making that up to you.

A lifetime? Isn't he getting married? I might as well end this conversation right now because his delusion is showing. I turn on my read receipts so he knows I saw the fuckery.

Maybe Jeremy: Tonight?

Oh, I'm not falling for that.

Me: Can't tonight. I have a date.

Before he could respond I put his number on do not disturb as well as my phone. I don't know what he expects to come of us talking. There is no plausible excuse for what he put me through.

I make my way upstairs to my room. It had a giant king-size bed and a 75-inch tv in it. Mariella had it furnished for me after I had the baby even though I protested heavily. I turn on Attack on Titan on the Tv and grab my laptop to do a little online shopping. I like to leave Mariella to have her time with Anya,

I think it's the respectful thing to do, plus she has raised two children, if she needed me she would come to get me.

I didn't even realize I had fallen asleep until I hear my phone ring. I look and see it's Isaiah. I look at the time its 5:02 pm

"Hello?" I said a little too loudly to pretend I was awake.

"Hey baby, I'm actually going to pick you up at around 5:40 so we aren't late for our reservation."

"Oh okay, that's fine."

"Okay bye."

Fuck. Bitch why are you always late. You wanna see some real speed?

I quickly run downstairs and grab the bag that I brought my clothes in. I came over in high-waisted sweatpants and one of Isaiah's T-shirts with a knot tied in the front. I dart into the bathroom in my room trying to shower as quickly as possible without getting my hair wet.

I run out of the bathroom to dry off and put on lotion. I didn't care if I was late I was not about to be ashy.

I throw on a midi white spaghetti strap body con dress with ruching in the back. I throw on some white block heels in the process. I'm pretty tall already so if it's not a pair of block heels, or my white wedges, I don't really like to wear them.

You thought I was finna throw them shoes out.

I redo my slick back puff, spray it with water and leave-in conditioner, and I finish it off by swooping and drooping my baby hairs. I end up pulling two little coils down on each side of my hair for a little razzle-dazzle.

I'm a little content with the way I look. I did miss my nipple rings though. I run to check the time seeing it was 5:37. I quickly walk out of the room while grabbing my white Brandon Blackwood bag, trying not to fall on my face in these heels as I run to Mariella's study. I notice she isn't there, and I curse myself for wasting effort walking all the way to the other side of the house in these heels.

I make my way downstairs to see her on the living room floor with Anya playing. Anya has some of the gift box paper in her hands and she looks like she is having the time of her life. Babies always have more fun with the gift wrap than the actual gift, I don't have a clue why. I walk over to pick her up and place kisses all over her face before telling her bye. "I love you my little bug," I say causing her to do the little half-smile I love so much. She only ever did it for me, well until Jeremy that is.

"You look beautiful Bambi," Mariella says to me as she stands looking at me lovingly.

"Aww thank you Glamma," I say kissing her cheek and handing Anya back to her.

I wave bye to the duo in the living room as I head out the door. I turn around to see a handsome man with perfectly white teeth against dark skin smiling at me leaning on the side of a black car. He is wearing dark grey dress pants with a white button-up shirt with the sleeves rolled up and the top buttons open. He is holding a single blue rose in his hands, I loved those. It fits him so well. I slowly walk to him biting my lips and taking the sight of him in.

I half wanted to fuck him on top of this car he looked so good, and he smelled so good. I walk up to him, grab the waist of his pants, and pull him to me so I can place a kiss on his lips. He holds my face strengthening the kiss. He sucks on my bottom lip before sticking his soft tongue in my mouth. I moan against it as our tongues start to sensually massage each other. I respond by slowly sliding my hands up his chest, from there to his shoulders, and then moving to wrap them around his neck. He immediately wraps his arms tighter around my waist pulling me closer to him and moving one hand to squeeze my ass. I feel his length start to grow against me and I get excited as I feel myself start to pool between my legs. This kiss has too much power. I take in his smell, his warmth, and I continue to dive deeper getting lost in the kiss.

I'm in a state of complete bliss before he abruptly stops the kiss.

I almost pout. I almost cry.

"If you continue doing that, we won't make it to dinner love," he says caressing my chin.

"But you taste so good," I say in a low moan going back in for the kiss.

"Don't tell me you only want me for my body love," he says avoiding my lips and giving me his cheek while placing a mischievous smile on his face.

I roll my eyes, "ugh fine, let's go then."

He opened the door for me but I don't take my eyes off him as I slide into the car. He closes my door and makes his way to the driver's side climbing in before humming the car to life. He grabs my hand placing a kiss on it as he starts to drive off.

We drive to a restaurant about 20 minutes away. From outside the restaurant just looks like a regular outdoor restaurant with flowers and awnings. We walk inside and the hostess directs us to the back of the restaurant. We go through and around a couple of hallways until we arrive to the back of the restaurant at a table that is near the river. The view is beautiful. The sun is setting on the huge body of water about 20 feet away from us and our table is set with wine glasses, flowers, and candles. The sight is almost breathtaking.

"Wow," I whisper. "It's breathtaking."

"Yes it is," he says causing me to divert my attention to him, but instead of looking at the view, he's looking at me in awe. He really is the sweetest.

We sit getting lost in conversation toying with each other's hands on the table, constantly smiling, and flirting with each other while we eat our food. At this moment I feel happy but I can't help but have a feeling that something is coming. Maybe it's just my anxiety? His phone goes off, he picks it up to look at it and his face immediately goes into a frown.

"Everything okay?" I ask. I wouldn't dare touch another man's phone. I like my mental health.

"Yea just something with work, nothing to worry about right now," he says offering me a small smile.

"I need to go to the bathroom," I said slowly getting up,

"Okay, I'll tell you what I had to tell you when you get back."

"I'll be quick then," I say as I sashay away swinging my hips so he can have a great view of me from behind. I look back to see him watching me while licking his lips and smiling.

I go to the bathroom feeling like a little schoolgirl. I was so happy at this moment I had almost forgotten about Jeremy." I quickly check my phone to see I have a text message from Mariella. I am pleased to see it's a picture of a very happy baby in a bath. I smile softly at my phone responding to her with many hearts. I notice about 10 text messages from Jeremy to but I don't have time to read those now. I'll deal with that later.

It's about Isaiah right now, the man that's been there for me.

I look at myself in the mirror, making sure I still look good. I can't help but smile at myself knowing I'm finna get some dick tonight.

I make my way out of the bathroom when I am greeted with a hard thud. I know this scent.

I bumped into this person way harder than I should have. "I'm so sorry," I say looking up slowly, hoping it's not who I think It is. I slowly look up to have dark blue eyes locked on mine.

"You've got to be kidding me," I said moving to walk away from him.

"Samantha we need to talk and it can't wait," he says sternly while grabbing my hand.

"We don't need to talk about shit right now. I am on a date, we will talk soon just not right now," I respond quickly as I try to walk away.

He sighed deeply keeping his grip only arm.

"Jeremy let me go what the fuck," I said turning around and eyeing him.

"Do you even know who you're on a date with?" He asked seriously.

" I do, I'm on a date with Gerald's son. I know him pretty well thank you very much."

"Samantha he's not who you think he is."

"I'm confused. Is he not Gerald's son?" I reply with the illest smartass attitude.

"He is but."

"Then what's your problem," I ask cutting him off.

He sighs deeply. "Look, let's just go somewhere and talk."

"No, I am on a date. A very nice date I should say. With a man who actually cares about my feelings, so if you don't mind, I would like to get back to that," I say as I yank my arm out of his grip.

"He's taking advantage of your Samantha," He calls out after I start to walk away. My feet immediately stop moving. Jeremy would really say anything, won't he? I think I am actually starting to hate him and his lies.

"How Jeremy," I ask annoyed. I stand there and wait for him to spew the bullshit so I can go back and tell my man everything he said.

"He's under my employment Samantha."

Yikes, didn't see that coming.

"What the fuck are you talking about?" I ask as I step back toward him. Cause now he finna make me mad.

"I really hate it when you curse." I shoot him a deadly glare. He stares at me for a second before sighing. "He was supposed to watch you and report back to me. I have been paying him for his services which are terrible by the way, but now I see he has been taking a little extra on the side."

I snap my head back at the comment he just said in disbelief. "I don't believe you," I said in an offended tone.

I started walking away as quickly as I could through the mazes while going to find Isaiah and ask him myself. I am not about to act on a whim.

I could hear Jeremy's quick footsteps behind me and it only urged me to move a little faster.

Isaiah smiled as soon as he saw me, but his face quickly changes when he sees the look on my face. He looks behind me, notices Jeremy, and quickly stands to his feet. His eyes grow worried moving from me to over my shoulder constantly as I walk straight over to him.

"Tell me he's lying," I said as I walked over to him. He looks back and forth from me to Jeremy blinking. Since he wants to be quiet ill speak again. "Tell me you weren't being paid to watch me by him and that he is just the liar we know him to be and we can go back to our date," I say seriously.

"Samantha let me explain baby." He said reaching for me I immediately pull back.

"No. The only thing you should be explaining is that he's a liar. Right?" I ask as I try to hide the emotion in my voice.

"Samantha," he says softly while taking a step toward me and I immediately take a step back and laugh. I can't be here.

"I trusted you," I said glaring at him. I grab my bag and phone and walk away while calling an Uber. I stomp past Jeremy who begins to follow me. "Don't follow me I yell back behind me."

"Please Sam let me explain," I hear Jeremy running behind me. I make my way outside the restaurant to the parking lot to wait for my Uber.

Everybody always wants to explain some shit to me.

"Samantha," I hear from behind me and it's Jeremy standing in the parking lot. "Baby come and get in my car and I'll take you home so you can cool off.

Cool off?

"Explain? You want me to let you explain?" I ask offended. "Did you let me explain when you threw me out of your house in the middle of the night? Did you let me explain anything to you after you shut me out of your life? You need to go explain to your finance why you are here with all of this fucking toxicity instead of being home with her. The one you actually love."

"Samantha, calm down, please."

Did this nigga just tell me to calm down? I know he ain't tell me to calm down. Am I bugging?

"Fuck you!" I yell at him shoving him hard in the chest away from me. "Why do you always find a way to ruin my happiness? Do you like seeing me like this? Crying? Heart Broken? It's like you get off on it, you're so fucking toxic!" I yell feeling the tears run down my face.

Fuck. Frustrated tears you couldn't wait like 5 minutes?

"It wasn't supposed to be this way. I didn't know what else to do," he said sadly.

Why is he so calm? How can he be so calm?

"What in the entire fuck are you talking about Jeremy. Why can't you ever be straight with me, Why can't anyone ever be straight with me, why is everyone always lying to me? Tell me what's going on then. Right now."

"I just need you to calm down first. You have to listen to me with a clear head."

"Calm down? You want me to calm down? Do I not look fucking

calm? I think I'm pretty fucking calm because if I wasn't calm then I would be putting my hands on you. Are my hands on you Jeremy?" I ask confused.

"No," he says while rolling his eyes.

"Exactly."

In the midst of my yelling, Isaiah comes running behind us while looking angry.

"Great," I said throwing my hands up in the air.

"What's your problem!" He yells while getting in Jeremy's face.

"My problem? I gave you one thing to do and you used it to get in her pants and act like a father to my baby? Why didn't you tell me she was pregnant? You knew it would change everything!"

"You didn't deserve to know," was all he said before Jeremy balled up his fist sending it straight to Isaiah's jaw causing him to stumble back.

Immediately Isaiah lunged toward him and the two of them started rolling around in the parking lot. I take the only sane route and ignore them. I ain't getting hit trying to separate two grown men having a pissing contest. Luckily my Uber pulls up and I quickly climb in. I don't even think they notice I leave they are so stuck on each other's dicks.

That ain't my business anyway.

I'm going to go to the only place I will find sanity at the moment. I take the Uber to my house run inside and grab my keys. I couldn't go to Mariella's house because they would just follow me there and I didn't need them around the baby. I couldn't stay at home because one or both will just show up here. I decide to go somewhere that I have found safe in the last few months.

I quickly jump in my car and drive off before either one decides to pull up behind me and try to follow me. I don't know if they had stopped fighting yet and to be honest, I didn't care. I turn off my phone location since I share it with Isaiah and Mariella. I quickly start to drive, calling the person I need the most right now hoping they pick up.

"Hello?"

"Can I come over for like an hour, it's an emergency."

"Sure baby I'm home."

Chapter 13

Samantha Kage

· ·

I quickly pull up to the Apartment complex pulling into the parking lot. I shoot a text to Mariella letting her know what's going on.

Me: Hey I'm gonna be home a little later, something happened but don't worry I'm fine.

Mariella: I was just about to text you. Jeremy came here looking for you. He just left.

Me: Everything is okay I promise. See you soon.

I walk out of the car, grab my keys, and walk into the apartment complex before I make my way to the second floor. I knock on the door quickly. I have been holding my emotions in up until this point, but as soon as the door opens my heart begins to swell in my chest and the tears come pouring out.

"Ms.Genesis," I said quietly through my sobs.

"Baby what's wrong? Come in, come in quickly."

We sit down on the couch and I tell her about the events of the last 2 days as best as I could without leaving out any necessary details. In this past year, she has surely become a mother figure to me in more ways than one. I couldn't call Annabelle because her first instinct would be to drive 40 minutes with a gun to threaten Jeremy and no one needed that.

"Baby it looks like you got a lot on your plate," she says to me handing me a bottle of water.

"What do I do?" I ask while sitting on the couch slumped in defeat.

"I can't tell you what to do, but If I was you, I would sit that boy down and figure out what the hell is going on. You deserve the truth baby. Not just for yourself but for your baby girl. Make sure you go in with listening ears. You need to know all the information before you know what to do next.

"But."

"No buts," she says holding up her hand in defense. "You finna do it on your terms too. You will do it when you are ready and how you want to do it. But like I said I can't tell you what to do. I'm also going to say I don't know though. So just in case this goes badly. you can't blame me," she said shrugging her shoulders causing me to laugh.

"I don't know if I'm ready for the truth," I say slowly.

"The truth will come out, either way, it's just up to you when and how baby."

"Thank you," I said looking at her and giving her a shy smile. "I needed to talk to someone about this."

"Of course mama, you stay as long as you need," she said placing a kiss on my forehead and pulling me in for a hug.

I sigh as I take up my phone. It's blowing up. Of course it is. I think know what to do.

I take up my phone ignoring the earlier messages from either part and shoot Jeremy a text.

Me: Meet me at Mariella's.

It was all I said. It was enough. I turn to Ms.Genesis telling her thank you before kissing her goodbye and making my way down to the car.

You got this.

I drive back to Mariella's house stopping at every stoplight to waste time. I wanted him to wait. When I finally make it back, I shoot Ms.Genesis a text telling her I'm home. I walk out of the car and walk up the stairs to see all the lights on.

I walk inside and a furious Jeremy stomps over to me. He has a small black eye on his face. I can see how that fight went. I wonder how Isaiah's doing. I'll deal with him later.

"Where the fuck were you! I have been worried looking everywhere for you and then you turn your phone location off?"

He's tracked my phone? He probably took his mom's phone.

"White boy you got me all types of fucked up if you think you finna talk to me like that," I said while pointing my finger in his face. "Sit down!" I urge him while pointing at the couch.

He quickly backed up walking to take a seat on the couch. He adjusted his pants and unbuttoned the top buttons of his shirt and he sat back.

Don't tell me that my yelling at him made his dick hard.

I kicked off my slides and made my way over to the living room to stand on the rug directly in front of him.

"Where's Anya?"

"Upstairs with my mom," he said quietly

Yea that's right bitch. Lower your voice while you're talking to me.

"Speak."

"You don't want to sit down?" He asked nervously

"Jeremy," I warn.

"I missed you," He says looking up at me."

"I hate you."

"I love you."

I squint my eyes glaring at him and kissing my teeth. "If the next words out of your mouth aren't the truth, I'm going to lose it," I say angrily.

"Fine," he started. " Do the words Zach Rivera mean anything to you." I immediately tense up as my blood runs cold. Maybe I should have sat down.

"How the fuck do you know that name?" My heartbeat quickens and I can't stand anymore, nor can I control my breathing. He stands up to comfort me but I quickly step back, I don't want him to touch me, it may only make this little mini-anxiety attack worst.

I walk over to the open kitchen to grab one of the chairs and move it to the middle of the living room to sit on it. I take a deep breath preparing for the conversation, "continue," I urge him.

"I'll start with the night you left Miami. I had a business meeting that night. However it was a business meeting with my miserable father, he came all the way down to Miami to meet with me when I was literally coming back to New York the next day. He knew about you for some time, he somehow found out that I was planning to propose to you when I got back to New York. I was serious about every promise I made to you that night baby girl" He paused to look at me searching for some sort of response.

Propose?

I don't give him the satisfaction of a reaction.

I roll my eyes letting him know that I wasn't in the mood right now.

He clears his throat before continuing. "At the dinner, we started talking business until he brought you up. He made it very clear that if I continue my relationship with a black girl, he would cut me off, which I didn't care about. He could keep his fucking money for all I cared. When he saw that I wouldn't listen and I would continue seeing you, it was almost as if he knew that would be my answer. He urged that I end things with you but I refused to listen until he said something that forced me to bend to his way. I know you were in an abusive relationship, but you never told me his name, we never even talked about it, and I never wanted to trigger you by asking. My father, however, did know his name. He made it clear that if I defied him and continued our relationship in secret, he would make it his duty to make sure that Zach found you, to which I still didn't listen."

"So what made you finally listen to your daddy," I say with an attitude.

"I didn't understand the severity of the situation until he showed me the police report and the pictures that were taken in the hospital. Samantha those fucking pictures scared me. My father also told me you never reported him. My father has a way of finding things out, you told the hospital it was a car accident but it clearly wasn't."

"He had the pictures, you saw the pictures?" I ask in disbelief. "How did he find all of this out ?" I ask.

I didn't realize I was shaking in my seat. The things that he who shall not be named did to me were unimaginable, It was pure luck that I was able to escape him. Zach, I haven't thought of that name in almost two and a half years.

Focus Samantha focus.

"He had people do a background check on you and they found out while you were in the hospital your current boyfriend was him. It didn't take a professor to do the math that he put you there. I was scared for you, I had to comply. His conditions were that I cut off all contact with you and he would be checking in. When you showed up to my office asking if anyone had heard from me, it helped my case with him that I had cut you off fully. It took everything in me not to go to you that day."

"So you knew I was there?" I ask and a tear falls out of my eye before I can stop it.

Piece of shit.

"I'm sorry," he says sadly.

"You say that a lot for someone who doesn't actually mean it. Please continue with the story."

He sighs looking at me sadly before he continues. "Apparently, Zach has been looking for you, and I have been trying to find him before he could find you. He was last heard from in Cali a little over a year ago. My father said he said you must have taken something from him or something which is why he was trying to find you."

I knew exactly what Zach was looking for, but I didn't have it anymore.

"I typically kept track of you. The day you went to see Gerald I had Isaiah on Instagram, his contracting company was one of the companies that were brought by mine. I called him into my office for a meeting to ask him to watch over you in case anything would happen. I told him to watch over an amazing girl I guess I can't be surprised that he fell in love," he said with a shy smile.

"He's not in love with me. We are not there yet," I say softly looking away. I hadn't even noticed I was hugging myself trying to find some sort of comfort at the mention of Zach's name.

"A blind man can see that man is in love with you Samantha," he said coldly.

I start to bite at my nails, a trait a picked up whenever I was nervous.

"But he never told me you were pregnant," he continued. "I told him to keep me updated with everything, I never knew you almost died giving birth or I would have stopped everything I was doing and been by your side. Thank god my mother was there for you. I will never stop apologizing for it. He would only tell me little things like you were fine or you were single, or that you were doing good at work. He never even told me you were seeing someone or that the someone was him. That's why when I saw you two together I got so angry. I want to also say sorry for all the harsh things I said that day. It was me trying to push you away out of fear of my father. I swear Samantha when my mom told me about the day you gave birth when I called her yesterday, I felt so bad. I cried finding out what you went through alone. I cried realizing I wasn't there for you when you needed me, You put your life on the line to give birth to my child and I wasn't there. I love you so much, I will never stop apologizing for this."

I roll my eyes dramatically as another tear sneaks away.

"Stop," I said holding up my hand and looking away from him while trying to hold back more tears. "I don't care," I responded coldly. "You weren't there, there's nothing else that can be done, we can't turn back time."

"Sam.."

"Please continue," I say cutting him off with a sniffle.

"When my father saw that I was serious, he made the decision to sign his company over to me earlier than planned, giving him a small share in it so he could keep making money but the condition was that I had to get married first, to Tiffany specifically because he likes her so much. Which is why we were engaged, and that's the only reason. I just didn't want my mom to hear it from a random person which Is why I came down here to tell her. As fate would have it, I ran into you and I was able to meet my beautiful baby girl. Fate keeps finding a way to bring us back together and we need to stop ignoring it."

This nigga got me fucked up.

"One more comment like that I am done listening to you," I snapped.

He cleared his throat. "Once my father signed over the company to me and lost all his power to aid with Zachary finding you, the plan was that I would find my way back to you. But until then I stayed away not trusting my father wouldn't keep good on his promises but now I don't care. My father doesn't know anything about you or the baby and I hope to keep it that way. I refuse to let him control my life any longer. I refuse to not be a father to that little girl. I refuse to be the father to her that my father was to me."

But you're okay with treating me like he treated Mariella?

"I am trying to speed the signing of the company over because I need to be in Anya's life. She's the greatest. I can tell she is amazing and I haven't held her yet. I didn't want to do it without your permission. That's something else I want to ask you. Can I hold her?"

I wipe away my tears looking away from him, I think to myself for a second. I realized that I would be taking away from Anya if her father wasn't in her life.

I roll my eyes.

Fuck it

"Angela!" I yell. "I know you're listening. Can you bring Anya down?" I hear her feet scurry. I knew she was listening the whole time. I spend a lot of time with her over the last 2 months, and I've begun to know her so well.

Mariella makes their way down the steps with Anya in her arms and walks over to me. She looks upset. She must have been listening to it too. She diverts her gaze to Jeremy to shoot him a dangerous glare.

She hands Anya to me with her pacifier in her mouth. She is awake and alert and looking around at everything going on. I move to stand and stare at Jeremy. He moves to stand looking around nervously as if he should have something in his hands.

"Come on," I said urging him to come forward.

He slowly walks over to me reaching out before taking Anya and cradling her in his arms slowly. She spits out the pacifier, pouting her bottom lip as if she is going to cry while looking at this random man. I step closer to them taking her hand and shushing her.

"It's okay mama," I said taking her hand, shaking it, and smiling at her causing Anya to relax a little.

My kid is cute.

"Oh my god!" Mariella yells out causing us to snap our heads around to her. Mariella is crying her heart out with Angela by her side wiping away her tears. Like literally ugly crying. "You. Guys. Look. So. Beautiful." She manages to choke out in-between dramatic sobs.

I turn my gaze back to Jeremy who is smiling at me with tears in his eyes. "She's so perfect," he says in a whisper looking at me. I offer him a small smile and then divert my attention back to the baby in front of me.

This feels weird.

I take a deep breath and step back. "Take some time with her before she goes to bed, It's almost 10. I'll come back down to get her in a few. I just need to be alone for a while. Mariella, I will be sleeping here tonight. I'm not in the right mind to drive." She just nods her head in understanding with a face full of tears.

I make my way up the stairs and lock my room door behind me. I strip out of all my clothes not wanting to have this day on me anymore. The shower is calling my name. I finally gather my thoughts together while making a list in my head in the shower.

Zach was looking for me. Jeremy's dad is a racist prick. Tiffany is stupid and likes the way my ass tastes. Zach is looking for me. Isaiah knew I was depressed and didn't tell Jeremy I was pregnant. Zach was looking for me. Do I forgive Jeremy for what he put me through? I need to talk to Isaiah. What will I tell Zach if and when he finds me?

I have always been the person to try to do the logical thing and think things through before making a rash decision but this was too much information to take in at once.

If I wasn't in therapy, the only logical choice would be to go lay in traffic.

I don't know how long I was in the shower. I exit, get dressed in some dad shorts and a T-shirt, and head downstairs to see Jeremy standing feeding a sleepy baby girl with his mother by his side. The sight of him with her almost makes me want to cry again. I feel the ball of emotion coming up in my throat but I choke it back down.

"Is she sleeping?" I ask causing all eyes to turn to me.

"No Bambi," Mariella said." I think she was waiting for you."

I walk over to see Anya in Jeremy's arms. They are just staring into each others eyes lovingly.

"If you two keep standing there together with that baby, I am going to cry again," Mariella said getting choked up."

We both let out a chuckle and I divert my attention back to Anya. "Are you ready for bed mamas," I say in a baby voice taking her into my arms. I say goodnight to everyone as I start to walk away with Anya in my arms.

"Umm Samantha?" I hear Jeremy say causing me to turn around. I stand there waiting for him to use his voice to speak. "Do you mind if I stay here tonight? I can't bear to be away from her."

For the baby Samantha, for the baby.

I didn't realize how tightly I was grinding my teeth.

As much as I wanted to say no, this isn't my house. If I said no, he would only stay anyway. I would only be taking away from the baby for my own selfish reasons so I might as well agree.

"Umm yes," I sigh. " You can sleep with Anya in her room," I said nodding my head to follow us.

I walk into my bedroom waiting for Jeremy to come behind me, I close the door behind him as he enters. With a full stomach, Anya has already fallen asleep in my arms. We make our way past my bed to the joining smaller room that had an oversized futon couch and Anya's crib in it. I slowly put Anya down in the crib. I watch as Jeremy takes his button-down shirt off revealing a white t-shirt underneath. He turns to me before dropping his pants, I snap my eyes away from him and start to walk away. He has a coy smile on his face as he turns to take his place on the futon next to the crib. I kiss Anya on the forehead before I walk out of the adjoining room to my bed and quickly climb in.

What a fucking day.

Chapter 14

Samantha Kage

I lay in bed with Jeremy and Anya sleeping in the next room. I couldn't get Zach off my mind. I started to wonder what he would do to me if he found me. Would he hit me again? Would he trick me into coming back to him? Would I go? Would he kill me?

 I think back to that day, the last day I saw him, the day I barely escaped with my life. It was the day I decided that enough was enough. I won't say I was strong that day because if I am being honest with myself, I debated going back to him. It's what a physical, emotional, and mentally abusive relationship will do. I am glad that I can I will call myself a survivor

I had decided to move to Cali for like 2 months before starting college. I was bright-eyed and 18 years old. That same summer is when I met him in California. We fell in love all too quickly. He was Puerto Rican, about 6'2 with tattoos everywhere, dark greenish-brown eyes, and a smile that could eat your heart out.

 When the hitting started, I would get showered with gifts, love, and empty promises that It wouldn't happen again. And for a while, it stopped, it really did. Until the day I finally left.

I feel like what we confused for love was lust and longing to be wanted by someone.

Someone had finally picked me. The girl who has never felt wanted in her entire life was finally picked. And I fell hard.

I take up the positive pregnancy test and hide it in the drawer of his apartment on his side of the bed. He lived on the 23rd floor, and the view was amazing. It was our inside joke that he was 23 and lived on the 23rd floor.

I was so excited to tell him about the pregnancy. I couldn't wait until he got home that night. He was out with the boys for one of their bachelor parties. I wasn't really sure which one, nor did I care.

I hung around the house for hours before he came home. By the time he got home, I had fallen asleep. When I finally heard the door open, I checked the time to see it was about 2:30 in the morning.

I was half asleep so I didn't move as he stumbled in drunk slurring his words. I hear something fall over and break. I look up realizing he had tripped over the chair in the room bringing the lamp down with him. I quickly move off the bed to help him up but he shrugs me off.

"I can do it!" He yells.

The way he yelled at me triggered me a little bit so I quickly oblige to go sit on the edge of the bed. I make sure to watch him so I can make sure he doesn't hurt himself. I wouldn't want to make a drunk person mad so I keep my distance. I watch him as he moves to stand while looking around the room. His eyes stop as they lock on me.

"Mmhmm" he laughs, "how did I get so lucky," he says walking over to me placing a kiss on my lips, and then moving down to my neck.

"Zach stop, your drunk," I say pushing him off with a small laugh. "Come on let's get you to bed baby," I said trying to step away.

I move to get up but he uses one arm to push my back into the bed. I shake it off as I get off the bed the other way. He reached for me causing him to fall into the bed and I was amused. He scurried to put himself in a sitting position. I move in front of him to kneel down and take his shoes off for him so he doesn't fall asleep in them.

He grabs the back of my neck pulling my hair to bring my face to his. He places a rough wet kiss on my lips, reaching his other hand down to take a breast in his hand squeezing it way too hard. I immediately push him off with all my strength. I quickly move to stand up using my hand to wipe the alcohol breath off my mouth.

I'm annoyed now.

I start to walk away as I hear footsteps behind me. He spins me around, grabs my shoulders, and shoves me hard into the wall causing me to cry out. "Zach stop!" I say pleading.

"Why are you not kissing me huh? You kissing someone else?" When I don't answer him he slams me into the wall again and yells in my face. I don't dare move, I just need him to get over whatever this is and fall asleep. I wait for him to let me go but he doesn't. I unintentionally start to cry as he squeezes my shoulders tighter.

This only makes him madder. I refuse to look at him. I keep my gaze on the floor waiting for this to be over. He releases one of my shoulders and I half expect him to let me go, but instead, he grabs my face in his hand roughly forcing me to look at him. "Look at me when I'm fucking talking to you Samantha."

His hand on my face starts to hurt I try my best to push him away. As a result of my squirming, he raises his hand to place a hard slap across my face causing me to fall on the floor. I look up at him and immediately I am met with another harder slap sending me back into the floor, this time my head hits the floor. I don't dare move. I am afraid of what he will do next.

I hear his footsteps walk away. As soon as I think it's safe, I slowly get up walking in the direction of the door.

He didn't mean that, he's drunk. I start to tell myself things to make myself feel better.

I just need to leave and let him cool off. I don't get far as strong fingers lace through the back of my hair yanking me back and making me fall on the floor. I try to fight but he just climbs on top of me to start his assault on my face. After the 3rd hit, I am numb to the pain, I just need to get myself out of there. I try to fight back the best I could, but that wasn't nearly enough. I don't want this. I cry out no over and over and try to push him away but nothing works.

I know I have ultimately failed when I hear his belt buckle moving. He ripped off my shorts, pried my legs open with his legs, and slammed into me causing me to scream. I felt no pleasure, only pain.

He must have not liked that because it ended up with more hits being placed on my face after being told to shut up and take it. I lay there crying until he was finished with me. You would think I was used to this because it isn't the first time it has happened, him wanting me and taking it whether I agreed or not.

He finally gets off me, my face is hot, and I can feel the blood running. I don't know where it's coming from but I don't care. I need to leave. I try to get up again but I am met with a swift kick in the stomach.

Oh my god. My baby.

I try to do everything to stop his assault but I couldn't. One kick, three kicks, he stops at six. The kicks only get harder every time.

I don't move from the curled-up position I am in for what felt like hours. I finally heard him mumble something and then collapse on the bed. When I was sure he is asleep I grab my handbag, passport, and wallet. I grab anything else that I could possibly need to get the hell away and dart for the door while in severe amounts of pain. Whatever I left here could be replaced.

It wasn't a good thing I had kept most of my stuff at his apartment. I look back at him before I leave feeling almost nostalgic. Then I look down to see all the blood on the floor and it goes away.

I am so glad I didn't forget anything important, I left all my clothes behind. I start to run down the back staircase needing to get away as far as possible. By the time I reach the bottom of the stairs, I can feel the wetness in between my legs, did I pee? I reach my hand down and my eyes widen once I see blood. The only thing keeping me going right now is my adrenaline, I am sure of it.

"Fuck," I whisper to myself. The nearest hospital is only 6 blocks away. I run straight there praying there is nothing wrong with my baby.

When I arrived at the hospital, I ran straight into the emergency room and got admitted when I told them I was hit by a car and started bleeding between my legs. I told them I'm pregnant so I ran here, and I didn't see the car. For whatever reason, I was still lying for him.

When the doctor told me I had a miscarriage, I couldn't stop crying. The police came and spoke to me but even though he has caused me to lose a child, I still made sure to only say it was a car accident.

They didn't hide the fact that they didn't believe me. The next morning I got up early and discharged myself. More like left the hospital as quickly as possible, went to the airport, and brought my ticket back to New York. I couldn't risk him coming to the hospital to find me. I didn't visibly relax until I got back home to my little apartment in New York.

"Samantha wake up!" I was being shaken violently. I open my

eyes to see a worried Jeremy. I immediately sit straight up alarmed.

"What's wrong, is Anya okay?" I yell looking around out of breath.

"Yes she's fine, it's you! You were crying out in your sleep."

I look around realizing that I was laying in a pool of sweat and the air was on. I look up at Jeremy feeling the tears in my eyes.

"I can't let him find me, Jeremy, I can't let him hurt me again," I whisper as I start to cry. He takes me in his arms in a bear hug giving me the comfort I desperately needed at that moment.

"I won't let him," he says pulling me in tighter nuzzling his face in my neck as I continued to sob uncontrollably.

"Do you want to talk about it baby girl?" I don't know why but the way he says that made a wave of comfort rush over me. I go back and forth in my mind debating telling him everything. There are parts of our relationship that I can't even bring myself to say out loud. There are some things that I still can't wrap my head around, some things I haven't even told Anna. He already saw the pictures and heard the gist of it, so I might as well tell him what I can.

I pulled away from him and told him the bare minimum. I actually told him less than the bare minimum if I am being honest with myself. I could tell he wanted to ask me more but he wouldn't pry and I appreciated that.

"Welp that's basically everything that happened the day those pictures were taken," I said through a sniffle trying to control my tears and emotions.

I was lying. I told him that Zach and I had a fight and he won.

"Baby girl, no one should have to go through any of that," he said looking at me with glossy eyes.

I shrugged and looked down. This is why I don't tell people my issues, it's the look, the look of pity that is plastered across their faces. They are not sure what to say or do but they want to make you feel better. It's actually quite annoying to me.

"Can I. Can I hug you?" He asked nervously.

I nodded my head before he pulled me into a deeper embrace causing me to break out into another heavy sob. He just held me, comforted me, whipped away my tears, and placed kisses on my forehead. I didn't know that's what I needed until he did it.

What am I even doing right now? I hate this man.

Chapter 15

Samantha Kage

• •

Jeremy's lips are slowly pressed upon mine. he uses his tongue to lick my bottom lip causing my lips to slowly part. He takes that as an invitation to slowly stick his hot wet tongue inside my mouth. I start to suck his tongue causing him to moan in my mouth while my hands slowly move up to fist his hair. He lets out a sexy groan as he pulls me to straddle his lap, I can feel his length pressed up against my inner thigh. I slowly start to grind my dripping sex against him as his hands tighten around my waist causing me to-

I snap my eyes open, thanking god that it was just a dream. I can't help but feel the moisture that has managed to pool in between my legs as I bring my thighs together.

I awake feeling more comfortable than I have been in a while. Why am I so comfortable?

I hear a soft snore in my ear and a warm body pressed against my back with a large remote stabbing me in my back. Was I watching television before I went to bed?

I look down and realize that strong arms are wrapped around my waist, hence the pool between my thighs. There is a soft breath on my neck. My back is pressed against his front, and his morning wood is unforgiving.

What the fuck.

There is too much going on right now.

I slowly move his hands off my waist, causing him to huff, tighten his grip and pull me closer to his dangerously hard length. When he finally relaxes a little I go for a second attempt. I am finally able to climb out from underneath him causing him to stir in his sleep letting out a groan.

I shrug it off, this feels like cheating on Isaiah even though we never officially gave each other titles. I walk into the adjoining room to check on Anya. My baby girl is still fast asleep with her little but sticking up in the air. Just the sight of her made me wish I had 2 of her. I have to wake her up and feed her.

I grab my phone to check the time but instead, I see a strew of messages from Isaiah. They are filled with I miss you's, I'm sorry's, and please talk to me's. I was going to give him a chance to explain his side of the story anyway, I just wanted him to stir a little. It's only been like a day. What an eventful few weeks I have had.

I walk downstairs to make a bottle for Anya, so she doesn't have to wait long when she wakes up. While the bottle is in the bottle warmer, I get lost in my thoughts.

Should I give Isaiah a chance? I mean he did agree with a man who broke my heart to watch me and report my movements back to him. But he also did not tell said man anything about what I have been doing, nor who I have been doing. Did he get so close to me because Jeremy told him to and he just happened to start liking me? Or was it the other way around? Was he playing me this entire time? Girl, you know where this man works just go ask him your dam self.

You right. You're right as hell.

I snap myself out of my inner dialogue when I hear fussing on the baby monitor. I grab the bottle and make my way back up the stairs quickly before she starts to scream. Sis really only cried for food. Sounds like her mama. I quickly enter the room to see the bed empty, I walk into the adjoining room to see Jeremy changing a very wet diaper of a fussy baby.

I sigh. "Do you want to feed her?" I ask eyeing him.

His eyes snap up to meet mine, and he nods slowly. I walk over to hand him the bottle. Cradling her in his arms, she graciously takes the bottle, grabbing his finger with her little hand. That action causes a smile to place across his face in awe, and I can't help but stare at the two. I lean on the wall just watching them bond over something so small. She doesn't even know what's going on but it still looks cute as fuck from where I'm standing. I didn't even realize a smile had sprawled across my face until he looked up at me offering a bright smile himself. I quickly changed my face and look away.

Bitch don't fold.

"Umm I'm going to go take a shower," I say quickly turning my back to him.

After a long shower, with my thoughts, and doing my morning routine, I have decided to go visit Isaiah at his office. I know he worked today so he could squeeze me in for 5 minutes at least to talk to me. I owe this man the benefit of the doubt, he has been there for me in more ways than one in the past few months. Plus, I want to hear his side of the story. My assumptions never do me any good.

I turn my location back on checking Isaiah's to make sure he was at his office. I throw on a grey T-shirt crop top and some high-waisted ripped jeans. I run downstairs to ask Mariella if she could watch Anya for an hour. Of course, she agrees no problem, but I still find it respectful to ask. I walk back upstairs to grab my baby girl to bring to her grandma. I need to go home tonight. I need some alone time with my girl away from all these crazy people.

I walk in and see Jeremy sitting on the bed on his knees leaning over and placing kisses on a giggling baby's tummy.

My poor ovaries.

"Umm, I'm going run a quick errand. Mar's going to watch Anya, so you can go to work or do whatever it is you do during the day now."

"Where are you going?" He asks handing Anya to me.

"About my business," I said turning away.

"Samantha," he starts but I am already walking out of the room. I don't have time for whatever nonsense he has for me today. Yes, we slept in the same bed last night but I am still royally pissed at him. The petty libra in me doesn't allow me to forgive easily or let shit go.

I walk downstairs and hand Anya off to Mariella, but not before placing a million kisses all over her face and neck. "I love you little bug," I say kissing her one more time before throwing on my grey Yeezys and heading out the door. I hop in my car and take off down the road.

I pull into the parking lot of the office building and make my way to the 15th floor. The first time he made me cum from his tongue alone was on top of that same desk in his office. I usually greet the receptionist on the floor but she isn't at her desk today, Liliana I think her name is.

He doesn't typically lock his office door so I make my way down the hall. I turn a couple of heads but no one really bats an eye at me. I have been here a couple of times before. Even before we started our *relationship,* I would come to visit him as his friend.

I take a deep breath and knock on the door.

"I'm busy!" He yells back sounding angry. Don't tell me he's brooding in his office because of what happened last night, I almost feel bad.

I sigh again before turning the nob and pushing the door open. "Isaiah we," I am silenced as I take in the scene in front of me.

Isaiah is half sitting on his desk, the same place I sat with my legs wrapped around his neck. His head is thrown back while biting his lips and on her knees in front of him is the Latina receptionist bobbing her head back and forth on his dick. The sound of slurps and gags is thrown in the air. His hand is tightly tangled into her hair shoving her head against his dick over and over again. His top few buttons are unbuttoned, her shirt is off and her skirt is hiked up. Her hands are pressed firmly against his thighs as she takes his dick into the back of her throat constantly. "Yea that's right baby," he says in a low aggressive whisper.

I am frozen I couldn't even move as I take in the sight.

This nigga healed like Wolverine. How long has he been fucking this bitch?

"I'm bout to cum," he says as he moves his head down to look at her but instead, his dark brown eyes stop halfway to meet mine. "Samantha," he says in horror, but my name rolls off his lips as he lets out a shaky breath, cums right in her throat right in front of me. Even goes as far as holding her head there while he finishes.

His eyes widen once he realizes what he has done.

I shake my head, roll my eyes, and exit the room leaving him standing there in horror. I walk back to the elevator hitting the button constantly. I was never one to cause a scene, not causing a scene sometimes is just as effective as causing one.

A text comes in on my phone as I look to my left to see the disheveled Latina stomping out of the room. She must be upset that a man said another girl's name while her mouth was on his dick.

Welp.

Isaiah makes his way out of the room quickly while looking a little sweaty. He makes eye contact with me and tries to make his way toward me.

I shoot him a blank look letting him know I feel nothing. I step into the elevators and quickly hit the close doors button before he can reach me.

What is it with the men in my life doing me dirty? I'm finna go find me an Asian man, maybe he will treat me right. Just got to find one that likes dark skin black girls first.

I walk back to my car with my phone going off constantly. Isaiah has called me three times. What could this man possibly have to say to me? I literally caught him with his dick in another girl's mouth the night after we had a fight. I can't even really call it a fight but he will be alright. I don't care to speak to him right now.

How am I supposed to feel if he does this after we have a fight? It makes me think that every time something happens between us, he will go out and find another girl.

Isaiah: I'm sorry. Please come back and talk to me.

No nigga.

I turn on my read receipts for occasions like this.

Boy, this nigga got me fucked up. I don't believe in sorry. If you were really sorry you would have never done it in the first place. He can really slap dick right now. I turn on the Bluetooth on my phone, and I drive back to Mariella's house with Boss ass bitch, by Nicki Minaj blasting. Fuck these niggas.

I make it back to Mariella's fairly fast. I was really only gone for not even 30 minutes. I walk into the house ready to grab mine and my baby girl's stuff and head home. I walk in to see a worried Mariella holding Anya with a stressed-out Jeremy rubbing his hands on his chin. I swear he looked like he aged 5 years since I have seen him this morning.

The fuck. Who died?

"Why does it look like someone died," I said as both their eyes darted to me with worried expressions on their faces. "What's going on? You guys are really freaking me out."

Jeremy rubs the back of his neck, a slight anger playing over his face, he looks to his mother for reassurance on what to do next. They offer each other weird glances.

What the fuck is going on now?

I stare back and forth between them waiting for them to say something.

"Samantha," Jeremy says taking a deep sigh. "You need to sit."

"Oh my god, what is it now?" I ask slamming the door behind me and throwing my hands in the air. Have I not been through enough in the last like 10 days? What else could possibly happen today? If you had told me at the beginning of the week that this is how my week would go, I would have said you're dead ass lying.

"Please Samantha," he pleads.

I walk over to the couch and plop down while looking at these two people in front of me with deeply concerned looks on their faces. Mariella hands Anya to me and I put her to lay on my chest.

"Samantha, Tiffany is pregnant."

OKAYYYYY?!?! The fuck that got to do with me?

"Okay? Why are y'all making it seem like it's the end of the world? Your illegitimate fiancé is pregnant. I'm sure y'all had to keep up some sort of facade and you never seemed to mind stinking your dick in her," I said with more disgust than I intended.

He rolls his eyes at me. "There's more."

I stare at him waiting. What is with this man and anticipation? Sometimes it's not needed. "She told my father everything, about the baby, about us running into you, everything."

The realization slowly creeps in, he would make good on his promise on telling Zach where I am. I felt the fear creep over my body. Before I can control it, my thoughts go into overdrive panic mode.

"Bambi please don't go home, stay here please," Mariella says pleading. "It will be safer for you and the baby."

"I will have guards outside the house to make sure no one tries anything," Jeremy adds.

"There is more than enough room here. You can have the entire side of the house to yourself if you like. Isaiah can even come over if his being here makes you more comfortable," Mariella says trying to convince me. Jeremy looked visibly uncomfortable at the mention of Isaiah's name. I notice he closes his eyes, tightens his jaw, and tilts his head to the side.

His reaction almost makes me laugh.

"Isaiah is a nonfactor," I said quietly causing Jeremy to visibly relax. I roll my eyes at him.

After considering for a second I just say fuck it. "I will need mind and Anya's stuff," I say quietly. I hate this but I can't risk Zach getting to me. The thing he wants back, I cannot give him.

"My guards and I will go with you," Jeremy affirmed.

Sir please okay, I know you just want to know where I live.

"So mothers day brunch is canceled tomorrow," I said standing to my feet entirely too fast causing Anya to grip my shirt.

"Yes"

"No"

The pair in front of me eye each other before breaking out into an argument for a second but Mariella clearly wins. She will have her mothers day brunch whether Jeremy liked it or not.

The rest of the day is spent with Mariella watching Anya and me going to pack as much stuff from my house as I could to bring to Mariella's with Jeremy and his two guards watching my every move. The extra breast milk in the freezer, the clothes Anya and I will wear for the mothers day brunch, toiletries, extra clothes for me, and diapers. You can never overpack when you have a baby. When we go back to Mariella's house, the guards take my stuff out of the car and bring it upstairs, with Jeremy following behind.

I finally make it to my room when I begin pacing back and forth trying to calm my nerves considering I am starting to get into my own head when suddenly he walks in. Before I can even protest him being in my presence, he quickly glides over to wrap me in his arms while placing a kiss on my forehead.

This man is brave for real.

I don't even fight it, I hug him back wrapping my arms around his waist. It's what I needed at that point, it had been a trying day. It's been a trying life.

"I'm sorry," he whispers against my hair. I feel the tears slowly coming to my eyes. This is a lot for one person to take in the course of a week. "I caused all of this, I will fix it I promise." He places one more kiss in my hair tightening the hug and darts out the door.

Chapter 16

Samantha Kage

Mariella has been in the kitchen with Angela cooking all morning. How much food could she possibly cook for six people and a baby?

I personally have been locked in my room all morning having snuggles with my girl watching Anime and Coco melon. I was not lifting a finger. It was my first mothers day as a mother. Today was about me and the little one who made me a mother.

I feel like I haven't spent enough time with her these last few days with everything that's been going on. This mommy-daughter time was much needed.

It was almost 1, the guests would be arriving soon, and I needed to get us ready. We had already taken showers, so the only thing to do was to get dressed. I put on a white dress with pink flowers all over it with a matching pink flower crown on Anya. I cover her in baby powder and put A&D ointment all over her face and legs.

Yes, I am one of those mothers with a shiny ass baby. Kiss my ass.

On myself, I put on an off-the-shoulder white fit and flare dress with a lace design. I place Anya on the bed with her Coco melon while I cover my hands in oil and say a prayer while I unravel this braid out.

My 4c hair was always a gamble when I did my braid outs. Sometimes it would work, sometimes I would cry and get depressed. Only one would end up with me just slicing it up into a pineapple puff.

Curls! Yes!

The new curl cream I have been using is actually working. Shrunken after a twist out, it barely reaches my shoulders, but shrinkage is a bitch because my hair really reaches a 3rd of the way down my back when I do my silk press which is rare.

I attempt a side part by using edge control to slick the edges on one side and using pins to hold it in place. I tease the front of the other side with a pick giving myself a fake side bang. By some miracle, my hair looks great.

I spray Anya's hair with water and conditioner while finger-coiling it as I go. She has a much looser curl pattern than I do. I touch up my eyebrows with makeup and put on natural lashes. I make sure to put Anya's bracelet on her that Jeremy brought.

I look at us in the mirror, a beautiful dark skin duo, one with soft brown eyes, and one with dark blue eyes. We look adorable. A knock on the door breaks me out of my admiration for her.

"Come in!" I yell, not really caring who it is or taking my attention away from the mirror.

"Hey are you almost-" Jeremy says as he stops. I look over to see him drinking me and the baby in my arms in. He blinks as his eyes widen while taking a hard swallow at the sight of us. He has on light grey plaid dress pants and a tight white shirt that hugs his muscles perfectly. "Are you almost ready, everyone's about to sit down," he says clearing his throat.

"Yea, let's go," I say walking towards him.

"Samantha," he says as I walk past him out the doors, I stop and turn around looking at him questionably.

"Hmmm?"

"The two of you look absolutely beautiful, Happy Mother's Day," he says nervously. The man is nervous, around me? The man who at one point stuck his dick all the way down my throat while my eyes watered is nervous around me.

Did I step into a black hole?

I offer him a small smile. There will be no hostility. Today. "Thank you, let's go," I say quickly turning my back. I hate to admit it but that had some sort of effect on me.

Bitch. Don't you dare fucking fold. This ain't a game.

We walk down the steps that lead into the living room where they have moved the table to. The table is decorated so beautifully with food that my eyes water. All eyes turn to us as we make our way down the stairs just the three of us.

"Oh, there they are," Mariella says with love in her voice as we make our entrance. At the table is Mariella at the head of the table, Angela to her left, with Jesy right next to her with an empty chair beside her. On the other side are two empty seats with a high chair in-between with extra padding inside to support Anya laying down on it.

Mariella is so thoughtful.

We make our way to the table sending smiles and greetings to everyone. I take my seat while Jeremy secured Anya in the high chair and handed her an orange filled pacifier. She could munch on that. Hopefully, it won't get on her dress and only her bib.

On the table, there are about 3 different kinds of pasta and four different kinds of meats, with antipasto on the tray. Jeremy's mom could cook some Italian food, but I always wondered if they never got tired of pasta.

We dive into our food getting into a light conversation about the house, the family, and the food. I was trying to keep all attention off me as much as possible, I wasn't in the mood. My mind was plagued with memories of Zach that I couldn't shake. Such a happy day yet I am in the deepest of negative thoughts. I started playing with my food for so long that I hadn't even noticed.

"You okay?" Jeremy leaned in and whispered to me.

I just simply nod my head and offer him a small smile. But again, I find myself needing to take the attention off of myself.

"Who is the empty chair for? Were we expecting someone else?" I ask diverting my attention back to Jesy.

"Yea my new boyfriend was supposed to be coming, but something came up. His name is Ari. "

"Ari? That's a stupid name for a man," Jeremy scoffed focused on a cooing Anya.

"Really?" She asks while squinting at him. "You want to start Remy?" He hated that nickname.

"You got nothing on me," He said shooting her a glare and holding up his hands in a come at me bro motion.

"Oh, really? I thought someone who prefers to stick their dick in random whores instead of being in their child's life said something." Jeremy glared at her and my jaw dropped.

"I'm sorry are you dating men or women this month, I can't

keep up with the number of times you switched in one week. Actually in one day," Jeremy said suggestively.

"At least I can keep mine."

"At least I can keep one."

"At least none of mine are plastic blonde cheating sluts who I am easily influenced by."

I purse my lips and looked down in an attempt to mind my dam business.

Dam bitch, Jesy came for blood.

I looked back and forth towards the brother-sister duo. I have seen them fight before and I just knew when something big and petty was brewing. The last fight I witnessed between these two ended with her throwing a 10-pound ashtray at his head. She missed but I don't want to know what would have happened if she didn't.

Maybe she would have knocked some sense into him.

Both of them looked like they were ready to pounce on each other. I just hoped I could get me and Anya out of the way fast enough. Two grown-ass people fight like kids who don't have any type of sense.

"Enough," Mariella said breaking the staring contest between the Bresset siblings.

"But," they both said at the same time but she cut them off again.

"Stop it, it's Mother's Day, it's about the mothers in the room, keep your petty banter to yourselves regardless of who has a good point," she said winking at Jesy with a smile.

"Mom," Jeremy says in protest.

"What?" Mariella asked innocently confused.

Jeremy sucked his teeth as he picked up Anya from the chair giving her kisses and cuddles. I guess he was over his food and just wanted to make as much time for her as possible.

"So, I have an announcement," Mariella said breaking the silence again. Everyone stopped and stared at her with concerned eyes. The first time I had dinner with his mother and she said she had an announcement, the announcement was that she divorced their father. This was around the early days of me and Jeremy's relationship. We all looked at her concerned because we never know what would come out of this woman's mouth.

"But I will tell you after the presents." She smiled clapping her hands. What is with this family and anticipation? "Jesy you can go first."

She hands her mother a box containing a Tiffany bracelet with an engraving of her name etched into it. Jeremy got his mother a Valentino bag filled with jewelry, cash, and Knick knacks. I got her the black and white Yeezys. She kept saying they looked really comfortable on my feet. I also got Andrea a new kitchen pot set. She was grateful and happy for every single gift she received.

Watching everyone give their gifts to Mariella warmed my heart, it made me happy to see how much children can love their mothers. It almost made me tear up a little.

"I actually got something for you," Jeremy said diverting his attention to me.

"Me? Why?" It may have sounded rude but I didn't want anything from him.

"Samantha, you are the mother of my child," he said pulling out a long velvet black box.

I mentally rolled my eyes.

I hesitantly took it but when I opened the box, I could have cried at how beautiful the necklace in the box was. It was a silver chain with a white opal heart on it. It was kind of huge, I won't lie. It looked to be a locket but I couldn't open it.

"Thank you, it's beautiful I really appreciate it Jer." I reached over to hug him, as much as I couldn't stand the man, my birthstone was my favorite jewelry stone. I never wanted diamonds I always wanted white opals. I tried to pull away from the hug but he only tightened his grip a little more.

"Umm Jeremy?"

"Yea sorry," he said awkwardly. He finally let go so he can put the necklace around my neck. "You're welcome Baby girl," he said before kissing the back of my neck sending chills down my spine. I look at him in disbelief, to which he responds by winking at me and I roll my eyes at him.

I knew what he was doing, and it wasn't going to work. Mans was going to have to work for this if he ever wanted me back. It wouldn't be easy this time, it may not even be an option now that I think about it.

What am I saying? I am done with this man.

"Baby girl? When did you two get back together?" Jesy asked while tilting her head to her brother.

"We aren't back together," I said before he could answer her. "He has a pregnant fiancé."

Jesy darts her eyes back to her brother dropping her jaw in

shock. Her shock turns into a full-out laugh. "Wow you're such a fucking dumb ass, you must wear condoms with sluts dummy." She continued to giggle to herself. Jeremy just let out a deep sigh rolling his eyes

"Anyways," Mariella said interrupting the tension at the table. "Back to my announcement. I almost forgot." She slowly pushed her chair back, stands up, and looks around at all of us.

Would she just spit it out already?

"Well, I am giving you the house Sweetheart. Happy Mother's Day!" She squealed in delight.

"Congratulation Jesy, you get this whole house," I said to her smiling, I don't know why she made me move in if she was just going to give Jesy the house.

"No, not Jesy, You," Mariella corrected while furrowing her brow.

"Who?"

"You."

"Me?!" I said as I pointed to my chest and looked around confused.

"Yes, this house is much too big for me. I have a smaller one not too far from here so I can still be in Anya's life, plus I don't need a house with 4 bedrooms and a pool. Plus I already put the lease in your name. This is your Mother's Day gift from me to you."

"Mariella, I don't mean to be rude, but I think one of your other children would expect to get your house."

"We knew," Jeremy said shrugging.

"Surprise!" Jesy said smiling.

Boy, do I hate surprises.

Is it crack? Is that what they smoke? It's crack, isn't it?

"I can't accept this gift, it's too much, it's a whole house for god's sake, I just brought a house a few months ago," I said looking around at everyone at the table.

"Well sell it, I'm sure you'll get a good price," Jesy said to me.

"She never did know how to accept a gift mother. Don't be offended," Jeremy said shrugging his shoulders while playing with Anya in his lap. He started tracing his fingers on her bracelet that he got for her.

"Kiss my ass," I mumbled under my breath so only Jeremy can hear.

"Gladly," he said so only I could hear causing me to glare at him.

"Well, either way, I'm moving out by the end of the week, sell it, don't sell it, remodel it, doesn't matter, it belongs to you, Bambi."

I sighed in defeat before walking around the table to go hug her. "Thank you," I said leaning down and kissing her cheek, she really was a little woman. I pulled her in for a tight hug and finally let go. I kissed Jeremy on his cheek too, thanking him for the bracelet. Before making my way back to my seat, he flushed red. That is when I knew I had to put down the wine.

"Well now that all the mushy stuff is over, how about we get to the dessert," Jesy said sitting up in her chair.

"There's more food?" No one seemed phased that we just had a giant meal, I was stuffed.

"Yes dear, we are Italian, I have tiramisu, Pumpkin pie, Ice cream, cookies, and carrot cake."

I tried a few of the desserts but no one's carrot cake will ever touch Ms.Genesis's handmade one. We were lost in conversation with each other when Jeremy's phone began to ring."

"Excuse me I have to take this," he says handing me Anya and walking away.

Jesy proceeds to ask me about me giving birth and I start to tell her to story but before I can make it halfway through, Jeremy stomps back in with an annoyed expression.

"What's wrong?" I look at him concerned.

"Security says you have a visitor," he says furrowing his brow.

Before I can ask who, the door is pushed open, with a small amount of commotion.

"Sir you need to leave," one of the security guards grabs his arm.

I catch a glimpse of Isaiah shrugging off security. Him and the security guard get close to each other huffing their chests in a stare down.

Men.

"It's fine," I yell back coldly rolling my eyes."

He shrugs off the security guards while side-eyeing them as he makes his way over to me. He proceeds to walk in holding a royal blue rose teddy bear, with a bouquet of a dozen red roses and two black and gold gift bags. I can feel Jeremy position himself to stand behind my chair leaning on it trying to assert some sort of dominance.

As if he actually has some type of dominance over me. I could feel Jeremy's anger and annoyance grow from behind me with every step closer Isaiah took. If they are about to enter a pissing contest it was one that I didn't have time for. There is a lot of testosterone in this room right now.

He walks over to Mariella and hands her the red roses, before making his way over to me and stopping in front of Jeremy.

"Excuse me," he says with an attitude as Jeremy stands blocking his way to me.

"Jeremy," I said in a warning tone causing him to huff and move out of the way.

He kneels down next to my chair, with all eyes on him around the table, he moves to kiss Anya's hand when Jeremy snatches her from me and steps away. I shoot him and glare and roll my eyes giving my attention back to Isaiah.

He is down on one knee just staring at me. I stare at him blankly just blinking my eyes trying to figure out what he wants with my hands folded on my lap in wait. "What?" I finally let out breaking the silence between us, and in the room. I have not an ounce of emotion on my face.

"I'm sorry," he says snapping himself out of whatever trance he was in. "Happy Mother's Day Sam," he says handing me the bags. I was hesitant at first but I rolled my eyes, sighed, and just accepted defeat knowing he wouldn't leave until I took them.

Inside both bags were 2 pairs of Top 3 Jordan retro 1's in sizes for Anya and me. "Wow, thank you. I appreciate it," I said with a straight face. I was still mad but inside I was bouncing around like a little girl. I wanted these shoes forever I was just too lazy to actually get them.

"Can we talk please?" He said clearing his throat while looking at Jeremy insinuating that he wants privacy.

Bitch he had a whole other girl's mouth on his dick and you literally caught him red-handed. Yesterday! But then again, he may have thought y'all were broken up. Then again, he may just not be shit. Then again, he could have been cheating this whole time.

I shake my head trying to ignore the voice of my indecisive inner libra goddess and just say fuck it.

"Uhm yea sure, let's go outside."

As I said that I heard Jeremy let out a grunt of displeasure. I move to get up as we make our way outside with Isaiah following close behind me.

Chapter 17

Samantha Kage

. . . .

I can't help replaying the moments of that office in my mind, in the same spot where he had another girl on his dick, a whole day after we had a fight was the same spot where he first made me cum from just his tongue. The man loved to eat pussy, and I loved that about him. That was the same day our friendship moved past a point of friendship into something more. It was about a month after I had Anya.

Mariella had Anya and I decided to go get lunch with Annabelle at a Mexican restaurant in the city. I had noticed I was by Isaiah's office when I asked him if he wanted me to grab him some lunch. At that time we had become really close with a few flirts here and there but nothing remotely serious, my oblivious ass thought he was being friendly and not that he actually wanted me.

I had made my way to his office with Birria tacos cause I was so excited for him to finally try them. I made my way to his office that day greeting Lilian as she offered me a small shady smile as she always did. I started to assume she got Botox in her face and she couldn't smile properly because I never did anything to that girl. I wasn't sure if she had a problem with me or not because she was always polite.

I chose peace and gave her the benefit of the doubt.

"Lunch is here! "I yelled entering the office and closing the door behind me. His eyes snapped up from whatever work that was on his desk that looked like it was frustrating him. However, his expression softened almost completely when he saw me.

He licked his lips while smiling. "Yes, yes it is," he said laughing to himself.

Did I miss the joke?

"Boy stop playing with me and come eat this taco."

I heard myself out loud but it was too late, he was staring at me with wide eyes and a shit-eating grin. Before we knew it we both broke out in a loud laugh.

I walked over to his desk with my white t-shirt, grey sweatpants, and pink crocs to drop the bag. As I walk towards him he looked at me up and down taking in my outfit, which of course I noticed.

"What? I'm comfortable," I said shrugging my shoulders. I didn't like the way he was looking at me, it made me feel like I looked more ridiculous than I thought I did. After having Anya, my main life objective was comfort and nothing else. Plus, I didn't plan on coming to his office, I only planned on grabbing a quick bite to eat with Anna and then going home to my baby.

I miss her right now.

"No, it's not that, it's just," he trailed off moving to walk from behind his desk.

"Just what?" I asked as he moved to stand in front of me.

"You look amazing love." He said taking my cheeks in his hands causing a smile to appear across my lips.

He has never not called me love.

"Awe, thank you."

We stood there staring at each other for what had to be about 5 minutes. If someone was to walk in on us they would think we were utterly weird, but we weren't. This was just something we did. This was our friendship, too close for comfort, being weird, watching anime together, laughing, and hanging out all the time. All together just blatantly showing our love for one another. He finally broke the silence again muttering something I didn't think I would hear him say, "Fuck it, I just wanna taste you love."

Before I could choke out the what from my throat, his soft dark lips were already on mine. Oh my God, his lips were so soft.

He broke the small kiss, looking for a sign in my eyes of some sort of continuance. I quickly responded by pulling him back in for another kiss this time sucking his bottom lip. He sucked in a sharp break of air inviting my tongue into his mouth. He tasted so fucking good I could feel the heat grow in between my legs. I was fully melting into his lips, his body, and his tongue. Our tongues were fighting for dominance but he was clearly winning by taking the lead. I didn't know how badly I wanted to kiss him until I finally did.

My pussy was hungry, she hadn't been fed for almost a year now. I grew wetter by the second imagining his tongue doing the same movements on my clit as he was doing to my mouth. It caused me to let out an unintentional moan against his lips.

I could tell he was trying to be a gentleman but the kiss quickly grew hungrier. I wanted him to touch me, I wanted him to take control but he didn't, he was gentle with me, he let me move at my own comfortable pace for him. Our kiss got sloppier and I let out another moan letting him know how much I was enjoying this. His grip on my waist tightened and I removed my hands from around his neck, grabbed his hands, and moved them away from my waist to my ass without breaking our kiss. He squeezed both cheeks tightly letting out a groan against my lips.

I knew I would have to come out for air eventually, but the moment was not here yet. He squeezed my ass again finally breaking the kiss and resulting in me panting. He moved to suck on that sweet spot on my neck causing me to throw my head back in pleasure. I had to put my hands back against the desk I was leaning on to support myself. My knees grew weaker as his tongue devoured my neck. I could feel his hard-on pressing up against me and it was driving me crazy. Who knew this whole time his flirting wasn't a joke, and that he actually wanted me?

"Sam," he said in-between kissing all over my neck.

"Mmhmm," I hummed. I couldn't even focus enough to form words his touch was just driving me crazy.

"If you want me to stop just say so."

He started moving his hands to pull down my sweatpants with my underwear following. At this point, he could do whatever he wanted to me. I was so horny I might have cried if he didn't touch me.

He removed my shoes and sweatpants throwing them in the corner, leaving me bare bottom in front of him. He lifted me and placed me on his desk pushing me to lay back and he lifted my legs in the air. I covered my face feeling so exposed to him at the moment. I feel like I haven't been touched in forever. I might cum just from him touching my clit alone.

"You with me love?" He says trying to get my attention as he places kisses from my calf down to my thigh.

I nod my head, my chest rising and falling heavily panting waiting and anticipating his touch. I feel his finger slide up and down my slick split, causing me to shudder under his touch.

"So perfect," he whispered as I look down to see him spreading me open with his fingers, he licked his lips and met my gaze.

"Look at me," he ordered. I looked down at him between my legs as he latched his mouth on my throbbing orb causing me to cry out with my breath hitches in my throat. He uses his lips to pull against my clit resulting in a sound escaping me that I forgot I knew how to make. He continued to suck on my clit without breaking eye contact with me, the pleasure was causing me to let out moans that I didn't know I could. The intense eye contact awoke something inside of me that I wasn't prepared for to come out.

"You like that baby?" He whispers in between licking my clit. I looked down nodding my head only to take in the sight in front of me.

He stared at me like a lion hunting his prey, slurping and sucking me like I was his last meal. I was a moaning mess. He used his hands to grip my thighs tightly to stop me from moving. He let go of one of my thick thighs to insert a finger inside me bending it slightly to torture my G-spot in a continuous motion.

"So wet for me baby. I want you to look at me while you cum baby," he whispered.

I tried my hardest to obey but I think at that moment I saw stars as I started to shake under him uncontrollably. He continued his assault on my clit and g-spot until I finally stopped moving. I was out of breath, and couldn't believe what just happened. My body would convulse every few seconds with the aftershock. He stood up over me sucking his fingers, and licking his palm that my juices had dripped down while making a slurping sound with his lips. He stood up pulling me off my back to stand up back at my feet. I almost collapsed but he caught me.

"Sam."

"Huh?" I'm snapped out of my daydream by Isaiah standing in front of me.

"Were you listening to me?"

"I'm going to be honest I wasn't, my mind drifted off just now."

"I could see, you were breathing hard and biting your lips. What were you thinking about?"

"I was thinking about you actually ."

"Me?" he said raising an eyebrow as a small smile appeared on his lips

"Yea, I was thinking about how you made me cum in the same spot you had your secretary sucking you off, how is she by the way?" I say with a mischievous smile on my face cocking my head to the side and folding my arms.

His smile quickly faded with him rolling his eyes at me as if that was going to make me feel bad. I've always been a very blunt person and he knows this.

"Look love, I'm sorry okay? I didn't know where we stood. And Lili, she was just there."

"Well, I hope you two are happy, is that all you needed?"

"That's it? No lash out, no yelling, did you even care about me? Dammit, I should've known considering you're with him right now, I bet it didn't take long for you to get back on your knees for him," he said in disgust.

See I was trying to keep my cool, what is it with men disrespecting me? One thing the men in my life will always undoubtedly have is the fucking audacity.

"Okay let's recap shall we? Who I am or am not on my knees for is now officially none of your fucking concern. I wasn't phased by that bitch because I knew you were upset and I just needed time to cool off before talking to you. But it seems you wanna press me while I'm still mad so fine. Fuck you!" I snapped." Go fuck that bitch who had her lips on your dick and leave me the fuck alone. Not even 24 Hours after we had a fight you literally had some thot on your dick, are you fucking kidding me? Then to find out you were watching me and reporting back to Jeremy, like a creepy little fly on the wall. You knew I was trying to tell him I was pregnant!"

"Sam he didn't deserve to know."

"That's not for you to decide! You sound like a bitch, all like I'm on my knees for a next nigga like you ain't do that same shit. And obviously I am in the presence of him, in his mothers house, on mothers day, for a fucking mothers day brunch! Do you even think before you speak or did you just want to insult me for petty reasons? It's giving very much small dick energy. You got me fucked up. Fuck! Is this what you wanted ? You wanted a reaction out of me so you can see me crying and broken over you? Are you happy now? Can you see that I actually care, Or do you need me to do something dramatic like put my hands on you, what is it you want me from me!"

I finished glaring at him with tears in my eyes. After I had Anya, for whatever reason whenever I get angry I cry, not cause I'm sad but because I get overwhelmed with emotions.

This is why I don't lash out at people, I cry and I don't like people seeing me cry.

"Shit Sam, I'm sorry! I just don't know how to feel. I lose logic when it comes to you. I never felt this way about someone before. I don't know how to act or react when I'm around you. You affect me in many ways. You're the first girl that has affected me this way. I know this wasn't the right way to tell you this but shit Sam, I hate seeing you cry. And I saw how broken you were after he left you. That's why I didn't tell him anything. I was afraid he would break your heart again." He took a deep sigh. "I hate seeing the people I love cry," he says taking a step closer to me with pleading eyes.

I take a much-needed step back. "How long y'all been fucking?"

"What are you talking about."

Nigga is you dead ass?

"Don't piss me off."

"We been on and off, but I never did anything with her while me and you were together."

"Sure," I said rolling my eyes dramatically and dragging out the word.

"I'm serious!" He said before letting out a deep heavy sigh. "I love you Samantha," he blurted out.

"Wow what a moment to say that for the first time, you don't even mean that," I said shaking my head.

He steps closer to me, taking my hands in his, his rough callused hands grab mine and he looks deep into my eyes. "I am in love with you Samantha, and I know you feel the same way too. Yea I fucked up but I wasn't in the right head space. The only thing in the way is him, it's always been him. Take some time to decide what you want, I will expect a choice soon, I won't wait around forever." His face is inches away from mine, and his arms are still wrapped up in mine.

Did this bitch ass nigga just give me an ultimatum? I know dam well he ain't telling me to choose cause at the moment, I don't want either of them.

"Did you really just tell me to choose because you won't wait for me after I literally caught you with wanna-be barbie on your dick yesterday? You not deadass."

"You know I'm right Sam. You know he's been the biggest dividing factor in our relationship, you were holding back from me because of him, I knew it and you knew it."

Before I could speak again to protest, the door is pulled open to expose an irritated Jeremy standing in the doorway, It startles me out of the obvious trance I am trapped in and I take a step back from Isaiah releasing my hands, turning my face away from Jeremy to hide my tears.

"You okay baby girl?" Jeremy says not taking his eyes off Isaiah.

"She's fine," Isaiah said rolling his eyes. "How is my other little baby girl," Isaiah said throwing a smirk at Jeremy.

"My daughter is fine," Jeremy answered tightly.

How did I get here?

"Can I see her Samantha, I miss my girl," he said turning his head back to me. Jeremy let out a low growl which we both ignored. I look between the two men trying to rack my brain on what to do in this situation. I can feel my anxiety rising, after this whole ordeal I must go call my therapist.

"Uhm yea," I said shyly causing Jeremy to snap his furious eyes at me, I give him back apologetic eyes and step past him in the house in search of my girl. I pick up Anya out of her Angela's arms assuring her I would be right back.

Isaiah perks up at the sight of both of us, but Anya lets out a scream of delight and starts bouncing in my arms excitingly at the sight of Isaiah. Jeremy looks visibly pissed off, but I don't really care. He's dam near only been around for like a week.

If that.

"Hey my beautiful girl, I missed you." He starts placing kisses on Anya's face and tickling her so she can giggle. Anya coos happily in his arms. I can feel the anger radiating off Jeremy, but It is what is it. He will be okay.

Jeremy lets out a low growl and walks away from the doorway. I stay with Isaiah for what had to be at least half an hour outside while he played with Anya in a weird silence while I watched them.

"Alright, I got to go. Take care of my girl. I'll see you soon, don't forget what we talked about," Isaiah said handing Anya back to me. He placed a small kiss on my forehead and walked away to his car to drive off through the gates.

When I got back inside, I handed Anya to Mariella so I can move my gifts upstairs. I was in the room placing the gifts down when Jeremy runs in behind me angrily. "What the fuck was that!"

I stop, take a second, and try to figure out who he is talking to. It's weird, I seem to be the only one here and I know he not talking to me. "Excuse me?"

"Where does he get off acting like Anya is his child, and you just letting him say things like "My girl," and getting away with it? What the fuck Samantha, She's Mine!"

What in the entire fuck did this albino penguin just say to me?

I had to blink a couple of times to get the confusion out of my head.

He's not talking to me like that? He could never be?

"No you dick, she's mine!" I yelled feeling the tears form again.

His head jerked back at my response. "I carried her, I almost died for her, I did it by myself without you! You left me you piece of shit! I don't care why you did it, you left me broken. You broke me!" I could feel the conversation finally happening, the conversation that so desperately needed to happen between us, who knows how this conversation would end.

"Baby girl what did you expect me to do? I did this for you!" I could hear Anya fussing down the stairs

"That's bullshit and you know it."

"Sam," He begins but I cut him off. I can still hear Anya fussing. Almost as if she can sense what's going on.

"Close the door." This argument needed to happen, and it needed to happen now.

Chapter 18

Jeremy Bresset

. . . .

The tension in the air was thick, so thick that a knife wouldn't be enough to cut through it. Maybe a chainsaw would be needed. We stare at each other for a few moments of silence. I am almost afraid of where this might be going. We rarely argued when we were in a relationship, but when we did it was bad.

Some arguments made me think we would never work out. Some arguments made me think I would never see her again.

"Do you know what I went through after you left? After you declared your love for me? After you gave me a ring full of false promises?" My eyes immediately dart to her hand clinging to a glimmer of hope that the ring was still there. I had constantly forgotten to check if it was there before, but it wasn't. I felt my heart sink a little. "Do you even care?" She said again while sounding broken. The small whimper that escaped her lips caused my heart to fall straight into my stomach.

"Baby girl," I began to protest but she cut me off immediately.

"Stop calling me that!" I feel a rush of regret, sorrow, and anger run over my body at her words. "I'm not your baby girl, you lost the right to call me that when you broke my heart over a fucking text." The sound of her voice cracking again at the end caused me to feel devastated. I could feel my eyes beginning to become heavy.

"Shit Sam, what do you want me to say? I said I was fucking sorry!"

"You could have talked to me! And you can not get mad that Anya has an attachment to a man that you made sure was supposed to be in my life!"

Is it weird that her yelling at me like this makes me want to fuck her brains out?

"He was never supposed to get that close," I grumbled.

"So what? He was just supposed to tell you If I was fucking another man? Or tell you if something you deemed significant happened in my life? So you were allowed to keep up with what I was doing for your own selfish reasons but I wasn't allowed to know anything about you?" She was looking at me like hated me and I couldn't take it.

"It doesn't matter because he didn't tell me anything anyway."

"That's not the fucking point Jeremy!" She sighs deeply and takes a second. I can see she is calming herself down. "How was it so easy for you to stay away from me?" She said in a soft whisper with a tear running down her cheek. "I was dying without you," she whispers defeated.

"You don't get it, you don't know what seeing those pictures of you in the hospital did to me. It struck a fear in me that would make me do anything my father asked. I couldn't risk anything happening to you Sam!"

"You happened to me though. You didn't hurt me physically but you broke me mentally," she said with disgust.

I cringed at her words. "I should have been there for you while you were pregnant. I know. Fuck!"

I'm just making myself mad.

It is silent for a few seconds until she speaks again.

"You have another baby on the way though. At least you will be there for her as always. She can get everything I never got. I should expect as much, she was always more important, and now she has won again."

"That's not fair Sam. I didn't know."

"It is fucking fair and you know it Jeremy. I never tried to hide the fact that I was pregnant. I went through hell and high water to tell you until I gave up and stopped trying to force a man into something you made it clear you didn't want to be in. Is the baby the only reason you want me back in your life? If Anya didn't happen, would you still want me in your life? Would we be here right now?"

"Of course I would fucking want you in my life. I never stopped wanting you what the fuck? Anya is just an added blessing. Samantha, I didn't know you were pregnant this is not my fault! I literally stalked your Instagram, I had a man watch you. You never posted you were pregnant, or anything related, and Isaiah knew and never told me!"

"So it's my fault? Is it Isaiah's fault? Everyone's to blame for me getting treated like shit except you right?" She sounds so disgusted with me.

"I didn't say that. Stop putting words in my mouth Samantha, you're really not being fair here."

"If you tell me I am not being fair one more time, I will walk out of this fucking room. I had no way to tell you, so it is fair, you blacklisted me from your life as I said before. Plus I know Mariella tried to tell you even though I told her not to. I just know your mother that well. But you're just such a dick that you didn't even answer your mother's phone calls. I almost hoped she would tell you to see how you would react but again, you do what you do best which is throw people away, even if it's your own mother."

"Samantha," I begin but she cuts me off.

"Oh wait! I'm lying. The one person you never cut off is your darling Tiffany," she says sweetly. "And then to find out your back with the one person who wanted nothing more than to see us fail. Maybe you're more like your father than you realize."

Her words felt like they were being spat at me in the calmest tone ever.

"I am here with you and not her, aren't I? As soon as I learned about Anya I was devoted to that little girl. I fell in love the moment I saw her. Knowing that you gave me that child is one of the greatest things that has ever happened. And don't you dare compare me to that man."

She rolled her eyes at me but immediately looked to the floor. When ever she looked at the floor like that she was internally debating something. I stood there folding my arms waiting for the most beautiful woman to say something.

She finally looked up at me again taking a deep sigh. "You know one thing about Zach, I never doubted that he loved me, even after everything he put me through, I never once thought he didn't love me. But you made me feel like I was nothing. Like I was some sort of challenge you sought out for yourself that you could fuck me again one last time after breaking up with me the first time."

Her words hurt, her words actually hurt me. How can she compare me to that monster?

"Are you fucking delusional, nobody does something like that to someone they love. You don't cause the person you love any pain. Don't you fucking compare me to him, Samantha! That's not fucking okay and you know it! Stop being so god dam petty all the time," I growled.

It's so unsettling seeing my beautiful strong queen like this. If she only knew that besides our daughter, she was the only woman I had ever loved. She's the only woman who I have ever been in love with. She's the only one I am in love with. I know she only said that cause she's petty as fuck but it still hurt a little.

She rolled her eyes at me before crossing her arms and walking over to the bed and plopping herself down. "But you did. You caused me pain. You broke my heart Jer."

"It was for the greater good."

"Fuck you," she scoffed as another tear rolled down her cheek. I could feel my face getting hot from he anger.

We both stood there in silence for a few minutes just staring at each other. This argument was going nowhere, we couldn't even fully focus on one topic. The argument almost felt repetitive, I just wanted us to move past this, I missed her. I needed her. Before I could counter the argument she speaks again in a softer voice than before making me ache at the deepest part of my core.

"I vowed to never let another man have that much power over me again. I had to go to therapy Jeremy, I was depressed, I was pregnant, and I was alone. I went through all of it without you and I have no problem with continuing to do it without you." She diverted her gaze away from me hanging her head down in defeat before she uttered words that shook me. "You have too much power over me. I lose all logic when I'm around you, we can't," she says stopping to clear her throat. "We can't keep doing this to each other, it's toxic. I think we should set up a visit schedule for Anya, maybe some distance between us may be for the best since we are currently getting nowhere. I can drop her off with Mariella and you can pick her up from here or something, I don't know. As much as we are bad for each other, I won't deny my little girl her father since I never had one. But me and you? We can't be around each other, it's too much and you know it."

Okay, fuck this.

I quickly take strides across the room to where she's sitting on the bed, so I can take her tear-soaked cheeks in my hands to raise her head to look directly into her beautiful brown doe eyes. Immediately she keeps her eyes down while refusing to look at me. I need her to see me, us standing so far away from each other is helping nothing. This argument is full of so much toxicity and it's literally going nowhere.

"You have all the power over me, don't you understand that!" I say to her in a pleading tone. Her eyes finally snapped up to meet mine with her lips parted a little, my eyes dart down to her lips distracting me for a second but I have to stick to my goal.

Oh, I would want nothing more than to taste her sweet dark lips at the moment.

I kneeled down in-between her legs as she was sitting on the bed, I took both of her hands in mine as I continued to speak. "I lose all logic when I'm around you! You are my light, my sun, my air, and the love of my life and I truly don't feel like I deserve you most days. You are the kindest sweetest person I have ever had the pleasure of being around. But make no mistake Samantha, I love you. You are the only woman I have ever been in love with, and will ever be in love with. I know I may go about things the wrong way but don't ever doubt what I feel for you. What I feel for you is way deeper than what people call love."

She stared at me quietly in tears. I could tell she was having an internal debate in her mind on what to do next. I just knew her that well. She was easy for me to read, always. My baby girl.

"I was devastated," I continued urging further to prove my point. " vowed to leave you alone for your own safety but I didn't, I couldn't. I even started working with that man just to know what was going on with you, just for the off chance that I could hear about your life. I even Instagram stalked you, as much as I tried to stay away from you, I found small ways to find out as much as I could about what was going on in your life. I know I hurt you okay? I know I broke you when I solely promised you I wouldn't." I could feel the tears welding in my eyes but I needed to bear my heart and soul to her at this moment so she would understand. "You have to understand where I was coming from, I didn't know what else to do Sam! I was scared for your life, I was a very selfish man, but never when It came to you, as much as I wanted you, your safety was my first priority. I've seen the things my father is capable of and I couldn't subject you to that kind of treatment. Make no mistake Samantha, I love you, I would do anything for you and our daughter. I promise you that. I'm not leaving your life willingly again, a visitation with Anya is not enough for you, I need you both in my life. Do. You. Understand. Me?"

"You've made empty promises to me before," She said in a voice so quiet, if I wasn't inches away from her face I would have never heard it. Usually, during our arguments, she was cold and distant but she is being very vulnerable with me right now and I can't handle it.

"And I will spend a lifetime making it up to you."

To my disappointment, she moved my hands away from her cheeks breaking our gaze and turning away from me. I throw my hands in the air in annoyance. "Do you at-least understand where I'm coming from?"

"I do, but it doesn't change how I feel, or how you made me feel. I need time," she said giving her back to me.

I move forward to wrap my arms around her waist from behind but she quickly steps away from me.

She's being petty, but I won't let her have her way. She likes to be miserable about something and drag it out until she feels like she's waited long enough to make me stir, I'm not giving her the satisfaction. What I say next even shocks me.

"You know Samantha, in a different time, I would have just fucked this attitude right out of you." I don't know what made me so bold but I was waiting for a reaction to what I just said.

"I hate you," she said as she started to walk away.

I wasn't going to make this easy for her, I grabbed her by the waist and pulled her back towards my front wrapping my arms around her from behind and nuzzling my face in the crook of her neck.

This wasn't fair to her, I know what my touch did to her, I know it made her weak.

I spin her around and tilt her chin up so she can look me in the eyes. Something is stirring inside her mind but I just can't tell what it is. I am feeling even bolder now because simply having her this close and not doing what I want with her is driving me mad. The things I would do to her if she gave me a chance. I slowly lean down and place a chaste kiss on her lips. It had been so long since I have done anything this bold. But I was always willing to take a chance with Sam. I was honestly surprised she even let me touch her.

To my utter surprise, she grabs my face and kisses me back, hard. I haven't taken in her scent or tasted her delicious tongue in so long that I get lost in the kiss. The kiss begins getting deeper with our tongues massaging each other so sensually. I feel my pants tighten as the kiss gets hungrier. She breaks the kiss looking up at me biting and licking her lips sexually to show me she is tasting me on her lips. This sets a fire inside me and I moan before I go back in for another kiss but she stops me with a palm on my chest. She pushes me back on the bed causing me to fall on it so she can straddle my hips. I rarely let her take control but after what we have been through, I need her to take the lead to see how far she will go with me. I have been bold enough I don't want to push too far.

She leans down to kiss me again. This kiss is even harder and hungrier at this point. It sounds so sloppy. Fuck she's a good kisser. I nearly come undone when she starts to grind her hips against my throbbing erection. Fuck I missed her, I couldn't control myself, I let my hands freely explore her body sliding under the dress she was wearing to feel for her ass but she immediately breaks the kiss and grabs my hands to stop me.

Fuck did I move to fast? Did I fuck this up? She must think I just want to fuck her. I mean yes I want to fuck her brains out until she cries and screams my name, shit I even might want to put another baby in her but Fuck! I just messed this up.

I just want her to sit on my face.

I continue the internal battle in my head getting ready to apologize but what she does next shocks me. She gets off my waist leaving me on the bed. Before I can sit up she uses her hand to push me back down as she goes for my belt buckle. "Sam, what are you doing?" I ask quickly. I'm not against this I just didn't expect her to do this or move so fast.

Fuck it, maybe my baby girl has forgiven me!

"Shhhh," she said looking at me hungrily. "Just relax baby," she says in the sexiest whisper I have ever heard in my life. I eye here curiously as she unbuckles my pants slowly lowering them freeing my erection from the hold of fabric. When my hard cock stands at attention, she licks her lips and I swear to god I see a spark in this woman's eyes. I don't want to get too excited but having this woman's lips around my cock again might make me pass out.

She licks her hand slowly coating it with spit before slowly wrapping her hand around my throbbing member and slowly stroking up and down. Her touch alone sets something off inside of me. I didn't realize how much I missed her touch until just down.

"Fuck," escapes my throat before I get the chance to stop it.

Her eyes never leave mine as she slowly strokes me from root to tip. She moves up to drag the tip of her tongue from the base of my balls to the tip of my dick dripping with pre cum. Seeing her do this sends a chill up my spine. I have missed her so fucking much. She swirls her tongue around the tip licking up any excess cum before slowly taking my entire length inside my mouth until I hit the back of her throat. I shudder at the feeling, her mouth feels so warm and soft, It feels like a million wet sexy hugs.

As she bobs her head up and down my dick I involuntarily let out moans. The sound of her choking on my dick as the spit drips down my cock is the most beautiful thing I have heard in a while. She slowly pulls my dick out of her throat with strings of spit and saliva following. Her beautiful eyes are red and tearing, and all around her mouth is covered in her spit. It is the most beautiful thing I have ever seen. She uses both hands to stroke, my cock while bobbing her head up and down my dick in quick circular movements while swirling her tongue around the tip.

"Fuck baby, just like that."

She lets go and moves down to place both of my balls in her mouth, sucking, as she continues to stroke my dripping-wet length. "Tell me when you're about to cum daddy," she says before taking my hard dick back into her soft hot wet mouth.

I let out a low groan as she takes me deeper in her throat than before. Her simply calling me daddy awaked something inside me that I hadn't even remembered was there.

"Just like that baby. Suck my dick like a good girl," I know she has a praise kink. She likes when I tell her she's doing a good job. And if I am being honest, I love telling her.

Even with her choking and her eyes watering she never lets up, she continues to suck my dick like she was starving and hadn't eaten in days without breaking eye contact with me. This type of pleasure was made for better men than me because I knew I wouldn't last much longer.

I tangle my hands in her coils as I could feel the pressure building inside when she pushed me all the way in her throat and just held me there. I grab her hair and shove my dick even further into he back of her throat bobbing her head constantly in little movements to attempt to shove my dick further. I love being rough with her.

The further I shove my dick, the farther her eyes roll back into her head. She looks so fucking pretty like this. I love how rough I can be with her and she will just take it like a good fucking girl. I yank her head off of my dick so she can take a breath and I am pleased to see how much spit is still connecting us. I want to lick up all of it but I don't have time right now.

She licks her lips while breathing hard. "Stick your tongue out and open wide," I say to her in a stern tone. When she doesn't do it quick enough, I slap her cheek while biting my lips. She smiles while biting her lips and opens her mouth wide and sticks her tongue out as far as it can go. "Your such a good fucking girl," I say quickly before shoving my dick back into her soft sexy mouth.

I love the way this woman chokes on my dick, the sound, the warmth, everything causes me to roll my eyes to the back of my head for a few. I suck in a sharp breath when the pleasure becomes overwhelmingly good. If someone told me this would have happened today, I would have told them they were lying.

I release her so she can take her own control again. She released me, took a breath, and continued to move her head up and down in slopping hot wet motions. I could feel her tongue circling my girth with every stroke. God dam this woman could suck some dick.

"Shit baby, keep going I'm going to cum." As soon as the words left my lips she released my throbbing cock from her lips with a dramatic popping sound. She stood to her feet looked at me while sucking on her finger and walked away from me right into the bathroom locking the door behind her.

What the fuck?

I hear the sink turn on and I have never been more confused before in my life. Is she coming back? I lay there confused, hard, and horny with a dripping wet dick not knowing what to do.

Is she brushing her teeth?

What the hell is she doing? I am laying in bed with the hard-on from hell and she has fully left me here with it. It won't go down either.

I can't stop picturing her lips on my dick from moments ago, and the look in her eyes as she held my cock in her throat.

Dude stop. Relax.

She finally comes out of the bathroom, making eye contact with me, looking unfazed. Her teeth are brushed, her face is washed, her curly coils are fluffed, and I am still sitting here slowly contracting blue balls.

"Now you feel a sliver of what I felt," she said before shrugging, walking out of the room, and closing the door behind her. I half debate running behind her, spanking her, and fucking her until she screams and can't take it anymore, but there are too many people home for me to fuck her as roughly as I want.

I can't wait to make her scream. I am going to get her back for this. I lay back into the bed in defeat letting out a deep sigh trying to think of things to make my dick soft but it won't budge.

I think she broke it.

I need to go take a cold shower. Finishing myself off would be an injustice to me considering my hand feels nothing like her mouth or her pussy, oh god I miss that pussy. I don't know how long I lay there waiting for my dick to go down but when I do I stuff it back into my pants and make my way downstairs after cleaning myself up. My balls are past blue, they are purple I am sure of it.

When I finally make it downstairs in a bit of pain, I hear music playing in the living room. Piano by Ariana Grande is playing while Anya is being spun around in the arms of my baby girl while dancing and laughing.

Look at her pretending she wasn't being a bad girl a few moments ago.

I can't even stay mad at this woman for what just happened because in some way I know I deserved it, but I knew I would have my revenge eventually.

I hope.

There was no denying this petty ass woman in front of me holding my beautiful daughter in her arms was the love of my life.

Chapter 19

Samantha Kage

It's been a few weeks since mothers day. Everyone in the house has gotten into a routine. I have been working a lot more lately since the destination wedding was in a couple of weeks. I have been emailing the hotel, the florists, and the bride and groom. I have been slacking lately since Jeremy came back into my life but I have found myself back on track and better than ever.

While I work in one of the rooms that I have made my office, Angela or Mariella will watch her. They were also preparing for their move out of the house. Angela offered to visit me a few days out of the week to work here being back and forth from me and Mariella.

I told her only if that's exactly what she wanted to do. To be honest, Angela should retire.

The security guards around the house have become part of the routine as well. To the point where their presence is often forgotten. I think it's a little much though. If Zach was going to pop up he would've done it already. Jeremy's father already knew everything.

Besides getting ready for this wedding, I have been getting ready to move into Mariella's house. Going back and forth, seeing what furniture to keep and sell, with Jeremy's help of course. I have almost already moved in.

The only thing left to do is just put my old house on the market but Jeremy's real estate agent has assured me that I would get back more than what I paid for it since Isaiah did many repairs on the house. Little things like fixing the pavement and repainting increased the market value.

Since our little sexcapade last week, Jeremy hasn't tried anything. I think he knows better by now. Plus he has a baby on the way. Me snatching his soul was to just be petty and nothing else. Or at least that's what I tell myself. I have masturbated enough times since that day. It kind of backfired but knowing he is in more pain than me is satisfaction enough. He does come over every day though. And if my calculations were correct, he was about to walk through the doors right now. He often comes here straight after work to spend time with Anya and then leaves.

And right on cue, Jeremy walks through the door searching for his little girl. Jeremy has been coming around a lot lately, slowly we have become accustomed to being around each other with the petty shit aside. I admire how he has made it his duty to spend as much time with Anya as possible. I am sitting on the carpeted floor with blankets in matching onesies with Anya when he walks over to us.

"Don't you two look beautiful as ever? What do we have here?"

"Daddy's here to join our pajama party. Let's show daddy the pajamas we brought him," I say in my baby voice to Anya. She giggles in response.

I'm going to be honest, these pajamas look fucking ridiculous. It looks like someone threw up sprinkles, glitter, and stars on a white unicorn. But I made sure to pick them out because they were so ridiculous and I wanted to see Jeremy in them so I could laugh. I leave Anya on the floor with Jeremy so I can grab the onesies. I made sure Jeremy's looked more ridiculous than mine or Anya's. He had a bright pink horn on his onesie.

I handed him the onesie and he looked at me like I had just suddenly grown 2 extra heads. "Put it on. For your daughter," I urge with a Cheshire grin.

He looks between me and the onesie having an internal debate with himself before letting out a huff of displeasure and grabbing it from my hands. He really could never tell me no. I can only imagine when Anya starts to be able to ask for things, she will have him wrapped around her little finger.

After a few moments he walks out of the back with the onesie on and I can't help but laugh. And when I say I laughed, I can't remember the last time I laughed as hard as I did. I was literally laying on the floor. I must take a picture.

"Shut up Sam," he says taking Anya up and cradling her in his arms. At the same time, Mariella walks down the stairs and immediately does the thing she does every time she sees the three of us together. She bursts out crying. The woman literally has to be dehydrated by now. Like it doesn't make any sense.

"Oh my god, take a picture, take a picture, take a picture!" She says quickly grabbing her phone.

The three of us pose with our smiles and she takes a few clicks with flashes. I look at the picture and we almost look like a normal happy family of three in the most ridiculous outfits ever. Like if I'm being honest, besides Anya, we look like fools. Mariella bids us our family time and headed back upstairs.

Not to ruin the moment but I need to know. "Jeremy, how's Tiffany?"

"She fine I guess. I don't know? Why?"

"Jeremy," I say in protest. "I know what it's like to be pregnant and alone. Go see the girl."

Did I mention that Jeremy called off their marriage and moved out? Or so he claimed. You know this nigga be lying.

He looks at me disapprovingly before turning his attention back to Anya. "Fine, I will go see her tomorrow. After I go visit my father to get some things settled. I won't be under his wing anymore. Once I have him off of our backs, I will do everything in my power to win you back and keep you safe."

I look over at him to see him looking at me lovingly.

"Are you hungry? I made Oxtail, rice and peas, and potato salad," I quickly say trying to change the subject. I will not let him distract me with his charm.

We are still mad at this man.

I think.

"I haven't had your oxtail in forever. Suddenly I am starving. I would eat anything you give me," he says licking his lips. I don't know if this boy wants to be with me or if he is just horny but he needs to stop.

"You need to stop," I quip as I start walking to the kitchen to make him a plate.

"Stop what?" He says mischievously. He sounds close. He sounds too close. I look back and he is standing directly behind me. I roll my eyes, finish making his plate and leave it on the counter before grabbing Anya from him to walk back into the living room. I set up the blankets on the floor with Anya's toys so she can have them within reach. I place her down grabbing my laptop so I can do some last-minute outfit shopping for Jamaica. Everything is basically settled. Jeremy takes his place next to Anya on the floor while he eats his food.

"You're going to Jamaica by yourself?" My fingers immediately stop scrolling.

Fuck.

Isaiah was supposed to go with me but we never fully confirmed. My plus one was already paid for.

Shit.

"Well, I guess I am now," I say shrugging my shoulders. I will probably ask Annabelle if she wants to come with me or something. I have already made arrangements for Anya to be watched by Mariella for the few days I will be gone. I don't know if I am ready to be away from her for 4 days but it was a start in the wedding planning direction I wanted to go.

"Nonsense, I am coming with you."

"No, you're not."

"I already booked my plane ticket, and changed your ticket to first class with me." I slowly turn my head to the man while looking at him like he was fucking stupid.

Girl, you ain't even mad. You love this crazy shit.

"And when the fuck did you do that?" I retort while trying to sound as annoyed as possible.

"The day after mothers day." He says it so casually while he walks away to put his empty plate in the kitchen. I'm surprised he didn't inhale the actual plate itself the way he cleaned it. I had taught that man how to suck the oxtail bones and that is exactly what he did. I quickly get up rushing behind him, but not before glancing at Anya to see that she is ferociously gnawing at her hand with her gums.

She's fine.

Before I can open up my mouth in protest he turns around to speak again. "You can skip the part where you complain and then just give in to me because whether you like it or not, I will be going to Jamaica with you, I would have just booked a room in the same hotel if you found a way to get me removed. Don't play with me today Samantha." I hadn't even realized he had backed me up into the counter. I press my legs together when I feel just how wet I have become in between my legs. This man should not have this effect on me. Like at all. Especially while he is wearing a unicorn onesie.

Are we like mad at him? Or like mad mad at him?

I roll my eyes and walk back over to Anya who is still determined to bite her hand off. She is so stinking cute. Jeremy and I really made something special. I can't help but think that if things had gone differently I would have had 2 babies instead of one. It affects me sometimes but I try not to think about it much. I had talked about it in therapy but not that much.

We sit there looking like a happy family in our matching pajamas watching movies comfortably when suddenly my phone goes off.

Unknown: I will have you muñeca perfecta.

I feel a chill go up my spine. I start to breathe heavier than I mean to. I need to calm myself down. Jeremy who is bouncing Anya on his knee notices my change in mood. Pretty doll, that's what he used to call me. Must be because a doll can easily be manipulated and that's what he thought of me clearly.

"Baby girl?" he says putting Anya back on her pile of blankets. "What's wrong?"

"It's him," I say handing Jeremy the phone with a shaky voice.

Jeremy immediately snatches the phone out of my hand glaring at it before dialing the number. The number was not in service. "Fuck!" He yells standing up to walk into the back room. His sudden outburst frightens Anya causing her to cry. I quickly grab her trying to hush her.

By the time Jeremy stalks back in, I am standing there with a calm baby, while he has changed back into his suit that he came in wearing earlier.

"I'm upping security," he says while typing on his phone.

"It's not necessary, we have enough around the house, I posted my number on my new planner website that's probably how he got it. It's fine Jer."

"Don't fight me on this Samantha. I will not allow anything to happen to you or my girl." I sigh in defeat. Even if I protested he would do it anyway. "I will see you soon, I have a couple of things to take care of, anywhere you go take one of the guards with you. Do you understand me?" His tone is so demanding.

Yes daddy.

"Y-yes." I choke out. He places a small kiss on my forehead and one on Anya's before continuing to type away on his phone and walking out the door.

I Head to bed for the night sleeping with my girl in my bed instead of putting her in the side room. She's spoiled so she has grown accustomed to sleeping with me sometimes. I needed her here for comfort anyway. I didn't feel like being away from her, nor did I feel like being alone.

I wake up in the morning to the feeling of a small hand slapping my face over and over again.

This little girl.

I wonder how long she has been awake. She leans in to attack my cheek. I guess she's hungry. I make my way downstairs in my shorts and T-shirt and I have never been more confused before in my life.

There are 2 men standing inside the doors with earpieces.

What the fuck?

As I make my way to the window by the kitchen I see about 12 men talking to our main security guard. Marcus, I think his name is. He's really sweet.

Angela is already waiting in the kitchen with a bottle ready for Anya. She shoots me a weird look. I hand her off and throw on my bunny slippers and storm out of the house. As one of the security guards inside opens the door for me. What the fuck is going on.

"Marcus!" I yell. I know I must look like a crazy person to all these men. I stand there tapping my bunny foot as he walks up to me.

"Good morning Ma'am, is there a problem?" He says smiling at me innocently.

"What's with the airport security Marcus?" My tone is clearly filled with agitation.

"Mr.Bresset said he needed more security for the house." Did he add this much security?

Oh hell no.

I run back upstairs to grab my phone, dial Jeremy's number, and run back outside to meet Marcus.

"Hello? Is everything okay?" He asks alarmed.

"Call off your airport security!"

"No," he laughs.

The bastard laughs

"I thought you meant like two more security guards. Not fifteen!"

"If I lower it to ten would that make you feel better?"

"I was fine with 1."

"How about eight?"

"How about Three?"

"Four, one for you, one for my mom, and two for Anya."

"Fine. But I want at least one black person." I hang up quickly before he can try to raise it to 6.

I glare at Marcus who has an amused look on his face. Before I can curse him, his phone rings.

"Yes boss... Yes boss, I understand......Yes she is boss..... The same pink bunny slippers boss..... Copy sir."

He hangs up the phone before shooting me a smile and heading over to dismiss the men. I roll my eyes and stomp back into the house but not before kicking out the two big men who were inside the doors. I slam the door behind me. I walk to the kitchen window to see the men scattering. Some are walking away and some lingering around. Ughhhh. This cannot be my life.

Let me go find my girl.

I start opening doors to find her in Mariela's room about to have a bath. I leave them to it and go do the same. It's been so long. I need to shave and have a nice long bubble bath.

Time for some much-needed me time.

Chapter 20

Jeremy Bresset

· ·

I wake up the next morning to a frantic phone call from my baby girl she is clearly upset about all the security roaming around but after she yells at me I agree to lower the number of security down to four. Four that she can see anyway. I stretch getting up from the bed in my hotel room. I own 2 hotels but this one is my favorite. The modern glass look is very beautiful to me. Yet it still feels homey.

If I am being honest, the place I really want to call home is wherever Samantha is.

I quickly call Marcus when I realize why I was awoken out of my sleep in the first place.

"Yes boss"

"Lower the number of guards visible to four and keep four more out of sight at all times."

"Yes boss, I understand."

"Is she standing right in front of you looking at you like she wants to kill you?"

"Yes she is boss."

"Is she wearing the pink bunny slippers or the sponge bob ones?"

"The same pink bunny slippers boss."

"Don't be looking at my woman Marcus. Protect my family at all costs."

"Copy sir."

I throw my phone on the bed and get dressed for the day. I had a plan today. I would go see my father letting him know that he either sign his company over to me now or I would just take it from him. I had enough dirt on him to have him exiled. It helped greatly that he was a racist fuck and I found a way to keep a record of it.

For the past few weeks, there have been a variety of recording devices in his office. Any negative data was being collected by a hacker friend of mine. He told me he had more than enough to have my father walk out quietly on his own. If he didn't sign the company over to me he would be ruined. Financially and in society. He would never recover.

By the time I make it to my father's office. I am full of energy. But I just can't shake this bad feeling. He doesn't know I am coming but his assistant that loves me assured me that he had no meetings in the morning. I walk with my stack of papers that I need him to sign. I am in such a good mood. Today I will finally get this bastard off my back and hopefully out of my life. I also need him to call off this Zach bitch. I'll just get whatever information he has on Zach and deal with it myself.

I'm on my way to the top floor in the elevator and I can't help but grin to myself like a child. I am overly excited. I can't wait to go home to my baby girl and tell her the good news. I can finally be with her again if she will have me. I quickly make my way down the hallway and smile at my father's assistant. I love her, she was the one who helped me place all the recording devices in the office. Such a sweet lady. I wink at her before flinging my father's office door open.

My jaw drops at the sight before me. I don't know whether to run, scream, laugh, or throw up.

EWWWWWWWWWW

He is on the couch in his office with his pants down while a blonde woman is bouncing on his dick repeatedly moaning. They haven't even noticed I have entered the room. This woman looks to be less than half his age. He is so disgusting. But wait.

That's not who I think it is, is it? I know that sound. I know that voice. I know that woman.

"Tiffany?" I ask in an unsettling tone.

Tiffany snaps her head around and my father looks over her shoulder. They are both glaring at me in utter shock.

"Oh my god," she says quickly getting up to get herself dressed along with my father who quickly pulls up his pants.

He was fucking the woman I was supposed to marry? Not that I really wanted to marry her but still.

Wait.

Why am I upset about this? I don't even care. I am more disgusted than anything.

They both frantically try to start explaining themselves but I don't want to hear anything. Only one question is weighing on my mind.

"How long?" I ask sternly

"Jeremy baby please listen to me," she says walking up to me with her shirt in her hands and pressing a hand on my chest. I grab her wrist, flinging it off me in disgust and I can see tears welling in her eyes.

"If you were fucking her right instead of fucking that monkey this would have never happened." My hand twitches but I ignore him. I need him conscious for the signing of these papers. I knew if I hit him one time I would relocate his jaw to another country and he would be out cold for weeks. I don't take lightly to people disrespecting my woman.

"How fucking long!" I yell this time not leaving room for any bullshit. She gives me a look with sorry eyes but I ignore it. "Tiffany," I warn.

"It started when you went to Miami. I missed you and you were there with her," she says while choking up with tears. "Your father was there to comfort me but then it just happened that one time. Until recently when she came back into your life, I went to him again for help to get you back in my life but this ended up happening again. How could I compete with a baby?" She is speaking frantically through her sobs but I feel not an ounce of feeling for her.

Then it hit me. They weren't wearing a condom. In the past year the two times me and Tiffany have had sex, we wore a condom. One of those times was recent. I was drunk, missing Samantha, and she was just there. We had drunk sex so I assumed the condom broke and that's how she got pregnant. "Is the baby mine?" This time I make no attempts to hide the disgust in my voice.

"Jeremy please," she cries while reaching out for me but I just take a step back. I don't know where her hands have been.

"Is the baby mine!" I ask again.

She just shakes her head and cries even harder. Welp that made this a whole lot easier then. She looks over at my father who is looking at her with disbelief. He finally works up the balls to speak.

"You're pregnant?" He asks as she nods her head at him with an innocent smile. "Abort it or I will sue you."

I tried to stifle my laugh.

I pray to god that is on the recording. I walk over to the desk where my father is standing and slam the papers down. "You will sign all the paperwork to hand the company over to me right now. Instead of keeping 20 percent shares in the company, you will keep 4. And that's only because I am feeling generous."

This made sense now. No wonder he wanted me with Tiffany so badly. It was so he could keep her close and fuck her whenever he wanted. This man was truly disgusting. "You will also make a public statement in one week letting everyone know you have signed the company over to me." I can feel the smile I have on my face. I have gotten rid of Tiffany and my father is about to be off my back.

"And if I don't sign this agreement?" He asks while folding his arms.

"Then I will expose you for the racist disgusting fucking pig you are. And make no mistake I have proof. So it's really either you lose your company to me or you lose your company overall. Only one way ends up with you still having some type of money. Next move is yours you old fat fuck."

He grabs the papers from the desks and signs them and shoves them back toward me. He is looking at me like he wants to fucking kill me but I don't give one fuck. Tiffany is still sobbing in the corner, and I really don't give a fuck.

I am content with my life at this moment.

"Also leave my future wife, my daughter, and my mother the fuck alone. I won't ask again." I turn to walk out of his office but not before Tiffany runs up to me grabbing my arm.

"You have a daughter?" He says curiously.

That's weird. Didn't he tell Zach about us? Isn't that why he texted Samantha?

"Oh, your whore didn't tell you?" I scoff. "I guess you were looking for any reason to just run and fuck my father weren't you?" I just shake my head and let out a chuckle. Well, I have to go. I know exactly where I need to be right now, and it is not here. "I will see you next week for the press conference, don't be fucking late," I yell over my shoulder at him.

"Jeremy please! I'm sorry." She is sobbing uncontrollably but I just look at her, then I look back at my father who looks highly upset but he knows better than to try anything. He has seen how serious I am. I shrug out of her hold and look at her like she is less than nothing.

I walk out of the office smiling and greeting his assistant who has without a doubt heard everything that just happened. I have assured her she will still have a job when this is all over. An even better job at that. To be honest I might expose him either way. I haven't decided yet. I have to go drop these papers off at my lawyer's office. Good thing my lawyers are right downstairs in legal.

After settling everything with legal, I make my way back to my car. I think I have more than earned the rest of the day off. I know exactly where I want to be. I stopped at the florist and picked up some white roses just like my baby girl loves. I make my way to the bakery to pick up some carrot cake cupcakes for her without cream cheese frosting but regular frosting because she doesn't like some people's cream cheese frosting. I don't know whose favorite cake flavor is carrot cake but I am not one to argue. I would do anything for her.

By the time I make it back to My mother's house I greet the guards and quickly make my way inside darting up the stairs taking three at a time with the flowers and cupcakes in my hand. I knock on her door and impatiently wait for her to answer. I feel like a giddy school child. She opens the door looking as beautiful as fucking ever. Her hair is slicked back into a high puff and her edges are laid. She is in a white lace bralette and some grey shorts resting on her waist. She has a scarf tied around her head. She looks so fucking cute I can't take it.

I unintentionally take in her scent. My god, she smells fucking good.

I don't realize how long I am standing there drinking her in until she clears her throat. I smile at her like I haven't seen her in months. "What?" She says in a confused tone smiling back at me as well. I hand her the cupcakes and flowers, she looks excited at the sight of them but confused at the same time.

"Where is Anya?" I add while scanning my eyes around the room.

"Oh. She's in your mom's room. Do you need me to go get her for you?"

"Nope."

"Well is everything okay? It's the middle of the day shouldn't you be at work?" She walks to the futon on the end of her bed and places the flowers and cupcakes down. I can't take my eyes off of her. My whole body has relaxed. I completely forgot I was even angry today. Her doe eyes on me are all I needed to see to calm me down. My god, I love this woman. I won't let anything keep us apart any longer.

Samantha Pov

"Are you okay? Why do you keep staring at me?" I can't help but chuckle nervously. He hasn't moved from the doorway.

 He is looking at me the way I look at puppies when they are cute as fuck.

"I'm perfect now," He whispers to himself before he steps into the room closing the door behind him. Within seconds he has crossed the room. He grabs my face in his hands and places a kiss on my lips that is so hungry, I don't have time to comprehend what's going on until I feel his hands all over my body.

Fuck fuck fuck fuck.

I couldn't even deny him right now if I tried. Our tongues are tangling in each other, my hands are fisting in his hair, and his arms are wrapped tightly around my waist pulling me forward so I can feel the unforgiving hard-on in his pants. He breaks the kiss and I am a panting mess. I am also confused. Why did he stop kissing me? He licks his lips while taking a deep breath and looking down at my body. I can't stop staring at his lips. I want more.

Bitch don't you dare fold.

"Take off your clothes." He sounds so fucking sexy breathing hard. He rips his tie off and starts to button down his shirt while pulling out the part that was tucked out of his pants.

"What?" I ask as I pry my eyes away from his lips to meet his bright blue ones.

Don't fold. Say no.

"I am going to strip down to my boxers. By the time that happens if you are still wearing any clothes I will rip them to shreds, do you understand?"

Girl, I folded like origami, drop them drawers.

I lick my lips nodding my head frantically. I watch him strip almost forgetting that I am supposed to do the same.

Shit.

I rip off my shorts kicking them off my feet. Of course one of the legs gets stuck on my ankle. I must look so fucking unsexy right now.

Thank god I just shaved and I am also not wearing any underwear to save me time. By the time I got to pull off my bralette, I don't get the chance this man is already in his boxers. How the fuck did he do that so fast?

He grabs my face again continuing the breath-stealing kiss that he trapped me in only moments ago. I quickly grant his tongue entrance. The kiss is ravenous. I can barely control my thoughts. His hands move down my body taking both my ass cheeks in his hands. He jiggles them a little before grabbing them roughly lifting me off the floor. I quickly respond by wrapping my legs around his waist and tightening my legs to hold my body up.

All without breaking the kiss for a second.

I let out a moan when he pressed himself against my throbbing wet sex. The only thing separating his dick from my dripping hole is the thin fabric of his boxers. I start to grind myself against him causing him to let out a deep grunt of pleasure.

He walks us over to the bed and throws me on it while breaking the kiss before climbing on top of me to continue it. I didn't realize just how much I missed kissing this man's sweet lips. He breaks the kiss moving down to my neck kissing and sucking as if he is searching for hidden treasure under my skin. I am a moaning mess. I might be highly loud. Even though everyone is on the other side of the house I don't want them to know how loud I am when it comes to Jeremy.

When he is satisfied with one spot he moves to the next. I know he is leaving marks.

Then I remember, I still have this lace bra on. He seems the realize this at the same time because he leans ups ripping it off with the tearing sound of fabric in the air. He pulls it off and throws it in the corner.

That was Fenty bitch.

I don't dare protest. I don't have the time. Before I can process how he ripped my favorite bra his tongue is wrapped around my nipples. Slowly he makes his way down my body savoring and tasting every bit of skin that his tongue can reach. Even though my piercings are gone, my nipples remained even more sensitive after giving birth. He nibbles on one causing me to arch my back in pleasure.

He stops at my C-section scar tracing a finger over it sending a chill up my spine. He places a small kiss over it whispering something almost inaudible. It sounded like he said thank you I think.

By the time he gets down to my pussy I am dripping wet. I can feel it running down my ass. He stares at my pussy licking his lips. I can't wait anymore. I need him to touch me. I raise my hips to meet his lips but he instead pulls back to stand up. He reaches down and places a hard slap on my clit that sends my back arching off the bed.

"Relax."

He places both of his arms under my thighs and yanks me forward. My breath hitches in my throat as I feel his tongue run from the crack of my ass to the tip of my clit with a flick of his tongue. This action alone causes my body to shudder. He continues to suck and lick me until I feel my first orgasm building. Within 2 minutes I am a shaking screaming mess and I come undone on his tongue. He doesn't stop, he just continues to lick me like I am the last thing he will ever taste. He inserts one finger inside me and I see black as my eyes roll to the back of my head.

He pulls his finger out slapping my clit tracing circles around it and slapping it one more time before shoving his finger back inside me curling it to play with my g spot. My chest is rising and falling dramatically, I can't catch my breath. My moans are coming out frantic, I think I have said his name, called him daddy, baby, everything. I couldn't even tell you at this point. This man has completely taken over my body with just his fingers and his tongue. I feel my second orgasm building and I can't sit still. He grips my legs tight to keep me from running.

It's so intense. I can feel it building from my core. He speeds up his finger and bites my clit causing me to scream uncontrollably. When he bit down on my clit I saw stars. My legs began to shake as my earth-shattering orgasm rocked my body. He released my clit from his teeth roughly sucking it so I can ride out my orgasm. I can't be held responsible for the sounds coming out of my mouth right now.

He rises to stand pulling me to sit up, his lips lower to meet mine, while his hand wraps around my throat. I can taste myself on his lips and his tongue. He lowers his hand to slip his finger back inside me. This time adding another finger. He doesn't break the kiss as he begins to finger fuck me rougher than before. I arch my back towards him opening my legs wider to give him as much access as he needed. He breaks the kiss pressing his forehead against mine while staring into my eyes as his fingers curl and he uses his thumb to brush my clit while continuing his assault on my pussy. "fuck daddy," is all I can muster out against his lips as I feel my third orgasm building. I don't know how much more of this I can take.

"Cum for me like the good girl you are," he says as he breaks the kiss. Yup that's it. From those words alone I squirt all over his hand and leg. I grip onto his arm for strength and the orgasm rocks through my body. I even feel it in my ears as they get hot from how much power that orgasm held. I grab his face and kiss him roughly. He breaks the kiss and takes a step back. "Face down ass up. Now."

Yes daddy.

I quickly obey and change my position on the bed as he commanded. I arched my back, legs open, and face on the bed just like he commanded. "Good girl," he whispers as he smacks my ass hard and I swear I almost cum again.

Before I have a second to take a breath. He is entering me slowly. Dangerously slow. "Fuck baby girl. You're so fucking tight."

He shoves his entire length inside me while letting out a moan that almost made me cum again. He lands a harsh slap on the other side of my ass. He doesn't continue his slow torture, he quickly changes his pace and slams into me roughly and continuously. The only sounds in the room are his harsh breaths, His pelvis slapping against my ass, my unrecognizable speech, moans, mutters, and the wet sound of my pussy. No other man can make me as wet as him and I am ashamed to admit it.

He takes a fist full of my hair as he speeds up his thrusts. I cry out at the pleasurable pain. "You like taking dick, don't you? You're doing such a job. Taking daddy's dick like a good fucking girl." I feel spit land on my asshole while he shoves his finger inside. His ungodly pace of fucking me has not let up at all. "Answer me!"

"Yes daddy oh my god!" I cry out.

"Yes what?" He says shoving his finger deeper into my ass moving it in and out.

"Yes daddy I love taking daddy's dick like the fucking good girl that I am." I cry out.

"You look so fucking pretty when you talk like that. "He pulls his finger out of my ass and places another slap on my ass cheek that is starting to burn but I fucking love it. He pulls out of me while yanking me backward by my hair until I am standing at my feet.

Jeremy turns me around to face him. Before I can even fathom what he will do next he hoists me up by my legs. I wrap my hands around his neck to keep myself from falling. "Put it in," he commands. I reach down and grab his dick slowly placing it at the tip of my entrance. He thrusts his hip forward entering me so suddenly that I scream. My body shuddered at the amount of pleasure that gave me. "Look at it." I look down to see my swollen clit being met with his pelvis constantly as he fucks me. This position allows him to get so deep that I can feel him in my stomach. "Your such a good fucking girl, you feel fucking amazing." He kisses me roughly slamming into me harder than before. He is swinging my body to meet his cock with every thrust. My legs are flying all around. How he has the strength to hold me up and fuck me like this is beyond me. I feel my fourth orgasm building. I pull him tightly against me and he throws his head back fucking me harder than before.

I let out a scream biting into his shoulder as my eyes roll back into my head and I cum harder than before. I feel myself clenching all around him. I could feel the wetness dripping down my legs as he continues to fuck me right through my orgasm. The sloshing sound from my wetness was turning me on so much and I could tell it was turning him on even more. I almost pass out when an aftershock hits while he is still fucking me. A few more hard thrusts and I feel him still inside me pushing himself as deep as he could go. I can feel all his hot liquids filling me up as I throw my head back. The feeling of his nut inside me almost makes me cum again. We both collapse onto the bed with him still inside me and both of us out of breath. I can barely keep my eyes open as he places kisses on my chest and my cheek.

I don't know who taught this man to fuck. But I wanna fight them. Doesn't matter if it was in the past I wanna fight her. I'm jealous.

"I love you so much baby girl," he says while continuing to lazily pepper kisses all over me.

"I love you too Jeremy." He snaps his head up looking at me with shock on his face. He eagerly kisses my lips while starting to move inside me again. I don't know how much more I can take. This man is hard again already. I am so sore, but I want him, there is no denying that. I make the kiss hungrier as he props himself up to get a better angle burying himself inside me deeper.

Chapter 21

Samantha Kage

. . . .

I lay in bed getting booty rubs after the spanking I just received for not letting him cum the other day. Let me tell you, it was worth it 100 percent. Besides the spanking, I had the pleasure of laying my head on pillows while he throat fucked me the way he see fit, this time he made sure to cum straight down my throat. You already fucking know I swallowed it and got called a good girl.

You go girl.

My left ass cheek was sore and my right ass cheek was sore because he kept hitting the same one over and over again. I am not going to lie I am wet again just thinking about it but I hope he doesn't know because after him cumming inside me 4 times, not to mention the number of times he came elsewhere, and me cumming god how many times, I can't go anymore. My puss feels swollen and my legs are sore. Not that I am complaining.

It was really the last round for me. When Jeremy had me in the air with my legs wrapped around his neck while he held me up by my ass against the wall devouring me. I came at least twice while I was up in the air. After he took me off his neck, he laid me down and fucked me on the carpet while I listened to my ankles. I am 80 percent sure I have a rug burn on my back.

Jeremy got up to check on Anya, but I stayed in the room

embarrassed. I know Mariella heard us, even across the house. We lay there together in comfortable silence. After he covered me in cum, like I'm not kidding, there was cum in my hair, my eyelashes, my skin, on my asshole, everything. We didn't do anal, but he released himself there during one of the only times he pulled out. I don't know if this man was trying to get me pregnant again but he was in for a surprise.

Got the implant in my arm hoes. Purr.

He drew me a bath and cleaned my weak body. He was so gentle, placing soft kisses on my lips and face as he washed my body. He got in with me sitting in front of him, while he wrapped his arms around me. We lay in the tub for about 30 minutes embracing each other's bodies. Not sexually but lovingly. I hate to admit it, but we still had a lot to work out, but my god did I miss this man.

Finally finding the strength to get up out of bed, I want to go see my girl. I get dressed, throwing Jeremy's clothes at him at the same time. I get Anya from Mariella's room to bring her back to mine after Jeremy changed the sheets. The three of us lay in bed together as the family we were meant to be for so long.

By the time Anya finished having her glamma time, she was all tired out and ready for a nap. She falls asleep first in my arms while we were snuggling, and I fell asleep shortly after.

I awake with the both of us wrapped in Jeremy's arms with him and Anya still asleep. I can't help but smile to myself. In the back of my mind, this was all I wanted all along. If only this could have happened sooner. I must enjoy this happiness because as usual, I don't know how long it's going to last.

My phone rang snapping me out of my bliss. I look at the phone to see it's Annabelle calling me. I quickly get up making my way to the adjoining room so I don't wake Anya or Jeremy.

"Sup mamas," She says with a smile.

"What's up? If your calling to see Anya, she's sleeping." Me and Annabelle, talk and text at least once a day. Even if it's just me sending her pictures of Anya, she still lives in the city.

"Come to the bar tonight. Leave my god baby with grandma and let's go. We outside sis. Let's make it a girl's night."

"I don't know," I quickly retort, I haven't really gone out much since Anya was born. We have gone to lunch and stuff but we haven't had nighttime fun.

"Come on for me. Pwease," she says pouting her lip.

"Ugh fine. It's a hot girl summer anyway. Text me which location. And what are you wearing?"

"Heels," she responds

"Got it." Me and Anna had a private language when it came to the what are you wearing conversation. If I asked what she was wearing and she responded heels, then it meant to dress up and put on heels too. If she said calm, then I could wear jeans and sneakers. If she said I don't know, that meant put on heels just in case, but I could dress it down with jeans. Finally, if she said sweats, that meant I could come outside in my pajamas.

"Girl we going to one of the restaurants. I just want hookah and food. Maybe jiggle my booty a little."

"Whose going?"

"I'm not telling you."

"I'm not coming."

"It's just me, you, Harper, Harper's cousin, and Aajklsl."

"I'm sorry who?"

"Angel," he says quietly. She knows I don't like that nigga, and I know that nigga doesn't like me. It was just always something about him that I couldn't put my finger on. Besides the fact that he is a walking red flag.

"It's a girl's night but Angel is coming?" I love Annabelle but sometimes she needs a reality check.

"Yea, he's just the designated driver though."

"Has he told his family you're dating yet?"

"Well erm no, but it's fine." Dude, it's been like 2 years. Then again they have been on and off for two years. Let me mind my business. I can't speak on her ain't shit nigga when mine was just inside me half hour ago.

I open my mouth, but then I realize I would just sound judgmental. "If you like it I love it. I support you sis," I respond.

"I'll see you tonight. Later," she says rolling her eyes at me before she hangs up. Well, tonight should be interesting.

I make my way back into the room to see both of my hearts awake and staring into each other's bright blue eyes. She is giving him one of the famous toothless grins. It's almost like they are communicating in their own language. I stand by the door gawking at the pair. I love how easily and quickly he fell head over heels for her. I leave them to let Mariella know I'm going out. I don't know what I will do when she moves out, granted she's moving like 2 blocks away but still.

Back in my room, I start laying my clothes out on the bed. I pick out a short red fitted dress with the back out and grab some nude open-toe block heels leaving them on the bed. Good thing I took a bath when I did. As I am fixing my hair and makeup on my vanity, I notice Jeremy looking at me through the mirror. His eyes dart from the dress on the bed to me.

"Where are you going," he says with attitude.

"Out with the girls," I say while continuing to primp myself.

"Looks like I didn't tire you out enough. You're not going." I laugh. I literally laugh at his words. Is he out of his cotton picking mind?

"And why per se can I not go outside Massa?"

"That's not funny."

"Yes, it is," I say laughing.

"Your safety is at risk, you are not going and that's final."

See now, I can play this one of two ways. I can just get dressed and go because let's be honest, who's gon check me? I technically don't have a man. Or I can mess with him a little.

I get up from the chair and slowly walk over to the bed. Of course, I am going to choose violence. I pull his lips to mine and immediately capture him in a greedy ass kiss. I stick my tongue fully into his mouth before he can stop me. My hands are in his hair massaging his scalp with him moaning into my mouth at the kiss. I go as far as nibbling and sucking his tongue. "Please daddy," I whisper against his lips while my hand gently strokes the bulge growing in his pants. He lets out another satisfied moan of agreement when I abruptly pull my lips away leaving him to blink at me in confusion. I place a chaste kiss on his lips.

"Thanks baby." He shoots me an annoyed glare. He knows dam

well he can't tell me no.

After some slight compromise, and when I say compromise I mean Jeremy bitching nonstop. I am sitting in the back of a car with Marcus driving me to my destination. I agreed he could come if he stayed out of sight. I agreed to let Jeremy sleep over tonight so he left to gather some of the things that he will need for my house. We actually agreed that he could have one of the rooms to sleep in after Mariella moves out and he comes over. Although, he has made it clear that he would much rather sleep with me.

I arrive at my destination to find Annabelle, Harper, Christina harpers cousin, and Angel waiting outside. I hop out of the car while Marcus goes to find parking. Good luck there is never parking around here.

I greet everyone with hugs and smiles, then I get to Angel.

"Angel."

"Sam." And that's enough conversation between us for the rest of the night. We enter, get our table, and get bottle service without dinner. We opted for a bottle of coconut Cîroc, a bottle of patron, and a bottle of champagne with passion fruit juice and lemonade as our chasers. There were only 5 of us, we could surely we could finish two bottles. Angel drove so he wasn't drinking. So 3 bottles for four people. Challenge accepted.

Things always seem like a good idea on paper clearly. A bottle and a half down and the DJ is playing the tunes. "Don't tell nobody by Tink comes on and it's over. I start singing into the empty Cîroc bottle and Annabelle starts to sing to Angel telling him he ain't shit. I was here for ALL the antics tonight. I might have drunk the majority of the Cîroc by myself, not gon lie.

As much as I was having fun. I was starting to miss my girl and my bed. But I hope she was asleep when she got home because I know I am drunk. Plus Jeremy's there. I wonder how they are doing. Actually, I am just going to head home. I leave the cash plus tip for my part of the bill and decide to dip out. I signal to Marcus that I am ready to go. Against his instruction, I wait outside alone while he goes to get the car from where he parked it. I was not finna walk anywhere in these heels plus I needed fresh air.

We got in the car and I start to complain that I want Taco Bell. I knew Marcus was tired of my shit cause I wouldn't shut up so he brought me. I got a cheesy gordita crunch, a crunch wrap supreme, cinnamon twists, and blueberry freezes. I got 2 of each for me and Jeremy. I love drunk food. Marcus got something to but I was too happy in the back drinking my drink to care about him any longer.

I knew Marcus was really over my shit when I made him start playing Cuff it by Beyonce on the way home. I was literally hollering in the back of the car. I bet he regretted coming out with me now.

By the time we got back to the house, I knew Marcus was ready to fling me somewhere so of course, I pushed his buttons even further.

"Marcus I don't want to put on my shoes. Can you carry me please?"

He gave me a look that was confusing.

"I will call Mr.Bresset to do it ma'am." He starts to place a call but I am ready to go now.

"Ugh fine. I'll walk barefoot then. Better hope I don't cut my feet otherwise Jeremy will be mad," I say through my tipsy slur.

I am drunk, but I am sober enough to know I am annoying Marcus. I think it's funny.

I move to open the door, but he quickly comes around to grab me. He throws me over his shoulder, grabbing my shoes, bag, and most importantly my Taco Bell. A security guard opens the door for him and he quickly puts me down on the floor. I look at his face and he looks alarmed. I turn around to meet a red face Jeremy looking at Marcus like he's nuts.

I look back and forth then I realize. It's because Marcus touched me. Got it. "Hi stinka butt," I say while biting my lip and looking at Jeremy. His eyes are still on Marcus who looks a little scared.

I do the only acceptable thing to do at that moment to defuse the tension. I walk over to Jeremy and grab his dick in my hands through his pants while sloppily placing wet kisses on his neck. A sexy groan escapes his throat when I touch him. Bet he won't ignore me now. My licks and kisses turn into nibbles and sucks. Now I am trying to leave a mark.

"You're dismissed," Jeremy says harshly. " I hear the door close and not a minute later, Jeremy wraps his arm around my waist lifting me and crushing his lips onto mine bringing me up the stairs to my room. We get to the room and he roughly tosses me on the bed.

Bitch we are bout to have drunk sex it's lit.

He rips my dress off my body. He stands there admiring me for a second before climbing to lean over me. He leans to my ears and whispers something. I am so horny it takes me a minute to hear. "Go shower, wash your face, and put your hair up before you regret it tomorrow." My jaw dropped.

"You're not going to fuck me?" I pout.

"Not when your drunk. Go shower, I'll get your food."

Oh, I'll shower and wash my makeup off but make no mistake Mr.Bresset, you are giving me cock tonight.

I put my plan in place. I grab my robe, my lace white lingerie set that fully has the crotch open, and I dart into the bathroom in my room. He wants to play? We will play.

I shower as quickly as possible, wash my face, and put my hair up. I lotion myself with Vanilla sugar lotion and spray myself with vanilla perfume. Vanilla is a natural aphrodisiac. Oh, I'm finna get him.

I come out of the bathroom in my fluffy robe to join Jeremy on the bed. I am horny but I still want my food. I ate my taco but then after that, I didn't want any more food. I was ready to go. We lay on the bed watching reruns of manifest when I make my move. I start to place kisses on his neck but he ignores me. He takes a deep breath inhaling my scent.

I slowly move my hand to go grab his dick but he grabs my wrist to stop me. "As good as you smell right now, your still drunk Samantha."

"I'm sober enough to know I want you in my guts." My words caused him to intake a sharp breath while his eyes closed. I could see the self-control leaving his body.

"Tomorrow baby girl I promise," he says as he wraps his arms around me snuggling me closer. I quickly wiggle out of his grasp to stand to my feet.

I got this.

He looks at me in confusion

"Fine," I said while unwrapping my robe. "I'll just go get dick from somewhere else." I drop my robe revealing my lace set and make a move toward the bedroom door. I know security was downstairs so he had two options, fuck me here or let me walk around the house like this. It was his choice.

Rough hands grab me and slam me to the wall. One hand is around my throat while the other hand is cupping my wet pussy. I smile at him biting my lip.

I have clearly won this game.

He crushes his lips to mine in a rough mind-blowing kiss. He roughly bites my lip and I taste blood.

Worth it.

He starts to rub my clit slipping one finger inside me, then two, resulting in me breaking the kiss to moan against his lips. He moves down to place rough kisses on my neck, and his fingers only move faster causing my knees to buckle a little bit.

This is all I wanted but he had to make it difficult. He breaks the kiss with my neck and steps back yanking his fingers out of me. I watch as he brings them to his lips and sucks off every last drop of wetness. Suddenly something changes in his eyes. It was like all he needed was a taste to set himself into overdrive.

"Fine Samantha if you want me to fuck you. That's exactly what I will do."

Shit. Is it too late to back down? I am a little scared.

He grabs me again pressing his lips to mine. He lifts me up and I happily wrap my legs around his waist. He walks over to the bed and throws me down for the second time tonight. I swear if he denies me again I might kill him. He stands there staring at me licking his lips and admiring my body. "You know

Samantha, something told me to go to the store today. I may or may not have gotten some toys for us."

I narrow my eyes at him. Okay, now I'm scared. The last toy he used on me partially had me stalking him. He walks over to the bag on the floor and pulls out a red and black bag. He takes out handcuffs and tape. You know when you're drunk and something immediately makes you sober up. That was me at the moment.

"You know what. You're right. Not while I'm drunk," I say before I start to get up. I sensed myself starting to lose this game.

"Don't fucking move Samantha."

Y'all I may seem scared but I will not deny that as soon as he used that tone with me, I was dripping. "Don't worry, Anya's down the hall, we won't have to worry about waking her up, so we won't need the tape," he says while spinning the handcuffs on his fingers. The smile on his face is highly devious but I will not deny I am turned on right now. "Give me your hands."

I listen quickly. He takes a handcuff snapping it on my wrist. He flips me over pulling my arms back and locks my wrists together behind my back. He yanks my body into the doggie position and places the palm of my hands on either ass cheek. "Spread your ass for daddy like a good girl, and keep it there."

I do exactly as he says. I feel the cool air brush over my clit causing me to shudder. I can feel how wet I am. "That's a good girl. Now don't move. If you move your punishment will be worst." I stay quiet waiting for a spanking. I actually enjoyed his spankings. I have gotten used to them.

I brace myself for my ass cheek to be slapped but he does something entirely different. He places a hard under slap to my clit causing me to arch my back and cry out. I didn't see it coming.

"What did I say Samantha? Move again and I won't let you cum tonight."

He doesn't mean that, does he?

After the 5th slap to my clit, each one harder than the next, I can feel how wet I am. The 5th slap almost made me cum, not going to lie. My wetness is dripping down all over my thighs and I can feel it. My pussy is just aching to be fucked. I brace myself for the next slap but instead, I feel Jeremy licking all the juices off of my thighs cleaning me up with his tongue. Right after he pulls away, 11 inches slam into me. I let out a loud moan when his thrusts kick into overdrive. He reaches down to rub my clit and the same time. I can feel my stomach tightening and my orgasm building. "Fuck baby girl, you're so wet. Wet ass fucking pussy," he says in between strokes and moans."

"Oh baby you feel so good inside me," I moan out. He roughly grips my ass cheeks yanking me towards him to meet each one of his forceful thrusts. My eyes roll in the back of my head as my legs start to shake. My ears start to ring at how powerful I become undone. I clenched myself around him as I cum which only leads him to fuck me harder. I can hear him moaning, I love when he moans. I finally come down a little from my high, my breathing becomes erratic as I try to remember where I am for a second. He yanks himself out of me and I can feel myself dripping down the back of my thigh.

He takes off the handcuffs, turning me over to lie on my back. He climbs on top of me taking my lips with his own in a rough passionate kiss, I fist my fingers into his hair pulling him closer as if it were even possible. He lifts my leg to place it on his shoulder slamming into me again.

The sound of him slamming into my wetness, my moans, and his grunts fill the room. He breaks the kiss to make intense eye contact with me while wrapping his hand around my throat and applying light pressure. I stare into his beautiful blue eyes like he is the only man in the world. He pulls his tip out to my entrance slowly and slams back into me. He does this repeatedly until I feel the tears roll down my cheeks. This pleasure is so intense I fucking love it. Especially when he lets out a grunt of pleasure with every thrust. He speeds up his pace leaning more into my body so my leg can go back further. I didn't think it was possible for him to go deeper.

He speeds up his pace and I feel myself about to cum again. Watching him enter me over and over while I hungrily eye his body is going to be my undoing. After a few more strokes I quickly become undone under him with my entire body shaking and my eyes rolling back into my head. A few more hard thrusts and he stills inside me throwing his head back and letting out a sexy husky moan. I love when men moan I want to know you're enjoying me as much as I am enjoying you.

Sing falsetto in my ear daddy.

We are finally relaxed and cuddling after the mind-blowing dick he just gave me. I am wrapped in his arms placing kisses on his lips, his chin, and his neck ever so often. I begin to fall asleep when my phone goes off. I ignore it at first but then it goes off twice, three times, four. It just continuously pinged.

What the fuck?

I grab my phone to look at who has the audacity to be texting me repeatedly like this in the middle of the night and my eyes widen in horror. I quickly sit up snatching myself away from Jeremy's arms. He shuffles out of his almost sleepy state.

On the phone are pictures of me from tonight from that unknown number. It's a picture of me with the bottle to my head, me standing outside when I first arrived, another of me dancing with Annabelle, me just standing around, me taking shots, and me standing outside alone waiting for Marcus to pull the car around. That was the last picture. At the end of the pictures was a message.

Unknown: You will be mine soon Muñeca.

"Oh my god!" I start to cry.

"What is it baby?" Jeremy asks while rising frantically to sit up next to me out of his sleep. He looks at the phone and sees the tears in my eyes. He grabs my phone out of my hand and his eyes widen in horror.

He grabs his phone forwarding everything to himself and frantically begins to make phone calls to his security, specifically Marcus.

Fuck! Something needs to be done. Something needs to be done soon.

Chapter 22

Samantha Kage

• •

Against my better wishes, security has gone up around the house. Mariella is staying in the house for another few weeks even though her house is all ready to be moved into. I am overly annoyed. Someone I thought I erased from my life is still affecting me years later. It's irritating.

Why can't I just be happy? At least I have Jamaica to look forward to. Jeremy and Marcus will be accompanying me while airport security will stay here with Anya, Mariella, and Angela.

The increase in security has literally driven me crazy. I should be focused on meeting with Jeremy's real estate agent today. Apparently, she got a good offer on my house, but no. Instead, I am currently standing in my sponge bob slippers in the living room with Anya on my side yelling at two idiot security guards who roughed up the mail guy, and now I don't have two of my packages for my trip. I leave for Jamaica in like 4 days.

I know I look ridiculous but I am tearing them new assholes.

"One of you better find my fucking package or you can fly to England and pick me up a new dress from the store I ordered it from. And it better be here in 2 hours. Figure out a way to get to London and back in two hours. I don't know how you will do it, you better fucking teleport or something! Get the fuck out of my face!"

They are looking at me with amusement on their faces. If I throw my sponge bob slipper at one of their heads I bet they would stop laughing at me.

Fuck it.

I reach for my shoe when I hear a voice boom through the house.

"Samantha."

I whip my head around with an irritated-looking Jeremy with his arms folded.

Bitch why are you irritated? You ain't lose a dress.

It's almost as if he knew what I was going to do. Dude needs to mind his business.

I whip my head back around to roll my eyes at the security guards. I hike Anya up properly on my hip and stomp away. I walk past Jeremy and go straight up to my bedroom. I put Anya in her playpen and collapse into the bed letting out a grunt of frustration.

"You can't throw shoes at the security guards," he said with amusement in his voice.

"You can kiss my ass. I needed that dress for the wedding Jeremy."

"I'll buy you 5 more dresses," he shrugs.

"I can buy my own dresses," I grumble.

"I know that," he says rubbing the back of his neck. "Look I just want to apologize for every single time I accused you of wanting my money."

"Why are you telling me this?" I sit straight up immediately. He twists his lips into an unsure face.

"I umm, was going over things with the real estate agent and,"

"You saw my bank statements!" I gasp. I had told Jeremy about my mom's death and that I was left money after she died but I never told him exactly how much. I think he thinks I have a couple hundred thousand lying around. But that was not at all the case. It was much more. "Jeremy that is an invasion of my privacy!"

"I know. I am sorry. But you know how much I make too so it's okay." Jeremy was a millionaire at the age of like 16. I always knew that. He got money from his grandfather and his father at a young age. He literally had a credit score of 830 when he was like 10. We love generational wealth. "Now I know why you won't let me spoil you. But I'm just saying, I like spoiling you. Can you just let me sometimes?"

I shrug. I'm annoyed now.

"Do you want some head to make you feel better?" He asks while winking at me.

"Umm no. One, your daughter is in her playpen," we look over at Anya who is aggressively biting a teething ring with her gums, cooing, and exhibiting her vocal play. "Two, you are officially back on pussy punishment. You ain't getting none." I fold my arms and collapse back into the bed. I start going over the things I need to do before I go to Jamaica. Braids, nails, shoes, and lashes. I hear Jeremy speaking to me but I zoned out for a second.

"What you said?" I ask while leaning up on my elbows.

"Do you want another baby?" I physically scratch my head blinking at him. Is it piss off Samantha day? What would possess this colonizer to ask me that?

"What would possess you to ask me that?" I snap.

"Because I want another baby." My giggles turn on and I can't stop them. I must have been laughing for 3 minutes. "Samantha, I'm serious."

"Oh. Why? Anya's not even 1 and you have a lot going and I umm. I don't exactly have the best memories while pregnant so I am kind of in no rush to do it again if I am being honest." He furrowed his brow at the thought. I was depressed for the entire beginning of my pregnancy, and I gave birth and did a lot without him. No, I wasn't alone, I had my friends and family but still.

"I mean, I was just saying because I noticed you haven't been taking birth control pills, and you haven't yelled at me for cumming inside you, and you haven't asked for a plan b. I was kind of getting my hopes up." I just noticed he hasn't moved from the doorway. Probably nervous.

"Why do you want another baby," I ask in a confused and irritated tone sitting fully up again. "I don't understand. And I have an implant in my arm. Missing birth control is how I ended up with Anya in the first place." I cock my head to the side waiting for his answer while he looks like he is lost in thought.

He sighs walking over to me to sit next to me on the bed. He takes my hand in his brushing his thumb on my hand with his head down. "It's just, I wanted to be there this time. I missed every appointment with Anya, every sonogram, the first time you heard her heartbeat, her first breath, her first cry, I wasn't there to rub your feet or your back. I missed her first shots, I just wasn't there for you or her. Most importantly, I missed her birth. If I had the balls to stand up to my father earlier none of this would have ever happened. It eats me up inside sometimes. I want to do it right next time."

I let go of his hand getting up from next to him. I sighed heavily. He looked at me with confusion and his tears brimming in his eyes. I walk over to the playpen lifting Anya in my arms. I walk back over to the bed as he watches me in confusion. I sit back down lifting Anya to stand on my knees and face Jeremy. She has a cheeky gum-filled smile on her face with her finger in her mouth drooling all over her chest as she starts to bounce on her legs since she can't stand up yet. My baby has become so smiley. I look over at Jeremy who is in awe watching her.

"Jeremy." He looks at me and his expression turns back to sad. "We forgive you for all the things you just said and more." His face twists into a hopeful smile that almost makes me cry. It's not his fault his father is a piece of shit. He places a kiss on Anya's head and one on my lips. He breaks the kiss leaning over and placing his shoulder on my head. I know he is crying he just doesn't want me to see.

"I love you baby girl," he whispers into my shoulder wrapping his arms around my waist and pulling us closer.

"I love you too Jer Bear." He snaps his head up immediately.

"You haven't called me that in forever," he says placing another long kiss on my lips before resting his head back on my shoulder. We were having a moment, it was very nice but it didn't last long. Right on cute Mariella walks past the doors and bursts out crying like she usually does when she sees the three of us together.

Lord.

"Oh my god! Don't move I am going to get the camera." We

laugh at her outburst as she immediately runs away in tears coming back 2 minutes later still in tears. We pose the exact way we were sitting while Mariella tries to figure out her camera. As we are posing, Anya does something unimaginable. It hurt me deep down in my core.

"Da...da." Anya sounds out in a forced whisper.

My mouth immediately drops in shock and Jeremy lets out an excited gasp jumping to his feet and taking Anya out of my arms spinning her around in the air causing her to burst out in giggles.

"I'm so proud of you!" He yells while placing kisses all over her face. My mouth is still dropped on the floor.

"I got all of that on camera!" Mariella screams in excitement. "I accidentally hit record!" She and Jeremy are two excited idiots. They are all happy, and I do the only thing I can do in that situation. I start hysterically crying.

I am bout to throw the whole baby away and start over. No way did I carry her for 9 months, have a c-section, and almost die for this little nigglet to say dada first. I am so mad.

"Don't be like that baby." He said grinning ear to ear like a fucking dumb ass. I was joking about pussy punishment but now I'm deadass." I get up to walk away with my arms folded and I am quickly grabbed at my waist in Jeremy's free arm. He places kisses on my neck in between his laughs.

This cannot be my life.

Does anybody want a baby?

We are sitting in the living room waiting for the real estate agent. Anya is napping with Mariella in her room upstairs. I'm still mad at the little nigglet. Jeremy hasn't stopped smiling since she said it. I'm sure he texted all his friends and posted the video of her saying it on Instagram too.

Security opens the door and in walks an olive-skinned green-eyed woman with strawberry-blonde hair. She is a white button-down shirt with her cleavage revealed and a knee-length light pink skirt with nude pumps to match. She is carrying a pink leather briefcase. I cannot deny this woman was honestly beautiful. I am literally wearing pink shorts and a long sleeve t-shirt. I was not getting dressed for this meeting. Jeremy had mentioned that they were friends. I don't know how I felt about it but I wanted to see them in action before I said anything.

"Good morning Jeremy," she says walking over to him and pulling him into a hug.

Sigh, here we go. Sis is bout to flirt with this man in front of me and then claim that they are best friends. She lets go rubbing his shoulders then turns her attention to me.

Here we go. She's probably going to shade me.

"Good morning ma'am," she says sweetly.

Fake ass hoe.

She pulls me into a tight hug as well. I guess she is a hugger. The only difference between my hug and Jeremy's hug is that she tightens her hold, she even slowly rubs my back. I realize she is holding on for quite a while. I look over her shoulder eyeing Jeremy with a confused expression. He seemingly looks annoyed. She finally let go when he cleared his throat. "Sorry," she giggled. "You're just such a good hugger," she said flashing me her pearly whites. "My name is Eloise, you must be Samantha." I nod my head awkwardly smiling at her.

What the fuck?

"So let's get started shall we." She said clapping her hands excitedly. She pulls some papers out of her pretty pink leather briefcase and lays them on the table. "Jeremy has already done most of the grunt work and paperwork. The offer has already been made on your house, all you really have to do is sign off on everything."

"How much am I getting?" I paid almost 1 million for the 2 bedroom 2 story house. Before you say that was a lot, we are in New York right outside of New York City. And to be fair, I have a living room, a den, 3 bathrooms, and a huge backyard.

"The house is selling for 1.9 million my dear. There was a lot of work done on the house inside and out in the short time you were there, and it brought the property value up high. Also, I am very good at my job," she smiled. I must thank Isaiah for that.

"Wow okay." I sign all the paperwork necessary while she pops a bottle of champagne. She pours us a glass, as well as Jeremy. Our fingertips brush when she hands me the glass and I swear she blushes red. She takes a sip not taking her eyes off me.

What is wrong with sis?

Jeremy gets a phone call and excuses himself quickly. I watch him walk away behind me. When I turn back around Eloise is standing right next to me leaning on the counter. "I must say, you are more beautiful than Jeremy said," she says with a smile.

"Umm thank you."

What a sweet girl.

Maybe she isn't so bad.

"I can't help but notice you and Jeremy aren't married. We are very close friends, hence why I use his first name," she says with a sweet giggle.

I nod my head slowly in response squinting at her. Where is she going with this? "Please forgive me."

"For wh," I am cut off when she grabs my face in her hands and places a kiss on my lips. She sucks my bottom lip. I open my mouth in shock and she uses it as an invitation to stick her tongue in my mouth. I go to push her away when she rolls her tongue around mine. I freeze instantly as I feel myself pool in between my legs. I won't lie and say her tongue didn't have me in a daze for a second.

No way she just gave you the super soaker from her tongue tricks alone.

"Eloise!" She smiles against my lips breaking the kiss as soon as she hears Jeremy's voice boom across the living room. I am still in shock and I must admit a little turned on.

"What? I couldn't resist, she tastes as good as she looks," she says while she wipes the corner of her mouth, sucks her fingers, and licks her lips.

Is this really happening right now?

My mouth is still dropped in shock.

She gingerly makes her way around the counter to grab all her papers and place them neatly back in her briefcase as Jeremy stomps across the room. I look over at Jeremy who is fuming.

"I'll see you soon bestie," she giggles as she gathers herself. She starts to walk away but turns back to look at me first. "Hopefully I see you soon too Samantha. I can show you what else my tongue can do," she says with a wink before strutting out the door. I will not deny I watched her ass as she walked away. I was lost in a daydream about the way she kissed me for a second when Jeremy interrupted me standing in front of me.

"What? She caught me off guard!" I say shrugging my shoulders.

He still looks mad but he looks like he is lost in thought for a second. He grabs my chair reaching down into my shorts. His eyes widen when his finger slips into my slit. "You're soaking wet? From a kiss from her?" He steps back rubbing his hand on his chin in thought, along with my juices. "I am going to fuck you until you forget about that kiss."

"Umm no, you're not. You're on pussy punishment," I said standing up and folding my arms.

"It can start later." He bent down and threw me over his shoulder, stomping up the stairs, and placing a smack on my ass every few seconds.

I can tell you not to fold but what's the point?

"You better not fucking drop me."

He throws me down on my bed upstairs shutting the door behind him. In no time my shorts are ripped off and my shirt along with it. I don't even complain. He grabs my legs yanking me to the edge of the bed while dropping to his knees. He flattens his tongue licking me from my dripping hole to my clit and back again. He slowly sucks on my clit slipping one finger inside me. He curves it flicking my g spot while sucking and licking on my clit at the same time. I feel the pressure build up inside me as my moans go loader. "Fuck baby," I moan out as I cum right on his fingers.

He strips down naked, lying on the bed, and pulls me on top of him. He places his tip at my entrance and slowly slides inside of me while looking deep into my eyes. I can see the fire within him. "Ride my dick like a good girl."

"Yes Jeremy," I say as I start to move up and down on his dick. I can feel it deep in my stomach, I almost can't handle it. He places a hard smack on my ass.

"Fix that."

"Yes daddy," I moan.

"Good girl."

I start to move myself up and down his shaft throwing my head back at the intense pleasure and pressure from having him inside me. "You look so fucking precious when you ride my dick like this." His words alone set a fire in me. I move to my knees so I can increase the motion of my strokes. I am bouncing on his dick when he sits up and starts to place kisses on my neck. He lifts himself off the bed a little thrusting into me meeting every movement of my hips. "You feel so fucking good baby."

His rough thrusts cause me to moan even louder. "Cum for me baby." He grips my hips taking full control of all the thrusts, I go to kiss him but he moves his head attacking my neck instead. The sloshing sound in between my legs sends me over the edge as I tighten and cum all around him. One hard thrust later he cums inside me not that deep this time. He must want to watch it drip down.

What he does next is something I didn't even see coming. He rolls me back over on the bed and leans down to open my legs and spread my wet lips. I figure he wanted to watch the cum drip out. It makes me a little self-conscious in this position, it was something he rarely did, but I guess that's what he needed right now.

Instead of watching it, he surprises me by sucking the cum out of my throbbing pussy. I can feel it leaving my body. The feeling of him sucking his cum out sends a chill up my spine and my legs to shake. He leans up grabbing my face in his hand to open my mouth. He spits the cum in my mouth along with his spit. "Keep being a good girl for me and swallow it," he says sternly.

I swallow all of it while licking my lips in the process. He stares at me intensely while I swallow all of him. He forcefully kisses my lips and I can taste everything I just swallowed. He bites my bottom lip before letting go.

"I don't want you to taste anyone on your lips except me. Are we clear?"

"Yes daddy."

To say I was soaking wet again was an understatement. This man was as nasty for me just as I am nasty for him. I am even wetter than I was before. I have completely forgotten about that kiss earlier.

Chapter 23

Samantha Kage

· ·

"Hand her over."

"No!"

"Bambi!" Mariella warns.

I start placing kisses all over my baby's face. The car is loaded and waiting and if I don't put her down now we are going to be late for the airport. I half debate if I want this job. I have left my girl for a couple of hours sure but never for 4 days. I don't know if I'm ready.

"Come on Samantha, we will be back in no time." Jeremy says as he slowly takes my baby out of my arms."

I give her one more kiss before I walk away not taking my eyes off of her. I only had to be down there for the wedding for 2 out of the 4 days. Jeremy wanted two days to ourselves.

I wave goodbye as we drive off. I immediately start to sob in the back seat. Jeremy pulls me into his arms and lets me cry dramatically until we get to the airport. I never used to cry this much. That little girl has clearly made me soft.

Finally, we arrived at our hotel. It was about 2 pm. The whole time on the plane ride I face-timed Anya, and just pretty much stared at her. Jeremy just did work on his laptop the whole time. He had to bring his office work with him, especially since he had a bigger workload now. Also as soon as we got back from Jamaica we had to make an appearance in public for Jeremy's father's press conference. Jeremy requested that me and Anya be there by his side. I don't really want to see his father but he said he needed us so fuck it.

Jeremy heads off to the room while I go to the bride and groom's room to meet with them. Before I head to the room I check with the hotel to make sure everything is on schedule for tomorrow's wedding and tonight's rehearsal dinner along with the two photoshoots I set up.

After checking everything with the caterers and the guests that have arrived, I make my way to the bride and groom's room to let them know I have arrived. I knock on the door and the groom answers.

"Samantha, you're here!"

"Yes, I trust everything went smoothly with check-in and the room?" I ask.

"Yes, and the rose petals were a nice touch thank you."

The bride and groom were getting ready when I walked in. The bride was in her robe doing her makeup for the photoshoot on the beach and the rehearsal dinner would take place right after.

I stayed with them until the photoshoot was almost over. They took photos all over the beach. She wore a white maxi dress and he wore a white button-up shirt with white linen pants. Their favorite picture of mine that they took together was when her blonde hair was hanging over his shoulder just right and she was laughing looking at him and he was smiling down looking at her from behind while the sunset hit them oh so perfectly. They looked so happy. The love was clearly in the air.

I leave the photo shoot to go change my clothes and shower for the rehearsal dinner. I gave myself enough time to get ready and I made sure the photographers would be at the rehearsal dinner. Everything was going swimmingly thank god.

I text Jeremy to tell me the room number. He tells me it's room number 601 in the Elite building. That's weird. That's not the room I booked at all. The bride and groom weren't even staying in the Elite building.

After some searching, I finally find the room, and my jaw drops. The room is twice the size of the room I originally booked. It is well-lit with a shower and a bath and a much bigger space. The room even has a hot tub on the balcony, and the view from the balcony was amazing. It was astounding, the sun was currently setting, and I couldn't pry my eyes away from the view. It's an ocean-view room but we are so high up you can see everything. The room was better than the room the bride and groom were in. I felt a little bad if I'm being honest.

"Jeremy! What is this?" He looks up at me from his laptop confused.

"What? I wanted the best for my baby girl so she got the best." He shrugs giving his attention back to his laptop.

"Jeremy this is too much. You don't have to spend all this money to make me happy. You're all I need to make me happy," I say as I walk up to him and wrap my arms around his shoulders putting a swift kiss on his lips. "I appreciate it though," I whisper against his lips. I quickly pull away from him when he throws me a knowing look letting me know that if I don't move he would make me late.

I run into the shower throwing my goddess braids in a bun. These braids are a definition of a hassle. The curls kept getting matted but the hairstyle itself was beautiful I will not deny. I made sure to give myself enough time so I wouldn't be late. I knew myself all too well. My blue maxi dress with the slit up to the waist and my sandals were already laid out. I applied light makeup getting myself ready as quickly as possible. I had to be there before the guests showed up. I drop my towel to slip on my v string and get dressed when strong arms wrap around my waist. He trails kisses down the side of my neck grabbing a boob in one hand while the other hand finds my waxed sex.

"Jeremy." I breathe out.

"Just let me taste it before you go, it feels like butter." He slips a finger in my fold rubbing my clit back and forth. I was already soaking wet from the simple fact that he was in the same room as me. He pulls his finger out of my folds bringing it to his lips and making a sucking sound with his lips. He lets out a moan of pleasure that makes my knees weaken a bit.

Focus bitch we can't be late.

"Nope," I spin around kissing his lips before I put myself out of his grasp. "I have to be there as soon as possible. But I promise tomorrow after the wedding I'll suck your dick on the balcony for the whole resort to see okay?"

"I'm going to hold you to that," he says placing another kiss on my lips.

I throw on my dress, grab my phone, and I am ready to go. I quickly kiss Jeremy goodbye. He will be meeting me there in about an hour. He is my plus one after all.

I arrive at the rehearsal dinner location and they are not fully set up. The guests will be arriving in 30 minutes. I rub my temple before I start shouting orders at people. I start moving the centerpieces to the tables while I make sure the hotel workers are setting up the flower in their strategically placed areas.

The caterers were laying out the food finally and the speakers and lights were finally set up. Thank god. The guests start to arrive shortly and everything runs smoothly with my help. I had to fix a couple of things here and there but everything else was A-okay.

Jeremy showed up just as dinner was being served. I appreciated having him by my side for this. I have done other events before, but my first destination wedding was a big deal for me. It was a step in the direction I wanted to go.

We were sitting down to eat but I barely touched my food. Every 5 seconds duty called and I needed to be somewhere doing something or helping someone fix some sort of crisis. I could relax a little since it was now time for the speeches. However, I was the one running around holding the mic.

"Thank you, everyone, for coming, at this time I would just like to personally thank the bride and groom for allowing me to be a part of their special day with them. I have come to know them very well in the past year and let me tell you I have never seen a purer connection of love between two people and I am honored to be here with you guys today." The crowd erupted in small applause at my words. "With that being said, would anyone like to say a few words on behalf of the bride and groom?"

The mother of the bride immediately steps up and starts her speech. Her uncles, her bridesmaids, and his families all follow shortly after. The love was clearly in the air. I was running around handing the mic to different people. I was tired as fuck. Finally, the groom goes.

"To my Beautiful bride Mandy. The day you stepped into my life everything stopped making sense. I couldn't understand how I had gone without you for my whole life, to be honest, I can't remember what life was like before you. You are the greatest thing that has ever happened to me. Tomorrow I will have the honor of being your husband and I don't think I have yet to come across a greater honor in life. You are the other half of my soul and I am in love with the person you are, and everything you do. I cannot wait until we are joined together as one." He places a kiss on her lips and the crowd erupts in applause, cheers, and tears.

I silently wipe the small tear trying to escape my eye. I look over at Jeremy who is staring at me with a relaxed smile on his face.

With that mic drop from the groom, the rehearsal dinner is over and everyone begins to leave. I kiss Jeremy goodbye as he heads back to the room. I have to stay and help clean up. Once the majority of the cleaning is done and I think it's good enough for me to leave, I check with the hotel again. Call it my OCD but I had to make sure that everything is all peachy fucking keen for tomorrow. They assure me at what time things will begin etc.

I finally make it to my room when I feel someone following me. I stop walking feeling brave and turn around when I am met with a dark figure walking towards me. Yes I know I am black and I should run but I got time today. I squint my eyes as my heart beats a little faster when the figure starts coming closer at a fast rate. Then I realize who is it.

"Marcus! You fucking asshole! Why are you lurking in the shadows?!"

"Why are you walking across the hotel alone, along the back way at that." I had been so busy that I had completely forgotten

Marcus was here with us. He looks rather nice, he actually looked like a normal hotel guest outside of his regular suits. He was wearing a white t-shirt and some Nike shorts.

"It was quicker and I was lazy. Have you been following me all day?"

"Yes, I have, now if you would continue to your room." I roll my eyes at him and continue to walk towards the elite building, it was on the far side of the hotel so excuse me for wanting to take a shortcut. I turn round to glance at Marcus to see how far behind he is and to my surprise, he is right behind me with his eyes trained on my ass. I stop walking and his eyes snap up to meet my gaze.

Really nigga?

"I'm ....er....Sorry Mrs. Bresset."

"Samantha's fine," I say rolling my eyes. " I think I can make it back to my room from here Marcus."

"Yes ma'am," he says before turning around and walking back in the other direction. I shake my head, but I choose not to tell Jeremy. Doesn't make any sense he loses his job over something so little.

I make my way back to my room and Jeremy is nowhere to be found. I look around confused until I see a note on the bed.

> *Join me on the balcony my sun & moon.*
> *- Jer Bear*

I smile as I open the door to the balcony to find Jeremy sitting on the chair in a towel and nothing else. The jacuzzi was bubbling while there was room service covered on the table outside and champagne. He smiles at me before getting up to place a small kiss on my lips.

"You need to eat and relax before tomorrow baby girl." He slips the straps off my dress dropping it to the floor and pulls the soft hotel robe on my shoulders covering my exposed body. He places a gentle kiss on my forehead before pushing me down to take a seat. I take a seat as he lifts the covered food to reveal breaded shrimp scampi and garlic bread. This man knows the way to my heart I swear. We eat in comfortable silence. I look up to notice that he is staring at me with his hand under his chin.

"What?" I ask smiling.

"Nothing baby girl, I just love you that's all." I blush with a cheeky smile at his words.

I finish eating, wiping my hands with the napkins. He moves to stand and reaches out his hand for me. I take it as he leads me into the jacuzzi, He drops his towel exposing that he is fully naked. I am only wearing my panties which is barely hiding anything. I lay inside the hot bubbling water on his chest while he wraps me in his arms and places a gentle kiss on my forehead. I love forehead kisses.

We lay there for I cannot tell you how long watching the moon in the sky. Touching each other's bodies not saying anything. I finally relax for the first time today and I truly feel happy in the arms of the man I love. I try to enjoy this peace as much as I could because tomorrow was going to be stressful.

If one more thing goes wrong I am going to cry. The bride's makeup artist got sick and can't come in so now I am currently doing makeup. I was already assured I would be getting paid extra for this. Good thing I know how to do makeup. The bride's veil is nowhere to be found. The best man is hung over. The photographers are here to take pictures and the bride is freaking out. Her bridesmaids are shady as hell. I am currently back and forth between the bride and groom's room making sure they are getting ready.

I had to get my own personal cart to transfer me across the hotel.

I might sound like I am annoyed but make no mistake, I love this shit. If I can help in any way to make a person's special day as special as possible, I will do it.

Once I finish the bride's makeup and she is happy with the outcome, I get the bridesmaids ready to take pictures in their robes. Once the photographer starts the girl's photoshoot I hop on my cart and make my way to the other side of the hotel where they have moved the groom to make sure the best man has the rings and their photoshoot is going well. The wedding is in about 45 minutes. The boys are basically ready to go. I walk into the room looking over in the corner and what do I see sticking out of a bag?

I am so stressed I just want to rub my temples but I refuse to mess up this face beat. "The veil!" I exclaim happily. The men look at me like I am crazy as I grab it hopping back on my cart and bringing it to the bride's room.

When I arrive she is getting dressed by her mother into her wedding dress while the photographer and videographer takes pictures. Her blonde hair is curled perfectly, immediately her eyes widen at the sight of me. "You found my veil! You are a lifesaver! I don't know how I would have gotten through this weekend without you," she says as she pulls me into a tight hug. I help her mother put her veil properly on her head. I also help her put on her earrings and hand jewelry.

"Okay let's go get you married!" I say smiling at her once I see she is fully ready. I hear a click and see that the photographer took a picture of us standing there together.

The groom is waiting nervously at the end of the beach. All the guests are seated and I am standing by the DJ booth. Jeremy is sitting in the back row looking at me and me alone. The instrumental for the original beauty and the beast starts to play as the bride makes her way down the aisle. A little cliche in my opinion but people want what they want. I mouth the words I love you to him and he does the same before I divert my attention back to the bride and groom.

The wedding goes off without a hitch. I went with the wedding party to take their pictures while Jeremy went to the Cocktail hour and reception.

Everyone was sitting down chatting amongst themselves. I make my way inside the reception to the DJ booth to grab the mic. "Ladies at gentlemen it is my pleasure to introduce to you for the first time, Mr. and Mrs. Nicholas Quails," I yell and the crowd erupts in applause as the bride and groom burst through the doors to the tunes of 24K magic by Bruno mars plays. They make their way to the dance floor through the crowd for their first dance as the song changes to Can I have this dance from High school musical. The entire dance was freaking adorable.

The mother-son dance follows, and then the father-daughter dance. She dances with her father to Isn't she lovely by Stevie Wonder. I can't help but tear up. I will never be able to have the father dance at my wedding. I find it unfair sometimes, but it doesn't mean I am not happy for others. Jeremy is immediately at my side wiping the tears from my eyes. "What's wrong baby girl." He whispers in my ear. I just shake my head smiling at him.

It's almost time for the bride's surprise. I grab a chair, bring it to the middle of the dance floor, and back everyone up. I dance over to the bride taking her hand to spin her around and put her in the seat. She looks at me like I'm crazy until the music comes on and the groomsmen break out into a choreographed dance to Soul for real by Candy Rain, Stand out by Tevin Campbell, and they finish the dance off with Boyfriend by Big time rush. It was the greatest thing I had ever seen. I couldn't stop laughing. The men were nervous and kept messing up.

But the bride was happy that's all that mattered. The rest of the wedding went on swimmingly with the cake cutting, more speeches and everyone seemed happy. I finally had a moment to Myself where I was doing goofy dance moves in the corner with Jeremy to Eye to Eye from a goofy movie. The couple really liked Disney movies. I was having the time of my life until It was suddenly interrupted.

"Excuse me, everyone!" I turn around to see the bride and groom holding the mic. Shit did I forget something? Fuck. Was I supposed to introduce their outro already? Nice fucking going Samantha. You relax for a second and something bad happens.

"I just want to say a special thanks to everyone for coming down here with us, we know traveling is a hassle but we appreciate everyone being here. We also want to give a special thanks to our wedding planner Samantha, for without her this hectic day would not have been possible. We appreciate you Samantha!" The reception erupts in applause and I stand there awkwardly waving. I turn around to look at Jeremy and he standing there with a dozen red roses to match my dress. I love this man.

But where the fuck he got those roses from?

Later that night I am finally able to relax. Well not really. Currently, I am leaning over the balcony facing the beach with towels hanging over the side of it. I am gripping the balcony for dear life as Jeremy roughly fucks me from behind. His grip on my waist is so tight as he slams into me over and over again. "Fuck baby, you feel so good! I love this fucking pussy," I moan as he places a hard smack on my ass.

He slows his thrusts to lean over peppering kisses on my back before he lifts one of my legs slightly turning me sideways and giving himself more access to me as his rough thrusts become much deeper. He slows his strokes making them long and deep and I feel myself about to cum. I throw myself back meeting his thrusts when I feel myself tighten around him. He leans down to kiss me roughly as his thrusts continue allowing me to sensually ride out my orgasm. He speeds up his thrust one more time before releasing himself deep inside me. I can feel it pouring out into me. His hot seed feels so fucking good. He pulls out of me and I almost collapse. I am so out of breath. This is the 3rd round since we have gotten back to our room.

I came back to the room with Jeremy and there were candles balloons and flower petals everywhere. You know I sucked the nut out of his balls immediately after. Yah girl was tired after the wedding but I was ready for the challenge. I almost fall asleep on the balcony after that last round.

Chapter 24

Samantha Kage

On the last day in Jamaica, Jeremy made it his personal goal to make me squirt on the balcony. I was currently in Jeremy's arms with my legs over his shoulders as he pounded into me relentlessly. Today is sadly our last day here. Yesterday we went swimming with the dolphins. I didn't enjoy it as much as Jeremy did because I can't swim and I have a natural fear of the ocean. He however turned into a fucking fish out of water.

We leave today so this morning Jeremy woke up to pack all of our stuff. I went to take a shower which he pulled me out of. He started by licking and sucking on my star until I was screaming and shaking. I really think this man wants to fuck me in my ass. I don't know if I am ready for that yet.

After he had his fill of my ass, he flipped me over and tongue fucked me while pinching my clit until I was screaming with my whole body shaking.

This man should not understand my body this well. And now here I am being fucked relentlessly on the balcony. I am pressed on the wall with my legs on his shoulders and my arms around his neck while he holds me up by my ass continuing his rough hard deep thrusts. Is this nigga the hulk? I am not light. I surely got thicker after I had Anya.

I start to tear up as the pressure of his thrusts erupts inside me. I throw my head back letting out a throaty moan as I cum harder than ever. He doesn't let up as I feel the pressure building inside my stomach. My stomach tightens and I can't hold the liquid that squeezes out of me with every thrust. It splashes all over my thighs and his legs and stomach.

I can't catch my breath as I am a panting mess when I find my release. His moans grow louder and I can feel him cumming inside me as his thrusts get sloppy. My arms and legs grow weak and I accidentally let go of his neck when my arms give out. I know he is lost in his ecstasy as he is cumming because when my arms give out and I let go he loses his grip and drops me.

To say I was mad was an understatement.

"Oh shit!" He yells reaching for me on the floor. I slap his hand away kicking at him. I jump to my feet and stomp past him ignoring the amused look on his face.

I know this man did fucking not.

I hear him yell out sorry but I ignore him and walk straight back into the shower. My skin stings when I realize I scratched the back of my thigh because of the angle I fell. I am so fucking mad.

"Baby you can't still be mad at me. You have been giving me the silent treatment since we left the resort. We are back in America now. Can't you forgive me for something that happened in another time zone?"

I snap my head at him glaring at him from the seat next to him. "It's only an hour difference."

Bitch.

"Ah, she speaks. Does that mean I am forgiven? I am so sorry baby girl. It's just that you felt so fucking good and I lost control of myself for a second," he says in a seductive whisper causing a heartbeat to flutter straight to my pussy.

I roll my eyes at him.

"How about I make it up to you? I can take my girls to dinner tonight. Or we can stay in and have a movie night. Whatever you want?" He says reaching over to take my hand in his.

"Fine. But I pick the movie."

"That's my baby girl." He picks my hand up to place a chaste kiss on it.

We finally arrive back at the house and I immediately run into the house searching for my girl. I spot her in her high chair covered in mashed orange sweet potato all over her face. She is literally a mess at the moment. "Is that my yum yum?" I yell getting her attention. Her face turns to me and immediately she gives me her loud toothless smile but I almost cry when I notice her smile is no longer toothless. My baby has a tooth coming in.

"I missed her tooth come in?" I take her in my arms immediately and start to cry hysterically.

"It's okay Bambi," Mariella says trying to calm me. "It's barely a sprout, you can just see the tip of the white." I start ugly crying even more. This cannot be my life. First I get dropped this morning and the back of my thigh is still throbbing, now I missed an essential moment in my baby's life.

My cry turns into a sob.

"Jeremy walks in with the bags immediately dropping them and rushing over to me to see the state that I am in. " What's wrong baby girl."

"Her tooth came in and I missed it," I managed to choke out through my sobs.

Jeremy lowers Anya's bottom lip to see her tooth and his face turns into a cheeky grin. Then he proceeds to turn into a bumbling fool of joy. Anya reaches out for him as she giggles.

Y'all new baby me, please.

Never is she more excited to see him than me. I immediately start crying dropping my jaw. Nah me and this little girl got beef now. I hand her to her father and stomp away.

"Baby don't be like that!" Jeremy calls out laughing hysterically.

"Fuck you, I am going to take a shower."

I come back downstairs in comfortable clothing. I look around the living room to see my girl on the floor in her little playpen with Mariella on her side with her. Anya is reaching for the toys above her and kicking her legs at the same time.

"Where did Jeremy go?" I ask looking around.

"He's taking a shower in one of the other bathrooms," Mariella said looking up at me. "Oh! Before I forget Jesy and her boyfriend whom we didn't get to meet on mothers day is coming over soon. They wanted to see you guys when you got back. The one with the name that Jeremy said was stupid. Ari?" I nod my head in understanding.

I take Anya getting her fully dressed before Jeremy can come downstairs. I have a surprise for him. I get dressed in some sweatpants and a T-shirt with my crocs. I let Mariella know my plan, also letting her know I will be back before Jesy gets here. I also text Marcus to bring the car around.

His name is saved under security dude number 1.

Jeremy comes downstairs with wet hair stopping at my appearance. "Where are you two going?" He says confused.

"We, as in you as well, are going outside for like 20 minutes. Put on a shirt. Marcus is waiting."

"Where are we going? We just got back." He asks curiously crossing his arms.

"You ask too many goddam questions. Get dressed and you will find out, otherwise, I will go without you," I say making my way to the door.

He doesn't hesitate to go put on a white t-shirt with his grey joggers and slips on some socks and slides before we hop in the car. Marcus begins to drive and I ignore Jeremy focusing on Anya in her car seat. Immediately she falls asleep as the car starts moving.

We arrive at the small mall near the house. It isn't big but it had exactly what I needed inside. We walk to a Jewelry kiosk where I urge Jeremy to sit down.

"What the hell are we doing here? Are you expecting me to get my ears pierced?" He sounds annoyed.

"No, you said you missed a lot of firsts in Anya's life so, I decided to give you a first. You will be here for the first time she pierces her ears," I say excitedly as I place Anya in Jeremy's arms while he is sitting in the chair.

His face morphs into a soft smile. "Thank you," he mouths at me, and I shoot him back a wink. Anya opens her eyes for a second before going straight back to sleep.

"Her eyes are beautiful," the piercer says to us. We both offer her our thanks.

The piercer gets everything ready and I immediately become nervous. I might cry I can feel it. Anya is still sleeping so hopefully she doesn't feel much.

Shit.

My mommy senses are tingling. Maybe this isn't such a good idea. I suddenly become very nervous the closer she gets to my baby with that needle gun.

I look at Marcus, who has an amused expression on his face as he notices my sudden change in mood. I start to record as the piercer instructs Jeremy in the proper way to hold Anya's head. She goes to pierce the first ear setting the gun up. As soon as the click sound goes off I swear my ear started hurting for her. She started to let out a cry in her sleep that I felt to my core. I felt so bad. Why would I do this to her? I am clearly a bad mother. I feel the tears welt in my eyes.

Jeremy starts to shush her and rock her back and forth slowly but she doesn't stop crying. "It's okay princess," He says over and over in a whisper and it warms my heart.

Anya is now crying in her sleep and my heart is starting to ache. The piercer instructs Jeremy to angle her head on the other side. She pierces the other side even faster and Anya lets out a tiny scream as she starts to cry again. When the piercer is finally finished screwing on the last ring, Jeremy Adjusts her position to put her on his shoulder in a tight hug. "It's okay princess, daddy is here, daddy loves you."

My ovaries.

He places kisses on her cheeks and forehead continuously to soothe her, and before you know it I am crying alongside my baby.

I always see videos of people crying when their baby gets shots or gets their ears pierced and I never got it until now. The shots for some reason I could handle but this? This is hitting differently. I feel my sob coming on my heart drops to my ass.

I look at Jeremy who is tearing up as he hugs and hushes Anya for dear life. I have seen this man cry. Before but not like this. It only makes me cry even harder. This cry was so sweet, he just wanted to ease her pain. I look over at Marcus and this man is red-eyed with a tear coming down.

It's almost instant how I stop crying and start my giggles. I turn the camera to Marcus who rolls his eyes at me and looks away.

"Aww Marcus come on you big lug," I say laughing and I pull him into one of those awkward hugs where I wrap my arms around his body with his arms at his sides. I cannot stop laughing. He looks down at me with a straight face and red cheeks which only causes me to laugh even more.

Why does he look constipated?

"I'm going to go pull the car around. Mrs. Bresset if you would please let me go," he says nervously.

In an instant, I stop laughing and look at him like he's mad. "Stop calling me that you tree!" I said before letting go. I look over at Jeremy who is looking at me and Marcus with a raised eyebrow and I see Anya has fallen back to sleep on his shoulder. Every now and then she lets out a shaky sigh of annoyance threatening to cry again.

The piercer instructs us on aftercare before we leave to make our way back to the house. In the car, I showed Jeremy the video of him crying. He tried to make me delete it but I bit him so I ended up winning that little fight. Plus I already sent it to Mariella.

We arrive back at the house with Anya in my arms as we walk to the door. He goes to open the door when he stops himself turning to me. "Why did you tell Marcus to stop calling you Mrs. Bresset."

"Because we are not married," I Shrug. Before he can start an argument I walk into a house pushing past him. I stop in my tracts to a sight that was not there 20 minutes ago. I look around the room when something pink in the corner of the room catches my eye.

There in the corner was a Giant pink box covered in light pink cellophane. It had an assortment of baby clothes, blankets, and toys. Next to it was a 4 tier diaper cake with pink bows and stuffed animals all around it.

Who the fuck?

"Who the hell sent that?" I say to Mariella who was sitting in the kitchen eating a sandwich. She gets up quickly to examine Anya's ears. She then places both hands over her heart and sighs with the tears welling in her eyes. Lord, I don't know how this woman isn't dehydrated. She cries for everything.

"Honey you wouldn't believe me if I told you," Mariella says shaking her head and wiping away her tears. I need her to focus right now but she can't take her eyes off Anya.

"Believe what?" Jeremy says walking over to us

"Someone sent Anya that assortment of gifts."

"Who the hell sent that?" He says confused.

"That's what I said." Mariella is still fully focused on a sleeping Anya fully ignoring us.

"Mother?"

"Oh! Sorry. Your father sent it," Mariella responds quickly.

"Who!" Jeremy and I both respond at the same time startling Anya awake and causing her to cry.

"Yup," she says. Y'all to say I was confused was an understatement. There was a note too if you want to read it." Me and Jeremy look at each other before racing over to the gifts to grab the note.

Dear Jeremy

I am sorry. Congratulations on your little girl.

- Justin Bresset

"What a load of crap. The press conference is soon, I pushed it back for Jamaica, and he must be hoping I change my mind. Pathetic."

"Yea it might be poisoned. Spray it with Lysol and leave it in the corner for a month before we touch it."

I go upstairs to change Anya when I hear the doorbell ring. Jesy must be here. The girl loves Her niece. She likes Anya more than she likes Jeremy. I throw the diaper in the diaper genie getting Anya dressed again so we make our way down the stairs.

I stop at the bottom of the stairs when I see Jesy hug her

mother. Her back is turned along with the male standing next to her. Anya lets out a loud squeal causing Jesy to spin around. Did she dye her hair red?

"Oh my god! Is that my favorite niece?" Jesy screams.

"She's your only niece." Jeremy snorts.

"And is that my annoying ass brother who doesn't mind his business?" She laughs slapping Jeremy on the back of his head. I walk over to her as she pulls me into a hug. "Oh before I forget, this is my boyfriend Ari."

I Look over at him as he turns his attention away from Mariella turning his body to finally greet me. I am met with the scariest pair of green eyes I have ever seen. The same green eyes that watched me bleed out on the floor as he beat me constantly.

"Zachary?" I say in a nervous confused whisper.

Chapter 25

Samantha Kage

. . . .

You have to tell yourself things like it's okay. He won't do It again. He loves me. It was probably an accident. What could I have done to avoid getting hurt?

After a while, you start to convince yourself that it's your fault. You try to figure out things to do to please him.

Then when you catch yourself apologizing to him for the abuse he is inflicting on you, you realize it's too late to leave.

I remember the first night it started. I remember it clear as day.

The night was great. We spent the night at a restaurant, wasn't that great of a restaurant but we made it fun nonetheless. The ambiance was okay, the food was mediocre, and the service was mid. But does that matter? Does it matter when the person you love is sitting next to you?

Everything seems minuscule when the person you love just makes everything better. I stare into his brownish-green eyes as he speaks to me. Our fingers are intertwined, we are lost in conversation, we are sneaking touches under the table, and the kisses he places on my shoulder and neck give me a constant stream of butterflies as he whispers sweet nothings in my ear.

It was all good once. Once upon a time. Who knew how the night would end?

We finally pry ourselves away from each other to leave the restaurant and get in the cab. Me and Zach had been together for about 6 weeks now, but it had felt like we have known each other forever. I am wrapped in his arms in the back of the car. That was also the first night he told me he loved me. Right in that cab.

Maybe it was my desperate need for connection and family after not having one of my own. I grew up in the system bouncing from different fosters moms, never staying long enough to get attached. When I did get attached to one, she died.

I started to think I was unworthy of want or love. I desperately wanted something consistent and he was that for me.

He was staring at me not saying a word while I comfortably relaxed into his body. Our bodies fit together like a hand in a glove. At one point in the back of that cab, we found ourselves staring into each other's eyes in silence. He finally broke the silence by blurting out the three words I think I have desperately wanted to hear.

"I love you."

I said it back with no hesitation. Love was something I dreamed of having, and I was happy. He loved me. Finally, someone chose me. Finally, someone loved me and I held on to that feeling with everything I had. I was desperate not to lose it.

It wasn't until we got out of the cab and we told the cab driver goodnight that the night took a turn.

We made our way up to his apartment, I dam near already lived there anyway. I walk ahead of him and drop my keys on the counter. I don't hear anything behind me. I turn around confused but I am immediately met with a hard slap to the face. I tasted blood from how hard he slapped me. He walked up to my face and said clear as day. "Don't flirt with other men in front of me." Then walked away. I later found out that apparently saying goodnight to the cab driver was flirting. That was the first of many times.

That's the only memory that plays in my mind while I stare into his eyes in front of me.

"Samantha?" He whispers while squinting at me

"Zachary?" Jeremy says with a confused tone. He quickly steps in front of me and Anya, grabbing his phone. I hear him yelling something into his phone, but I can't process what's happening. I am frozen in place. I don't know what I feel. I just know it isn't fear. I am not afraid of him.

I do however feel anger. Anger at myself for endangering Mariella, my baby, and everyone in this room. Angry at Jeremy's father for taunting us with gifts and still sending Zach here. He put my daughter's life in danger, who knows what Zachary is capable of?

I am livid.

I am snapped out of my thoughts when Marcus rushes in with 2 other people on his security team. Everything happens so fast. Jeremy leaves my side as the guards come in. He quickly makes his way over to start arguing with Jesy.

Jeremy gets into a heated screaming match with Jesy, both guards grab Zach shoving him into the wall one arm on each shoulder. Marcus rushes over to me and Anya. He immediately pulls me into an embrace to lead me away, but I refuse to budge. He is talking to me but I can't hear. I cannot take my eyes off the green-eyed devil before me.

I feel like I need to watch his every move. Mariella is confused as hell. Everyone is yelling and Anya starts to cry. I can't deal. I want to wrap myself in a ball. I won't move a muscle unless he does. I won't run from him. I have run enough.

Marcus seems to understand my body language. Instead, he places a protective arm on my shoulder in case anything happens. "Sir, you need to leave. I won't ask twice." Marcus scared me a little with his body language when he said that. I never heard his voice so deep and scary before.

"Why? Because my ex is here? What does that have to do with me?" Zachary said struggling against the guards.

"Because you have been stalking her and texting her for weeks now," Jeremy yells turning his attention away from a crying Jesy.

"What the fuck are you talking about? No I haven't!" Zach yells still trying to break free of the guard's embrace. "Samantha, what have you been telling these people!" He yells at me and I flinch.

I flinch at him raising his voice but I say nothing. I feel Marcus's arm tense against me.

"You dated! You abused her?" Jesy says yelling at Zach.

"No? What? Yes? But I have changed baby I swear. I hardly hit her, I would call what we had fights. I have never put my hands on you. You know this! Tell them now!"

"Stop," I say in a voice so quiet that no one heard me. I'm trying to find the courage in my voice.

"You sent her pictures of herself, a few weeks ago! You have been texting her! You used my sister to do it?" Jeremy yells.

"I have never. I haven't tried to contact her in over a year. I had given up! It wasn't me!"

He what?

Marcus hasn't moved from by my side. Jeremy is standing in the space in-between Zachary and me. Everyone is still yelling over me and arguing.

"Stop," I repeat again a little louder. The only one who hears me is Marcus. He turns to me raising an eyebrow. Yet the arguments continue. No one is getting anywhere. Everyone is just yelling. Mariella is consoling a distressed Jesy, I can see Jeremy is trying everything not to lunge at Zach. Jeremy shoots a confused look at Marcus with a protective arm around me.

Not the time dude. Read the room.

"Everybody stop!" I yell out. Everyone in the room freezes and looks at me. "Mariella, can you take Anya upstairs, please? Clearly, we all need to talk."

Mariella nods her head and walks over to me taking Anya from my arms. My eyes are stuck on Zach. In the back of my mind, I can't help but worry that he will attack me. I finally pry my eyes away from him to watch as Mariella heads upstairs. The room is completely quiet until we hear the door close upstairs. My daughter is safely away thank god.

"Talk," I say as I turn my attention back to Zach. I don't know where this bravery is coming from but I will hold on to it as long as possible.

"Can you tell me, guards, to let go of me first?" Zachary quipped.

"Not a fucking chance," Marcus and Jeremy say harshly at the same time.

"Tell the truth. Were you stalking her?" A frustrated Jesy spat at him.

"No! I don't even know what you are all talking about!" Zach yells again. He tried to move but the rough arms shove him back against the wall.

"Over the past few weeks, someone has been texting me and calling me muñeca perfecta. I went out the other night and the same person texted me pictures of myself out. No one called me that except you!"

"What night was this?" He says confused. This man is the best actor I have ever seen he genuinely sounds like he has no idea what I am talking about.

"Two Fridays ago, the 12th," Jeremy snapped. " I know it was you, you fucking piece of shit. Why can't you just leave her alone? Haven't you done enough!"

"The 12th?" He asks weighing his mind. "It wasn't me I can prove it! I swear I stopped looking for you over a year ago," He spat.

"He was with me. All day and night." Jesy finally spoke looking down. "We were on our way to Cali. We got away for the weekend and didn't tell anyone. We were on a flight that night." She finished quietly.

"He still could have had people watching her," Jeremy growls to his sister. "And you. How the fuck did you let him get in the house!" Jeremy growls at Marcus. He stops and eyes the two of us. I only notice now that I am hugging myself and Marcus's arm is wrapped around my body protectively.

I ignore him. I don't have time for that right now. So does Marcus.

"Have people watch her? Who do you think I am? That I would have people? What is this a mafia book?" Zachary says Putting emphasis on the word people.

"Why tell my sister your name is Ari then? Why lie? Unless you knew who she was all along and how close she was to Samantha."

"Jess calls me Ari all on her own. She knows my name. She prefers to call me Ari because she thought it was cute. That I was cute," he says offering her an apologetic smile. She immediately looks away from him and down at the floor. "You know what. I don't have to stay here. Jesy baby let's go home and talk."

"No," she says quietly. I can hear her voice cracking.

"No?" He says angrily. He turns his attention back to me. I feel Marcus tense beside me at the same time Jeremy's fist clenches. "This is your fault you stupid bitch!"

"Call her a bitch again, and I will break your fucking jaw," Jeremy growls.

"You think your so fucking perfect walking around these people. I see you have a pretty little baby. Did you tell these people what you took from me? The reason I was looking for you in the first place? How would they feel if they know what you took from me? How would everyone in this room look at you? Huh Muñeca!"

I flinch slightly at his raised voice. "I didn't take anything from you!" I say as my voice cracks. I can feel the tears welling in my ears. I wasn't ready for them to know. Marcus turns his head to look down at me as Jeremy looks at me with sad eyes.

"Tsk tsk tsk. Don't be like that Muñeca. Tell these people the truth. You're afraid they will know the real you?"

"What the fuck are you talking about?" Jeremy snaps at him.

"You want to tell them or should I?" He says with a devious

smile.

"I said," I pause taking a deep breath, "I didn't take anything from you! Don't do this. It won't end the way you think it will," I yelled. I could feel the tears rolling down my cheeks. I have only really ever spoken about this out loud in therapy.

"Are you threatening me? The truth will set you free princess."

"Anything she may or may not have taken, I will pay you back for it. Just leave her alone," Jeremy interrupts.

"Please. What she took cannot be repaid for in diamonds or gold. Can it Muñeca? You wanna try to ruin my relationship with my girl? I am going to ruin your relationship with everyone here."

"Zachary you don't know what the hell you are talking about," I say quickly. He doesn't know the truth himself.

"Fine, I will tell them then since you want to play stupid. Actually, I am not entirely sure you're playing stupid or you just are."

"Hey," Jeremy says in a warning tone that even scares me.

"I know you were pregnant Muñeca!" Both Jesy and Jeremy's eyes snap to look at me. I can feel my cheeks burning with the tears. "One ought not to put a pregnancy test in someone's drawer that they keep everything in. Tell me did you run away knowing you were pregnant? Did you give my baby up for adoption or worst, abort it? But you chose to raise another man's baby instead? While your baby is somewhere in the world maybe, I don't know. How about you tell me where my child is yea?" The room has fallen into complete silence as they take in his words. "Yea I know everything! Where is my child Samantha? Dead? Or living with some random family because you didn't want it. What kind of mother throws a baby away?"

"You had another baby?" Jeremy says shocked with a hint of bitterness in his voice.

"You had his baby?" Jesy says shocked.

"You're so stupid," I say chuckling darkly. I cannot stop crying but the laugh came out. It quickly turns back into a sob.

"Stupid? Me? What's stupid is you leaving fake blood all over the room so I would think something happened to you. I thought you were dead! How could you take my child away from me? Why don't you tell the truth huh? Tell your precious white people. All we had was a little fight."

I look around at the faces judging me around the room. I might as well come clean right? I don't owe anyone in this room an explanation but I feel a golden opportunity to break Zach. Fine. He wants to do this we will do this. I rub my hands up my face wiping away my tears in frustration. I rest my hands on the top of my head and step away from Marcus's embrace while shaking my head. I need to calm down a little. I am way too worked up.

My mind is on 100.

I start to laugh. I actually start to laugh hysterically and the people in the room look at me like I am nuts. "You're so fucking stupid!" I say while trying to hold it together. "You want the truth? Fine. "I was pregnant." All eyes are on me now. I take a deep breath before I continue. "The blood wasn't fake you fucking idiot! And a little fight? You beat the shit out of me that night I left. The blood all over the room was mine! Let me refresh your memory since you don't seem to remember what the fuck happened that night. I don't know how you could anyway. You were drunk as fuck! You beat me dam near bloody and unconscious, then you raped me because I assume that the only way you could get your tiny dick hard is when a female is beaten and bloody. Then you proceeded to kick me in my pregnant stomach over 5 times. Then you passed out. Then I had to pry myself off the floor and drag myself to the hospital to make sure that my baby was okay. I finally made it to the hospital on foot and in pain. I had to tell them I was hit by a car. Just for them to tell me that the accident I was in caused me to miscarry. You killed your own fucking child you piece of shit."

I know I must have sounded crazy because I kept laughing and sobbing through that whole monologue.

"You're fucking lying you stupid bitch!" He says as he lunges towards me, he breaks loose from one of the guards. He tries to run past Jeremy but before he can even make it to him muchness me, Marcus runs up to him and tackles Zach to the ground. Hard. If I wasn't mistaken I think I heard a bone crack the way he slammed his body.

Zach cried out in immense pain. "Restrain him!" Marcus yells at the other two security.

Marcus looks up at me with sad angry eyes. Jeremy slowly takes steps towards me with red eyes. Jesy is in the corner crying uncontrollably. I never wanted the truth to come out like this. I need to go. I need to be with my baby. Jeremy takes a step towards me, but I immediately back up and shake my head. "Please leave me alone," I say as best as I could. My voice was weak. I felt defeated. I never wanted any of them to find out like this. I don't know if I wanted any of them to find out at all.

I take one last look around the room before running up the stairs. I go straight to Mariella's room to find her laying on the bed with Anya. Anya is holding her feet with her hands playing while Mariella is next to her reading a book. I make sure to lock the door behind me I do not want to be disturbed.

I climb into the bed pulling Anya into my embrace. I start to cry harder than I was crying downstairs. "Bambi what's wrong," Mariela coos pulling both of us in her arms. I lay there crying trying my best to tell her the gist of everything. Just like when I had Anya, she was there for me. She placed her kisses on my forehead and tried her best to make me feel better.

Shortly after Mariella got me to calm down. There is a knock at the door. I roll my eyes. "I don't want to see any men right now," I whisper to Mariella. She nods her head getting up. She walks to the door stepping outside the door. I heard hushed whispers before the door is open and closed again.

I turn around to see Jesy standing by the door with tear-stained cheeks. We stare at each other in silence for a while. I half expect her to yell at me for messing up her relationship but she doesn't. She stares at me for a few seconds before breaking out into a sob. "He hit me too," she whispered before fully breaking down. I quickly get up pulling her into a tight embrace. I understand what she went through. This poor girl

A short while passes and we have finally relaxed with a sleeping Anya in between us. We were both laying down just facing each other in comfortable silence. We don't know why, but it's just what we needed.

"Where did they take him?" I ask her finally breaking the silence.

"I don't know. Marcus and the other security left with him."

"I can't believe your father allowed that man to come into your life."

"My father? My father never met Ar..Erm..Zachary. It's so weird to say his name. He forced me to call him Ari and would hit me when I didn't," she said whispering to herself

"The reason Jeremy left me was because your father threatened to tell Zach where I was if he didn't."

"Yea, that's weird. I showed him a picture of my father once. He showed no signs of recognition," she shrugged.

Don't tell me this man affected all of our lives on a fucking bluff.

"Where is your brother?"

"Sitting in the living room with a bottle of whiskey."

"Great," I roll my eyes. I take Anya to make my way to the door. I need to talk to Jeremy. I know how he gets. "There's one thing I'm confused about?"

"What's that?" Jessy replied.

"How did you and Zach meet?"

"Oh, me and my ex went out to a club in the city. Britney. I miss her," She said as she trailed off in thought. "But anyway, he was there and he pursued me, he actually made me break up with Britney. If only I could see how manipulative he was back then," she said shrugging her shoulders. "I mean he even forced me to dye my hair red."

"What the hell was Zach doing in New York anyway," I say shaking my head. Something is not adding up.

"Oh, he was out with his cousin that lives out here. Angel, I think his name is." My eyes widen at her words.

"Angel? Brown eyes? About Ye high?" I say while raising my hand. "Kind of dick?"

"Yea that's the one. He tried to talk to Britney while Zach pursued me. How do you know him?"

"He's my best friend's boyfriend," I say with disgust.

"Oh wow. I don't think he's anything like Zach though. He seemed really sweet."

I roll my eyes.

"And how long ago was this?"

"Me and Zach have been together for almost 2 months now I wanna say."

"Interesting," I say to myself.

I'm going to snitch.

But later. I need to work up a way to properly tell her.

I make my way downstairs to see Jeremy sitting on the couch with his head down with the bottle of whiskey in between his legs.

I roll my eyes.

Oh this should be fun. Knowing Jeremy he will probably be mad at me. Well, Might as well dive into this conversation now.

Chapter 26

Samantha Kage

· ·

"Are you mad at me or something?" I ask finally breaking the silence. I have been standing in front of him for about 5 minutes now.

"How could you not tell me," he says with a sniffle.

"It's not something I talk about often Jeremy. Losing a baby took a toll on me. I was really young," I say as I pull Anya a little closer to me and mutter my words.

"I should be the person you can confide in. I'm more upset with myself for not making you feel safe enough or comfortable enough to talk to me. You went through something terrible. I am so sorry. I will try to do better to be someone you feel safe enough to talk to."

"It's really not you. It's just me. I barely talked about it in therapy."

"How long have you been in therapy?" He asked snapping his head up.

"That's a conversation for another day."

He doesn't need to know that he was the initial reason that caused me to go.

"You know I love you, right baby girl? I would do anything to protect you. You know that right?"

I know he feels like he failed today. I just know him so well. He feels like he could have done more to protect me. Zachary should have never been able to get in the house much less through the gates with all this security.

I simply nod my head giving him a small smile. "So do you believe Zach?"

"Believe him about what?" He says snapping his head up at me.

"That he isn't the one stalking me," I said rolling my eyes at his attitude.

"I don't know. I mean who else could it be?"

"Let's see if I get any more messages and we will go from there. We will know if it was Zach or not. I am sure Marcus found a way to have him arrested or something."

"Yea. I guess," he said shrugging. "Come on, you have gone through a lot today. Let me draw you a bath and put Anya to bed. I will order us some dinner."

He walked over to me placed a small kiss on my cheek and led me up the stairs to the bedroom. He put Anya in her crib after drawing me a bath with candles. The water smelled like lilacs and vanilla. It was what I didn't know I needed at that moment.

I lay there in my peace and quiet in the tub for what felt like an hour. It was comfortable and relaxing. I couldn't get over the fact that everyone in the house found out my secret today. I needed to clear my head.

Marcus, the other guards, Jesy, and Jeremy all know what I have been hiding. Mariella was the only one I chose to tell without being forced to.

While sitting in the tub I started to go through my head of anyone besides Zachary who would try to hurt me. I can't help having a gut feeling that this isn't over. Could it be Tiffany? She's relentless but I don't think she's capable of stalking me.

Jeremy's father? I am not even sure he knows what I look like outside of photos. He seems to be the type to confuse all back people with each other if I am being honest.

I am snapped out of my thoughts by a small knock on the door. Before I could answer Jeremy enters with a giant towel, he was wearing grey sweat shorts and no shirt. He must have taken a shower in one of the other bathrooms. I step out of the bath with him wrapping the giant towel around my body. Before I can step out he scoops me into his arms bridal style and walks into the bedroom. He places me on the bed gently telling me not to move. I sat there wrapped in my big towel as I watched him maneuver around the room. He handed me the pasta he ordered while he grabbed everything he needed.

He grabbed my African whipped shea butter and my bonnet. He placed my bonnet over my head and proceeded to rub my body with the African whipped shea butter. I was bare for him. He massaged every inch of my body while placing small kisses on my forehead, hands, thighs, and lips.

We were quiet.

He massaged my feet kissing those in the process as well. He was trying everything to make me feel better and I was just going to let him.

He dressed me in silk shorts and a lace bra set with a silk robe to match. He pulled me onto his lap laid my head on his chest and we just sat there in silence. The longer we sat the tighter his hold got on me. I didn't mind. He needed this as much as he did.

"I love you," I whispered looking up at him and finally breaking the silence.

He placed a chaste kiss on my lips. "I love you more baby girl. I am so sorry you had to go through everything you went through. I will never hurt you the way he did. You know that right?"

"I know Jeremy, I know," I whisper against his lips while nodding my head. We lay down keeping our eyes focused on each other before we fall asleep in each other's arms.

I wake up hot with the feeling of a weight on my chest. I try to shuffle but I can't move. I am on my back and Jeremy's head is on my right titty. I look down to see that this man has a monster grip on my other titty with his whole hand under my top. He is even snoring. Well, the best sleep you will get is sleeping with a hand full of titty I have heard.

I try to wiggle out of his grip but he doesn't move. His hand on my boob only tightens. I reach down and stroke his dick through his pants until he is fully hard. He lets out a moan in his sleep and shifts. He shifts just enough for me to wiggle out of his grasp. My arm hurts like a bitch. I go to Anya's crib to check on her but she is not in it. I walk down to Mariella's room to see it empty as well.

I make my way down to the kitchen to see Anya drinking a bottle with Angela and Mariella.

"When did you kidnap my child?"

"This morning while y'all were sleeping. My grandma's senses were tingling," she said with a big smile on her face.

I decide to let Anya stay with Mariella while I went to the kitchen to make breakfast. I looked outside the window noticing the guards are still there. I decide to make them breakfast along with Jeremy.

I whip up scrambled eggs, sliced fruit, Omelets, bacon, sausages, and waffles because I don't like pancakes at all. I make French toast as well because I craved it towards the end. I spread out all the food on the counter with plates and forks. I make a plate for Mariella and Angela and bring it to them in the living room. I made coffee, squeezed orange juice, and placed apple juice on the table. I look down at my outfit before inviting the men in and just decide on closing my robe.

I open the door gaining the attention of Marcus and his two guards leaning against the car and talking. Marcus's eyes widen at the sight of me.

Okay, maybe I should have changed.

Nah, this is my house. They'll be alright.

Actually, I am sure they have seen woman's legs before. Fuck it. "Marcus, can you and the others join me inside for a second?"

Marcus starts to walk and notions his head for the other two to follow him. I walk away and they follow me over to the island in the kitchen where the food is spread out.

"Ma'am?" Marcus says stopping in his tracks at the sight before him. I turn around smiling at him.

"I made you guys breakfast!" I say spreading out my arms with a smile. But they look at me confused.

"Ma'am you didn't have to do this," One of them said.

"Yea but I wanted to. You guys were such a big help yesterday. If I am being honest." I trailed off looking down. " I would have never raised my voice at him, or even talked back to him if you guys weren't there to make me feel better and safe. And for that I thank you. You guys protected me and my family and I am forever grateful for that. I know you were just doing your jobs but I felt you guys deserved something even if it's just a simple home-cooked meal so don't let my hard work go to waste please?" I said nervously. Imagine I made all this food and they don't want any.

"Thank you ma'am, we appreciate it," One of the men said. Marcus shoots him a glare to which he responds with an apologetic look.

The men take seats around the island and begin to dig in. I go back to the stove to make red velvet waffles for Jeremy because of how he made me feel loved last night.

"You're still cooking?" Marcus asked.

"Yea, I know Jeremy likes red velvet waffles so I'm going to whip some up for him." Marcus just stares at me blankly. I shrug and return to what I am doing. "So what are your names my saviors?"

"I'm Rich," the dark skin taller one said. "And that's Vincent." I don't know why but Vincent looked German to me.

"Nice to finally put names to the faces," I smile.

Me and the boys get lost in conversation about little things while I continue to cook. Anime, clothing, movies, you name it. When I was younger people always told me I was one of the boys. I never knew how to feel about it.

"You're really telling me that DC is better than marvel?" I ask annoyed.

"Yes!" Rich exclaimed. "They literally have better stories."

"Your movies are literally dark. Like not in a gloomy sense, but in the sense that your movies need better lighting. Can't y'all afford light edits?" Marcus quipped.

"Exactly! Dark-ass movies make my eyes hurt," I said laughing.

I finally sit down across from the men after wrapping up Jeremy's food for when he wakes up. Today is the day his father makes his announcement about the company so he doesn't have to go in as early. I would much rather let him sleep in until we all have to get ready. I start to eat my omelet, waffle, and French toast when I hear feet patter down the stairs.

I look over to see Jeremy stop to take in the sight before him. He furrows his eyebrows before making his way over to me. He grabs my face in his hands and places a kiss on my forehead. "Good morning baby girl."

"Good morning baby," I smile turning my head to towards him.

"Gentlemen," Jeremy said clearing his throat as he walked over to the island. He places a kiss on my lips and then reaches down to whisper in my ear. "Why are you naked?"

"Good morning." They all respond in sync. That was weird.

I roll my eyes at him and ignore his comment once what he said actually registered in my mind. The rest of breakfast goes on without a hitch. I tried to wash all the dishes but the men did it instead. They thanked me and went back to their positions, or whatever it is they do in their downtime.

Jeremy, Mariella, Anya, and I make our way to the building. Unintentionally we all ended up wearing blue. Jeremy is in a dark blue suit, I am in a dark blue strappy body con dress with a cardigan over, Anya is in a navy blue dress with a matching navy blue and white flower headband, and Mariella is wearing a navy blue pantsuit with some Jays. My mother-in-law is stylish.

We decided it was best to be here for Jeremy, not just for the photo op but because we support him in everything. Also, Jeremy said having me and Anya here would help him stay calm and not slap his father. Although I wouldn't mind seeing it.

We are walking down the hallway in the building to the open conference room where the announcement will be held when we spot Jeremy's father making his way toward us. I keep shifting Anya between my arms uncomfortably. I can't get over this pain I have in my arm.

Immediately Marcus and the other two guards switch positions. Jeremy walks ahead while Marcus walks in front of me and Mariella with the other two trailing behind until we come to a stop.

"Father," Jeremy says harshly.

"Jeremy. My beauty," he says winking at Mariella. He then turns to greet me, "Samantha, and is that who I think it is?" He says smiling. I grip Anya a little tighter.

"Please don't address my mother, my woman, or my child," Jeremy says annoyed.

"Boy, she was my woman for 22 years, don't mistake it."

"22 years too fucking long," I heard Mariella grumble beside me.

"Anyways. Samantha, may I speak with you?"

"No," Jeremy answers.

"In private it's important," he says rolling his eyes at Jeremy.

"Umm. Okay." Jeremy and Marcus whip their heads around to look at me in disbelief." I shrug my shoulders handing Anya off to Mariella before proceeding to walk toward him. Call it curiosity but I genuinely want to know what the fuck he will say. He wouldn't dare threaten me, I would hope he knows better so I want to know. Jeremy grabs my arm to stop walking while Marcus stands in front of me.

I look at Jeremy like he is stupid causing him to let go while I step past Marcus. Jeremy may control me in bed but I will drop-kick him if he tries it in public.

I walk behind Justin as he takes a few stops away from the crowd until we stop.

"First, I want to say, I fought hard against this but I can see my son really loves you. Also if you tell my son any of this I will deny it."

Okay, move on old man.

"I should have never threatened you with that monster to come back into your life. I know I seem like a bad guy but I would never intentionally harm a woman. I was a terrible man but I never put my hands on Jeremy's mother. There is no denying that."

"So why send Zachary to the house? Why make him date Jesy? Why give him my location"

"What are you talking about? I never did any of those things. He's dating Jesy? That monster is with my daughter!" His sudden raise in voice causes me to hear footsteps behind me. I turn around to see no one other than Jeremy and Marcus walking toward me. I hold up my hand for them to stop which they do. Reluctantly I might add, but they stop nonetheless. Once I am assured they will not move again after sending them a bunch of death glares I turn my attention back to Justin.

"They broke up don't worry." So if he didn't send Zachary, and Zachary claims he wasn't stalking me. Then who the fuck is stalking me.

Someone needs to talk to the author in control of my life. Cause a bitch is tired of being in danger.

"Good. I just hope they stay broken up. I was sick to my stomach seeing what happened to you. Again, I'm a shitty person for using it against you and Jeremy but I assure you. I never made contact with him. Either way, I do want to apologize."

I just nod my head in agreement. He won't be given forgiveness. Fuck this man.

"Your daughter really is beautiful. She has our eyes," he adds.

Aww, that was sweet. I offer him another small smile. "Thank you. If only her father was there when she was born and didn't abandon me to endure my pregnancy and birth alone because of his father." I shrug with a bitchy smile.

"I deserved that. But hey, at least you didn't get rid of it as the other one did. You stuck it out alone. It's admirable."

"Other one?" I say confused. Did Tiffany really get an abortion I thought to myself?

"Yea, I wasn't sure if Tiffany's baby was mine or his, either way only one woman gets to carry my seeds, and that woman is standing right over there," he says motioning to Mariella with a smile.

This man really has a weird ass way of showing how genuine he is. It's like one second he's wholesome and two minutes later he's a fucking asshole. And I really feel like in his own mind he is honestly being genuine. He needs help. No wonder Mariella left him.

"Well, if that is all," I say as I start to walk away.

"Yes. I have said my peace. I am ready."

We walk back over to the group that is eyeing us curiously. I ignore them walking back to my place next to Mariella and taking Anya back into my arms. I wince a little at that stupid pain in my arm again.

"Are you okay baby girl?" Jeremy asks concerned.

"Yea, it's nothing, just a pain I have. Let's just get through this."

He nods his head in response. The doors open for us to enter a room full of cameras and a bunch of staff. Jeremy's father moves towards the mic while Jeremy stands next to him. Me, Mariella, and Anya stay a few steps behind with Marcus, Vincent, and Rich moving about the room assuring nothing goes wrong. Jeremy's father proceeds to begin his speech by praising his son and making jokes about retirement. The crowd obviously eats it up.

He finished his speech off with, " it is now my greatest honor to hand over everything I have built to my only son. He worked hard for this, and he deserves it. He never lets anyone stop him from getting what he wants and I admire that. I love you son." They go into a fake handshake and hug for the cameras before Jeremy takes over the mic and his father steps aside. If I didn't know the father was a terrible person, I would think the way he was looking at Jeremy was very whole-hearted. Too bad I know him well.

I still can't get over the feeling of someone watching me. I am so lost in my thoughts I didn't hear a word Jeremy said in his speech.

If Zachary wasn't stalking me, who the hell was being weird and creepy like that? Then again Zachary could just be lying since I haven't received a weird message since he has been gone. Maybe that really was the end of it. Maybe Zachary was lying and he was actually stalking me. Yea that's it. Don't worry about it too much.

The sound of applause snaps me out of my thoughts. I look up to see Jeremy walking toward me with a smile on his face. He takes Anya from my arms putting her on his side while he takes his other arm to wrap around my body placing a kiss on my lips. He then poses for a photo for all the cameras flashing. Way too many at one time for me.

Anya buries her face in Jeremy's shoulder as the lights start to irritate her. As soon as that happens, we make our exit back into the previous hallways we were in before. I am so ready to go back home. My arm is killing me.

The four of us make it back to the car. Mariella and Anya go in one car to go home while I decide to go to urgent care. The pain in my arm has been unbearable these last few days but today the pain is so intense I can't help it. I feel like I want to throw up.

I offered to go alone but Jeremy insisted on coming with me

of course. Sitting in the car my phone goes off. It's probably Annabelle I think to myself.

But of course, it's not Annabelle because why would my life be that simple?

I open the phone to see a picture of me staring off into space while Anya leans on my shoulder with her pacifier. Under the picture, the message scares me even more.

Chapter 27

Samantha Kage

• •

Jeremy is currently laying behind me in bed while rubbing his dick on my ass, squeezing my breast, and placing love bites on the back of my neck.

Fuck he feels good. He goes as far as pinching my nipple and I feel his precum on my ass.

I am trying to resist but I must say it's becoming harder with every thrust of his dick on my body. I am dangerously wet between my legs.

I had to get my birth control removed yesterday and I need to wait a week for the pill to kick in. This man has made it clear that we will not be using condoms and he will not be pulling out, so I decided we should abstain from sex.

I think he almost cried when I told him no more sex.

When we arrived at urgent care, they had to remove the implant in my arm because it shifted. Turns out that was the cause of my severe amount of pain. I don't think I would have made it another day if I didn't get it removed.

After a painful 30 minutes, it was finally out, and I have prescribed the pill instead as well as pain medication for the new scar on my arm. The bandage around my arm is giving me some discomfort but it wasn't anywhere near as bad as the pain that I was feeling while it was in.

I let out a small moan as Jeremy reaches his hand in my shorts to rub his middle finger up and down my slippery slit occasionally brushing my clit.

"Come on baby girl just the tip," he whispers against my ear. "You're already so wet for me."

Just the tip my ass. Do not give in. You are strong bitch. You have the pussy. You have the power. Tell him no.

My thoughts are cut off when he presses himself closer to my ass while nibbling on my ear. An unintentional moan escapes my lips. I can feel his mouth turn into a smile.

Resist bitch. Resist!

I am winning this one. And he knows it. I mentally cheer myself on for not giving in. Then of course Jeremy being Jeremy uses one finger to slide inside me. "So fucking tight and wet baby girl," he grunts against my ear.

Dam bitch just take a plan B. Or be petty.

A throaty moan escapes my lips as I reach behind me and start to stroke him through his boxers but to my surprise, he is completely naked. I spit on my hand and start to stroke him from behind my back. He lets out a groan as he speeds up the thrusts of his finger inside me.

"Fuck me daddy," I whisper like the weakling I am.

He wastes no time moving my silk shorts to the side so he can adjust himself perfectly aligning his tip at my entrance while spreading my ass and giving him more access. He grips my hip as he slides into me at a dangerously slow pace. He begins his slow thrusts while peppering kisses on my back and the back of my neck. I throw my head back from the overwhelming sense of sensual pleasure. "Oh baby, just like that," I moan out.

I can feel myself dripping on my thigh. "Fuck baby girl, you're so fucking wet for me." Jeremy moves to grab my leg to lift it up to place it on top of his, opening me up more for him to thrust deeper. His thrusts speed up as he grabs my throat from behind. The only sounds that can be heard are Jeremy's grunts, my soft moans, and the sloshing of wetness as he pounds into me. I can't help but moan loudly as this position allows him to slam into my G spot directly and constantly. I reach back and grip his thigh with one hand and grab onto the hand on my throat for support. I just needed to grab something to hold on to for dear life.

"Shit baby girl I am about to cum," he says as he quickens his thrust. He reaches down with his other hand to rub my clit while his dick assaults my G spot at a rapid pace. I can feel the pressure building up in my stomach. "That's it baby girl, cum for me."

My body starts to shake and convulse as my eyes roll back into my head. I reach my earth-shattering orgasm while inaudible noises escape my throat. Jeremy continues to fuck me roughly through my orgasm until I come down from my high. "Fuck baby! You feel so fucking good," he moans as he continues to pound into me.

I quickly move to pull him out of me. He is so wrapped up in his high that I move off the bed before he has time to grab me. I almost fall on my wobbly legs but I quickly grab the edge of the bed to catch my balance. I didn't realize how weak I was until now.

"W-What's wrong?" He stutters out of breath.

"You don't listen. I told you not to cum inside me until my birth control kicks in after a week. Now you won't be allowed to cum until you have my permission. Two can play this game king," I say feeling fairly pleased with myself.

"Are you kidding me? You're going to give me blue balls Sam!" He argues while holding his fully erect dick in his hand.

Dam his dick is pretty.

"Oh, okay fine," I say smiling. I walk around to his side of the bed leaning over to place my lips on his throbbing pink tip. I lick and kiss the tip causing him to throw his head back in pleasure. Before he can grab my hand to throw me back on the bed I move out of his grasp and make my way toward the bathroom to do my morning routine. "See, you don't listen. Now don't make yourself cum, or I won't put out for a month. Understand? And I will know," I yell over my shoulder.

I turn around to see his eyes filled with hatred, lust, and admiration as he nods his head.

Oh, this is going to be fun.

I get in the shower after locking the door because I know him, and I continue to rack my mind on who the fuck would be stalking me.

Jeremy has instructed that I don't leave the house without him or the guards, but mostly not without him. I honestly think it's not that serious and that it's just a weird peeping tom. He or she has only ever taken pictures of me in public settings anyway, it's not like he is taking pictures of me outside or inside the house or anything. Now that would alarm me. This person hasn't done anything dangerous but send me a few pictures. I understand the severity of the situation but at the same time, I think Jeremy is overreacting a little bit.

I come out of the shower wrapping myself in a small towel to see Jeremy laying on the bed with a fully erect dick looking frustrated.

"You're still hard?" I ask confused.

"What do you expect from me when the most attractive woman in the world is naked in the next room dripping wet? I couldn't stop picturing you touching yourself in the shower or how your body looks as the water ran over you. Fuck," he says shooting me a glare.

"Oh, that's unfortunate." I shrug dropping my towel on the floor in front of him. I maneuver around the room slowly getting everything I need. I come directly next to his face and bend over to check something on my toes for no reason giving him a great view of my ass and pussy. It isn't long before I feel his lips on my pussy from behind. As good as it feels I want to torture him. And I don't know how long he will actually let me do this so I have to milk it.

I snap my body up stepping away for a second before my petty senses kick in. I get back on the bed straddling his waist and place my dripping-wet sex on his semi-erect member. I grab his throat as he uses his big hands to grip my waist. "Fuck yes baby," he whispers all too excitedly. I start to slowly rub my wetness on his member as my hand tightens around his throat. I continue my grind leaning forward on his body so that my face is in his.

"Did I say you could touch me?" He just shakes his head no with lust in his eyes. "I didn't think so," I say releasing his throat and getting off of him to get dressed. I throw on his grey sweatpants and white bralette. This is too much going on at like 7 in the morning but I am enjoying every minute of this. I know once this is over he will find a way to make me pay, and honestly, I look forward to it.

He relaxes into the bed in defeat before getting up and stomping to the bathroom slamming the door shut.

He better not wake my baby with all that noise.

I still can't believe he's letting me do this. Usually, he would have thrown me over his shoulder by now. Maybe I can make him so hard that he fucks me until I pass out. Hmm, I wonder what that's like.

I check on Anya who is still fast asleep in the next room of course. Once we moved out of the newborn stages, she sleeps through the night and into the afternoon if I don't wake her up. Sis loves her sleep. I run downstairs to make a bottle so I have it ready since I will be waking her up soon.

I walk back into the room to see Jeremy sitting on the bed typing on his phone looking annoyed with his towel around his waist.

"You okay baby daddy?"

"No. My balls hurt," he grumbled. "And today is my first day officially as CEO. I'm stressed out," he pouts.

He looks so cute sitting there. His back looks like it needs some scratches.

Dammit, I knew this wouldn't last long. I am dam sure about to give in to him and It's only because I don't want him to be stressed out on his first day of work.

I drop my sweatpants on the floor and walk over to the other side of the bed to stand in front of him. He looks up from his phone eyeing me up and down. "Stop messing with me Samantha," he snaps.

I unwrap the towel from around his waist as I admire his 6-

pack and take his phone out of his hands throwing it on the bed so I can straddle his legs. I start to kiss him ever so passionately. He grabs my hips to bring me closer to him as possible. I hold myself up to slide him inside me without breaking the kiss. I attempt to slide down on him dangerously slow but he lifts his hips up to meet me instead.

I grab his throat pushing him down into the bed. "Relax. Or I'll stop," I say seductively.

I start to ride him dangerously slow. His eyes stare into mine intently. With every stroke, my hand tightens a little on his neck while his hands grip tightly on my waist. I lean over to whisper dirty things in his ear.

"Oh, baby your cock feels so good inside me."

He moans in response.

"I love feeling every inch of you deep inside me."

He digs his nails into my hips and I moan out. I kind of like pain a little bit.

"No one can ever fuck me as good as you can." I continue moaning my dirty whispers as I begin to roll my hips taking him deeper. I can see his eyes rolling back into his head as a sexy moan escapes his lips. I lick the side of his face from his chin to his ear placing a hard nibble on his ear. In return, he moans and slaps my ass.

This is kind of fun.

I feel like a bad bitch right now.

"Beg me to let you cum," I say as I continue to nibble on his ear while I slow down my rhythm to a dangerously slow pace.

"Fuck baby. Please let me cum," he struggles to say while he leans up to pull a nipple into his mouth.

"Say it again for me daddy," I moan.

"Please let me cum baby girl," he moans. I still can't believe he's letting me take this much control.

"Okay, you can cum, but only if you fuck me as hard as you can daddy."

Without a second passing, I am thrown off of him into the bed. Both my legs are placed above my head as he slams into me. One large hand holds both my ankles over my head pressing them into the bed, while the other hand is wrapped around my throat. The pounding I am getting right now is surely justified.

I let out a moan with every deep hard thrust he gives me. "You like that baby girl? You teased me and this is what you get. This is what you wanted, isn't it? You like when I fuck you like this don't you?" He says as he pounds into me harder.

"Fuck! Yes!" I moan out. I didn't think he could be so rough.

"Open your mouth," he orders and I open my mouth and stick out my tongue.

He tightens his grip on my throat and pushes himself to my deepest point as he leans forward and I watched the spit slowly drip onto my tongue.

As soon as I felt his spit on my tongue my eyes rolled back into my head immediately. I swallow it the best I could with his monster grip on my throat.

"I fucking love you," he says before he leans down to assault my lips with a dominating kiss never once easing up from her speed of fucking me. He lets go of my throat and uses his hand to rub my clit while his other hand continues to hold my feet in place. I can feel my second orgasm of the morning building.

"Fuck me baby oh my god!" I cry out as my walls clench around him and I cum hard for the second time that day. He pulls out releasing my legs as he shifts his body to straddle my chest. He places his dick in my mouth and wasted no time before he began to slam into my throat. After about 5 good thrusts he stills himself in the back of my throat and I can feel his hot seed sliding down.

"Fuck," Jeremy whispers as he empties himself. I swallow everything and keep sucking him off until his body starts to shake and he pulls away.

"I fucking love you baby," he says before leaning down and pulling me into a harsh kiss.

I love when he kisses me when I have cum in my mouth.

This has turned into a great morning. Watch me be smiling for the rest of the day.

I hang up the phone with Steven from our usual weekly catch-up. Andrea is currently 3 months pregnant and they have officially moved to Miami. He asked me about Isaiah but I basically shrugged it off and said we were no longer speaking. The man basically cheated on me and then gave me an ultimatum. Like child, please. He must have really thought he was doing something that day. Not to mention he lied to me for months. Yea fuck that man.

He did give really good head though.

I called Gerald today to check on him too after Jeremy left. He is having a BBQ this weekend and wants to see me and Anya. I had to tell him me and Isaiah were no longer together. To be honest that's the real reason I was avoiding Gerald but he understood and said he still wanted to see me which I happily obliged.

I need to go stop by the office today. I have a small wedding coming up but I need a few catering numbers and stuff that of course, I left in the office building. I like having a job where I can work from home. Everything I need is on my computer and my boss is great so it's a win-win. Plus my extended maternity leave is coming in handy. I have about a month left until I have to start actually showing up again. I might as well enjoy as much time with Anya as possible until I have to go back and before I can be my own boss I have to build my event portfolio.

I can run to the office, then the mall to get Anya a swimsuit, and then spend the day in the pool with my baby girl. The kiddie pool we ordered for her finally came. Me and Jeremy agreed not to bring her into the big pool in the backyard yet. No one even uses it. I am not even sure I have been in the backyard yet as long as I have been here.

I throw on a short baby blue sun dress and I make my way downstairs to find one of my security talking with Mariella while they both play with Anya. They look a little too close for comfort but let me mind my business.

I am in such a good mood. I love it.

"Good morning," I interrupt getting their attention.

"Good morning ma'am," Vincent says stepping back quickly. Mariella turns around with a small smile but I can see that she was clearly blushing. "Do you need to go somewhere?" He says eyeing my outfit. I am fully dressed with my bag on my shoulder. I was going to try to sneak out away from the guards but it seems that's not happening.

"Yea I was just going to fun a few errands," I say skeptically.

"I will drive you Mrs. Bresset."

"Y'all gon stop calling me that," I quickly responded.

"Sorry ma'am but I insist on driving you, otherwise I can call Mr.Bresset," he trails off.

"No, it's fine. Trust me I would rather go alone."

"Well if you don't feel comfortable being with me alone, I can call Marcus or Rich," he begins. I would rather Vincent alone than the entire convoy. If you call one, then they all will show up and I don't need that type of excitement right now. Too many different energies around me are annoying sometimes. I am assuming they are not here because they went to the office with Jeremy and I didn't tell Jeremy I was leaving or he would have made all 3 of them stay home.

"Nope! That's okay you can drive me. Let's go. Mariella, I'll be back in about an hour, unless you want me to bring Anya with me?" I feel bad leaving her with Mariella sometimes.

"No. You know I love spending time with her. Go enjoy some kid-free mommy time," she says sweetly.

"Okay as soon as I come back, we will take Anya to her first pool day. Is that okay with you?"

"Yes Bambi, love you," she says as she walks ups to me and places a kiss on my cheek.

I place a million kisses on her and Anya before walking out the door. "Love you both."

We make our way to the car where we take off down the road. My office is only about 25 minutes from the house. 15 the way these men drive especially when you take the back roads like I usually do when I go to the office. I suddenly remember to ask the question I have been wanting to ask forever now.

"Hey Vincent."

"Yes ma'am."

"What happened to Zach?"

"Zach ma'am?"

"The man you guys hauled out the other day after he tried to attack me?"

"Oh, that sorry excuse for a human? He was handed over to the proper authorities. He is in a cell and if he tries to leave we will know ma'am."

"Interesting." So he's been in a cell this whole time. I notice Vincent doesn't drive as fast as Jeremy, Marcus, or Rich. Rich drives like he's staring in a Fast and Furious movie. He is honestly the worst of the four.

Caribbean men man.

"Ma'am, I know it isn't my place to say, and I am terribly sorry if I am overstepping, but I am so sorry for what that monster did to you." This big angry German man is such a sweetie.

"It's okay Vincent, thank you. I have risen above." He nods his head in the rearview mirror turning his attention back to the road.

I am scrolling on Instagram in the back of the truck on my phone when suddenly all I hear is "What the fuck?" Before there is a loud crash. The impact sent the car flying and flipping over. I was thrown in every direction but painfully held in place by my seat belt.

By the time I understood what was happening the car had stopped rolling. I was in severe amounts of pain but still conscious. The car was upside down and I could see blood. Not my blood but blood coming from the front of the car. That's when I realize the car was directly hit on the driver's side.

I struggle with my seat belt to try to grab my phone that was thrown from my hand. I finally get it off falling to the floor hard seeing that I was hanging upside down. I am in even more pain now and the ringing in my ears isn't helping. I look around to see if I see anyone calling 911 but I see not a soul on these back streets.

I yell out for Vincent but he doesn't answer. I reach around to check his pulse finding a small one. He is covered in so much blood. I need to call 911. Focus Samantha.

As I am reaching for my phone the door flies open. Someone wearing all black and a ski mask drags me by my ankle.

I start to scream as I reach for my phone but the person yanks me harshly pulling me out of the car. I scream for help and for Vincent but there is no one around and Vincent is still unconscious.

I start to fight as best I could considering the amount of pain that is radiating through my body. I am instead met with a damp cloth placed over my face. I fight as hard as I could before my arms and legs felt weak.

I keep fighting until everything goes black and the darkness takes me.

Chapter 28

Jeremy Bresset

• •

"I'm sorry sir there was no one else in the car."

"What the fuck do you mean there was no one else in the car? My wife was in that car. Her phone was in it."

"There were no cameras on the street where the accident happened. The driver was lucky someone just happened to drive down the road and find him."

"Fuck!" I cry out. I can't do anything else but that. My baby girl is missing. What the fuck? How could this happen? I have to stay strong. Marcus and Rich are on their way to the hospital now as we speak. I am now speaking to the useless cops in the room but of course, they don't care enough to help when a black woman goes missing.

"Sir, if you would be kind enough to provide a picture of her we will see what we can do. Trust us when we say we will do everything in our power to find the missing woman."

"My wife," I snap the correction at them. "She is not just a missing woman, she is a wife, a sister, and a mother," I snap at them.

At the same time, Marcus and Rich rush into the hospital room to see Vincent unconscious. Marcus's eyes widen and Rich looks broken. "What happened?" Rich snaps.

"He was driving Sam somewhere when a car hit them and she was taken."

I finally say it out loud. She was taken. My baby girl was taken from me. "I already sent extra guards to watch Mariella and Anya."

"How long has she been gone?" Marcus asks.

"A little over 2 hours," I answer. "Where is Zachary?"

"Still in jail," Marcus responds not taking his angry eyes off Vincent. "Is he going to live?"

"They don't know. He's in a coma the doctors say. He hit his head pretty hard who knows if he will even remember anything," I say rolling my eyes.

I am so frustrated I don't know what to do.

"I will put together a team to find her sir. Rich take Mr. Bresset home."

"No. I am staying here with Vincent." Rich snaps through his tears. "I'm not leaving my best friend man." Marcus hesitates but nods his head in response.

"Please let me know any and everything you find." I say to Marcus." He nods his head before quickly walking out the door. I look back at Rich who has his head down in Vincent's bed.

I walk over to put my hand on Rich's shoulder. "He's strong, he will make it. Call me if you need anything," I say as Rich looks up at me nodding his head. I walk over to the nurse's station and tell them to call me the minute the patient wakes up before walking out. I need to see Anya.

I hop in my car and make my way back home. I need to be with my baby girl. I must be doing a mile a minute until I get to the house. I couldn't focus on anything else but making it to the house. Tears were brimming in my eyes the entire way home. I needed to see her and make sure her and my mother were safe. I don't know how I will survive if something happens to Samantha.

I park the car in front of the house, run inside past the guards, and run straight inside. I see my mom is in tears while holding Anya. I relax a little knowing they are safe.

"Oh Jeremy," she runs to me in tears. "Where is she? Did they find her?" She says frantically through her tears.

"No," Is all I can mutter out before I collapse into the floor with tears in my eyes. I let out a cry releasing everything I have been holding all day since I got the call that my car had been hit and her phone was found. My chest hurts and I can barely breathe. I need her. My mother tries her best to console me but nothing works. I failed. I failed Anya, I failed her mother. If I had never come back into her life, none of this would have happened. I was selfish and couldn't stay away from her.

Fuck.

I just want my baby back in my arms.

My mom finally got me to calm down a little as I sit with Anya. It's like my baby can sense what I need. She is holding on to my neck with her head on my chest while she quietly sucks her binky. Samantha always says babies can sense energy. I guess she knows this is exactly what I need at this moment. She is the only thing bringing me comfort while we wait. I hug her tightly before I begin to sob again.

I haven't prayed in a while. But lord, if there is someone out there listening, please bring her back to me. I can't go on without her. Please don't take the love of my life away. Please don't take the mother of my baby away. I love her. I start to sob even harder at the end of my silent prayer.

I look at Anya admiring all the features she has gotten from her mother. Her curly hair, her beautiful dark skin, her perfect smile, and how she wears her bracelet the way Samantha always wears the necklace I got her for mother's day. I trace my fingers over the bracelet on her wrist that spells out ANYA that I got for her that she never takes off just like her mom doesn't take her necklace off.

Wait.

Bracelet.

Necklace.

Air tag!

"I put an air tag inside the heart of the necklace I got her for mother's day!" I yell out loud at the realization startling Anya. Anya fusses a little as I shush her. She can curse me out about it later.

After she turned off her location after me and Isaiah had that fight, I took extra precautions. I was scared as hell not knowing where she ran off to that day. She will kill me when she finds out but it's okay. She always wondered why she couldn't open the locket. It's because I glued it shut with the air tag inside.

I quickly put Anya down in her bassinet and grab my phone to call Marcus, but I don't get the chance because at the same time, my phone rings, and it's Rich. Mariella stares at me intently as she takes Anya into her arms consoling her.

"Yea, how is he.... He saw who hit the car?...... Are you fucking serious?.... Come to the house right now and bring your gear I have an air tag in her necklace. "I couldn't believe what I was hearing.

"FUCK!" I yell out this is all my fault. "No no no fuck!"

"Jeremy what happened!" My mom yells out.

"We know who took her."

"Who?"

Samantha Pov

I open my eyes letting out a groggy moan. I feel like shit. I try to rub my hand on my throbbing head, but I can't move it. I look up to see that I am zip tied to the side of a bed. This isn't my bed. I instantly panic. I look around to see that this bedroom looks oddly family to mine and Jeremy's.

What the fuck?

I check my body for any cuts and scrapes from the accident but there is nothing visible. Surprisingly though, any cuts I did have from fighting were bandaged up. Who the fuck would kidnap me and then cater to my wounds? I start to fidget with the zip tie the best I can to see if I can get loose.

"Stop that," A voice booms across the room. I snap my head forward to meet big green eyes.

"What the fuck? You did this? Why?" I ask confused

"It was the only way. We can finally be together now." He says smiling. "I have waited so long for this Samantha," he adds while walking towards me. He yanks the sheet off of my body exposing me still in my dress. Thank god I am not naked. He climbs on the bed to start placing kisses on my legs. "I have

302

waited so long to taste you," he whispers against my skin.

I try to kick him but he grabs both my ankles pinning them under his legs causing me to cry out in pain.

"Marcus please stop this! You're hurting me." He immediately let's go.

"I would never hurt you. I am sorry. I am nothing like those monsters you have been with in the past. See I am better than both of them. Jeremy broke your heart then got you pregnant and left you, then he put you in danger over and over again. The first time I laid eyes on you I knew you were meant to be mine. I would never hurt you like either of those other men did."

You're hurting me now dipshit.

"Marcus just let me go, I promise I won't tell anyone," I start to cry. Please tell me everyone is safe. I hope he hasn't gotten to Anya.

"Why would I let you go princess? We will be together from now on. I will protect you the way that Jeremy never could. When I found out what that disgusting man did to you that day, I made sure he regretted it. I made him scream how sorry he was as he bled out.

"What? No no! Zachary's in Jail," I whisper confused.

"Yes, that's what my men were told but I couldn't help it. Finding out he hurt you made me so angry. Don't worry I took my time with him. I made sure he felt every ounce of pain he inflicted on you twice over until he took his last breath. It was honestly a little fun," he says smiling as he lays next to me pulling my body to his. He starts to play with the coils of my hair.

I pull my head away from him. Not only is he touching me but did this white man just touch my hair? I know I have no right considering the situation I am in but I look at him like he is nuts.

"Oh sorry, I was just so fascinated by it. I did research on type four hair and brought all the hair products that recommend for your hair online. I figured you would need them since you will be living here now," he smiled at me.

"Live here? You're a killer. I can't live with a killer. You killed Zachary," I spat at him.

"Don't tell me you are angry that he is gone? He deserved it. He hurt you. I won't let anyone get away with hurting you."

"You hurt me. You literally hit me with a car, kidnapped me, and drugged me."

"That wasn't hurting you. That was saving you."

This nigga...

I want to ask so badly if he took Anya, but if he didn't then I didn't want to give him any ideas. I look away from him staring at the ceiling with tears falling from my eyes. How am I going to get myself out of this?

"To be honest Samantha," he whispers tracing a finger up and down my cheek. I really wish he would stop constantly touching me. "I loved you from the very first time I laid eyes on you. You can pretend you didn't want this too but I know you did. From the very first time you came outside in those sexy shorts and those cute little bunny slippers and you yelled my name," he said while tracing his finger up and down my thigh under my dress. "Ugh," he moaned out. "I could picture you screaming my name over and over again. I knew you wore those shorts for me. I would listen to when you and him had sex and how loud your moans were. I know you were moaning that loudly so I could hear you. I know you were doing it just for me. You were challenging me to see if I could make you moan louder and I surely will be doing that today," he says as he sniffs my neck.

"Your scent is so captivating," he continues. "That night you made me carry you, I knew you just wanted to touch you, I could smell you that night, I imagined stopping the car and fucking you in the back of it until you cried from your orgasms. Touching you that night awakened something inside me. I will make you feel things that he never could," he whispers into my neck as he traces circles on my stomach.

I could feel the tears running down my face as he spoke. This man is nuts.

"But I still wasn't sure if you wanted me or not. You seemed a little infatuated with him on your trip. I was there for you always. I even watched him fuck you on the balcony. I hid as I jerked off imagining it was me who was fucking you on the balcony. You can deny it princess but I know you only fucked him in the open so I could see. I know you were walking alone that night cause you knew I was following you. You wanted me to fuck you right there on that beach. Sending mixed signals wasn't nice princess. You would send me signals then go be with him. It wasn't fair to me, to us, to our girl, or our future children."

"I already see Anya as mine I just have to go get her later." I start to sob uncontrollably at his words.

"No please!" I cry out. "I would rather have our own kids, leave Anya with Jeremy so he can have something to remember me by. Please."

"Anything you want princess. I will do anything for you.

Except let you go," he says smiling at my words. I visibly relax knowing he will leave her where she is, but that one piece of relief doesn't stop the tears from rolling down my face. "I also started calling you princess because that monster called you Muñeca. It's not special to me anymore. Do you like it princess?"

I don't answer I just continue to cry. As long as Anya is safe I no longer care about myself.

"Don't cry, princess." He says moving to softly pepper kisses on my shoulder in an attempt to console me. I immediately flinch and shrug him off in response. "You know that day we shared a moment together in the mall when you got her ears pierced? I was going to take you that night I just couldn't find an opening. But now everything is good. I have you all to myself. Finally, we can be together." He says as he moves to kiss my neck. I instantly flinch away. "Stop running from me princess, I don't like it."

This man isn't nuts, he's bat-shit crazy. I quickly scurry away from him in fear. "Get away from me," I manage to choke out through my tears

He lets out a deep sigh. "I knew this wouldn't be easy. I know what to do. You keep crying but I am going to make you feel better don't worry princess. I wanted to wait until after we were married to try for babies, or at least until we leave the country tomorrow. But you look so beautiful laying there that I just have to have you right now." My eyes widen in fear as I watch him get off the bed. He stands to rip his shift off before climbing back on top of me placing kisses on my chest and face.

Fuck.

"No please Marcus," I cry out as I try to wiggle from under him.

"Shhhh," he says lowering himself to the bed. I start to kick and cry the best I could but he held on to my ankles. I try to use my other hand to push him away but I don't succeed.

He huffs as he takes another pair of zip ties out of his back pocket to bring my ankle up to hook it to my wrist. I am so fucking uncomfortable like this. But that's when I notice it. I am in a compromising position.

He lifts my dress and rips my panties off throwing them in the corner of the room. I continue to move around the best I can but it's no use. I can't break free. I keep moving and hoping he will get annoyed that I am not keeping still but it's no use.

"I have waited so long for this princess. I have waited so long to taste you," he said before leaning his head down between my legs. I scream and cry at the top of my lungs but there is no use. My body betrays me.

He stayed there with his head between my legs for what felt like 15 minutes. He wouldn't stop. I eventually gave us fighting and screaming after my throat got hoarse. The tears however wouldn't stop.

When he finally stopped, I think I had already shut down mentally.

I only found my fight again when I heard him unbuckling his belt. "I am going to make you feel better than you did 2 minutes ago princess," he says smiling, licking his lips, wiping off his mouth, and sucking his fingers off. I look at him in disgust. He finally opens his pants but thank god for his phone rings at the same time.

He rolls his eyes and jumps off the bed to walk to the counter to pick it up.

"What?...... Vincent got hit by a truck?.. She's missing?... Oh no," he says with a smile on his face but he keeps his voice concerned. "Okay, I'll be at the hospital in about 10 minutes," he said before hanging up the phone.

"I'll be back to you in no time princess, I have to go put on an act so no one suspects it's me. As much as I want to tell Jeremy about us, he is a good boss so I will let you do it when you're ready. Not today but soon. Once you have accepted us. I have to make sure Vincent is dead too. No witnesses. No one will come between me and my princess." he walks over to me and starts to rub my legs. "When I come back, I am not going to stop. I can't wait to be inside of you. I love you."

He buckles his pants and released my ankle from the zip tie but cutting it with a box cutter. My leg is in pain from the ridiculously uncomfortable position I was just stuck in.

He grabs my face as I turn away from him to place a lingering kiss on my lips. I try to fight him off and tighten my lips until he lets go.

He grabs his keys and his phone before looking back at me with a bright smile. He looks so pleased with himself and I am so disgusted.

I use this as my opportunity to try and break free from the zip tie. My hair is in braids so I have no need for body pins. I start to tug against the zip tie as hard as I could but it was no use.

I go in for one final attempt, using whatever energy I have left, and pull on the zip tie as hard as I can. I think this is one of the most painful things I have ever done in my life.

The zip tie digs into my skin causing blood to start to flow but I refuse to stop. I have to get out of this.

I sigh with a pain-filled relief as the zip tie pops but not without causing significant damage to my skin and wrist.

Honestly can't believe that worked. I dart straight for the door after wrapping my wrist in a piece of cloth I found but of course, it's locked from the outside.

Fuck me.

I run to the curtains but there are no windows behind them only lights. I look for anything that can get me out of this room. I would much rather kill myself than have to endure this man when he gets back.

I must have been searching the room for at least half an hour. I settled on breaking a vase to use the shards as a weapon to stab him in the neck when he comes back. I wait patiently until I hear footsteps. I tried looking for anything to help me communicate with the outside world but I never wear my apple watch and I remember leaving my phone in the car. Fuck I hope Vincent is okay.

I have nothing on me that can be tracked or used to communicate. The only thing I am wearing is a dress, I am barefoot, and I am wearing that stupid locket that Jeremy got me that won't open.

I am startled when I hear footsteps.

Fuck.

I take my position behind the door. I plan on stabbing him straight in the neck when he comes into the room. No questions asked. The footsteps grow closer and I try to slow my breathing. I can do this. The lock shimmy and I heard a voice so sweet. "Samantha!"

My eyes widen as I break out into a sob. "Jeremy!" I cry out.

"I'm going to break down the door. Move!" I quickly back up from the door.

After a few loud bangs, the door flies off the hinges. Jeremy storms in with his eyes searching the room until he finds me. He pulls me into his arms first examining my body to make sure I am okay. He relaxes a little before pulling me into a tight embrace as I cry into his shoulder.

"Shhh, baby girl I am here now. We have to go baby," he says kissing my hair. He starts to lead me out of the door when the sound of a gun is cocked back. We both look up to see Marcus stepping towards us with red eyes.

"You couldn't just let us be happy could you?" He says to Jeremy. Jeremy quickly pushes me behind him. "Come to me princess," he snaps at me. I shuffle behind Jeremy instead.

"What are you doing Marcus? You were supposed to protect her!" Jeremy yells.

Umm Jeremy hun. Tone it down crazy dude got a gun.

"I am protecting her!" He yells raising the gun at Jeremy. I can protect her where you never could. Now come here to me princess! I won't ask again! Don't make me do something I will regret," he pleads.

"Please Marcus, don't hurt us. Just let me go, please," I cry.

"Look at that. You made her cry you piece of shit. She doesn't want you Jeremy. Tell him you don't want him so we can be happy together princess," Marcus says angrily.

"Marcus, please," I cry as I hold on to Jeremy a little tighter. I keep looking back and forth between him and the gun praying he doesn't use it.

"I could never let you go. I love you way too much," he says as he looks back and forth between me and Jeremy before he starts to chuckle. Oh, I see, if you're dead then this will make it easier for her. Don't worry princess, I will do anything for you." He raises his gun again.

This time I heard a loud bang as a body dropped to the floor. I immediately let out a blood-curdling scream.

Chapter 29

Jeremy Bresset

· ·

I am sitting in the hospital hallway covered in blood with my hands clasped over my face with my leg shaking. I must have prayed 100 times since she was shot and until now. I have died a thousand times in the last 48 hours, first the kidnapping now this. Now she is in emergency surgery and I have no update on her condition. She was perfectly fine and in my arms one second then down the next.

A few hours ago...

A gun went off as Marcus collapses to the floor groaning. Samantha screamed immediately grabbing me and making sure I wasn't shot. Rich kicked the gun away from Marcus. He is throwing curse words from the floor while the rest of the guards swarm in. Once Samantha is finally done checking my body to calm herself. She relaxes a little pulling me in for a hug and sobbing into my shoulder. We pull apart for a second when another gun goes off. I snap my head down seeing Marcus with an evil smirk on his face while spitting up blood pointing a gun in the air. "If I can't have her, no one can," he manages to choke out. The cops release a slur of bullets into him and attack and restrain him.

I look down and see Sam covered in blood on the floor.

What the fuck?

I am in so much shock. I don't even know when I had gotten on my knees to apply pressure to the bleeding wound on her chest. There was so much blood I couldn't tell you exactly where she got shot. Was it her shoulder? Her chest? I couldn't tell you.

My main focus was to stop the bleeding. Was he aiming for her heart? I start to cry and yell for help when I see her starting to grow pale. Her glowing dark skin was now a color close to grey.

"Talk to me baby come on!" I yell. She tries to say something but she just takes a shaky deep breath instead, I can feel her body starting to shake from under my hands. "Come on baby, please. Hold on for me okay!" I can see the sweat growing on her forehead. The ambulance was already on its way just in case anything wrong happened thank god because it only took them 2 minutes to get into the room.

Rich had to pry me away from her so that they could work. I couldn't stop crying. Seeing her like this was the most heartbreaking thing I have ever experienced. My heart has been breaking nonstop since yesterday.

"Be careful she's prone to blood clots!" I finally yell to the EMT. They nod their heads in response as they continue to work.

I drove behind the ambulance with Rich all the way to the hospital before they rushed her into emergency surgery.

Now here we are.

The nurses in the hospital and the guards that came with us kept offering me ways to clean myself up but I don't dare move, I just ignore them. It's been 3 hours and I haven't heard a single update. I don't want to move a muscle until I know if she's okay. My mom is on her way with Anya after Rich called her but I don't want to see Anya.

I don't want to see Anya knowing I failed her mother. Because of my own selfish ways, she may lose her mother. I love Anya with all my heart but I don't deserve to look at her.

"Jeremy!" My mom runs down the hall with Anya pushing her in her stroller. The tears that had finally stopped have started flowing again without warning. She stops for a second so she can take in my appearance. She hands a sleeping Anya in the stroller to Rich as I put my head down sobbing uncontrollably. I can tell she wants to hug me but I am still covered in her blood.

"Family of Samantha Kage," a voice says. Everyone stands including the guards. The woman eyes me curiously since I am covered in blood but I don't have the time. Can she get on with it already?

"I am her mother-in-law." My mom speaks since I just can't find the voice to do so.

"The bullet was lodged in her clavicle but we were able to remove it. It was a little touch and go for a second but she is going to pull through. She will be in an immense amount of pain for a while." I visibly relax for the first time in 3 hours. Before I can think another sob breaks out. She's okay. She is going to be okay. Thank god. "You guys can see her in ICU in about an hour. She won't wake up for a while though." My mother thanked the doctor and I finally walk over to Anya to look at her in the stroller. I lean over whispering to my sleeping baby that her mom is going to make it.

"Jeremy I brought you a change of clothes. Go get cleaned up, she cannot see you like this," my mother says softly. The nurses bring me to another side of the hospital so I can clean up and shower. I break down one more time in the shower. I couldn't get the image of her bleeding out of my head. I shower and change my clothes as quickly as possible putting on black joggers and a black hoodie with some black socks and Nike slides.

I walk back up to the area where everyone is waiting to go into ICU. I walk up to my mom to see she is on the phone. I eye her curiously. "The name of the hospital?.... Umm hold on." She turns to me. "What's the name of this hospital?" I shake my head saying I don't know, plus I don't know who she is talking to. We walk over to the nurse's station to ask.

"Excuse me what hospital is this?" She asks the nurse.

"Oh, this is Serenity Kage memorial hospital," the nurse says with a smile before going back to type on her computer. My eyes widen at the realization. This is the hospital where her mother died.

"Serenity Kage memorial... Okay... See you soon." She says sadly as she hangs up the phone.

"Who was that?" I ask her curiously.

"Gerald. I called him to let him know. He is coming with Isaiah and Ms.Genesis." I start to roll my eyes at the mention of his name. Fuck it, this isn't about me, she needs to be surrounded by people who love her.

"You guys can see her now," the doctor says. "We moved her into a private suite room per your request Mr.Bresset." I nod my head as we follow the doctor. My mother, Anya, Rich, and I leave the other guards behind to come into her room.

My heart breaks upon entering the room. she has a visible cast under her hospital gown on her chest. Her color had come back a little thank god. Even laying there she still took my breath away. My mother breaks out into a sob at the sight of her. I take up Anya and take a seat next to the bed. Maybe hearing Anya's coos will help her wake up. My mother pulled the chair up on the other side of the bed as she started to pray.

We sat in comfortable silence for a while with the machines

beeping in the background, and Anya drifting in and out of sleep.

Suddenly the door flies open and an older black man stomps in with red eyes. Rich immediately stands to stop him, but my mom holds up her hand.

"Gerald. I wish we would stop meeting like this." He looks like he models older men's clothes for Versace. My mother stands pulling him into a tight hug. He looks over at Samantha on the bed tearing up while looking back and forth between her and Anya.

Anya perks up reaching for him. I stand to hand her off as she giggles. My poor girl doesn't know what's going on and I am glad. She always knows who needs to be held. She is very comforting that way. My baby is an empath.

I watch as he wraps his arm around Anya pulling her to him as he starts to sob. "This is the floor her mother died on," he choked out. For the 50th time today, I feel the tears come into my eyes again. My girl deserves better than this.

She deserves better than me.

Ms.Genesis walks in with Isaiah behind her. Immediately Ms.Genesis walks over to Samantha, kisses her forehead, and starts to fix her hair into a braid bonnet. Shit, why didn't I think of that? Samantha had explained to me a while back that her first name is Genesis but they just call her Ms.Genesis because she is sassy and its respectful.

Everyone takes their seats around her keeping her company until she wakes up in silence. We often pass Anya around so she can do the thing she does where she brings comfort to anyone that is holding her. My little girl truly is special. Samantha blessed me with a great girl. "What happened,"

Isaiah says with an attitude that finally breaks the room's semi-comfortable silence. All eyes turn to me with curiosity.

I proceed to tell them the story of the text messages and about how one of her security guards turned into a stalker and kidnapped her but I got her back. I was hit with disapproving looks.

I couldn't help feeling like everything that has happened to her was my fault. I could blame my father because he was the gust of the wind that made the first domino fall making the rest of them follow falling behind, but that's not the case. The blame is on me. If I had never forced myself back into her life twice then none of this would have happened.

"She was safer with me," Isaiah snaps.

"Isaiah!" Ms.Genesis and Gerald snap at the same time.

"Sh- shut up."

"What? He knows it's true. She was never in danger when she was with me. The clear danger was always him," he said shooting me a glare.

"shut ...up."

"You're still upset you couldn't trick her into loving you?" I snap.

"Jeremy!" My mom snaps at me.

"Shut up. Oh my god," I hear a raspy voice say. All of our heads snap around to see Samantha opening her eyes weakly. I am frozen in my seat. Why do I suddenly feel worst?

Samantha Pov

"Oh my god!" Mariella yells grabbing my hand and squeezing it. Here sis go with the tears. "How do you feel Bambi?"

"Ow, water," is all I can mutter out. I was trying to tell them to shut up for a good 4 minutes. Yelling like my dam head doesn't hurt. Rich leaves quickly to go grab water. I look around taking in the faces all around me. Ms. Genesis, Gerald, Isaiah, Jeremy, Mariella, and my baby girl. I pray this isn't a dream. I was having terrible dreams about Marcus the whole time I was asleep. I cringe at the memory of him touching me.

Rich comes back with the water and a straw quickly. The cold water going down my throat feels like heaven. I drink quickly while taking a deep breath as everyone greets me with smiles, nods, or tears, except Jeremy. Jeremy has a stone-cold expression staring at me.

"I am going to go call the nurse," Jeremy says standing quickly exiting. I am a little hurt that he hasn't said anything to me yet.

"What happened?" I ask, directing my question at rich who is red-eyed standing in the corner.

Rich looks around the room for a second before looking back at me. "Marcus is gone, and you are safe that's all you need to know Sam." I smile at him saying my first name. Suddenly I remember something.

"How's Vincent? Please tell me he's okay?" Rich simply smiles and nods his head. I look over at my girl, I have missed her all too much. I go to reach for her in Mariella's arms but the movement of my arm sends pain through me that I can't fathom. I fall back into the bed letting out a groan of displeasure. Then everything comes back to me.

Me getting shot, Jeremy crying, Marcus getting shot again. The last thing I remember is getting in the ambulance. Must have been when I passed out. At least me and my baby girl are safe now but I can't move my shoulder in this cast.

This is ghetto.

"There she is!" My doctor comes in with Jeremy walking behind her with his head down. She looks at my chart for a few seconds then proceeds to check the machines. "Everything looks to be okay, we do want to keep you here for at least a week since you are prone to blood clots and the trauma to your body wasn't good for the fetus considering the complications with your last pregnancy. We want to keep a close eye on both of you."

What the fuck she just said?

"Oh, I don't have a fetus I have a 7-month-old. Right there." I say giggling and denying her claims while pointing my chin to Anya and smiling.

"Nope, my records show you're about 3 weeks along. I take it this is news so congratulations." She says smiling after checking the cart one more time.

I blink at her confused.

"You sure you got the right chart?"

"GSW to the clavicle," she says reading the chart. "Yes, I am sure."

The fuck?

I start to laugh. I wince at the pain but it doesn't stop me from laughing. "Oh, I see I am still dreaming."

"No my love. I promise you that you're awake." I look at her like she's crazy. Mariella, Ms.Genesis, and Gerald look happy meanwhile Isaiah looks annoyed. Jeremy however looks just as confused as I do.

"Lady I got my birth control out like 4 days ago because it shifted in my arm. I cannot be pregnant," I said blinking at her as if the answer is going to magically change.

"Yea, sometimes it shifts a while before you feel any pain, and also it's only 99 percent effective. Well if you want we can explore your options, I will come back and talk to you when everyone leaves. But for now, no stress and try not to move your arm." She nods her head before walking out but stops at the door. "You wouldn't happen to have any relation to Serenity Kage, would you?" She says turning around to me.

"Yes, she was my mother why?" I ask looking around the room.

"Wow, you're one of the Kage twins?" She says curiously.

"Why are you asking me this?" Like lady stop questioning me. I just went through a lot.

"Well this is Serenity Kage memorial hospital and your mother's story is the reason I became a doctor. It is my honor to be your doctor," She says nodding her head and offering me a smile before exiting.

I'm pregnant? This is the hospital my mother died in? I don't know which one is the more shocking at this point. What kind of supersonic sperm does Jeremy have to counteract my birth control?

I have nothing to say. My mouth is just sitting there hanging open. I know it's not Isaiah's because I am only 3 weeks along, plus we always used condoms. Now here comes Jeremy's John Wick level sperm to come and impregnate me. I am mad. I mean am happy and blessed, but I'm big mad.

The room is silent for a few seconds.

"Congratulations!" Mariella squeals. Gerald and Ms.Genesis follow with their congratulations but I am still in shock. Apparently so is Jeremy because he hasn't moved from his spot or said anything.

"I think we should leave these two alone so they can talk," I hear Ms. Genesis say. I can only assume it's her since I am not paying attention and have been staring at the wall for the past 5 minutes because I don't know where else to look. I hear everyone finally get up to leave. As soon as the door closes my eyes snap to him.

He stays in his spot saying nothing not even looking at me. I'm over this. I move to try and sit up, I groan in pain when he rushes over to me.

"Oh, now you acknowledge me. What's your fucking problem?" I snap at him. He makes sure I am comfortable before stepping back and looking at the floor saying nothing again. "Now you can't even talk to me? Do you hate me or something?"

His glossy eyes finally snap up to meet mine. "I hate myself," he says quietly.

"Why Jeremy?"

"This is my fault. If I had stayed away then none of this would have happened, and none of this bad stuff would have happened to you. You would be happy and safe. I should have stayed away in Miami. If I had then."

"Then we wouldn't have Anya," I say cutting him off. His eyes widen with realization at my words. "Then we wouldn't have this baby growing inside me. This isn't your fault Jeremy. I don't blame you for any of it," I say holding back my tears. Is this what he has been carrying on his shoulders? How can he blame himself for Marcus getting obsessed with me?

"I'm no good for you Samantha," he says as he breaks out into a sob.

"Jeremy come here." He slowly walks over to me. "Climb in on my good side." He shakes his head no but I huff and he complies. I move over as best I could as he lays next to me in the bed. "Jeremy I do not blame you for anything. You do know that right? I kind of blame your father but that is neither here nor there. I love you, and you are not going anywhere. Okay?"

"How is it that you have been kidnapped and shot yet you're the one consoling me? I love you so much Samantha don't ever scare me like that again." He reaches up placing a kiss on my forehead. Slowly he reaches his hand over while placing it on my stomach. "I meant what I said though. I really don't deserve you. You're too perfect for me." I place my hand on top of his.

"I am far from perfect."

The door creeps open and Mariella pokes her head inside. "Okay the coast is clear, they look fine!" She yells as everyone enters the room again.

Everyone stays for a while just talking to each other. Mariella takes Anya home, while Gerald and the rest head out. Finally, it is just me and Jeremy in the room. He is laying next to me when It finally comes out.

The realizations hit me all at once. I was kidnapped, Marcus t-touched me, if he had taken me out of the country I would have been pregnant and Jeremy would have never known. I might have never seen my girl again. Before I can do anything about it, all my feelings hit me all at once and the tears start to flow nonstop.

"Let it out, baby girl." Jeremy pulls me as close to him as possible as I sob into his chest.

Chapter 30

Samantha Kage

It's been almost 3 months since I got out of the hospital. Anya is growing and developing every day along with my little bundle of kicks. She has become oddly attached to me as if she is afraid she is going to lose me. Jeremy has been working a lot more lately but as CEO it was understandable. He tried to make as much time for me and Anya as he could but sometimes he would just come home and go straight to bed. I honestly didn't mind, I knew he was working hard and I appreciated the time he managed to spend with me when he could. I am proud of him. I hope he knows that. I should tell him more often.

Rich and Vincent still work for us. But only them because we trust them fully. We got rid of everyone else. Jeremy decided to take no chances, plus I can see the budding friendship between Mariella and Vincent. She visited him in the hospital often.

What was really annoying is Jeremy treating me like I am a fragile little thing. He won't even let me walk down the steps without him next to me. Like sir, I had a whole baby before this. I think I can manage simply walking down carpeted steps since I wasn't allowed to walk down the wooden ones. It was worst when I first came out of the hospital though. He wouldn't even let me walk while I had my cast on my arm. He took a week or two off from work and carried me everywhere. I had to draw the line at the bathroom but he would still help me get in there and then come back and carry me out. It's not like my legs were in a cast.

I had trouble handling Anya while I had the cast on. I spent most of the first few weeks laying in bed with her crawling around me. It made me a little sad. Almost as if I was neglecting to hold my girl.

In the last few months, Annabelle has left Angel. You best believe I told her everything I found out as soon as I could. And when I say as soon as I could, I mean as soon as she came to visit me in the hospital I sang like a fucking bird.

She now has a new man and she is actually happy thank god. His name is Timothy I think.

I have fixed my relationship with Isaiah, we are now good friends again. He is also Steven's son's godfather. He did however tell me that if Jeremy fucked up, he would be waiting.

Steven offered to come to visit me but I declined. Andrea needs him more but we still have our weekly phone calls.

Today I decided to go visit Jeremy with Anya and my almost 4-month-old belly at work to bring him lunch. Then I have a doctor's appointment with a new doctor Jeremy recommended. He is a private doctor who is much closer to the house. As much as I loved the doctor at Serenity Kage Memorial, she is just too far to travel to as often as I need.

I throw on a short white sundress that showcases my bump. My bump seems a little big for 4 months but the doctor assured me that It was normal. I will just ask again when I go to Jeremy's doctor later. I don't know why Jeremy was so adamant about using this doctor but it is what it is.

I get myself and Anya dressed to head down the stairs. Mariella moved into her new house officially, but she is still here almost 5 days a week to help or just stare at Anya. She was here a lot more when I had my cast on. The lady really does love her granddaughter.

I was carrying her diaper bag on one arm with Anya on my hip walking down the wooden stairs when Rich immediately ran up to me to grab the bag and wrap his hand around my waist. I rolled my eyes dramatically.

"Sorry Sam, Mr.Bresset's orders." I sigh continuing to walk down the stairs. I am about to just start sleeping downstairs until I give birth because Jeremy is annoying me. Actually, that doesn't sound like a bad idea. I don't know if he is annoying me or if I am just horny and mad because of these pregnancy hormones. Sure the sex is great but he gets upset when I don't allow him to give me head. I haven't let him put his lips down there since that day. The first time he tried to give oral pleasure I cried.

I was immediately taken back to that room and I dam near had a panic attack when he tried.

He seems bothered by it but he doesn't push it. I will let him do it when I am ready. I grab the food I packed on the counter before heading out the doors.

I strap Anya in her car seat and climb in with the help of Rich. I currently want to do nothing more than sleep in this car but the baby just keeps kicking the shit out of me. It feels like he or she has a foot in my bladder, a foot in my ribs, and its arm pushing on my back. This baby better be a future gold medal gymnast I tell you that much.

We arrive at Jeremy's office and park in the private garage. I grab Anya while Rich grabs the diaper bag and the food. We make our way to the private elevator going straight up to Jeremy's office. I walk in to see him on his phone and typing away on his computer at the same time. I must have been standing there for 5 minutes before he looked up at me. He holds up his finger to tell me one minute. I nod at Rich who walks over to the desk to place the food down. He leaves the diaper bag on the floor next to the couch before exiting the room.

I walk over to the couch to sit with Anya until he is done on the phone.

"I am sorry baby," he says to me. I look up with a small smile before he walks over to me resting a hand on my stomach and kissing my lips.

"It's okay. Please eat something before we go to the doctor," I beg.

"Did you eat?" He says concerned.

"I tried. I can't keep anything down today." He nods in response going back to the desk to eat and taking Anya with him. The morning sickness that comes with this pregnancy is a bitch. I made him Shrimp scampi along with stuffed shells just like Mariella taught me. He would occasionally stick a piece of pasta in Anya's mouth. Watching them bond was so cute. It warmed my heart. I couldn't wait to watch these two bond as well.

I lay on the couch falling asleep. I am so exhausted and I don't know why but Jeremy's office couch is so comfortable. A little commotion with the door rattling causes me to fly awake. I look over at Jeremy who looks alarmed. He quickly stands with Anya and walks over to me to stand in front of me. He grabs his phone making a phone call. I am assuming it's to Rich.

"What the hell is going on out there!" He yells. I stand to try and hear what's going on but to no avail. Jeremy rolls his eyes. "Let her in," he says annoyed.

Out of habit, I rest two protective hands on my stomach unaware of who is on the other side of the door. The door flies open with a blonde idiot stomping inside with Rich on her tail. "Calm down ma'am," Rich yells. She pauses when she sees me and Jeremy. The tears begin to gloss her eyes.

Why is she here?

Her eyes shift from sadness to anger when her eyes dart from me to my stomach to Jeremy over and over again.

"What do you need Tiffany," Jeremy says sounding annoyed.

"Jeremy I," her eyes dart to me. "Can we speak alone?"

"No," I answer for him.

She rolls her eyes. "Jeremy I miss you okay? I am sorry. Please can we talk? I know what I did was wrong but you have done some bad things to me too." She says taking a step closer to us. Rich immediately pulls her back shooting her a warning glare when she turns back to look at him.

"What exactly is it you want Tiffany?" He said sounding bored.

"I want us. I miss us. Please just give me another chance Jeremy," she pleads.

"No," he simply answered. I swear this man has never looked sexier than he does right now. "Is there anything else you needed?"

She looks back at me with anger. "This is all your fault. If you never came back into our lives we would not be in this mess. If you didn't trap him like the slut you are,"

"That's enough!" Jeremy snaps.

"Hey!" Rich yells startling her.

"How come she gets to have a Bresset baby, and I don't huh? I was never good enough for you Jeremy you made me feel like shit. And I couldn't keep my baby but she gets to have 2?" She says sounding broken.

"Tiffany you and I both know that baby wasn't mine."

"I loved you Jeremy. Then you left me for her. How do you think that made me feel? You pushed me to do what I did. You treated me like shit toward the end of our relationship. Are you really going to choose her? After everything we have been through? You can throw us away like that? We fight, we break up, and we get back together. That has been our pattern for years. We need to come back to the get-back-together part."

"Not that it was a choice, but I have already chosen her," he said point blank period.

"You know the only person in this world for you is me. Because deep down you're just as fucked up as I am Jeremy. The *Toxicity* is what made our relationship so fun," she says with pleading eyes.

"Are you done?" Jeremy says bored again. Man, this girl needs help.

"He will do the same thing to you. He always finds a way to fuck up," she says turning her attention toward me. "I just hope for your sake that you get out before he ruins you too. I really wasn't always like this," she said sounding heartbroken. "He broke me," she said looking at Jeremy. "Fine. I'll leave. I just hope you know the way I am is on you Jeremy." She turned on her heels stomping out of the door.

How do you go from begging him to come back to telling him that he was a terrible boyfriend in a matter of seconds? She needs help and I will pray for her.

"Anyways," Jeremy breaks the silence, "ready to go to the doctor?" I simply nod my head. I don't have any energy to react to what just happened.

I am currently sitting on the table in the small private doctor's office with my dress up and a sheet over my lower half while Jeremy plays with Anya on the chair. The doctor finally comes in to place the cool blue gel over my stomach to check on the baby with a sonogram. He is a young white man with blonde hair. He looks fresh out of med school. I would have preferred a black woman doctor but it is what it is.

He takes the gel and places it on my stomach before putting the remote on it.

"Oh, would ya look at that!" He yells with a smile on his face while clicking buttons on the computer.

"What?" I ask nervously.

"It looks like we are having two babies, not 1."

"What!" Jeremy says standing to his feet way too quickly to look at the monitor. A wide smile appears on his lips before he places two kisses on my forehead and one on my lips. I love it when he's happy.

"That explains me feeling like I am being kicked in 5 different spots at the same time."

"Yes but that means they are active. It's a good thing. Remember that." I nod my head. He eyes me curiously for a second. "Are you okay? You don't seem happy you are having twins. How are you feeling, any depression?"

"No I am happy," I assure him and Jeremy who both look at me concerned. "It's just that I am tired."

"What did you eat today?" The doctor asked concerned.

"Nothing," I respond quietly. "I can't keep anything down at all. I would just rather not attempt to avoid throwing up. I have no appetite anyway," I say sheepishly.

"Sam seriously? I thought you said you tried to eat something." Jeremy says. I simply shoot him an apologetic look. He doesn't understand throwing up every 5 minutes, my nausea, or the loss of appetite while being hungry at the same time.

"I am going to prescribe you something for your nausea but you are eating for 3 now. You must eat as much as possible. I don't want you or the twins in danger okay?"

"Okay," I say nodding my head. "Can I go now?" I am just ready to sleep and eat after taking whatever medication he gives me.

"Actually there is one more thing, I would like to do an Amniocentesis. Right now actually."

"Why? Isn't that for like genetics or something?" I ask confused.

I watch greys anatomy hoe.

"That among other things. One of the twins is a little smaller than the other, I just want to make sure there is no underlying cause for that," he says sternly.

I look over to Jeremy who nods his head at me. I don't know how I feel about a doctor I just met today performing a procedure on me but fuck it. It is what it is. If it will keep my babies healthy then that's what's important.

After a little over an hour, the procedure is done. I was scared the entire time. I felt like the needle was going to hurt the babies. The procedure itself only took about ten minutes. But I had to be monitored for about an hour after to make sure there was no bleeding or anything. Jeremy stayed by my side looking worried and concerned the entire time. If a monitor would beep too fast for a second he would panic. Hell, if I would shift uncomfortably he would panic.

I had to keep reassuring the man that I was fine. Which I was. The procedure was a little uncomfortable but I am okay. I will feel better once we get the results in a few days.

We leave to pick up my medication for my nausea and it really did help a lot. When I got home I ate everything in sight and was able to keep it down with no problem. Jeremy sat on the couch with me rubbing my feet while I ate a mango. I don't know if I was moaning because of the mango or because of my feet but I can see the fire in Jeremy's eyes. My feet were so sore after today. He placed a kiss on each foot after he was done rubbing it.

However, after I ate all that I felt sluggish and decided against walking up the stairs and stayed downstairs on the giant couch with Anya. I woke up in the middle of the night to see Anya laying next to me bathed and clothed with Jeremy sleeping behind me with his hand on my stomach. My little family is almost complete.

I smile to myself before going back to sleep.

Chapter 31

Samantha Kage

It's been a week since I saw that doctor and I have been feeling a lot better. I have officially moved downstairs for the time being. Besides the fact that Jeremy doesn't want me around the steps, I don't want to walk up them anyway, and I am officially four months pregnant with my twins.

It's too much dam work to walk up them dam stairs.

My mood has improved lately and I think I owe that to Jeremy. He has been around a lot more. It's like everything changed after we found out I was having twins. I half debated suing the birth control company because ain't no way they let twins slip through. I was happy about the twins don't get me wrong, but check your birth control ladies.

He stopped working late and has been around the house more often. Sometimes he works from home but he still makes time for me even when he is busy upstairs. I think I was just having a little depression but things are really starting to get better and I couldn't be happier. I am finally happy. I really hope I stay this way.

"Hi Bambi," Mariella says walking in while I am sitting in the kitchen eating.

"Hi mom!" I squeal, I am in such a good mood today I don't know why. I am sitting in the kitchen eating donuts stuffed with ice cream, with a tank top and boy shorts on. I couldn't be happier at this moment. Anya was sitting next to me in her high chair eating watermelon and apple slices. We were having a ball. "I thought you weren't coming until tomorrow?" I ask raising an eyebrow.

"You know I can't stand staying away from my four babies for too long. Oh and Jeremy, I forget about him sometimes," she says causing both of us to giggle. "Also you have a date. You need to get ready. I will be watching Anya."

"What date?" I ask confused.

"The one you have to get ready for in one hour. Come on Bambi go shower, comb your hair, and look pretty. Richard will bring around the car soon," she says excitedly.

"Uhm okay?" I get up from the chair making my way to the downstairs room to see if I have anything decent in my closet occasionally looking back at Mariella like she's a little crazy. If Jeremy and I had a date tonight why wouldn't he just tell me so he could have grabbed me something from upstairs or I could have gone shopping earlier? I am a little annoyed.

Luckily I find a white off-the-shoulder dress and some white platform sandals. Even though I don't remember bringing them down to the downstairs bedroom. Then again baby brain causes me to forget stuff. Who knows what I even did 20 minutes ago?

I shower after staring at myself in the mirror getting a little depressed at how my body looks. I wasn't that big with Anya but the stretch marks on me now are ridiculous. There are marks on my stomach, thighs, and but. The only place I don't have them on is my boobs. Thank god because I love showing my boobs, but not so much now since they have gotten so much bigger. Jeremy shows a lot of love to my growing boobs, he loves them wholeheartedly. The other night he didn't cuddle with me, he fell straight asleep on my breasts after placing a kiss on them. I have been wearing more clothes around the house to hide my stretch marks though.

I lotion my legs, arms, and face. I throw my hair in a high curly bun and fix my edges before tying them down. After my hair is tied down, I start my makeup on my eyebrows.

I slip on my dress looking at myself in the mirror. "My god I am fat," I say to myself disappointingly. I actually don't want to go anywhere at this point. I feel so awkward in my own skin. I fight with myself for a moment and decide that food is more important than my insecurities right now. At least I am hoping this date involved food because if Jeremy drags my pregnant ass out of the house for something nonfood related I am going to be pissed.

I grab my purse and make my way into the living room. Mariella looks up at me and immediately starts to cry. We seriously have to get this lady checked out by a doctor. How is she not dehydrated? She quickly rises to her feet off the floor with Anya in tears. She runs over to me pulling me into a tight hug. "You look beautiful Bambi. I love you," she says through her tears. She seems so genuine and sincere behind her words. She has said these things to me before but this time just felt a little different. She looks me up and down admiring me sweetly causing me to smile.

I feel the tears coming down before I can even think. " I love you too Mariella, thank you for always being there for me and Anya. Most days I don't know where I would be without you. I love you so much." We stand there for a moment in tears in each other embrace. Words will never express how much I appreciate this woman. She has a special place in my heart.

Mariella's one of the best grandmas a girl could ask for her. She really has my entire heart. I trust this woman with my life. She wipes away my tears placing a kiss on my cheek.

"Okay!" She sniffles. "Rich is waiting for you outside. I don't want you to be late for your date!" She squeals excitingly. Did I mention she is bipolar too? She can switch her mood in a heartbeat.

I walk outside meeting Rich who is holding the car door open for me. What the hell is going on? It's a freaking Thursday, it's not even an actual date night. Whatever, I'm just going to go with it. I didn't put on underwear for no reason.

We drive for about 15 minutes pulling up to a restaurant along the Hudson. When we pull up I see Jeremy standing outside with a bouquet of a dozen white roses. Rich stops the car coming around to open the door for me and help me out of the car.

"Thank you," I say to rich as I walk towards Jeremy. "Jeremy, what is all this?" I say greeting him with a kiss.

"It's just an I love you. It's just a day to show you how much I appreciate you Samantha," he says smiling sweetly. Fuck it I guess my man just wants to spoil me on a random Thursday. I should stop questioning it. He hands me the roses and at the same time offers me his arm. I interlock my arm with his as he leads me into the restaurant. The restaurant is quiet and romantic. Inside of the restaurant is candle lit with purple and pink flowers hanging from the ceiling. Outside the window are the views of the city and the sunset along with the river giving us an amazing view.

Jeremy had wine while I had sparkling cider. Jeremy ordered Lamb chops with risotto while I ordered the medium filet, with mashed potatoes and lobster Mac and cheese. My pregnancy hormones were controlling the way I was ordering from this menu. But Jeremy did tell me to order whatever I wanted and he added a baby girl to the mix so how could I say no?

I cleaned all my plates with a little bit of help from Jeremy. I moaned at the first bite of everything I took, I swear things don't taste as good while you are not pregnant. It should be a sin for food to taste this good when you are pregnant and just go back to regular tasting after you give birth. It's disrespectful is what it is. And ghetto.

Me and Jeremy shared a cheesecake mousse for dessert. It was so good. By the time I was done eating I was stuffed and happy. And appreciative of Jeremy. "I love you. Thank you for all of this. I really needed it," I said to him lovingly. I felt like he was neglecting me a little bit for the past few weeks but I didn't complain. "Jeremy I just want to let you know I am so proud of you. Everything you are doing, how hard you are working, and how much you are being there with your busy life isn't going unnoticed. I love and appreciate you much papa."

"Anything for my baby girl, I love you more," he smiled. "I know I have been busy these past few weeks but I am here now. It means a lot to hear you say that. This will get better baby girl. I promise." I reach around the table placing a kiss on his lips.

"Thank you."

The waiter took some pictures of the two of us with the beautiful restaurant background. Some pictures of Jeremy holding and kissing my belly. Some pictures of us staring into each other eyes. However, my favorite picture of us is him standing behind me with my hands on top of his hands while they are on my stomach. I made it my lock screen and Jeremy made it his home screen

We get in the car to go back home. While we are driving, I stare at the phone in my hand at the picture we just took admiring it. "Can I have a photoshoot? A pregnancy shoot? But as a family, I want you and Anya in the pictures as well," I ask Jeremy.

"You can have whatever you want. Just tell me when."

"Wow, thanks, baby. I love you." I say kissing him sweetly. The kiss quickly becomes hungry before we go into a full make-out session. We only pull away for air. The kiss is broken when Rich clears his throat to let us know we have arrived home. I get a little excited that we are home because my panties are soaked and I want to be fucked like a slut.

Jeremy leads me inside the house after carefully helping me out of the car. I guess we are back to the part where he treats me like a fragile doll. I didn't mind that much tonight. I feel loved.

"Oh you guys are back!" Mariella squeals. She carries Anya over to us giving her to Jeremy. "Okay, I got to go." She says as she quickly flies out the doors without another word.

What the fuck?

She didn't even let either of us say goodbye.

Weird.

I look at Jeremy who just shoots me a shrug. I start to walk in the direction of the downstairs bedroom when Jeremy grabs my hand to stop me. "What is it?" I ask confused.

"I have another surprise for you?"

"What?" Y'all know I don't like surprises.

"You'll see." He takes me to the carpeted staircase next to the kitchen leading me up the stairs to Mariela's old room.

"What are we doing up here?" I haven't been in the master

bedroom since Mariella moved out. Mostly cause I am lazy and that was a lot of fucking stairs.

"Open it," he says smoothly shooting me a smile.

I look at him and Anya curiously before turning the door nob to the room. I open the door and to my surprise, the room is beautifully decorated with 3 cribs. All three cribs are white. There is a bedazzled A above the crib decorated with pink blankets, ballet slippers, and pink stuffed animals. The other two cribs are decorated with yellow blankets and neutral-colored stuffed animals since we don't know what the gender of the twins are yet. There are 3 changing tables and 3 rocking chairs with white elephant blankets folded over them.

The walls are decorated with glow-in-the-dark stars, moons, and elephants. My favorite animal. I feel the tears in my eyes fall as I step closer inside the room and take everything in. There is a giant stuffed elephant in the corner of the room along with the giant teddy bear that Jeremy had got for Anya months ago. "Jeremy when did you," I start to say through my sobs as I turn around.

I blink at the sight before me. Jeremy is down on one knee with Anya sitting on his knee while she is holding a black box up for me. "Jer," I can barely get anything out without me sobbing uncontrollably.

"Samantha. I have loved you from the first night I met you, even I couldn't deny what I felt for you after first laying eyes on you. There is no mistaking you are the love of my life and I love you more than life itself. You have not only blessed me with one but three babies. You are the woman for me and I would be lost without you. Thinking back on the night we first met, god himself pushed you into my life. You are what I needed, you are what I need, you are my everything Samantha. There is no Jeremy without Samantha, I trust you with my whole life. I would go to the ends of the earth to protect you and our babies. I would do anything for you the same way I know you would do anything for me. I. Love. You. Samantha. Will you do me the honor of becoming my wife?

"Y-yes." I choke out as best I can through my sobs. He quickly lifts Anya taking the box out of her hand and putting the huge diamond on my finger. He places a kiss on my lips and pulls me into a tight hug but not tight enough that we are squishing Anya as I cry my heart out into his shoulder. I occasionally look up from his shoulder to kiss him again. My god, I love this man.

"She said yes!" He yelled out. Suddenly the lights turn on and Mariella, Rich, and Vincent come inside the doors. I get congratulations and hugs all around. I couldn't stop crying. Now I know how Mariella feels.

Everyone has gone home. Mariella took Anya for the night so me and Jeremy can have some much-needed alone time. I stare at the ring on my left hand admiring it for a second. It is a Radiant cut diamond with a diamond band alternating between opals and diamonds in every other spot. It truly is beautiful.

I am fresh out of the shower standing in front of the floor-length mirror trying to work up the courage to leave the bathroom. I am wearing a white lace bra with a pink silk robe over it with matching white underwear. My stomach is annoying me. I don't feel sexy right now. I start to tear up a little.

"Sam, you okay in there?" Jeremy knocks on the door. I don't answer I just stand there staring at myself in tears. He opens the door slowly but quickly and makes his way over to me to stand behind me in the mirror. "Baby girl what's wrong." The man literally looks like a god just standing there in his boxers.

"I don't feel sexy," I sniffle. I watch Jeremy look back and forth between my eyes and my body in the mirror. He places both his hands on my hips looking me up and down before leaning to place a kiss on the crook of my neck. It sends chills up my spine immediately.

"You are the sexiest woman I have ever seen in my life. And this," he says placing his hands on my stomach, "only makes you more beautiful and sexy." He presses his hard dick into my back moving to grab my boobs. "You are so fucking sexy it drives me crazy, I would fuck you where you stand baby girl." The feeling of his erection on my back and the massaging of my boobs along with him kissing my neck causes me to let out a throaty moan.

I whip my head and body around capturing his lips in a heated kiss. We slowly walk out of the bathroom not breaking the kiss. He leads me to the bed pushing me to lie down. He climbs on top of me capturing my lips once again taking it dangerously slow. He moves down my body pulling a nipple out of the lace bra and circling it with his tongue before sucking on it slowly. I can feel myself growing wetter between my legs. My nipples are more sensitive now than they ever were with my piercings.

"Jeremy just like that," I whisper letting out a soft moan. He lets my nipple go moving to the other one giving me the same amount of pleasure. He moves down tracing and kissing down my belly leaning up to pull off my panties.

"Can I?" He whispers. I want it but I am a little self-conscious because I have been having trouble shaving with my stomach. But also I think I will be okay with him putting his lips there now. Therapy has been helping.

"I don't know, I haven't shaved in like a month."

"I am a grown-ass man baby girl, a little hair ain't nothing. Let me taste that sweet pussy."

I hesitantly nod my head as he dives between my legs. I feel the cool air hit my moisture as he spreads my lips apart. The first flick of his tongue is almost my undoing. The simple flick of his tongue causes me to arch my back while taking a sharp breath. I don't ever remember this feeling so good.

He continues to lick and suck me slurping up everything I have to offer. My moans are so loud I can feel Jeremy smiling against my throbbing sex. Not too long after, my legs start to shake along with my arms as I come undone on his tongue. My words are incoherent after the mind-blowing orgasm. He continues to suck and lick all my juices up going right back to my clit. "Wait Jeremy," moan out. He moves to add a finger while continuing to lick my swollen clit.

I wasn't sure where one orgasm ended and the other began but I had to have cum 4 times already squirting once. "Baby please I can't again," I said squirming under him. He grabs my thighs holding me in place.

"You can and you will," he says passionately. "I have been starving for months," he says as he licks his lips going right back down to suck on my clit. My stomach tightens as I feel my next orgasm building. My breath became shaky as he sped up the motion of his tongue and his fingers. I could hear the wetness from his fingers. He uses his other hand to reach up and pinch my nipple. I scream his name as I cum undone for the 5th time in a row.

He finally stands up to suck off his fingers while looking at me seductively. He wipes off his face licking off his hand as well. "You taste so fucking good baby."

I am laying there a panting mess while still having after-shocks. He just stands there staring at me smiling looking satisfied with himself. I finally move to sit up to pull down his boxers but he stops me. "No baby, there will be time for that later, we are nowhere near done. I am going to fuck you now," he says as he pushes me back into the bed.

Dam I was just trying to suck a little dick.

He drops his boxers stroking his length that is glistening with precum. Without skipping a beat he lifts up my legs on his shoulders squatting down and sliding inside of me. He slides inside of me dangerously slowly causing my breathing to become erratic. He quickly moves to slam into me over and over throwing his head back in pleasure. "So fucking tight for daddy baby girl," he whispers harshly speeding up his thrusts. He pounds into me relentlessly. It feels so good I can feel tears in my eyes.

"Oh fuck!" I cry out as my walls start to tighten around him. Pregnancy has made me so much more sensitive. I cum around him with my legs shaking on his shoulders. He lowers my legs slowly leaning over to place a wet kiss on my lips while continuing to pound into me. My body is becoming overrun with pleasure.

He flips my leg over to the side so I am laying comfortably on my side. I start to play with my nipples as he watches me. He slams into me once again throwing his head back. The sound of my thighs slapping, my dripping wet core, my screaming moans, and Jeremy's aggressive grunts are making music in the room. He starts to thumb my clit when I feel my stomach tightening again. "Be a good girl and give me one more," he says through his grunts. I throw my head back in ecstasy and my walls quiver and tighten around him one more time before he pushes himself deep into me stilling himself. I can feel the ropes of his hot cum shooting inside me.

After 2 more rounds, I am half asleep while Jeremy is in the shower. The third round was more sensual and more like love-making with Jeremy showing loving attention to my body. I was in complete bliss at this moment.

I hear a pinging that won't stop going off. Half asleep I groan and reach over to grab my phone seeing two emails. I swipe up unlocking the phone to see what it is. It's just junk emails of course. I go to exit the email when another flagged email catches my eye. I click the email chain causing my eyes to widen as I read the emails. It may sound like prying but I couldn't look away. I am so confused, why would this be sent to my phone?

Then I realize this isn't my phone. It's Jeremy's. He doesn't have a password on his phone but he should have if he was going to do something like this. I look back and forth to the bathroom in disbelief. How could he do this?

I quickly forward the emails to myself before he gets out of the shower erasing any trace of me ever sending them. I take screenshots for good measure and send those to myself as well, I am going to need proof for this one. Deleting the text messages, the screenshots, and even the recently deleted photos out of his phone to make sure he doesn't know.

What the fuck do I do with this information?

I never thought he would do something like this.

Chapter 32

Jeremy Bresset

I can't believe I am getting married. The thought of Samantha being my wife has put a permanent smile on my face. There was no doubt that I loved this woman. I am so thankful for the time we spent together last night. It pains me that my baby girl doesn't feel beautiful. She is the most beautiful thing I have ever seen. Especially while carrying my kids. I cannot be more thankful for this woman. I stop and pick up flowers and Krispy Kreme for my babies. This morning when I left she was still sleeping but I am going to feed her and take care of her tonight.

My future wife, those words just sound amazing. I can't wait to see her. It's been a long work day, but knowing that at the end of the day I get to come home to my fiancé has made it go by quicker. I quickly exit the car to run inside the house eager to greet my girls.

I open the door to search for my girls, but instead, I find Samantha sitting around the island kitchen looking lost in thought. Her eyes look bloodshot with tears.

"Baby, are you okay?" I say nervously. But she doesn't answer. "What's wrong, is everything okay? Are the babies okay?"

She just sits there leaning on her hands staring off into space.

What the fuck is going on?

Samantha Pov

I had a lot of trouble falling asleep last night. What would lead him to do this? I talked things over with Mariella and we decided on the best course of action. I needed to know why. But what good reason would he have? I just feel like history is repeating itself. But I know what I must do. I

n the past, I have done things rashly. I would like to think I have grown since then. Today I will wait and I will talk it out. I left Anya with Mariella and I waited at home for Jeremy to come.

He walks in the door but I can't bring myself to look at him. I have been crying all day. Maybe I was being dramatic and overly sensitive because of the pregnancy hormones but I was hurt and again, I just wanted to know why.

One man can not hurt me this much.

I don't know how long I am sitting there in my thoughts before the door finally opened. I can hear him talking but I can't bring myself to speak or even hear what he is saying. I am hurt. I know if I don't answer him soon he will come near me and that is the last thing I want. I look over at him meeting his worried eyes on the other side of the island before I finally find the courage to speak.

"Do you have something you want to tell me?" I try to say as best as I can while choking up. I clasp my hands on the table waiting for him to respond.

"Samantha? What's going on? What do I have to tell you?" He responds in the most confused tone I have ever heard. I could toy with him but I have had all day to deal with this I just want him to say it.

"Do you trust me?" I ask impatiently.

"With my life. Why are you asking me this? Baby girl just tell me what's going on, you're scaring me," he responds frantically.

"Why did you select that doctor?" I ask angrily. There is a split-second spark of realization in his eyes, if I wasn't paying attention I would have missed it.

"Sam," He trails off walking over to me.

"Don't come near me," I say while chuckling bitterly. "Stay where you are please," I say while averting my gaze away from his.

I can't even look at him.

We stay there in silence for a second. He knows that I know. I am just trying to calm myself down enough to not cry when I start speaking. I am not sad I am angry, and when I am angry I cry.

"So today I researched amniocentesis a little more. And guess what I found out," I scoff.

"Sam," he begins but I cut him off.

"Guess!" I snap at him. But he says nothing. He just stares at me with his famous glossy eyes. Fuck this man. "Well since you don't seem to know, let me tell you what I found out," I say as my voice cracks a little. "The amniocentesis procedure is not only used for genetics and health testing but it's also used for intrauterine DNA testing. So I ask myself. Why would Jeremy specifically need the results of a DNA test? I also asked myself why he would secretly use my medical condition to his advantage to get a DNA test. But I said no, Jeremy wouldn't do that to me because I haven't given Jeremy a reason to not trust me. Care to elaborate?" I finish with a sniffle. He just stays quiet, I can see he is debating his next words. "Why!" I say slamming my fist on the table when he doesn't answer.

"Baby girl," I roll my eyes at the nickname. "I-I don't know okay, I was just really in my thoughts one day and I don't know one night you were sleeping and you whispered Isaiah's name, and then my mind went elsewhere and one thing led to another. Once the doctor told me that you needed the procedure I was being stupid and asked if we could use the results for a DNA test as well. I regretted it immediately. I was stupid, I was in my own head." He is leaning on the counter at this point but I don't think I want him that close to me.

"All I heard was bullshit just now. You're telling me, that because I whispered Isaiah's name in my sleep that I slept with him and cheated on you? That's the logic you came up with? That's the stupidest fucking thing I have ever heard. Really Jeremy?" I ask annoyed.

"Baby," he says starting to come around the corner but I hold up my hand in protest.

"Don't you fucking come near me. You know I have put up with a lot of bullshit in the past few years Jeremy. I look past a lot too. Like when you called me a gold-digger, when you abandoned me, and broke up with me over a text message. When you would do little petty shit, I forgave you for all of it. Yet you go out of your way to ask our doctors to do a DNA test on our twins because you didn't trust me?" I can feel the tear rolling down my cheek.

"Baby I am so sorry, I never meant for you to find out this way. It was one of my weakest moments. I regret everything. I never meant," he started but I cut him off.

"I was never meant to find out at all was I?" I snap cutting him off. "Well did you get the results you wanted? Are you happy with them?"

"What does that even mean? Of course, I am happy, I never doubted it."

"You did, otherwise you wouldn't need the test. But now I have another question. What if they weren't yours?"

"What the fuck do you mean by that Samantha."

"What. If. They. Weren't. Yours? Surely you knew there was a fifty-fifty chance, so what was your end game here if they weren't yours? Huh?"

"I don't know," he says softly. "Sam it was a stupid thing for me to do!"

"I think I do though. I have had some time to think about this and the only conclusion I can think of is you wanted an out. Right?"

"Jesus Samantha, I wouldn't have proposed to you if I wanted an out. Think about it, come on baby you're scaring me, your stressing yourself out with this. The stress is not good for the babies!"

"I also noticed you waited until after you got the results before proposing but I digress. But that's what you would have done right? If the twins were yours? You would have left. Am I correct?"

"It doesn't matter." I shake my head letting out a dark chuckle at his words. This man can't even give me a straight answer.

"You know I think in our relationship I thought we have come far, don't you? Especially coming far from when you broke up with me after accusing me of sleeping with a random man who turned out to be my brother. I thought we built up some type of trust in that time but I was clearly wrong." I start to play with the engagement ring on my finger while I am talking. He is staring at me intently but I do not care.

"Sam let's just talk this over before we do something rash." He says as his eyes dart from my eyes to the ring over and over.

"You were looking for your out. Shit, you were probably looking for a way to get back to Tiffany," I say with a pause. "Well I am going to do you a favor," I say while nodding my head in understanding. I start to pull the ring off my finger. "You can have your out." I leave the ring on the counter. "Jeremy I love you. But you have hurt me so much and time and time again I have forgiven you and taken you back, but this? This one really broke my heart. I cannot forgive you for this," I say with my voice cracking. I let out a deep sigh before I say what I have to say. "I can't do this with you anymore." I get up to walk away when I can no longer look at him

Jeremy doesn't skip a beat as he circles the island coming up behind me to wrap his arms around my waist from behind burying his face in the crook of my neck. "Baby please, I am so sorry, don't do this. I am sorry, I love you, I can't lose you." I stand there unmoving with his arms around me while my silent tears fall. "Please baby, please," he whispers moving his kisses up my neck bringing his body around trailing kisses up to my lips.

Before he can reach my lips I push him away quickly. "Get off me!" I yell out as best as I could through my tears. His hands burned my skin.

"No, we are going to work this out. We are going to fix this baby girl." I let out a dark chuckle at his words. I think I am going crazy.

"Why is it so easy for you not to trust me? I have never done anything to lead you to believe otherwise!" I snap

"I have trust issues I am sorry baby, they are fucked up, they lead me to do stupid things. There's no excuse, just can we sit down and talk about this baby? I'm sorry."

"What are you going to do next time you make up a scenario in your mind? If you would go as far as to do this then what will you do next time? If you were feeling unsure why didn't you just talk to me!"

"Baby I'm so sorry, can we just," he says reaching out for me but I pull away immediately

"No! I deserved better than that. All the times you accused me of wanting your money, I gave you chance after chance and every single time it was nothing but I'm sorry. Do you really think this little of me? Marriage is supposed to be a union between two equal parties but you have made sure to always try to make me seem smaller than you."

"I have never seen you as smaller than me. You are my life Sam. You are much bigger than I am, a bigger person with a much bigger heart. You are smart and kind. I feel like most days I don't deserve you because you are too good for me. I could never understand why I was fortunate enough for you to choose me. Out of all the people in the club that night you picked me and I have been forever grateful. Baby please we can work this out. We can go to therapy, I'll do anything. I am willing to work to fix my mistake."

Bitch I am in therapy. You need therapy, not us.

"I don't know Jeremy," I say skeptically

Bitch if you don't stick to the fucking plan. We are done with him. Do not fall for it! We deserve better. The babies deserve better. Your

mental health deserves better. Fuck him. We have given him chance after chance and he still doesn't know how to fucking act. You deserve better, choose yourself for once!

My inner monologue only angers me.

"Jeremy I am pregnant. The risk is literally higher for me to carry your children. All you do is stress me out and that is physically and mentally dangerous for me. All you do is hurt me and I deserve better than that. I deserve better than you. It's a constant pain that hits me over and over again. I won't let you hurt my babies the way you hurt me over and over again. There is some good in you, I know it. But there is also your father in you. He used to hurt your mom over and over again, and that's what you are doing to me and you can't even see it. You never have and I am not sure you ever will be you need help."

"I need you."

"I am not the thing to fix you, trust me I have tried," I respond sadly. "Get some help Jeremy. But do it without me."

I walk over to the ring on the counter grabbing it. I walk over to him and drop them in his pocket. "I made Rich move all my things to the downstairs bedroom. I don't want you sleeping on the same floor as me. I really want you gone but I won't deprive my kids of their father. If you want to leave you can but that's your choice. Like I said, take the out if you want, or don't. I don't think I care anymore. I never thought the man I was in love with would do something so terrible to me yet here we are. I do love you Jeremy, and I thought you loved me and trusted me but I was wrong. I hope you find the help you need."

I grab my keys off of the counter but he snatches them from me. "You are going to stay here and we are going to talk this over Samantha, you are not leaving me, I know what I did was fucked up but."

"Do you though?" I ask in the calmest tone while cutting him off. I don't think I have the energy to be mad anymore.

"Samantha please. We can work this out. We have been through too much. There isn't anything we can't get through."

"I am going to leave for a few days to clear my head, don't worry, Rich has agreed to go with me. I won't take your kids away from you, I will be back soon. I just need time away from you."

I walk over to him placing a small kiss for the last time. He grabs my face to try and deepen the kiss but I pull away." I know Rich is waiting outside for me and he already has a bag in the car for me. I am only going to Mariella's house, but Jeremy doesn't need to know that.

I walk around Jeremy so I can walk out of the house. I take a second and stop at the door. I look back at him over my shoulder to see he is staring at me with a heaving chest and red glossy eyes.

"Goodbye Jeremy," I say softly before shutting the door behind me

The end.

Epilogue

Jeremy Bresset

2 months later

I leave work like I did every day at around 5 to stop and pick up fresh flowers for her. Ever since she left me I have regretted everything I did to lead me up to that point. I fully stopped talking to my father because, in my opinion, this was from the effects of something he started.

I started going to therapy for my trust issues about a month ago. I stopped drowning myself in my own sorrows and started to fix myself, not just for her but for me. I wanted to feel like I was someone she deserved. I love her with all my heart but I hurt that woman repeatedly.

Although she gave me back my ring, she never kept the kids away from me. She made sure I didn't miss an appointment with the doctor. Every blood test, sonogram, and even finding out the gender, she worked with my secretary whom I had kept from my father to make sure I was present for all of that. I didn't know Samantha was the one who was helping make my schedule, but I should have expected it. The woman has the biggest heart I had ever seen.

She didn't even kick me out, she just treats me like an acquaintance. She makes me stay upstairs while she sleeps downstairs. After she came back from my mom's for a week and a half with Anya, while ignoring my phone calls and texts, she set some rules.

She told me I could not try to win her back until I have gotten help. I am keeping therapy a secret, I just haven't told her yet. She kind of stays away from me in the house unless she absolutely needs me for something which is rare since my mother comes around often.

It's typically good morning or goodnight with little to no words uttered in between. She will text me and ask me if I want some time with Anya but that's it. She really won't talk to me directly unless necessary.

The other day my mom came over at 12 at night to bring her honey chipotle wings and cottage cheese. Samantha hates cottage cheese but I guess that's what the babies wanted. I wish she had asked me for it though. I feel like I am failing her pregnancy, I wanted to be the one up all night rubbing her feet, fulfilling her cravings, and rubbing cocoa butter on her stomach. It breaks my heart but I refuse to go against her wishes.

My therapist gave me suggestions like taking emotional risks, facing my fears, and negative feelings that I have from my trust issues. I mean my own fiancé was fucking my father and carrying his child. Why wouldn't I have some sort of trust issues? But she helped me see that I was deflecting those feelings for Tiffany onto Samantha and that wasn't fair to my baby girl.

I have to do something and something fast. I do not want my twins to come into this world without me and Sam together.

I finally make it home carrying the flowers. I send greetings as I walk past Rich outside by the car. I am pleased to see Samantha sitting in her love sack while Anya is standing next to it gripping on for dear life. Did I forget to mention that my baby girl is walking? Thank god I was home when she did it. It was about a month ago, and we were having family movie time that Samantha suggested. We were watching Moana when Anya stood up and walked towards the television reaching for the green seashell. She had been standing and holding on to things before but she never took a step. Not until that day that is. Samantha screamed and cried and I had never felt more proud. We called my mom and she came over 10 minutes later crying her heart out as usual. I didn't tell her to come over, she simply flew over once I told her that Anya took her first steps.

Anya's little pitter-patter of her feet was the only thing I heard as she screamed running over to me. I pick her up kissing her on her cheek. I really love my blue-eyed little girl. She is amazing, to say the least. I walk over to the counter where we have three vases to switch out the flowers I bring her every other day. The flowers never stay for more than a week. It keeps the counter fresh and beautiful.

With Anya still in my arms, I walk over to Samantha kissing her stomach and then her forehead. It's the most she will allow me to do. After the first time she left, she didn't allow me to touch her for like 4 weeks. It wasn't until the twins started kicking that she allowed me to touch her for the first time.

"What are you doing?" I ask curiously.

"Ordering the final stuff for Anya's birthday party next weekend," she says not looking at me as she continues to type on her computer.

"Need help with anything?"

"Nope," she said sounding annoyed.

"What's wrong with you today?" Usually, she was very cordial with me but right now she sounds pissed.

She takes a deep sigh and closes the laptop to look up at me. "Nothing," she says with a shaky voice. She climbs off the love sac as best she could and waddles away from me. I put Anya down in her bassinet so she doesn't run around and grab anything as I run after Samantha.

"Sam, what's wrong with you?" She is standing in the corner of the room downstairs facing the wall.

"I can't tell you! Ugh fucking pregnancy hormones, I hate it!" She yells at me with tears in her eyes.

"Baby tell me what's wrong, please? Are you in pain, do I need to call the doctor?"

"No! Ugh!" She screams. I stand there dumbfounded confused as hell. She sits on the bed folding her arms and pouting. "I'm horny you idiot. And I am still mad at you!"

"I mean I can help you with that," I say boldly, I miss her and it's worth a try.

"No it's okay, I'm huge and you're probably not that attracted to me anyway. I haven't showered, I'm tired, and it's okay," she says with her head down. I have never seen Samantha like this. These pregnancy hormones are no joke clearly.

I think for a second then I got it. I know what to do for her. "Stay here, relax I know what to do," I say quickly before rushing out of the room. I grab my phone calling my mom asking if she can come to get Anya until tomorrow, of course, she asked me why Anya wasn't already at her house. I grab Anya and her diaper bag and hand her over to Rich who brings Anya back and forth sometimes to my mom's no problem. Anya already has a million and one clothes at my mom's house so we never have to send her with much, plus she only lives like 5 minutes away. Or Vincent, but Vincent prefers to be stationed at my mom's house, so I don't complain. A few minutes later My mom texts me a picture of her and Anya letting me know she arrived.

I run upstairs, change my clothes, throw on some grey sweatpants, and head back down. Within 15 minutes I am back in the room downstairs. She eyes me curiously as I walk past her with no shirt on and I head straight into her bathroom. I turn on the bath not too hot, and not too cold while dropping her lavender bath oil soap in the tub. I open Sam's little thing of lilac rose petals and sprinkle them in the water while lighting a couple of candles for her. Once the tub is filled and ready I go get Sam and tell her to undress. She looks at me like I am crazy for a second but complies. I let her know I sent Anya to My mom's and she doesn't mind.

I leave the room as she gets undressed but I end up going back in when she calls for me. I try not to stare at her beautiful naked body as I help her in the tub, I chose a bad time to wear grey sweatpants, I hope she doesn't notice my raging hard-on. I place soft towels behind her back and dim the lights and leave her in there. I call rich asking him to pick up tacos and grab something for himself as well. I let him know to just come in and leave it on the counter.

I lay out clothes on the bed for Sam, Just a long t-shirt since she doesn't like wearing clothes this pregnancy. She says they are too much work.

Within thirty minutes the food is here, and Sam is ready to get out of the bath. I pick her up bridal style and bring her to the bed placing her on the towels I laid out. I would rather not have her slip.

I dry off her body which she allows me to do, and I pull the oversized t-shirt over her head also making sure to massage her body with her African shea butter. I make sure to massage every inch of her body that she will allow me to touch. I make her sit in the middle of the bed while giving her the tray of tacos. She clapped and squealed at them while she happily ate. Finally, I am able to do something to help her.

While she ate I massaged her feet with African shea butter as well, to which she responded with a moan, and boom just like that my dick is hard again. I put fuzzy socks on her feet after I was done just in case she got up while I was upstairs I didn't want her to slip.

We were sitting in a comfortable silence eating and watching Bleach until I broke it. "I have been going to therapy for over a month now. I just wanted to let you know," I say looking over at her. She simply nods her head in response.

We finished eating and I took the trays out of the room. Now that she was comfortable I could leave her alone. I walk back into the room to see her laying on her side comfortably. I walk over to her kissing her forehead before I head back upstairs. I start to walk away when she grabs my arm.

"What is it baby?" I ask nervously.

"Please stay." She whispers. I nod my head in response and climb under the covers with her on the other side of the bed

Book 2 Preview

Samantha Kage

. . . .

"Samantha if you don't get down from there right now!"

"I need to get all these decorations up before the kids start arriving, leave me be." I roll my eyes at Jeremy as I continue to reach over to place the streamers properly while standing on the chair.

"It's literally 8 am, Anya's party doesn't start until like 4. You have been up decorating the house since 5am, this baby brain of yours is ridiculous. Go take a nap or something."

I was too busy focusing on Jeremy instead of the streamer and the streamer fell on the floor. I look down at the streamer on the floor that I worked so hard to put up and I look back and Jeremy who is standing there wide eyed.

Before I can stop it, the sniffle comes right out.

"You made me drop it," I whine before I burst out into a full-blown cry.

"Oh my god come here," he responds in an annoyed tone before walking over to me. I slowly step off the chair and grab the tape before throwing it at his head.

"What was that for?" He asks annoyed after dodging it against my better efforts to make it connect with his head.

"You yelled at me!" I argue as I continue to cry again. It took so

359

much work to get my 6 month pregnant ass on top of that step ladder for it to just fall out of my hands.

"Are you two at it again?" I hear Mariella come in the house.

Ever since that night me and Jeremy laid in bed with each other, things have been awkward and tense around the house. Jeremy took it as getting back together and I took it as a warm body that I needed at the time.

My hormones clouded my judgment that night and I should have never let him get that comfortable even though it was what I needed at the time.

It's been so weird. I love Jeremy there is no doubt that he is the man I am in love with, but I don't like him right now. Like at all. I always want him ten feet away from me but at the same time, I want him near me. I want him to give me body massages, but I don't want him to touch me. I feel like I am constantly going back and forth in my mind and this baby brain is not helping

I know he has been going to therapy and working on himself but the distaste I have in my mouth from him is still there from what he did.

I look over at Mariella and huff a little before I glare at Jeremy once more. Time to be petty.

"He yelled at me and made me cry!"

"Really Samantha? I am a grown ass man, and you are tattling to my mother about me?"

Right on cue Mariella grabs the remote and throws it at him and once again he dodges it.

Why the fuck do we keep missing?

"Why are you making a pregnant woman cry? Have you no shame? I raised you better than this."

I try to stifle my giggle; I knew she would take my side.

"Mom, I yelled at her because she is 6 months pregnant and she was standing at the top of the step stool reaching across the fucking ceiling."

Fucking snitch.

"Who are you cursing at? And so instead of telling her to get down nicely, you yelled at her? What if she got startled and fell? What would you have done then?"

I sit back and watch Mariella curse him out. I knew exactly how this was going to play out and I let it. That's what his bitch ass gets for yelling at me. He knows I'm sensitive.

"I-" he begins but Mama Mari cut him off instead.

"I nothing, apologize to the mother of your children!" She snaps at him, and I look over at him while fighting everything inside me that is telling me to laugh and or smile.

He slowly looks over at me and I see his jaw tick and I swear that action alone makes my clit throb.

Whoa, down girl.

"I am sorry I yelled at you and startled you Samantha," he grits through his teeth.

I place an innocent smile on my face while rubbing my belly and I don't miss how he scowls.

"It's okay, just don't let it happen again," I coo sweetly while doing an about-face and giggling back to grab the streamer on the floor. I don't miss the sound of his footsteps walking away quickly.

Okay, even I noticed that mood swing. Maybe they are as bad as Jeremy says they are. But then again his bitch ass isn't carrying twins so he can get the fuck over it.

"Absolutely not," I hear from behind me. "You have guards all around this house, if you need something done ask one of them," she scolds me before looking around the room.

That's when her eyes widen and she sees just how much work I have actually done since I had woken up. I put up streamers and blew up balloons. Blew up the pool floats that are just piled in the living room.

The theme of Anya's first birthday is bubbles.

There are pictures of Anya everywhere from a photo shoot we had a couple of days ago. The biggest picture is of her with a head wrap towel on her head and a towel around her tiny little body and she is soaking wet and smiling her bright 2 tooth smile as if she is in a bubble bath. The background of the bathroom is a light blue color that brings out her beautiful blue eyes and her dark skin looks amazing against the contrast.

There are pictures of her cake smash which was an ombre blue cake with an edible rubber ducky topper surrounded with bubbles. The cupcakes have little balls on top in different sizes and colors to resemble bubbles as well.

I even went and made the bright pink balloon arches for the party, as well as stuffed the goodie bags for the kids.

"My god, you got a lot done. Did you start last night?" She asks curiously.

"No, I started this morning. I got up a little early," I pout innocently.

"What is a little early?" She asks raising an eyebrow at me.

"5 am," I whisper under my breath.

"Okay, I am going to make you breakfast, and I am going to wake Anya up so she can be napping again by 12 and be up for the party. You are going to eat and then go back to bed." Anya has been sleeping a lot lately. Like she gets angry when you wake her up. Just like her momma I suppose.

"But," I begin to protest but there really is no arguing with this woman.

"No buts! Kitchen now!"

I pout but I sit in the kitchen and watch her whip me up pancakes eggs and bacon and it smells so good I only pray I don't throw it up.

While I am waiting for the food, Jeremy comes back down the stairs in some grey sweatpants, no shirt on with his hair dripping wet, and I almost drop the fork I am holding. I don't miss his bulge swinging in his pants.

He is doing this on purpose he knows how horny I am lately. How dare he come down the stairs looking fuckable and with no underwear on to make things worse.

He pulls up a stool right next to me without looking at me and I don't miss the smile that plays on his face.

Fuck him.

I eat my food basically scarfing it down and immediately the itis hits me. I sigh before I thank Mariella for the food and sluggishly walk back to the bed and lay back down on my side.

I can't wait until this is over and I can lay on my stomach again.

I start to go over everything I need to do when I wake up from my nap. I must call the cake lady and make sure she delivers the cake by no later than 2 pm and I have to set up the tables and decorations outside by the pool as well as get Anya dressed and myself.

I try to fall asleep, but I can't and I hate the reason why. In the last week, since the moment that happened between me and Jeremy, I can no longer sleep until something happens and I hate my body for it.

I grab my phone and call him. He doesn't even say hello, he just says, "I'm coming," then hangs up.

I don't know why, but I can't go to sleep until he kisses me on my forehead. The other night we got into another argument about foolishness. I will fully take the blame for that one. I wanted him to go get me a steak from a steak house that was like 8 miles away and he was not having it.

I cried and we argued but even that night when I was lying in bed he still came in and kissed me on my forehead and told me goodnight before he left, and now it's a thing.

He walks in the room still looking fuckable as ever and leans over the bed placing a sweet lingering kiss on my forehead and within no time, I am fast asleep.

Coming Early 2023.
Xoxo

Made in United States
North Haven, CT
28 March 2023

34695666R00200